"Lynn Blackburn's done it again. She made me read way past my bedtime and owes me several hours of sleep! What a fabulous story with characters who will live in your head—and heart—long after the last word. I'm eagerly awaiting the second book so I can return to Gossamer Falls and catch up with all of my new besties!"

Lynette Eason, award-winning, bestselling author of the Lake City Heroes series

"With an exceptional gift for writing relatable characters who touch deep places of the heart, Lynn Blackburn's voice is unrivaled! I quickly fell in love with Landry, Cal, Eliza, and, in fact, the entire compelling cast of characters in this brand-new romantic suspense series. A must-read, *Never Fall Again* delivers the emotionally gripping romance, riveting suspense, and captivating characters readers love!"

Elizabeth Goddard, bestselling author of *Cold Light of Day*

"Lynn Blackburn is a rising voice in romantic suspense! This book had it all—a delicious romance, obsession, found family, redemption and reconciliation, edge-of-your-seat suspense, and the kind of ending we all root for! Don't miss this first book in what I believe will be a fantastic series."

Susan May Warren, *USA Today* bestselling and RITA Award–winning author

NEVER
FALL
AGAIN

Books by Lynn H. Blackburn

DIVE TEAM INVESTIGATIONS

Beneath the Surface

In Too Deep

One Final Breath

DEFEND AND PROTECT

Unknown Threat

Malicious Intent

Under Fire

GOSSAMER FALLS

Never Fall Again

GOSSAMER FALLS · 1

NEVER FALL AGAIN

LYNN H. BLACKBURN

Revell

a division of Baker Publishing Group
Grand Rapids, Michigan

© 2024 by Lynn H. Blackburn

Published by Revell
a division of Baker Publishing Group
Grand Rapids, Michigan
RevellBooks.com

Printed in the United States of America

Library of Congress Cataloging-in-Publication Data
Names: Blackburn, Lynn Huggins, author.
Title: Never fall again / Lynn H. Blackburn.
Description: Grand Rapids, Michigan : Revell, a division of Baker Publishing
    Group, 2024. | Series: Gossamer Falls ; 1
Identifiers: LCCN 2023031284 | ISBN 9780800745363 (paperback) | ISBN
    9780800745585 (casebound) | ISBN 9781493444724 (ebook)
Subjects: LCGFT: Christian fiction. | Romance fiction. | Novels.
Classification: LCC PS3602.L325285 N48 2024 | DDC 813/.6—dc23/eng/20230713
LC record available at https://lccn.loc.gov/2023031284

Baker Publishing Group publications use paper produced from sustainable forestry practices and post-consumer waste whenever possible.

24 25 26 27 28 29 30   7 6 5 4 3 2 1

For Sandra Blackburn,
my extraordinary mother-in-law, for loving me like
your own and for living a life that is a beautiful
example of the hope we have in Christ.

And in memory of Gary Blackburn,
my father-in-law, who packed a lifetime of love
and laughter into far too few years.

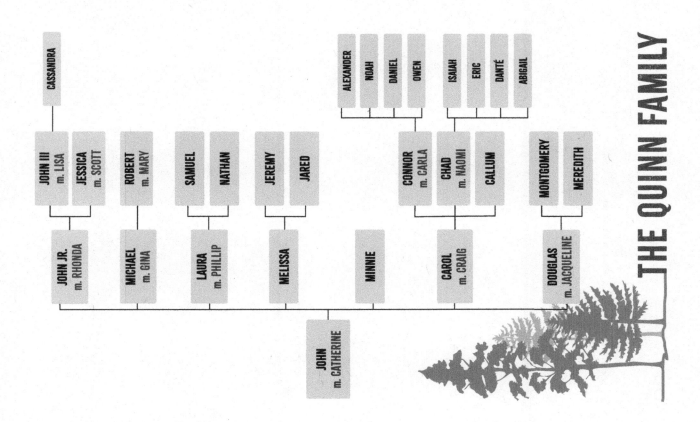

THE QUINN FAMILY

ONE

Landry Hutton didn't believe dreams came true anymore. She'd had dreams a long time ago. They'd nearly destroyed her. Still might.

But this was the first step toward the answer to a prayer she hadn't known to pray. And, oh, how she'd prayed. For safety. For a future. But never for this. She hadn't dared ask for it. Hadn't imagined it was possible. Over the last three years, she'd kept her head down and worked hard. Despite the tears and the occasional meltdown, she'd persevered. And now, somehow, she found herself here.

She took several slow breaths and stared through the windshield at the building ahead of her. Could she do this? Should she do this? Was it too soon?

Was she truly safe here?

Those were the wrong questions. She couldn't hide from the correct question. How much longer would she let the past keep her in a stranglehold? She'd been given an opportunity to make their future stable and beautiful.

And the first step was to place this fragile slip of an idea in front of a man she'd never met and ask if he could turn it into something real.

Landry had been putting this off for six months. Would still be putting it off if Bronwyn hadn't promised her Callum Shaw was the man for the job. "You don't have to interview fifteen contractors," she'd said. "He'll tell you the truth about what will work. He won't take advantage of you. He's a gentleman. He's great with kids. He loves his family; I trust him completely. You can too."

If anyone but Bronwyn Pierce had said those things, Landry would have smiled and resisted the urge to tell them no one could be trusted. But they'd been friends for longer than most people realized, and their friendship had been forged in a crucible of pain that had left them bonded for life. Bronwyn knew where Landry's skeletons were hidden and how important it was for them to stay that way.

Bronwyn didn't trust many people outside the Pierce family. In fact, she didn't trust many people *within* the Pierce family. But Callum Shaw had made her short list. It was high praise and had given Landry the push she needed to make the phone call. That and the fact that Bronwyn stood across from her, eyes flashing, and refused to leave until she dialed the number.

Landry was unprepared for the woman on the other end of the phone to say that Mr. Shaw had time this afternoon. She dropped everything and rushed over. Maybe it was for the best. She had no time to continue overthinking this, and instead of coming alone, she had her best girl with her. "Eliza?" Landry turned around to make eye contact with her five-year-old daughter.

"Yes, ma'am?"

"Remember what we talked about?"

"Best behavior." Eliza's tone sounded like expecting good behavior was a doomed effort.

"I know you're tired, but Mr. Shaw had a cancellation in his schedule, and I couldn't pass up the chance to talk to him today. After we leave, we'll get pizza and have our movie night. Okay, doodlebug?"

Eliza grinned. "Okay." She waited for Landry to open her door, then climbed from the back of the car. She squinted at the sign beside the door as they walked. "S-P-Q." She spoke each letter one at a time. "What's the next word?"

"SPQ Construction. Established 1982." Landry squeezed Eliza's hand, then pulled open the heavy wooden door and looked around. The business may have been established in the eighties, but the decor was what she'd taken to calling "modern mountain chic."

No one decorated this way in Arizona. The desert had its own beauty, and that aesthetic would always be a part of her soul. But the mountains of North Carolina made for a soothing palette, and the person who decorated the offices of SPQ Construction embraced it. Walls of the palest blue. Large prints of local vistas. And in the corner— "Oh!"

"Mommy!" Eliza darted past her and paused at the edge of a flowing water feature that took up an entire side of the room. "It's Gossamer Falls!"

"I think it is." Someone had created a replica of the waterfall for which the town was named. The lacy cascade originated one foot from the ceiling, then ran down a water-smoothed rock face and into a river that flowed along one wall until it disappeared into the far corner.

Eliza trailed a fingertip in the river and grinned. "Can we put one of these in our new house?"

A gentle laugh came from the other side of the room. "The Shaw brothers nearly lost their collective minds on that project and have sworn a solemn oath never to re-create it." The woman behind the reception desk widened her eyes at Eliza. "But I know for a fact that Cal has been itching to make a smaller version. And he has a soft spot for beautiful ladies such as yourself. If you ask him, he might be able to get an exception granted."

"Don't encourage her!" Landry left Eliza by the waterfall and walked toward the woman. The desk she approached was fifteen feet long, with a slight curve. When she got closer, she saw that the top was made from a massive slice of a tree, varnished to a high shine with a vein of blue running in a lightning pattern throughout. She'd seen this type of woodwork in a few of the shops in Gossamer Falls, but always on a smaller scale. Vases, bowls, bookmarks. This desk was a work of art, and Landry couldn't stop herself from running her hands along the glossy surface.

Her eyes met those of the woman on the other side. "This is amazing."

A soft smile split her face. "Cal does beautiful work. He nearly gave his mother a heart attack when he started electrocuting the lumber, but he has quite a gift. You must be Landry Hutton. I'm Carla Shaw."

"Nice to meet you."

They shook hands, and Carla pressed a button on what must have been some type of intercom device and said, "Callum?"

"Carla?" The voice was deep, and that one word was infused with humor. Landry had the distinct impression there was a joke between them that she wasn't privy to.

"Ms. Hutton is here to see you."

"Send her back."

Carla stood. "I'll walk with you. It's a bit of a maze to Cal's office."

Landry and Eliza trailed behind her. The walls held framed photos of homes ranging from modest starter homes to extravagant estates. Each with a plaque underneath that listed the construction dates.

They passed several offices before they reached an open door.

"Maisy. Stay." That same deep voice from the intercom floated to the hallway.

"Oooh! A dog!" Eliza dashed into the room.

Her little sprite was fast and already halfway across the office before Landry realized what was happening. "Eliza, wait!" Fortunately, she stopped at Landry's words.

"I know, Mommy. Never touch a dog without permission. I just want to see."

Eliza turned her big brown eyes toward the man who had come around his desk and knelt beside a dog now quivering with excitement.

The man—Callum Shaw, she assumed—met her daughter's eyes and said, "Your mom's right. You can't ever rush at a dog, even dogs as gentle as this big baby. But if it's okay with your mom . . ."

His eyes, which were as blue as the Carolina sky, now met hers. There was humor and gentleness. And shadows. Something dark flitted across his gaze. But then he blinked and it was gone.

Landry nodded her permission, and he turned all his attention back to her daughter. "This is Maisy. She's a golden retriever. She's three years old. She loves long walks in the woods, sunbathing, peanut butter, and belly rubs." He demonstrated the belly rub. Maisy melted under his touch, and Eliza crept closer. "You can pet her. Maisy doesn't bite my friends."

Eliza dropped to her knees beside Callum and held out her hand toward Maisy's nose.

Maisy took a quick sniff and rewarded Eliza's good behavior with a lick. Callum stayed where he was until it was clear to everyone that Eliza and Maisy were set, then he rose to his feet and extended a hand. "Ms. Hutton."

"Landry. Please."

"Landry. A pleasure."

Landry kept the contact brief. "Sorry, my hands are rough." She turned them palms up. "Hazards of the job."

Why had she said that? What did it matter if her hands were a bit on the crispy side? She didn't have to prove anything to this man. Embarrassment crept across her and burst through her pores, heating her neck and face, and now she had no idea what to do with her hands. Should she put them down? Tuck them behind her back?

Callum glanced at her hands and turned his own up. "Same here." He heaved a dramatic sigh. "It's to my eternal despair that I'll never land that hand modeling contract I've always hoped for."

His easy humor made it automatic to tease him back. "Well, there's always ditch digging."

"Good point. If this construction gig doesn't work out, I'll have something to fall back on." Callum turned his attention to Eliza. "And I gather your name is Eliza?"

She giggled with the abandon unique to happy children. "That's right, but sometimes Mommy calls me Liza or ZaZa, but never Lizzy because that's too close to Landry, and it gets confusing."

Landry tried to keep a straight face as Eliza parroted what she'd heard Landry say too many times to count.

"It's a pleasure, Ms. Eliza." Callum pressed a hand to his chest. "I'm Cal Shaw. I'll answer to Callum, but not LumLum because"— he dropped his voice to a stage whisper—"that's just not dignified."

Eliza's laughter filled the room. Bronwyn hadn't been wrong about Cal Shaw. He was very good with children. Even now, he kept his attention on Eliza. "Are you good here with Maisy while your mom and I talk?"

"Yes, sir."

Cal grabbed a legal pad and pen from his desk and took the

chair opposite the one he directed Landry to sit in. From their seats, they could both see Eliza and Maisy.

She waited for him to start the conversation, but maybe she was supposed to go first?

"She's a beau—"

"Land—"

They both stopped talking, and his smile seemed genuine as he nodded to her. "Please. Go ahead."

"I was going to say your dog is beautiful." She willed her body to stop flushing scarlet, but it refused to cooperate. She didn't have to see herself to know that her face, neck, chest, and even her feet were on fire. This was why she did best behind the walls of The Haven. She could interact with the patrons there with minimal difficulty. But put her out in public, and she became a tongue-tied, socially inept disaster.

Cal's grin held mischief, and he leaned toward her. "If all goes as planned, she'll be pregnant soon. I bet Eliza would love a puppy for Christmas." His voice was cajoling and teasing, but at least he had the good sense to keep it too low for Eliza to hear.

He winked in a way that was friendly and not flirtatious, and Landry understood why Bronwyn liked him so much. He leaned back and in a normal voice said, "I gathered from your conversation with Carla that you're going to build nearby."

"Yes. I have three acres on the edge of Pierce land." She watched him carefully as she spoke and was unsurprised when his grip tightened on the pen at her words.

"How long have you lived in Gossamer Falls?"

"Long enough to know the Pierce and Quinn families don't get along. And long enough to know SPQ stands for Shaw, Pierce, Quinn Construction, but your father and uncle bought out the Pierce in question two decades ago. And while your last name is Shaw, your mother is a Quinn."

"That saves me some potential awkwardness." Cal's smile didn't reach his eyes. "Because I'm afraid if you're building on Pierce land, they may object to having us as the contractor."

"No. They won't. The land is mine now. And Bronwyn Pierce told me to call you. She insisted and told me if anyone in the family gets their shorts in a wad over it, she'll take care of it."

Cal studied her for a long moment.

She couldn't stand the silence. "I gathered that you and Bronwyn are friends."

This time the smile was genuine. "Bronwyn and I grew up together. I have two cousins, Meredith and Mo, and the four of us were in the same grade and did everything together. The family drama made things difficult at times, but we've remained good friends."

"She's mentioned Meredith and Mo. Said the four of you were like a small gang as kids."

Cal laughed. "It's true. We were terrors, but our pranks were mostly directed at soft targets." He tapped his pen on the legal pad. "Where exactly is this land?"

"It's on the far edge of Bronwyn's land. There's a right-of-way to a state road, so that's not an issue. Bronwyn's land is on three sides—she carved out a three-acre spot for me. There's a river on the fourth side. I'm not sure who owns the property on the opposite side of the river."

Cal dropped the legal pad, sat back in his chair, and ran his hands through his hair. "I do."

"You know who owns it?"

"Yes." A huff. Several shakes of his head. "I do."

A deep thrill of foreboding shot through her. He'd been easy and light since they walked in. Even her mention of the Pierces garnered only a small amount of tension. But well-controlled . . . something . . . radiated from him. She didn't think he was angry. But he wasn't happy. "Is it a secret or something? Is it owned by a terrible person? I don't think Bronwyn would have sold me land that wasn't safe, but—"

"Landry."

She reined in her babbling. "Yes?"

Cal leaned forward and rested his elbows on his knees. "I'm trying to tell you who owns the land across the river from yours."

She wanted to scream at him to spit it out already when he looked at her and pointed to himself.

"I do."

TWO

"But . . . Bronwyn said no one lived there. That it was isolated. Safe. No one would be around me, and the only people who might ever build there were longtime residents, I guess I assumed. Oh dear. I can see you aren't happy about having me as a neighbor. I'm not sure what to do about that." She shook her head in dismay. "I'm sorry."

Cal counted to ten in his head. He'd mucked this up and then some. He could blame it on shock. But the more Landry rambled, the more he found himself stuck on the words she'd spluttered. *Isolated. Safe. No one . . . around.* "Landry?"

"What?" No hostility or temper was in her voice. No hope either. It was flat and despondent. Nothing like the laughing woman who'd entered his office moments earlier. He hadn't meant to, but his reaction had made her turn in on herself until she looked like she was trying to fade into the chair.

"Please. Forgive me. I was surprised on too many levels to explain at the moment. But I promise I'm a great neighbor. Or, I mean, I will be. Someday. Maybe. Not maybe about being a great neighbor. I'm the best neighbor. I know how to fix things, and I have a dog."

Landry didn't say anything, but somewhere in the middle of

the verbal debacle he'd just subjected her to, a glimmer of light returned to her eyes, so he kept going. "And Bronwyn's right. It *is* safe. Isolated. There's no one for miles who doesn't have the last name of Pierce, Quinn, or Shaw."

"I'm not sure that's the ringing endorsement you seem to think it is, Mr. Shaw." The words were formal, but the tone . . . Was she messing with him now?

He sat straighter and turned on the Southern charm. "I assure you, Ms. Hutton, that while the Pierces and Quinns don't get along, our feud has never devolved into violence. You never have to worry about getting caught in the crossfire. We're polite about our disagreements, and there's not a Pierce or a Quinn who wouldn't come to your aid."

"Or a Shaw?"

"That goes without saying."

She sighed and relaxed in her chair. "I appreciate what you've said, but I can tell you aren't happy about this. I think I must be missing some key information."

She was. He was going to strangle Bronwyn for putting them both through this. He had no idea how much Landry knew, but if she was going to live in the middle of Pierce land, across the river from Quinn land, she had a right to the truth. "The river that runs along our property line is on the far edge of Pierce and Quinn lands. Most of our families live on the outer edges, as far away from each other as possible. But when we were sixteen, Bronwyn, Meredith, Mo, and I hatched a plan to ask for that land. Both of our families have a tradition of giving a plot of land to the children, and now grandchildren, when they turn twenty-one."

"Bronwyn said the Pierces own a lot of land."

"They do. And the Quinns do as well. Enough to continue breaking it up and handing it down for several more generations.

The theory is that by the time it's all split up, the older generations will have died so their land will be available."

"So you wanted the land at the far edges of your family's property? Why?"

"Partly because of the river. We grew up playing in and around it."

"I can see that." Landry's smile was back, her eyes soft as they flicked to Eliza. "It looks like a place a kid could spend hours exploring."

"And we did." The river was so tied to their childhoods that they'd wanted to live there so their kids could grow up the same way. Although at the rate they were going, there would be no kids.

"You said partly?" Landry's question pulled him from the dark direction his thoughts had taken.

"Yes. There were many reasons, but the biggest was that the four of us wanted to be neighbors. We'd decided by then that our grandparents, parents, aunts, and uncles could carry on with their drama for as long as they wanted to, but we wouldn't let it get in the way of our friendship."

"Did that work?" Her question held an undercurrent of knowledge. He'd have to ask Bronwyn how much she'd shared with Landry.

For now, he'd stick to the publicly known facts. "We all left home after high school." Before in Bronwyn's case. "We aren't the same people we were when we left." None of them had escaped their twenties unscathed. "Now that we're all back home, we're trying to figure out what our adult relationships look like. And I must be honest, Bronwyn selling a piece of her land, especially land adjoining mine right in the heart of our little enclave without saying something? I didn't expect her to do that. It's her land, and she can do whatever she wants with it. But I didn't see that coming. Quinn land can't be sold to anyone who isn't a Quinn. I thought the Pierces had a similar expectation."

Landry's expression grew guarded at his mention of Bronwyn, and Cal was unsurprised when Landry rushed to defend her. "Oh, they do. There was a family meeting about it before Bronwyn offered it to me. And there's a binding contract that should I ever sell the land, Bronwyn has first right of refusal."

Cal should have expected that, but he should have heard this from Bronwyn, not Landry. "I'm trying to explain my earlier reaction and bad manners. *You* don't owe *me* an explanation."

"Based on what you told me, I think I do." Landry didn't give him time to argue. "I'm not a Pierce, obviously, but I've been living on Pierce land for three years. I'm settled at The Haven. I don't want to leave, but I've had lucrative offers from other resorts." A faint tinge colored her skin. "I'm not sure how to say this without it sounding conceited, but I suspect the land was a small way to ensure that I stay."

Cal leaned toward her. "I know the Pierces, and I know they excel at business decisions. I'm certain they'd pull out all the stops to keep you. But you should also know that while the desire to entice you to remain may have been a contributing factor, they wouldn't sell a blade of grass of their land to someone they didn't trust and care about. It isn't a small gesture. It's huge."

Landry flushed again. Her fair skin turned pink with the slightest provocation. This was a woman who would never be able to hide her emotions. Time to get the conversation into safer territory. "Just to get this out in the open, I've seen your work. I own one of your vases. It's remarkable."

She smiled hugely. "Thank you for saying that." She gestured toward the door. "That means a lot. Especially coming from an artisan like yourself. Carla said you made her desk. It's stunning." "Thank you."

"And, to get this out in the open, I've seen your pieces in town. I have a bookmark, and a bowl I keep Reese's Pieces in."

"A peanut butter fan?"

"Peanut butter with chocolate fan. I like peanut butter fine, but I love it with chocolate. And"—she narrowed her eyes at him—"despite your change of subject, you should know that I have my eye on two of your vases. They're works of art. How long have you been perfecting your craft?"

Was *he* blushing now? What was wrong with him? He cleared his throat and again pushed the conversation into shallow water. "I started messing around with woodworking in my late teens. When I moved home after I left the Marines, I had way too much time on my hands in the evenings. Meredith and Mo hadn't moved back yet, and I could only handle so many evenings with my nieces and nephews."

Landry's eyebrows lifted in amusement and confusion. "You were so good with Eliza, I expected you to be the favorite uncle." Her voice dropped. "Eliza isn't usually comfortable with strangers, especially men. But she opened right up to you."

There it was again. A hint of past trouble, maybe even present. Cal caught himself before he asked if Landry was okay. He wasn't going there. He'd jumped in with both feet before, and his heart still bore the shrapnel scars.

Landry Hutton was beautiful. Blond, about five feet five. Neither skinny nor chubby. Her eyes brown. Her handshake had been firm, and while she apologized for her rough hands, he hadn't noticed that they were particularly abrasive.

Eliza was adorable. Her skin was brown, her hair was dark brown and curly. Her eyes brown. Her father must have had dark skin and hair, and his genes had overridden Landry's. Except for the shape of her face, which was a miniature of her mother's.

Was Landry's husband/Eliza's father the reason for her fear? It didn't matter. They were potential clients. Members of the community. Soon-to-be neighbors. Maybe someday they would be friends, but that was all they would ever be.

With his thoughts firmly corralled, he answered her question. "Carla's married to my oldest brother, Connor. They have four boys. My other brother, Chad, has three boys and one girl. They're all awesome. And, as a matter of fact, between you and me, I *am* their favorite uncle."

Landry mimed zipping her lips.

"But my nephews are so loud that a recording of them could be used to torture political prisoners to great effect. My niece has this high-pitched squeal . . ." He shook his head at the thought of it. "Thirty minutes of that chaos, and the terrorists would be begging to spill all their secrets."

Landry laughed. "Not exactly the best way to wind down at the end of the day."

"Definitely not."

"But electrocuting trees is?" Her eyes widened. "Seems a bit dangerous."

"It can be, but that's only a small fraction of the work that goes into each piece. I spend hours sanding and finishing after that. It's a long process and quite therapeutic."

Her eyes shone. "I feel the same way when I'm at my wheel. Sometimes it's hard work. But sometimes it's exactly what I need to rein in my emotions and scrub off the day."

"Do you have a pottery . . . what's it called? A studio? And a kiln?"

"Yes. At The Haven. Eliza and I live in a cabin on-site, and my pottery is stored in a small building where my wheel and kilns are set up. We sell the pieces at Favors—that's the name of the gift shop at The Haven—and they've done so well that I'm in a position, financially and otherwise, to have my own place."

Cal didn't miss the *otherwise.*

"What I have at The Haven is wonderful. But I want our own house, a studio I can set up exactly the way I want, more room to create, and maybe, theoretically"—she stopped talking and mouthed the words—"for a dog."

Cal zipped his lips and threw away the key.

Landry grinned. "Eliza started kindergarten a few weeks ago. And while The Haven is lovely, it takes a long time to get to town from there. I want to live in a location that's still private but a bit closer to town, school, and activities. She wants to play soccer in the spring, which means multiple trips to town on certain days."

"That all makes sense." Or did it?

The Haven, the source of the feud between the Pierce and Quinn families, was a lush getaway for the rich and famous. With only twenty cabins, the exclusivity appealed to the upper crust of society. The Haven had a zero-tolerance policy for anyone who violated their nondisclosure agreements. Rumors abounded, of course, but few knew for sure which A-list movie stars, musicians, and politicians had found solace at The Haven.

While there, guests could do absolutely nothing, or they could take private classes on everything from rappelling to pottery. That was where Landry Hutton came in. She'd joined The Haven staff three years earlier, and her pottery had quickly become the talk of the town. Her pieces sold for astronomical amounts, and the patrons of The Haven were happy to plunk down their money to have her work shipped to their LA and NYC homes.

Within a few days of Landry's arrival, Cal had heard about the pretty art teacher who taught pottery, sculpting, and painting lessons. He'd heard she had a little girl. And with the way people gossiped in small towns, he'd heard no husband was in residence.

His interest had been limited to her art, and he wasn't lying when he told Landry he appreciated her work. The vase he owned was extraordinary, and he'd used the shape to design a similar piece out of wood.

Other than that, he hadn't given her much thought. But now,

with Landry sitting across from him and Eliza doing her best to win Maisy's heart, he couldn't help but ask himself what would bring a single mom to an exclusive enclave in the mountains of Western North Carolina, and what would still be haunting her three years later?

Landry Hutton wanted him to build her a house where she could get to town easily but also stay hidden forever.

Why?

THREE

Landry couldn't shake the sensation that Cal Shaw still wasn't happy about the prospect of having her as a neighbor. The way he looked at her. It wasn't . . . unpleasant. But it was intense. Like he was trying to see behind her walls.

There was curiosity in his eyes, and even though he kept his questions to himself, she was certain he would be asking them. Sooner rather than later.

She'd closed that door and rarely spoke of what lie behind it. Nothing in the past needed to be pulled into the present.

"So, Landry." Cal retrieved a legal pad and pen from a small table between them. "What do you have in mind for your home?"

Whatever questions he had about her personal life, he'd obviously decided to leave alone for now. Landry pulled a sketch from her purse. "I'm not an architect, but this is a general idea."

Cal took the paper from her and opened it. He didn't speak, but his face reflected a series of responses that shifted from mild interest to intense scrutiny until he lifted his gaze to hers. "Landry. This is extraordinary. It's functional and practical without sacrificing elegance and beauty. We'll need to talk to an architect about a few of these design elements, but I'm sure she can figure out how to make this work."

Landry didn't try to hide her relief. "Really?"

"Really. You can certainly contract with your own architect, but we have one in Asheville we use for our custom designs. She's a mountain girl at heart and knows what's important in a home up here." He glanced at her drawing. "She'll love this."

Why did the thought of this architect send a trill of something not nice through her veins? She didn't know this woman. And Cal obviously thought highly of her. What was her problem? She shook it off. "I don't have any contacts with architects. If you trust her, I can't see why I wouldn't at least talk to her."

Cal stood and walked behind his desk. He opened a drawer and rummaged around for a few seconds before he produced a business card, which he handed to her, and resumed his seat. "I'll talk to her next week. Her people will call you to set up an appointment. You'll need to spend time with her fleshing out some of the ideas here so she knows what to do." He glanced to the corner of the room where Eliza was asking Maisy to shake and giggling when Maisy immediately went through her entire repertoire of tricks. "Feel free to take Eliza when you meet her. Rachel won't mind. She has grandchildren who run wild in her office on a regular basis."

Rachel was a grandmother? Well, wasn't that nice? Very nice. "Sounds good."

Carla peeked her head through the open office door, and even though Landry had only met her a few minutes earlier, she knew from the expression on the woman's face that something was wrong. "Cal. Sorry to interrupt. Please answer line three."

"Excuse me a moment, Landry." Cal stood and leaned over his desk, lifted the receiver to his ear, and pressed a button on the base. "Callum Shaw."

Landry watched in morbid fascination as his eyes widened with surprise, flicked to hers, then back to the drawing that sat on the table, then back to her. His lips, which were quite full—and why she'd noticed that she had no idea—went white around the edges as his skin paled under his golden tan.

"What do you need me to do?" The question was clipped. A pause. "I'm not going to leave her to face it alone." No compromise in that. Whoever the *she* was, and *this she* was clearly in trouble, she would have Cal Shaw at her side.

And then her world tilted sideways when Cal said, "She's sitting in my office. Eliza's playing with Maisy."

She. *She* was the she? "What happened?" Was that her voice? She swallowed and tried again. "Cal?"

He held up one finger. "Got it." A pause. "Yep." A nod. "Beep, breathe. I've got it. I'll take care of Landry and Eliza. Go."

He placed the phone back in the cradle and walked to her. He squatted beside her chair, and while he didn't touch her, his presence was a wall of strength and security. "That was Bronwyn."

Landry managed a small nod.

"Favors is on fire."

On fire? That didn't make sense. How could it be on fire?

But Cal wasn't done.

"The fire is currently contained to the shop, but Bronwyn says it went up like someone poured lighter fluid all over it. It's looking like a total loss."

Landry knew she should say something. "Did everyone get out?"

"Bronwyn said everyone is safe."

"My pottery . . ." Her voice trailed off as Cal shook his head.

"One of the firefighters who was inside told Bronwyn that from what he could see, most of the shelves had fallen."

Her work. Her art. It would have shattered. All of it.

Gone.

Landry's eyes burned, but she wouldn't cry. She hadn't cried since . . . She wouldn't cry.

Warm dog breath, a damp nose at her knee, and a low canine

whine announced Maisy's presence a moment before she shoved her face against Landry's stomach.

"Good girl," Cal whispered to Maisy, and Landry found herself weaving her hands through Maisy's soft coat.

She heard Carla speaking to Eliza in that cheerful voice adults use with children when they're trying to keep them from picking up on the tension in the room. Cal leaned closer. "Do you mind if Carla takes Eliza to our break room for a snack? Does she have any food allergies? Anything off-limits?"

"No allergies. That's fine."

She pulled it together and turned to Eliza. "Doodlebug, Mrs. Shaw is going to take you to grab a snack. Best manners, yes?"

Eliza was halfway to the door before Landry finished speaking. She called out a quick "Yes, ma'am" and kept going.

Carla paused by Landry and placed one hand on her shoulder. "Take all the time you need. Eliza and I will keep ourselves occupied." She hurried after Eliza, calling out, "Second door on the right. Yep. That's it."

Then Landry was alone with Cal Shaw. He still knelt by her chair. Maisy continued to give Landry the doggy version of a hug. She forced herself to look at Cal. "Is she a therapy dog?"

When Cal hesitated, Landry realized what she'd asked. "Sorry. That's none of my business. My mouth gets me in trouble sometimes. I'm trying to make conversation and rein in my scattered thoughts, and instead of keeping things light, I ask something personal. Don't answer. Ignore me. I'm fine. I mean, I'm not fine. But I'll be fine. I'm going to shut up now."

Cal didn't say anything, and she couldn't bear to look at him. But then Maisy's body vibrated against her, and she risked a peek—only to discover that Cal had a hand over his face and was failing to hold in his laughter.

"It isn't funny."

A chuckle escaped from Cal.

"It isn't."

Another chuckle. And she had no idea how it happened, but his laughter must have been contagious because she conceded, "Maybe it's a little funny." And then she was laughing.

And for the next thirty seconds, they both tried to stop laughing. And if a few tears escaped from her eyes in the process, well, that was what happened when you laughed through your pain.

Landry Hutton was an attractive woman. Anyone with a pulse could see that. But Cal had seen her true inner beauty in the last two minutes. She was hurting, but she hadn't lashed out. She was determined to be strong for her daughter. She had the good sense to accept comfort from his dog. And she wasn't afraid to laugh at herself.

Cal needed to talk to Bronwyn about her matchmaking skills. It was time she put them to use for Landry. It was obvious that she was more than capable of taking care of herself and Eliza. But it was also clear that the monsters under the bed had been real at one time. Maybe they still were. A woman like her should have someone in her corner. Someone who appreciated her strengths. Someone who would cherish her the way she deserved to be cherished. And someone who would adore Eliza the way all daughters deserved to be adored by their daddies.

And the sooner this lucky man came along and made them his, the better.

He stood and returned to his chair. Maisy stayed with Landry. "To answer your question, I had a few difficult experiences while in the military. Maisy isn't fully trained as an emotional support dog, but she's quite good at picking up on emotion. Most people find her soothing."

"She's wonderful." Landry leaned down and rested her cheek on Maisy's head. "Thank you for giving me a few minutes to order my thoughts before I have to talk to Eliza. I'll be okay now." She sat up, but her hands continued to smooth Maisy's fur. "I'll get Eliza, and we'll be out of your hair."

"No need for that. I'm coming with you."

"What?"

Cal couldn't decide if Landry's question held confusion or fear. Probably both. "I'm coming with you."

"I appreciate that, but Eliza and I will be fine. Thank you."

"Landry, if you leave, I'll follow you."

The expression on her face was disbelief mixed with a gorgeous helping of defiance. She scooted away from Maisy and stood as she spoke. "Mr. Shaw——"

"It's Cal. And hear me out. I'm not trying to take charge. I'm trying to keep the peace. Bronwyn's exact words were 'Don't let her out of your sight for a second.'"

All the fight seemed to leave Landry's body, and she lowered herself back into the chair.

Cal had so many questions, but Landry and Eliza weren't his mystery to solve. "I promised I would stay with you. It will be chaos at The Haven. Bronwyn's dealing with guests, some of whom undoubtedly think they can fight a fire because they play a firefighter on TV, while still others are convinced this is somehow all about them, and others are packing their bags and fleeing the mountain as fast as their fancy cars can take them."

Landry huffed out a humorless laugh. "I didn't think you'd spent much time at The Haven."

"I've only been on the property a few times. But Bronwyn's like a sister to me, and we sometimes hang out and gripe about our jobs. So I know what she's dealing with. Making sure you and Eliza make it back safely is the only way I can help her right now."

She gave him a small nod.

"You heard what I told her. I promised. I won't break my word. Even though you're holding up quite well, there's no way you're not distracted and a bit disoriented. I would prefer it if you would allow me to give you and Eliza a ride back to The Haven. I'll make sure we get your car back to you either later tonight or tomorrow."

"I appreciate your offer." Landry's voice was low and husky. "But you don't know me. It's Friday night. I'm sure you have plans that don't involve chauffeuring me around because Bronwyn's afraid I'll see the fire trucks and have a panic attack." She pinched her lips closed.

"Why—" He shook his head. "Never mind. I think we both know you're going to accept my offer. Not for yourself, but for Eliza." He forced himself to lighten his tone. "And because I can offer you the company of a not-officially-trained emotional support dog."

Maisy had her head back in Landry's lap, and Landry had been stroking the retriever since she'd resumed her seat. "My, um, my husband"—she paused and took a breath—"died in a car accident. Small town. Fire trucks and response vehicles from every corner of the county descended on the scene." Landry's skin had turned bright red, and she chewed on her lower lip before she finished in a rush. "I've had a hard time with fire trucks ever since. It's irrational."

"In my experience, anxiety is never rational. That doesn't mean it isn't real. And anxiety rooted in trauma is particularly difficult to displace with rational thoughts." It would be wildly inappropriate for him to pull her into his arms and hold her. But that didn't mean he wasn't tempted. Instead, he stood, slid his phone into his back pocket, then tapped his front pocket to confirm his truck keys were there. "I'm not sure what we'll find when we get to The Haven. Do you want Eliza to come with us?"

Landry's look was one of confusion. "Where else would she go?"

"She could hang out with Carla."

"Thank you. But I think—"

"Mom!" Eliza ran into the room with another little girl hot on her heels. "Mom! This is Abby, my friend from school!"

Landry looked from Eliza to Abby, then to Cal, then back to the girls. "Hi, Abby. I've heard a lot about you."

"Hi, Ms. Hutton. Nice to meet you." Abby's eyes flicked to Cal, and he gave her an encouraging nod. Her mom would be pleased that she'd remembered her manners. Her decorum lasted another two seconds before she broke and ran straight to him. "Uncle Cal!"

He scooped her up, her legs hanging closer to his knees than ever. When had his niece grown so tall? "How are you?" He rubbed the scruff of his beard against her cheek.

She squirmed away, pressing her small hands to his face. "Uncle Cal! I didn't know you knew Eliza! She's my best friend. Can she come home and play with me?"

FOUR

Cal glanced up and saw both of his sisters-in-law in the doorway. Carla winked at him and nodded. She'd probably called Naomi the minute she left Landry in his office. Naomi entered, hand outstretched. "I'm Naomi Shaw. Abigail is our youngest. I'm married to the middle Shaw, Chad."

Landry stood and shook Naomi's hand. "Landry Hutton. Pleasure to meet you."

The adults all stood staring at one another for a second before Carla chimed in. "Abby, why don't you and Eliza take Maisy out for a few minutes."

Abby went straight to the door behind Cal's desk and opened it. Maisy darted through and Eliza quickly followed.

Landry watched them go with obvious concern.

"It's a fenced-in yard that I created so Maisy could go outside while I'm working," Cal told her. "They'll be perfectly safe. The fence is six feet high, and the entire area is monitored by security cameras."

Carla tapped the doorframe. "Cameras I'll go keep an eye on."

"Thank you, Carla."

"Landry, I know you don't know me at all." Naomi perched on the edge of a chair and Landry resumed her seat. "But we've heard so much about Eliza since school started. I wish we could have met under better circumstances, but Carla called and told me what was going on."

Naomi was one of those Mother Earth women you knew was an amazing caretaker. She was short, slightly plump, and her eyes shone with sincerity. She'd been that way since the first time Chad brought her home when they were in college. Cal was a freshman in high school, and after spending a weekend with her in their home, he told Chad he'd be an idiot if he didn't marry her.

His brother was no idiot.

Naomi dropped her voice. "Chad and the boys are on their way into town. We're going out for pizza. We try to go a little early to beat the crowds. We'll probably wind up going for ice cream after." She spoke with maternal indulgence that belied the fact that Naomi Shaw ran a tight ship. "We'd love to take Eliza with us."

Landry, for her part, wore the look of a woman who had too many things hitting her at once but was determined not to be taken under. "Naomi, I—"

"I know you're hesitant. Feel free to call Bronwyn for a character reference. But please consider it. The smoke could be seen from quite a distance." Naomi glanced at Cal. "Chad heard it from Nick."

Nick was a paramedic, and he was also Chad's best friend from high school.

Naomi turned back to Landry. "We've fostered and adopted four children. We've been checked out by every state agency imaginable. We know how to appropriately interact with children who aren't our own. We'll keep her in public spaces at all times."

Naomi's sincerity couldn't have been any clearer, and Landry raised her hands in defeat. "You've convinced me. Thank you. Taking Eliza into that situation with the fire, not knowing what we're facing . . . I don't want to do that."

Naomi and Landry exchanged numbers, and before they finished, the door flew open with Maisy in the lead, followed by Eliza and Abigail.

"Abby," Naomi said in a tone that said "I love you more than my own life, but this is not the time to sass me."

"Yes, Mama."

"Come with me for a few minutes. We need to talk to Aunt Carla."

Abby caught his eye, and he gave her a wink and a thumbs-up. Her grin lit the room before she turned and skipped down the hall.

"Eliza"—Landry knelt beside her daughter, presumably so they would be eye to eye—"I need to talk to you about something."

Cal froze. He shouldn't be here. But Maisy rubbed against his leg before making her way to the small huddle formed by the Huttons. She wiggled between them, and Eliza laughed. Cal took the opportunity to go to the window and give them a semblance of privacy.

Not that he didn't strain to hear every word.

"What is it, Mommy?"

"I don't know everything yet, but there's been a fire at The Haven."

Eliza's muffled cry of fear had Cal turning around before he could stop himself. Her eyes bounced from her mother's to his.

"Do you know what happened?"

Cal followed Landry's lead and took a seat on the floor. "Not much. We're going to find out. I think that's what your mom wants to talk to you about."

Landry gave him what he took to be a grateful smile, then spoke to Eliza. "Abby's invited you to go with her family for pizza. Would you—"

"Yes! Can we leave now? Please? I can go, right?"

Landry pulled her daughter in for a hug. "It's fine with me if you want to."

"I want to. She said she wanted to invite me over, but her mom said she had to meet you first."

"That's true. But now I've met Abby and her mom. So you can go."

Eliza threw her arms around Landry's neck and squeezed.

"Thank you!" But as she pulled back, her face morphed from joy to concern. "Will you be by yourself?"

Landry pulled Eliza until she sat in her lap. "I won't be by myself. You go have fun with your friend, and I'll come pick you up in a little while."

Eliza snuggled into Landry. "I love you, Mommy."

An echo of a memory, a young voice, a blond head, chubby hands . . . and sharp pain pierced him. Cal shook it off.

For the present? He would help Landry Hutton because Bronwyn had asked him to. But only because Bronwyn asked. He'd learned hard lessons in the past. He had no plans to make the same mistakes in the present.

Five minutes later, Landry waved goodbye to Eliza and then paused by the door of the large black truck Cal indicated was his. Cal opened her door and pointed to the step that would allow her to climb in without needing a boost. "Thanks." He closed the door, and she took a few seconds to breathe.

The truck smelled like sawdust, earth, something clean and fresh—maybe Cal's shampoo or soap—and the faintest hint of golden retriever.

The golden retriever responsible for that scent scrambled into the truck when Cal opened the driver's-side door. Maisy flopped down half in Landry's lap and bumped her muzzle against her chest.

"Persistent, isn't she?" Landry stroked the dog's soft fur and took a moment to rest her face on Maisy's head.

"She's a nag." There was no heat in his words, and Cal reached over to pat Maisy before he cranked the truck and pulled out of the parking lot.

"Don't listen to him," Landry crooned to Maisy. "He's jealous because you're giving me all your attention. Yes, he is."

Maisy's tail beat a rhythm on the truck seat, and Cal's throaty chuckle filled the space. "Nah." He turned onto the main road out of town. "Maisy's love tank can't be depleted. She has enough to go around."

They drove in silence, and Landry appreciated the time to gather her thoughts. This wasn't the first time her life had been turned upside down in the space of a heartbeat. As bad as this had the potential to be—loss of property, loss of income, loss of time—it was unlikely to have the same world-altering impact as the last time.

And she had real friends this time. Not the fake friends who'd refused to believe her when she told them she was afraid.

Her phone buzzed, and she scooted Maisy over so she could retrieve it from her back pocket. The text was from Naomi, and the photo made her heart stutter. Not in fear but delight. Eliza and Abby were ensconced in the center of a huge round booth in the corner of what she recognized as the pizza restaurant/grocery store that she still found charmingly bizarre. In front of the girls were the hard, red plastic cups so common in pizza restaurants, and the text said, "Don't worry. It's lemonade. No caffeine for these two." The girls were laughing, and even through the photograph Eliza could sense their abandon and freedom.

"Everything okay?" Cal's deep voice rumbled from her left.

"Naomi sent a picture of the girls. Looks like they're having a good time."

Cal's grim expression lightened by an almost imperceptible fraction. Landry suspected that for all his assurances that Eliza would be fine, he was relieved by this news. But the determination of his features gave her pause. "Do you know something I don't?"

He frowned and glanced in her direction before returning his attention to the road. "No. Sorry." He shook out his shoulders, and Maisy twisted around in the seat until her head rested in his lap, while her tail flounced across Landry's legs.

So it wasn't her imagination. Maisy had noticed it too. Cal's right hand fell to the top of Maisy's head, and he scratched behind her ear. He cleared his throat. "I apologize if I worried you. It's force of habit. My brain's in mission mode. There's a problem, and I'm bringing a civilian into a hot zone. I'm running through contingencies. It's unnecessary. Gray is on-site, and he knows his stuff."

"Gray? You mean Chief Ward?"

Cal didn't respond until he'd navigated through a tricky curve. "Gray and I served together. When the chief's position opened up, I was thrilled he went for it. He's a good man. Great soldier. Saved my life. He'll be all over this."

He paused and glanced at her again. "I think my paranoia is high right now because I've never heard of an incident like this at The Haven. Their buildings were built to the highest possible standards. And that includes fire suppression systems. It makes no sense that the building went up in flames the way Bronwyn described it."

"I'm still trying to wrap my mind around it." Landry turned her unfocused gaze to the window, the trees nothing but a green blur as they passed. "I want to believe it was an accident. I've been there three years. The staff is content. The Haven pays well. People get along with each other for the most part. There's the occasional overbearing guest, but most people who come to The Haven want to be left alone. They appreciate the high-end amenities, of course, but they aren't looking to be doted on. It's not unusual for some- one to check in and literally never leave their cabin."

Cal snorted.

"Is something wrong with that?"

"They could stay home and never leave their house and save themselves a ton of money," Cal shook his head. "If you come here, you should come to experience the area. Hike to a waterfall or three. Drive around. Enjoy the view. Wander through town. I've seen the porches on the cabins at The Haven. The very least they could do is sit on a swing and read a book."

"Are you more offended at the waste of money or the waste of the opportunity to see something beautiful?" Landry couldn't tell.

"Both." This time when Cal caught her eye, there was a glimmer of amusement. "My family isn't wealthy by The Haven's stan- dards, but by the mountains of North Carolina standards, we're filthy rich. But we were raised to be frugal. I think that's why some of the older generations of Quinns and Pierces clashed. The Quinns couldn't see the sense in providing a space for rich people to waste money. The Pierces figured if they were going to waste it, they might as well waste it here where the people of Gossamer Falls could benefit from it."

"Who was right?" Landry asked.

"My opinion? Both. And neither."

"A very politic answer."

Cal grinned, and Landry caught her breath. The man had a dimple. Just one. And when he grinned, the focused soldier dis- appeared and a younger, lighter Cal emerged. "I've been dancing between the families since I was born. When Meredith, Mo, and I met Bronwyn, we were too young to understand the implications of a family feud. We liked each other, and we were in the same grade at school. They couldn't keep us apart."

"Did they try?"

Before Cal could answer, they rounded a curve and were met with a wall of emergency vehicles. Lights flashed from the top of fire trucks, ambulances, and random pickups. Landry took a deep breath. Then another. But the next one was shallower than she'd intended.

"Landry?" Cal's hand wrapped around her bicep. "You with me?"

Maisy's wet nose nudged Landry's cheek, and Landry didn't hesitate to wrap her arms around the dog's neck. Her breathing steadied. "I'm okay."

Cal hadn't removed his hand from her arm, and now he squeezed it. "Would it help if I told you wildly inappropriate stories about the firefighters in this town?" He didn't wait for an answer. "The two guys who usually run that truck"—he pointed to a truck on the left side of the road—"are brothers. Mike and Jack Dwyer. They fought so much as kids that one year they almost failed a grade because they'd been suspended from school so many times. You might assume they hate each other, but you'd be wrong. They're best friends, but they still fight. They got thrown out of the Pizza Palace two weeks ago."

"No."

"Yes. It was quite a scandal."

"What was the fight about?"

He spoke with the solemnity of a news anchor. "They fought over who would pay the bill."

A giggle bubbled through Landry, and she was shocked to hear herself laughing. "Seriously?"

"Yep. They're currently serving out a six-month ban. Denise, the owner, even refuses to allow them to order takeout." Cal released her arm and drove in a slow creep toward the main gate. When they passed an ambulance, he pointed. "That paramedic,

43

Valerie, was in my class in school. She once led a raid of the boys' locker room during football practice. She and several other girls took everything they could find and put it all in big bags, which they dumped over the back of the bleachers."

"Were you on the football team?"

"No. I played basketball in the winter. During the fall and spring, I worked with my dad after school."

"Did Valerie get in trouble?"

Cal grinned again. "See, no one could ever be sure who did it. This was before there were cameras everywhere. And it was raining. The coaches were giving the guys some practice in inclement weather. The girls wore raincoats with the hoods up, so no one could prove anything. Needless to say, Valerie was a legend with the girls and despised by the football team."

They'd reached the front gate and were waiting.

"What was her motivation?"

"Revenge. The quarterback had done something, and she was getting him back. The specifics were never made known."

"How'd he take it?"

Cal winked at her. "Married her after graduation. They have three kids."

When he rolled down his window, smoke and the stench of melted plastic blew into the cab of the truck. They both coughed as they watched a man approach.

"Cal. We've got a bit of a situation here."

"I can see that, Mick. But I have Ms. Hutton with me. Bunch of the stuff in that store was made by her. She needs to get in there. You know where Bronwyn is? Or the chief?"

"Hang on." Mick stepped away and keyed some kind of walkie-talkie contraption.

Cal leaned toward her. "Mick once streaked through a baseball game."

"No!"

Cal laughed. "To be fair, he was four."

She slapped his arm. "That doesn't count! You're exempt until you're five."

"Is that a rule?"

"Yes!"

"Well, don't tell Mick. He's almost forty, and it's a story still told to the great delight of the hearers and Mick's great embarrassment."

Mick returned and scowled at Cal. "Stay to the right and follow the path. Chief Ward is down there. So is Bronwyn. And some of the other Pierces showed up about fifteen minutes ago."

Cal stuck his hand out the window, and Mick shook it. "Preciate the heads-up. We'll be careful."

"You do that. When you leave, make sure you get signed out. Don't need to be hunting you down later just to find out you're back at your little house on the river."

"Will do." Cal left his window down and eased through the gate.

It took several minutes to reach the perimeter, and Landry kept her hands twisted in Maisy's fur the entire time. She thought she'd understood the words *fully engulfed*, but she hadn't.

Where an elegant shop had stood a few hours earlier was nothing but the vague outline of a building being swallowed by flames shooting into the darkening sky.

FIVE

Cal was no expert on fires, but he'd seen more than a few.

This was no accident.

He parked behind a vehicle that he guessed was one of the Pierces' personal cars and made sure he left plenty of room. No sense in tempting them to "accidentally" back into his truck. He unbuckled his seat belt and tossed Maisy's lead to Landry. "Why don't you hang on to her?"

He climbed down and hurried to Landry's door. She hadn't had a chance to open it yet, and he waited until she made eye contact. Her nod was a bit shaky, but her back was straight, her shoulders were set, and her expression had settled into a "take no prisoners" variety. He opened her door and helped both Landry and Maisy to the ground.

Then he stayed close as they walked toward the police perimeter.

"Landry!" He could barely make out Bronwyn's voice over the sounds of burning wood and spraying water.

Bronwyn gave him a quick pat on the arm and threw herself at Landry. The women hugged and whispered something to each other that Cal couldn't hear. When they pulled back, Bronwyn bent down to speak to Maisy, then bumped Cal's shoulder. He pulled her in for a hug and murmured, "She's okay. Are you?"

Bronwyn stepped back. "I'm furious is what I am. Gray says this isn't an accident. But for the life of me, I can't think of any reason why anyone would do this."

Cal pulled Bronwyn back into a hug. "Calm down, Beep. You can't run ahead of this. First step, get the fire out. Second step, figure out what set the fire. Third step, figure out who set the fire."

She narrowed her eyes at him, but before she could comment, Landry chimed in. "Did you call her 'Beep'?"

Cal gestured toward Bronwyn. "Bronwyn Elena Elizabeth Pierce. B-E-E-P. Beep."

Landry turned to Bronwyn. "Is that your full name?"

Bronwyn huffed. "My family is full of drama. Which is why I wound up with more names than anyone should have. But according to my mother, it kept them on speaking terms with the family, so . . ."

"Is Beep a joke, a term of endearment, or is it mean-spirited?"

Bronwyn gave Cal a mildly disgruntled look. "From Cal? It's a teasing term of endearment."

A man in a police uniform approached. Gray Ward extended a hand to Cal that turned into a bro hug, then he nodded at Bronwyn and Landry. "Ladies. The fire chief tells me that despite appearances, the fire is contained. They expect to have it out in the next hour or so." He glanced around, then beckoned them closer. In a lower voice he added, "Off the record, the fire chief is convinced it's arson but says it will be days before he has a conclusive result. The resort itself can stay open, Bronwyn, but we'll need to cordon off this area, and you'll need to provide easy access for investigators."

Bronwyn groaned.

"I'll do my best to keep the number of people to a minimum." Gray looked toward the remains of the building, and Cal followed his gaze. It was bizarre how quickly the flames had died down in the few minutes since their arrival.

"I don't want you to do anything of the sort, Gray. I want a full investigation. You tell your people, the fire chief, and whoever else needs to hear it that we'll continue to protect the privacy of our guests, but we won't do anything to impede the investigation."

"I appreciate that," Gray said before turning fully to face Landry. "Landry, sure am sorry about the loss of your pottery."

Since when was Gray on a first name basis with Landry? Was there something going on between them? And why should Cal care? Gray was a good man. In fact, he'd be perfect for Landry and Eliza. Maybe he'd talk to Bronwyn about setting them up on a date.

Cal gave himself a mental slap. What was wrong with him? He wasn't a matchmaker. It was none of his business who Landry was friends with. Or Gray, for that matter. And Gray was even more of a confirmed bachelor than he was.

Cal didn't date single moms. Gray didn't date. Full stop.

"Cal?" Cal pulled his attention to the present and found Gray, Bronwyn, and Landry staring at him.

"Sorry. What do you need?"

Gray gave him a look that Cal knew from years of experience. Gray would bring this up later, but for now, he had more important things to address. "I said that all the other structures are fine, but it will be several hours—maybe even a couple of days—before the smoke clears enough to make breathing easy for anyone with compromised lungs. And that's a problem because Eliza has asthma."

How did Gray know *that*? No. Not the point. Cal didn't hesitate. "They can stay at Meredith's."

Both Gray and Bronwyn smiled in relief. Landry took a step back. "What?"

Bronwyn led the charge. "Meredith Quinn. You've met her. She's the dentist here in town. But she's on the rotation at her mom's this week."

Landry's confusion hadn't cleared, so Cal took over. "Aunt Jacqueline, Meredith's mom, has cancer. All the women in the family are taking turns staying overnight with her for a week to help if she needs anything. Meredith's week started tonight, so she won't be in her place until next Friday. It's sitting there empty. Right between Mo's place and mine. It's small, but there's plenty of room for the two of you."

"I couldn't . . ."

Gray chimed in. "It's perfect." Something about his tone set all of Cal's nerves on end. "You'd have Mo and Cal as neighbors, and Maisy would love it."

Landry took two steps back and rested her hands on her hips. "Gentlemen. Bronwyn. Please. I appreciate this. But please stop talking and let me think."

Everyone hushed. She turned her back on them and walked toward Cal's truck. Gray tilted his head to one side, and Cal followed him a little closer to the tape while Bronwyn stayed put.

"You need to convince her to stay at Meredith's place." Gray pulled his hat off and ran his hands through his hair.

"What aren't you telling me?" Cal asked.

"If you were a civilian, I wouldn't be telling you anything." Gray frowned.

"Then I guess it's lucky for both of us that you had the good sense to hire both me and Mo as consultants."

"I'm not sure your consulting role applies here."

"As the consultant, I think I should be the judge of that."

Gray studied him for a long moment. "There was a note."

Landry took ten steps away. With every step, she fought the compulsion to go back and apologize. Maybe she could have been nicer, but these people were coming close to killing her spirit with kindness. She'd been on her own for three years. Emotionally on her own for three years prior to that.

She didn't lean on people. She didn't take handouts. She didn't need anyone.

Needing people was dangerous.

The wind shifted, and the smoke from the fire wafted over them. She coughed. Then coughed again. If the smoke was making her cough, what would it do to Eliza?

Bronwyn approached but didn't speak. She didn't even make eye contact.

"Beep?"

That earned Landry an exasperated grin. "Don't start."

"Sorry about before. I think I can be rational now."

"No apologies needed. We weren't trying to be unkind, but we were. You aren't a child. And your child is your responsibility, not ours."

"I know you mean well." Landry waved a hand toward the burning embers of the boutique. "And Eliza can't stay here. But crashing at a stranger's house? It's a lovely offer, but I'd prefer to grab a room at the inn in town."

Bronwyn shoved her hands in her pockets. "About that."

"Don't tell me there's no room at the inn." Landry wasn't serious, but when Bronwyn grimaced, she understood. "You moved some of the guests there?"

Bronwyn threw her hand toward the smoldering heap. "I didn't have a choice. A few guests packed their things and drove to Asheville. One had her driver take her to Charlotte." That the idea of a guest having a driver didn't faze her was a testament to how long Landry had worked at The Haven. "But a few of them hope to salvage their stay. They asked if there was anywhere local, no matter how primitive"—Bronwyn put air quotes around the word *primitive*—"where they could stay for tonight. Melissa had three rooms, and the only reason she had them was because a wedding party cancelled when the groom called off the wedding this morning. She even let me have the locals-only room."

Melissa Wright owned the town's only inn that normal people could afford. It was an open secret that even when the inn showed "no vacancy" on the website, a small room on the backside of the house was usually available. Melissa had an understanding with the police and church leaders that if a vulnerable person needed somewhere to sleep, she had a place for them.

Landry pressed her palms to her temples. "Bronwyn." She tried not to whine. She was unsuccessful. "There are no words for me to tell you how uncomfortable this makes me."

Bronwyn put an arm around Landry's waist. "I know, sweetie. I would come stay with you if I didn't need to be on-site. And it pains me to say this, because I love my family, but I wouldn't be comfortable sending you and Eliza to any of their houses."

Landry rested her head against Bronwyn's. "I don't want to hurt your feelings, but I think I'd rather go to Meredith's than your parents'."

"I wouldn't let you go to my parents'. Talk about a disaster. My family built The Haven on principles of Southern hospitality. Sadly, while we do well with total strangers, we aren't famous for open doors with anyone else." She stepped away and pointed to where Cal and Gray stood talking. "But this is how the Quinns and Shaws operate. Over-the-top generosity and in-your-face hospitality are ingrained. I think it comes from Granny Quinn. If you ever get invited to a family dinner, you *have* to go. There will be sixty people there, and at least fifteen of them will have been brought by a Quinn who thought they shouldn't be alone."

Landry couldn't quite picture it. It wasn't that she didn't believe

Bronwyn, but nothing in her life gave her any frame of reference for a family that operated that way.

"Trust me, if Meredith wasn't out of her house already, she'd move out for you. In fact, she'll probably rush home, change her sheets, and leave you a plate of brownies." Bronwyn reached for her phone and looked at the display. "Speak of the devil." She answered the phone with a quick "Meredith! Were your ears burning?"

A pause. A nod. "You're the best." Then a frown. "I'll let Cal handle—" Her lips pinched together. "Not now, Mer. Please. I can't—" Another pause during which Bronwyn's eyes remained closed. A long sigh. Then, "Thank you. Don't go home and change the sheets. Landry can—"

Bronwyn mouthed "told you" to Landry. "Fine. Okay. You're the best. Love you too."

With that, she slid her phone into her pocket. "All taken care of. She had run home to grab something, so she was there when Cal texted her. She's leaving clean sheets on the beds and food in the fridge."

"How could she possibly be leaving food? She found out a minute ago."

"She brought food from her mom's house for Cal and Mo."

"What?"

Before Landry could protest more, Cal spoke from behind her. "I hope she brings more of the chicken pot pie Mrs. Stewart made. That stuff is amazing."

Landry whirled toward Cal. "That's just . . . wrong."

Cal and Gray rejoined their circle, both of them grinning.

"This isn't funny. I can't take food that was intended for a woman with cancer."

The grins disappeared, and Cal held out his hands in a placating gesture. "If it'll make you feel better, I'll have Mer take a picture of Aunt Jacqueline's fridge. She's begging us to take the food. I stopped by yesterday, and she sent me home with vegetable soup, corn bread, macaroni and cheese, and an entire chocolate pie. They appreciate people bringing food over, but Aunt Jacqueline doesn't have much of an appetite, and Uncle Douglas can't eat it all. You'll be doing them a favor."

Gray shifted closer. "They've been feeding me too. I went by on Monday and haven't had to cook all week."

Landry didn't understand this. "If it's too much food, why don't they say they don't need it?"

"They have. Many times. Doesn't matter. Folks around here show love with food. They leave it on the porch and slip away. It's better to share the food with family than to let it go to waste."

"But I'm not family!"

For reasons that made no sense to Landry, this statement sent Cal, Bronwyn, and Gray into a laughing fit.

"Oh, honey. I didn't realize how isolated you've been here." Bronwyn raised a hand when someone called her name. "Just a minute!" she called back, then turned to Landry. "Eliza's with the Shaws right now, and you're staying at Meredith's house tonight. You didn't ask for it, but you've been adopted. It's what they do. Just go with it."

Gray nodded in agreement. "I've been invited to every family gathering since I moved here. I didn't go the first time because I didn't want to impose. The next day, Granny Quinn marched into the police station with a to-go container filled with the leftovers from the low-country boil they'd had and told me I'd been missed."

Bronwyn snorted. "That's Granny Quinn's way of saying she was offended you didn't come."

"Believe me. I got the message. Made it a point to attend the next time. It was hamburgers and hot dogs. I ate a burger, a hot dog, and all the sides before I had to leave on a call. Cal here was sent to bring me dessert at the station because Granny Quinn was worried that I hadn't had enough to eat."

There was nothing but affection in Cal's voice when he spoke. "No one tells Granny Quinn no. It's not the done thing."

Gray laughed, but his expression grew somber as he turned to Landry. "I hate to run, but I do need to get back in there. We'll get to the bottom of this."

"Thanks."

"I have to go too." Bronwyn gave Landry a hug. "I'm sorry, Landry. We'll get this sorted."

"Not your fault." She turned from Bronwyn to see Cal and Gray in a low discussion. Or maybe a disagreement. Whatever it was, it looked serious. And she couldn't afford to be kept out of the loop. "Gray? Is there something I need to know before you go?"

Gray ran a hand through his hair. "Nothing I can share right now. Stay alert and aware of what's going on around you."

"Do you think I'm in danger?"

"You specifically? No reason to think that. But someone isn't happy with The Haven right now. So everyone associated with it needs to be cautious until we figure out what's going on."

SIX

Gray cleared the way for Cal to drive Landry to her cabin on The Haven grounds. He was prepared to wait outside, but she waved him in. "I'll just be a minute. Make yourself at home."

She disappeared into a bedroom on the left side of the living area. In less time than he thought possible, she came out with a small bag and a massive stuffed tiger. "Eliza won't sleep without him." She dropped the items on the sofa and entered a room on the opposite side of the living area. Five minutes later, she reemerged with a bag and a pillow.

"Let me guess. You're one of those people who can't sleep without her own pillow."

"I *can* sleep without it, but I don't *want* to."

Cal took her bag, threw Eliza's over his shoulder, and grabbed the tiger. "Ready?"

"I think so." They walked outside. Cal opened Landry's door, then put everything in the back of his king cab. "Just a minute." She turned toward the house. "The weather's been so nice, we had a few windows open. I need to make sure—"

"I'll help." They moved through the house and found two open windows that they closed and locked, then returned to the truck.

"Good thing you thought of that," Cal said as he held Landry's door.

She buckled her seat belt and didn't speak until he had maneuvered through The Haven and was heading toward town. "I don't leave the windows open often, but it was so deliciously cool last night, I couldn't resist."

"It doesn't bother Eliza?"

"Not this time of year. I have to be more careful in the spring with the pollen. But fall is usually a good time for her."

"Does she have an inhaler?"

"She does." A small smile flitted across her lips.

"What's funny?"

"You surprised me. Not many single men think about things like inhalers."

Her words were a kick to the most bruised part of his heart, but he kept his voice light when he responded. "When I was a kid, my mom was the only doctor in town. We didn't have an urgent care facility, so I grew up seeing kids on our front porch when their parents brought them to Mom at all hours. I've seen kids in the middle of an asthma attack. It's terrifying for everyone."

"Understandable."

"Fortunately, the air here is so clean, we've had very few issues. But a couple of years ago when that forest fire went through Tennessee, there was enough smoke in the air to mess her up, so now I'm a little paranoid about it."

They made small talk until they arrived at the ice-cream shop where they were cajoled into joining the party, Eliza's delight at getting to have a sleepover at "Abby's Aunt Meredith's house" was infectious. Cal was sure Landry was still feeling the stress of the evening, but her demeanor was more relaxed by the time he took her and Eliza back to her car, which was still at his office. Landry followed Cal to his home and into the small, covered parking area he shared with Mo and Meredith.

Cal had barely made it out of the truck when Meredith came out of her house, Mo right behind her. "Welcome!" Meredith smiled huge at Landry and Eliza as they climbed from their car.

Mo gave everyone a nod but stayed back.

Eliza ran straight to Cal. "Which one is yours?"

Cal pointed to the tiny house on the left.

Eliza's eyes lit. "It's cute!"

She pointed to the house in the middle. "Is this Dr. Quinn's?"

"It is."

She narrowed her eyes at Mo, frowned, and took two steps closer to Cal. "Who's that?"

"That lump of jocularity is Mo. He's Meredith's brother. My cousin." He dropped his voice and in a whisper that would carry across the yard with no difficulty said, "He currently looks like a grizzly bear, but he's more of a teddy bear."

Maisy chose that moment to bump against Mo's legs. Mo dropped to one knee, pressed his face against Maisy, and ran his hands over her head. Maisy's tail wagged exuberantly before she lay on the ground and rolled over. Mo's grumbled "Spoiled rotten dog" didn't fool anyone watching.

"Mo's the reason Maisy's addicted to belly rubs." Cal pointed toward his cousin. "Maisy thinks he's her personal masseuse."

Eliza wrinkled her face. "What's a masseuse?"

Mo answered. "Someone who gives massages."

"Is that what you do? Give massages?"

Cal wished he had a camera to catch Mo's reaction to Eliza's innocent question. He stared at her for a few seconds before he managed to say, "No. I'd scare away all the clients."

"What do you do?"

Clearly, he wasn't scaring Eliza. Mo gave Maisy one final pat before he stood and answered. "I'm a forensic accountant. Which means I spend most of my time sitting in front of a computer."

Landry walked up to Eliza and put her hand on her shoulder.

"Baby, let's not bother Mr. Quinn."

That got a grumbled "She's not bothering me. She's asking questions. Showing off how smart she is." He winked at Eliza.

"You can ask me anything, Miss Eliza."

Eliza giggled, and Mo grinned at her. At least, Cal thought Mo did. It was hard to see his mouth under all the facial hair. Meredith met Cal's eyes, and hers were wet.

Leave it to a five-year-old to pull Mo out of his funk.

"Thank you again for allowing us to invade your space." Landry directed her remarks to Meredith but included Mo and Cal with a wave of her hand. "We'll be out of your hair tomorrow."

"No rush." Meredith clapped her hands. "Let me show you around."

Cal should have stayed outside, but he couldn't seem to stop himself from trailing behind as Meredith gave them the lay of the land. Meredith's home had two lofts. A small one that contained a twin bed and not much else. Eliza didn't seem to mind at all. The other loft was more spacious, and unless he was very much mistaken, Landry was relieved to have her own space for the night.

When Meredith finished getting them settled, Cal didn't linger.

"Good night, ladies. If you need anything, holler."

"Good night, Cal. Thank you." Landry gave him a weak smile and closed the door.

He joined Meredith and Mo where they stood talking by Meredith's car. "How's Auntie J?"

"Tired. Dad came home around three this afternoon." Meredith crossed her arms. "She told him tomorrow he needs to go to work and not come home until six."

Mo frowned. "Tomorrow is Saturday."

"I know. Mom said she didn't care. That she was sure there was something he could do. He said he wasn't going in on a Saturday. So now I'm going to have to deal with both of them tomorrow. I'm not looking forward to it."

Mo crossed his arms and in that moment looked so much like Meredith that Cal had to fight not to comment on it. "He's worried about her."

Meredith leaned against her brother. "She knows that, but he's driving her nuts. It's a combination of Mom being annoyed that she can't do what she wants to do and Dad hovering so much that they're on each other's nerves."

"Anything we can do?" Cal asked.

"Give him a job that will keep him busy. Please. I'm begging you."

"Might do that." Cal pointed to Meredith's door. "Landry wants us to build her house."

"No kidding? Where's she wanting to build?" Meredith asked.

Cal kept his eyes on Mo as he pointed to the river. "Right over there."

Mo's jaw clenched. "What?"

"Yeah. Shocked me too. Bronwyn sold Landry three acres. The house will be right across the river from my land."

"Why?" There was a sadness in Mo's question, and Cal knew Meredith had heard it when she shifted to put her arm around her brother.

"Landry's looking for land that's private but closer to town. She used the words *safe* and *isolated*."

Mo frowned at that.

"I don't like it either. Something's up with her. She says she's a widow, but when I was in her house earlier tonight, there were no pictures of the husband. None. I thought maybe she didn't have any in the living area, but when we went back inside to check the windows, I was in both bedrooms. There were no pictures of a man."

"What're you thinking?" Meredith asked.

"I'm thinking there's a lot more going on with Landry Hutton than we know. She's running from something. But whether she's the victim or the one who walked away from the dad, I can't say for sure."

Mo and Meredith shared a look, and somehow Mo must have gotten the signal to be the one to speak. "Man, we get it. But she's not—"

"Don't say her name." Cal glared at Mo, but Mo carried on.

"Fine. But from what Meredith's told me, Landry and Bronwyn are good friends. I don't see Bronwyn bringing her into the Pierce fold if she was a shrew. She sold some of her land to this woman. There's nothing about this situation that says Landry is anything other than what she claims to be. A widow. A single mom. An employee at The Haven."

"And what do you make of the fact that there's no evidence there was ever a husband? Or that she's clearly running from something?" Cal asked.

"Not all widows mourn their husbands," Meredith said. "Her reasons are her own. She seems nice. Her daughter is adorable. I'd say you're projecting your own issues onto this." Meredith released Mo and hugged Cal. "Right now, your job is to keep an eye on her for Bronwyn. Then build her a beautiful house. And if possible, be her friend. It's always a good idea to be friendly with the neighbors."

"You're related to all your neighbors, Mer."

"Doesn't change the truth of what I said. Just makes it harder sometimes." With that, she kissed both Cal's cheek and Mo's before she climbed into her car and drove away.

Landry tucked Eliza into bed and eased her way down the short flight of stairs. When Cal mentioned that Meredith's house was small, she'd automatically pictured something like a bungalow. She was completely surprised when they came around the curve and she got her first glimpse of the three tiny houses arranged in a semicircle.

Landry had never been inside a tiny house, and it was so much more than she'd expected. Meredith's home was a masterclass in the efficient use of space. The alcove where Eliza slept was just big enough for a twin mattress and a few shelves. But did the guest area need to be any bigger? Not really.

The master bedroom was reached using a different set of stairs, and while the low ceiling would take getting used to, it held all the accoutrements of Landry's own room. A queen bed, a TV mounted on the wall, a closet. There was even a reading nook with a lamp, a side table, and a squashy chair that would be a lovely place to decompress at the end of a long day.

The rain that had teased them on the drive over decided now was the time to make a bold appearance. Landry closed her eyes and concentrated on the sound. She loved rain. Always had. And tonight, when everything had spiraled out of control, it was like God was reminding her how much she was cherished. As if her Father was singing her a lullaby, his instruments the rain and a tin roof.

She didn't waste time with a lengthy bedtime routine and was under the covers with the lights out ten minutes later.

Her phone buzzed on the pillow beside her. It was Bronwyn.

Settled?

Yes. Eliza's in bed. So am I.

Sorry. Sleep tight.

I will. The rain? It's going to be good for the smoke, but not the investigation. Should I be worried?

Jesslyn McCormick is in town visiting her grandparents. She's a fire marshal from a town an hour or so away. She came by and volunteered her services. Gray said she was a big help, and she's going to come back in the daylight tomorrow. The rain won't do any more damage than the fire suppression foam from the sprinkler systems. And it will help clear the smoke from the air. Don't worry about it.

Well, that's good. But the worrying part. That's going to happen.

Go to sleep.

Good night.

Landry set the phone back on the pillow and listened to the rain. Why would someone set fire to Favors? She'd picked up on the tension in the Pierce family and knew there was a faction that didn't want Bronwyn in charge. They might be devious enough to try something like this. But wouldn't burning down an income source be counterproductive?

The guests at The Haven were, for the most part, incapable of burning down a building. Well, of burning it down on purpose anyway. Those twins who visited in July managed to destroy the stove in their cabin while attempting to bake cookies. Break-and-bake cookies. Instead of placing them on a cookie sheet, they put them in the oven, still on the tray they came in. She supposed it was a small mercy that they took them out of the exterior wrapping first.

Not counting the twins, who despite their destructive cluelessness were quite sweet, most of the guests wouldn't bother with such a violent approach. If they were angry, they might hire someone to sabotage The Haven. But she couldn't see it. They'd rather use the vindictive powers of social media to run a smear campaign.

If it wasn't the Pierces, and it wasn't the guests, who else would have a vendetta against Favors? Or against The Haven?

Or, maybe, against me?

Landry had avoided that question all night. Whenever her mind had hinted at it, she'd firmly shoved it away. But here, in this cozy bed with the pouring rain providing a protective cocoon, she stared it in the face.

Could someone be coming after her? There was only one possibility.

But she was safe. Eliza was safe. The attorney had assured her when they spoke this summer that Dylan's family had zero chance of ever taking Eliza from her.

At least not legally. Would her in-laws stoop to kidnapping?

A shudder rippled through her as she considered the depths of depravity and deception she survived during her three-year-long marriage. They were wolves in sheep's clothing. They were the worst kind of Christians. The kind who smiled on Sunday and dared you to tell anyone about the knife they stuck in your back on Saturday because no one would believe you. Not even if you showed them the gaping wound.

Landry squeezed her hands into tight fists, then released them. The downward spiral of her thoughts slowed, and she refocused on the facts. Dylan's family hated her. But destroying Favors was too tangential an attack to have anything to do with her. Or Eliza.

Dylan's family might still be a threat, but they weren't behind this.

What could the endgame be? If someone was trying to flush her from the protection of The Haven, they'd succeeded. But no one, herself included, could have foreseen a scenario where she and Eliza would be sleeping in the middle of Quinn land.

They were alone in the house, but not truly alone. Cal was in his house on one side of her, Mo in his on the other side. She didn't know either of them, but she strongly suspected they were armed and a lot more dangerous than they appeared on the surface.

Well, Mo did appear to be rather dangerous. But Bronwyn had said he was gentle and kind. And Cal was . . . Cal. She wasn't sure how she knew, but she knew he would protect them.

With that thought, Landry rolled onto her side, closed her eyes, and allowed exhaustion to drag her into the bliss of a dreamless sleep.

———

The next morning was chilly and gray, which was the only excuse Landry had for the way she'd slept in. She checked on Eliza, who was sound asleep, hurried through her morning routine, and slipped out the door of the house. Mo and Cal sat around the firepit, steaming mugs in their hands, feet propped up on the stone rim. But . . . no fire.

They both stood as she approached.

"How'd you sleep?" Cal asked.

"Pull up a chair." Mo motioned to the empty seat to Cal's left. She nodded her thanks to Mo and sat. "I slept great. I didn't mean to sleep so late though. I probably need to get to The Haven."

"No rush. Coffee?" Cal pointed to a thermos and a mug on the edge of the firepit.

"Sure."

"Cream? Sugar?" Mo asked. "We drink ours black. You know, because we're manly men and all that."

"Right." Landry fought back a grin.

"But Meredith is into the girly stuff. Creamers, sweeteners, milks that come from things other than cows."

"I would take some cream. The cow kind. No sugar."

Mo hopped to his feet and before she knew what was happening, he dashed inside Meredith's house. He returned thirty seconds later with a pint of cream. "Will this work?"

"It's perfect. Thanks." She doctored her coffee, took a sip, and tried not to sigh in pleasure. She did love a warm beverage in the morning. Coffee. Tea. Hot chocolate. Chai. She was an equal opportunity morning beverage drinker. As long as it was hot. She didn't want anything cold when she first woke up.

She opened her eyes and found both men staring at her. "You're looking at me like you've never seen anyone drink coffee before." Cal looked at Mo. "You saw it, right? She liked it."

Mo's expression was smug. "Indeed she did."

"Is there something wrong with the coffee? Is it made from bark or beetles or something horrible? If it is, don't tell me. No. Tell me. Never mind. I don't want to know." She took another sip. It tasted like coffee. "Okay. Tell me."

Cal laughed. Mo's lips quirked, giving Landry the distinct impression that he wanted to smile but was holding back. Why, she didn't know. But she suspected it was good that he had at least given the idea some thought. "It's just coffee. Nothing more. But Mo orders these beans from somewhere in South America, and I think they taste burned. Kind of sour. That's the real reason Meredith has all those creamers. It's the only way she can stand the stuff."

"Meredith is weird. This is documented fact. Ergo, her opinion on the matter is invalid." Mo stated it as fact, but his lips twitched again. She knew it. Mo did have a sense of humor. He'd buried it. That much was certain. And Landry suspected it was rather dry. But it was there.

Cal took another sip.

"If you think it tastes bad, why don't you make the coffee?" Landry wrapped her hands around her mug to try to pull some of the warmth into her fingers.

"Because he refuses to drink mine. Says the beans I buy are mass-produced corruptions of coffee. Inauthentic. Unfit to drink. So every Saturday morning I sit out here and try to drink this swill."

"I think it tastes like coffee." She turned to Mo. "But it's not great coffee. It's just coffee. I hope you don't pay a lot for it. Because it doesn't seem like it would be worth that."

"Ha!" Cal crowed in triumph.

Mo sat up straight, favored them both with a haughty expression, stuck his pinky out at a ridiculous angle, and took a slow sip. "You're both uncivilized barbarians." He delivered the line with an atrocious British accent.

Landry laughed so hard she had to set her cup down. Cal's cup joined hers. Once she had herself under control, she pointed to the firepit. "Do you always sit out here with no fire? Or was it too wet for one?"

Mo, pinky back to normal, took a drink.

Cal picked up his cup. "We weren't sure if the smoke would bother Eliza."

Oh.

Tears pricked the backs of Landry's eyes, and she took another drink to give herself a few moments. "That was . . . you didn't have to . . . thank you."

A spot inside her heart burned. It was the same sensation as when she ran freezing fingers under hot water. For a moment, there was a bite of pain, followed by searing relief when true warmth chased away the chill. Or, in her case, when it eradicated the frostbite left from people who never cared.

"I don't believe the smoke would be a problem. She's been around the firepits at The Haven plenty of times. Bonfires and things like that aren't an issue. A short exposure isn't going to mess her up the way sleeping in a smoky room would. If you want to build a fire, she'll be fine. We won't be here much longer anyway,"

"There's no rush." Cal had said that before.

"Why not? What do you know?"

"Nothing much. Talked to Gray this morning. He said the site's a soggy mess. He wants everyone to gather at his office at one o'clock and informed me in not-so-nice terms that he didn't want to see me before then because I would be in his way. He didn't say you couldn't go home, but he did say you should feel free to take it easy this morning. He'll be updating everyone in full and developing an action plan at the meeting. And he specifically requested that you attend."

"He did?" Landry was thrilled to be included. While Favors didn't belong to her, it was hers in so many ways.

"He asked Beep who needed to be brought in. You were at the top of her list. He asked me to come in case there are construction-specific questions that need to be answered."

"Did you build Favors?" She hadn't thought to ask last night. She'd assumed they hadn't, but maybe she was wrong.

"SPQ? No."

Mo snorted, and Cal shot him a "shut up" look.

"Then why does he want you there? I mean, I think it's great, of course. It's not like I have a problem with it or anything like that." *Shut up, Landry.* "I'm curious why you would have to attend. It's your Saturday. Seems like an awfully big ask."

"Nah. I don't mind. Like I mentioned before, Gray and I go way back. When he became police chief, he took a rather unusual step. Our town is small. Our police force has always been tiny. But it's a new world, and Gray needs more people than he has available on the police force. He can always call in people from Asheville if he needs something done in an official capacity. But sometimes that kind of delay can be catastrophic."

Mo humphed. "What he isn't telling you is that before Gray came, we had a missing hiker situation. The police chief wouldn't ask either of us for help because we're Quinns, and he firmly sided with the Pierces. Cal did a lot of search and rescue in the Marines. And he also did some crime scene investigating. He has skills that could've been useful, but he was kept out of the investigation."

"What happened to the hiker?"

"Cal went out on his own and found him. But . . ."

Cal stared at the ground. "It was too late. I don't know if I could have gotten to him in time regardless. But the people in town were furious with the police chief. Gray heard all about it when he was being interviewed for the position. So he told them that if he was hired, until he could rebuild the police force to appropriate levels, he wanted to hire a few people as consultants."

"So you work for Gray?" Landry was confused now.

"My consulting fee was $1. So was Mo's. We have no jurisdictional authority. We don't carry guns. We aren't officers. But Gray knows he can call on us if he needs something when time is a critical factor, or when he thinks our knowledge of the town and the people here would be beneficial."

"Gray's a smart guy." Mo sipped his coffee. "And he's not proud. He wants to do his job. He wants to do everything legally and correctly. But he also doesn't want the wheels of justice to be bogged down in red tape. Which is why Cal will be attending the meeting. He knows everyone, understands the dynamics of the town, and is respected."

"Yeah, and Beep needs someone she can trust to give her straight answers and not try to take advantage of the situation."

Now it was Mo's turn to stare at his feet. Landry decided not to dig into that mystery right now.

"We're friends. It's the least I can do." Cal said this without a hint of sarcasm.

"If that's your definition of *least* . . ." This time she managed to stop herself. Who was this guy? He was going to give up his Saturday to sit in on a law enforcement conversation about a building owned by the family his family had a low-key feud with.

"It's not a problem. I want to help. Your livelihood was in that building. The sooner they figure out what's going on, the sooner you can get back in business. I don't mind. I like to take care of my friends."

"I appreciate that. But you barely know me. We're practically strangers."

"Yeah. He likes taking care of them too." Mo stood. "I'm off to my own fun day filled with spreadsheets and numbers. Y'all have fun fighting crime and all that stuff."

SEVEN

Eliza woke up moments after Mo disappeared, and Landry went back inside the house to help her get going for the day. Thirty minutes later, she knocked on Cal's door to let him know that she and Eliza were headed to The Haven.

Cal spent the rest of the morning clearing his email inbox and planning his schedule for the coming week. At 12:30, he and Maisy walked to his truck.

Mo met him in the carport and handed him a stack of papers. "What's this?" Cal scanned the documents. "Mo!"

"You weren't sure. I checked. It took five minutes. And now you know." Mo shoved his hands in his pockets. "You're welcome." He walked back to his house and went inside.

Should he thank him? Or strangle him? Cal climbed into his truck and studied the pages. One page was a copy of Landry's wedding license to a Dylan Flores. There was also a copy of a wedding write-up that had been published in an Arizona paper. Cal studied the photo. Landry had been a beautiful bride.

The second page was a copy of Dylan Flores's death certificate. Based on the date, he died a few weeks before Landry moved to Gossamer Falls. There were copies of two other newspaper clippings. One detailed the fatal accident that took Dylan Flores's life.

The other was his obituary, which listed Landry and Eliza as his "beloved wife and daughter."

A photo of the accident explained why Landry had such a negative reaction to the scene last night. The black-and-white image showed the presence of numerous emergency vehicles.

The photo used for Dylan Flores's obituary gave Cal pause. He'd been a decent-looking guy. Fit. In his thirties at the time of his death. Maybe he was reading more into it than he should, but he didn't like the look of the man, who had a haughty and calculating expression.

As Landry had pointed out earlier, he and Landry were still practically strangers. But Landry was so warm and vibrant. Cal couldn't see her being happy with the man in that photo.

He'd tell Mo to quit snooping in other people's business, but he wasn't sorry he had the proof in front of him. She'd been married. She was widowed. She moved to Gossamer Falls after her husband's death. So she wasn't on the run from him.

But he still had so many questions.

He'd be willing to bet her marriage hadn't been a happy one. Why had she married the guy in the first place? Not that he had room to cast stones. He'd come close to making a huge marital mistake. He wouldn't fault anyone who'd been fooled by someone who claimed to love them.

And having a dead husband didn't eliminate the possibility that she was on the run. Who moves across the country mere weeks after burying their spouse? Maybe if they were returning to their family or their hometown or something. But Landry was a talented artist. Surely she could have found employment closer to home.

Unless she didn't want to stay close to home.

Cal kept the folded pages in his pocket until he got inside Gray's office. He released Maisy from her leash. Glenda, the station receptionist, kept treats for Maisy, and Maisy bounded toward her.

While Maisy and Glenda did their thing, Cal sent the papers Mo had given him through a shredder beside Glenda's desk.

He'd seen what he needed to see. If he wanted more information, he'd obtain it from the source.

Gray sat behind his desk, and Cal tapped on the doorframe.

"Permission to enter, sir?"

Gray threw a stapler at him. "Shut up and get in here."

Cal caught the stapler. "I may have you arrested for assaulting a civilian. That stapler was loaded. I could have been pierced through."

THIS IS JUST THE BEGINNING.

The words were written in red. "The beginning of what?" Cal didn't expect an answer, and Gray didn't give him one. "And why leave a note? What could they hope to accomplish?"

Again, Gray didn't answer.

"Have you shown the note to Bronwyn yet?"

This time, Gray responded. "Yes. Neither she nor Landry have any idea what it could mean."

Cal considered that before he asked, "Where's the investigation stand?"

"Nowhere. I'll get into the details once everyone's here. But right now, beyond the near certainty that this was arson, we have a big fat goose egg for evidence."

"What do you need me to do?"

Gray ran a hand over his head. "Just pay attention. Keep your

Gray didn't even smirk. Not good. "Sit down. Where's Maisy?"

"She's with Glenda. She'll be here in a minute." Cal placed the stapler on Gray's desk and took a seat. "Who spit in your cornflakes this morning?"

"Whoever left this note." Gray slid an evidence bag toward him. Inside was what looked like a broken piece of pottery. "We found this at the base of a tree near the entry to Favors."

ears open around town. And tell me when we're done if you think of anything I'm missing."

"You're the chief, Gray. Not me."

"And you know everyone in town. Not only do you know them, you know their parents, grandparents, second cousins twice removed, and the people who are related but don't know they are because someone's uncle fooled around with someone else's aunt."

"That only happened once."

"Sure it did." Gray tapped his pen on the desk. "I've watched you plan and execute missions. You think of everything, I need you to reverse engineer this thing."

"You want me to think like the arsonist?"

"Or the person who put the arsonist up to it."

Cal sat back in his chair. "You don't think the person who started the fire was working alone."

"I don't know. What I do know is that Jesslyn was back out there this morning. Her exact words were 'This was elegantly done.'" Gray rubbed his hands over his face. "How many skilled arsonists could be walking around Gossamer Falls? I'd say not more than one. But how many people have enough money to hire one?"

"If you include the people who frequent The Haven? A lot. If you're talking about Gossamer Falls natives?" Cal considered the people of his community. There were a handful sitting on small fortunes that few knew about. Still others who could be wealthy if they sold their land. But none of them would set fire to The Haven.

"There's my family. Quinns and Shaws."

Gray nodded.

"The Pierces."

Gray nodded again.

"The McClures have the money. So do the Nelsons. But the only ones who might have motive would be the Statons."

Gray put his pen to work on the yellow legal pad he had on his desk. "Tell me why you focused on them."

"I'm not accusing them—"

"Didn't say you were."

"Fine. There's a man. He'd be about fifty now. He went to school with some of my older cousins. He was raised as a Staton, and he looked like his mother when he was young. But as he got older, some people noticed a resemblance to a certain Pierce. The rumors have flown fast and furious over the years that he was illegitimate."

Gray wrote for another minute before looking at Cal. "I'm guessing your family had an opinion on the matter?"

"Their opinion was that it wasn't any of our business, and we should stay out of it. That it was unkind to gossip, and we should be nice to all the people involved."

"Sounds like Papa Quinn was behind that." Gray took a sip of his coffee.

"Probably. I wasn't born yet when it all hit the fan."

"So why mention it?"

"Because that man has kids. They're in their twenties, and they hate the Pierces."

"Names?"

"Julian and Jeremy Staton."

"Twins?"

"No."

"Mean?"

"As the devil."

"Great." Gray closed his eyes.

Cal looked at his friend closely. He was in clean clothes. He didn't smell like smoke. He'd had a shower. But that didn't mean he'd been home. "Have you slept?"

Gray pointed to the corner of his office. "I caught a few hours on the sofa. I thought Meredith was nuts when she redecorated this place, but that sofa has saved me more than once. Now, why am I just now hearing about the Staton boys? They haven't hit my radar yet."

"They're mean, but I've never known them to be criminals. Bullying. Snide remarks. Pretty sure they would have vandalized The Haven if they could have gotten on the property. I'm not accusing them of anything. I'm just trying to give you the full picture. Their granddaddy died three months ago, and he left some of the money to their mom, but a big chunk of it went to them directly."

Gray quirked an eyebrow. "Do I even want to know how you know that?"

"It's not a secret. They bragged about it everywhere, from the church fellowship hall to The Dry Gulch."

"How do you know they bragged about it there?" The Dry Gulch was the oldest bar in Gossamer Falls, and not the kind of place any Quinn, Shaw, Pierce, McClure, Nelson, or Staton should be seen in. Not that they weren't.

"One of the guys on my crew came in talking about it. Said those two fools marched in, ordered drinks for everyone, and toasted to their good fortune."

Gray glanced at his watch. "Okay. Let's sum up before everyone else gets here. The Quinns have a perpetual beef with the Pierces but have never stooped to any sort of criminal activity. This doesn't look like something a Quinn would do."

"Glad you see it that way."

"The Pierces have two distinct branches of their family. One is on the straight and narrow. The other seems a bit wobbly to me. But lighting the place on fire cuts into their profits and serves no clear purpose."

"Unless they're trying to damage Bronwyn's standing."

"True." Gray scribbled something on his notepad. "We have a total of five families in town who might have the financial resources to hire someone to do this, but only the Statons have any possible motivation, and that's thin."

"Agreed."

"Anyone who's stayed at The Haven has the resources and might have the contacts."

"True."

"And bottom line, someone started that fire. Whether they did it in person or remotely, at some point someone was inside and left behind flammable materials."

Cal's skin chilled. Getting inside The Haven grounds was no small feat. "Are you leaning toward a guest?"

"I'm not ruling anyone out. But based on what we currently know, I'm leaning toward a guest, a Pierce, or a disgruntled employee."

━━━

Landry and Bronwyn walked into the police station at 12:58 p.m.

"Good afternoon, Glenda." Bronwyn spoke to the woman behind the desk.

"Good afternoon, Bronwyn."

"Glenda, this is Landry Hutton."

Landry extended her hand. "Pleasure to meet you." A low woof came from under the desk, and then Maisy came around the desk.

"Maisy!"

"You know Maisy?"

"We're great friends." Landry held Maisy's head and brushed her nose with hers. "Aren't we, girl? Yes, we are." Maisy had kept her sane last night. She made a mental note to find out what kind of treats Maisy was allowed to have. She needed to stock up. They were going to be neighbors, after all.

Glenda pushed a button on her phone and spoke into the receiver. "Gray, Bronwyn and Ms. Hutton are here." She looked behind them and said, "Looks like the rest of the party's on their way in."

Landry turned and saw four men approaching. One was a silver fox–type of man. In his fifties. Gray hair. Handsome. Two were probably in their twenties. They wore black cargo pants and T-shirts that declared them to be members of the Gossamer Falls Fire Department. The fourth man was in khakis and a navy-blue polo shirt. The belt at his waist carried a gun and a badge. Maybe one of Gray's officers?

Behind her, Glenda replied to something Gray said, then hung up the phone. She pointed to the men. "Y'all are going to meet in the conference room. Go on in. I'll bring coffee and tea in a few minutes." Then she turned to Bronwyn and Landry. "Follow them."

"Thank you." Landry took a few steps toward the side door, and Maisy stayed glued to her side. "You coming with me, girl?" Maisy leaned against her leg.

Landry looked at Glenda. "Is it okay if she comes back?"

"Sure. She has the run of the place. She's kind of our mascot." Glenda pressed a button and a buzz indicated the door was unlocked.

Landry followed the others down a short hall and into a small room. The table was oval and had eight chairs. Landry suspected that it was rare for all eight seats to be taken, but they would be today.

She and Bronwyn took two seats near the door. Maisy slipped under the table and lay down with her head on Landry's foot. "Cal told me I should get one of Maisy's puppies for Eliza. If her puppies are anything like her, I'm going to have to have one," she said to Bronwyn.

Cal and Gray walked in. Gray took the seat at the head of the table. Cal took the seat to Landry's right. He pulled the chair out and grinned. "There you are." Maisy's tail banged against the floor in a quick rhythm.

"You trying to steal my dog?" Cal winked as he took his seat. Maisy shifted her body, and Landry peeked under the table. Sure enough, Maisy now lay with her head on Landry's boot and her body across one of Cal's feet.

"Thinking about it."

Bronwyn leaned around her. "She needs one of the puppies. You have to give them one now."

"In my head, one already has Eliza's name on it."

Before Landry could respond, Gray called their meeting to order with introductions. He started at his left. "I think everyone knows Bronwyn Pierce, CEO of The Haven Corporation and owner of Favors. Then we have Ms. Landry Hutton, artist-in-residence at The Haven. Much of her work was destroyed in the blaze." He paused. "I'm truly sorry about that, Landry."

She couldn't speak, so she nodded in acknowledgment.

"Y'all know Cal."

No one in the room seemed surprised or upset by Cal's presence. They all did that chin-lift thing guys have perfected as a means of nonverbal communication.

Gray pointed to the end of the table. "This is our fire chief, Steve Jensen. Then we have two of our volunteer firefighters who were on the scene last night, Mike and Jack Dwyer." He grinned at Landry. "Yes, they're brothers. No, they aren't happy about it."

Everyone chuckled, and the brothers shot Gray identical "not funny" glances before returning their attention to her. "Pleasure to meet you, Ms. Hutton. Sorry it's under these circumstances," Mike—or was it Jack?—said.

The other Dwyer chimed in and directed his words to both her

78

and Bronwyn. "Sorry about your shop. There wasn't any way to save it."

"I appreciate that, Jack."

So the guy beside the fire chief was Mike. Then Jack. Landry repeated their names several times in a vain attempt to memorize them.

"And then we have one of our officers, Brick Nolan."

Did he just say *Brick*? Was that the man's name? Really? No one else seemed to find anything strange about the name, so Landry kept her question to herself.

Gray picked up a legal pad. "I don't want to keep anyone here longer than necessary. But we all need to be on the same page."

He began with a rundown of the events of the evening, none of which Landry would ever forget.

Then he covered what the fire marshal had discovered. "Jesslyn thinks there was at least one cell phone, and possibly two, used to initiate the fire. This indicates advanced planning and skill and that the perpetrator knew the building's layout."

"Not a stranger to The Haven, then." Chief Jensen also had a legal pad and made notes as he spoke.

"Either they've been there before, or they were well coached as to where to plant the devices."

"Hard to get onto The Haven grounds." The officer, Brick, directed his words to Bronwyn.

"Either we've had a massive security breach or someone with permission to be on-site is responsible. Given what I know of our security, I'm leaning toward it being either a guest or an employee."

Gray flipped the page on his legal pad. "There's also the matter of the note." He held up a photocopy of the message. "We have no context for this beyond that it's tied to the fire."

The discussion that followed was vigorous but never heated. Landry stayed silent. She and Bronwyn had discussed her fears about someone coming after her. But they'd both agreed there was no evidence to support the idea and it was just her imagination running wild.

Despite that, she planned to share her concerns with Gray. He should have the full picture as he investigated.

An hour later, everyone stood and filed out of the conference room. The fire chief, officer, Cal, and Bronwyn had been given specific assignments. Landry's part was to provide an estimate for the losses, both financial and regarding how long it would take her to replace the inventory.

"Gray, could I have a word?" Landry stopped Gray before he left the room.

"Of course. Come to my office."

She followed him, and it wasn't until she took a seat that she realized Maisy had come with her.

Gray chuckled. "I sure hope you like dogs, because Maisy has decided you're hers to protect."

"I do." She stretched a hand down to rub Maisy's head. "I don't know if it's anything or not, but I thought you should know. I left Arizona under a cloud. My husband's family hates me. They hated me before my husband's death, and my decision to leave Arizona cemented it for them. I've spent the last three years trying to keep a low profile and avoid any attention, and I'm fairly certain they don't know where I am."

"Or where Eliza is." Gray's observation cut to the real issue. "Dylan's family despised me, but they loved Eliza. I was afraid for a long time that they might try to take her from me."

"You don't think so anymore?"

"I think they would if they could. But I'm not alone. I have friends. A business. Any attempt to portray me as unfit or unable to care for Eliza would fail." She held her hands together to keep them from shaking. "And despite their treatment of me, I can't believe they would stoop to this kind of violence."

"What are their names?" Gray pulled out his pen and wrote down Dylan's family's information. Everything she could think of. Names, addresses, even phone numbers.

"I don't want this to be public. I don't care for myself, but for Eliza—"

"It'll go no further. I won't assign anything to my officers. Unless—" Gray fixed her with a dark look—"I uncover information that makes me suspect his family is involved. If that happens, I'll warn you before I share it. I appreciate your desire for privacy, but nothing good can come from keeping this under wraps only to find out too late that you *were* in danger."

"I agree. Thank you, Gray. I'll get out of your hair." If she didn't get out soon, she'd start rambling. What was it about cops that made honest citizens feel guilty?

"Landry?" Gray's voice stopped her before she could get away.

"Yes?"

"Don't hesitate to call me if you see or hear anything suspicious. Call me if you even get a weird feeling. If you don't want to call me, call Cal. If you're alone, get somewhere with people."

Landry's mouth went dry. She had to try to swallow twice before she managed it. "You're kind of scaring me."

"I'm not sorry." Gray looked out his window, and Landry got the feeling he wasn't seeing the same thing she was. When he turned back to her, his face was troubled. "I'd rather you call me twenty times with false alarms than second-guess yourself and not call me when you need to."

"Okay."

"Promise me, Landry."

"I promise."

EIGHT

The next two weeks were exhausting for Landry on every level. Even though she was back in her own bed, sleep eluded her. And when she did sleep, her dreams were unspecific but dark and frightening.

Her hands, neck, shoulders, and arms ached. Her fingers were stiff. She'd spent the first week after the fire at her wheel, throwing as many bowls, vases, and pumpkins as she could. The pumpkins were a seasonal offering, and all but three had been on display in Favors. They were a favorite of current and former guests of The Haven, and she had orders to fill. They were also one of her more lucrative items, so she couldn't afford to wait until next season. Especially with the way things were proceeding with her new home.

Despite the turmoil and chaos, she'd had two meetings with the architect and three meetings—two in person, one over the phone—with Cal Shaw. The plans weren't finalized, but the architect had given Cal a rough estimate for the measurements of the footprint of the house she'd designed.

Last week, she met Cal on the site to discuss the general location for her house. While there, she marked the trees she most wanted to keep. If it was up to her, she'd live surrounded by trees. But she also wanted a yard for Eliza to play in.

Cal had pointed out that if she kept all the trees, there would be so much shade that she wouldn't be able to have much grass or a vegetable garden. She'd glumly accepted that there was no way to build her home without cutting down more trees than she'd originally planned.

Now, Landry walked around her property, searching for the markers Cal had told her were in place to indicate where the outer perimeter of her new home would be. They were red. There was another perimeter marked in blue that delineated the yard. Everything inside the markers would have to be cleared. But everything outside would remain.

A joyful bark reached her ears, and moments later Maisy bounded across the river and straight to her. Maisy had the decency to shake the water from her fur before making her final approach.

Landry dropped to her knees and threw her arms around the dog. "Hey there, girl. What are you doing home?" It was only 11:00 a.m. She'd assumed Maisy would be with Cal at a job site.

Cal appeared on his side of the river. "Hi." He gave her a small salute and scrambled down the bank. She lost sight of him, and when he emerged, he was a hundred yards to her left. As he grew nearer, she could tell that he was completely dry.

"Hey! How'd you do that without getting wet?"

He smiled, and her heart did that annoying flippity-flop thing it had been doing every time she'd seen him for the past two weeks. Not everyone smiled with their whole face, but Cal did. Usually. And since she'd noticed the difference between his real smile and his polite smile, she'd learned something new about herself.

She was a sucker for a man with a gorgeous smile. One that reached his eyes and hid nothing.

Not that she was interested in Cal. Or, well, she was, but she couldn't be, so she wasn't. She was single and content. She and

Eliza had everything they needed. They were going to have a house in the mountains, on a river, with kind neighbors. A house that would be a girls-only residence.

Because while Landry had healed enough to consider someday risking her heart, she wouldn't—she couldn't—risk Eliza's. Eliza had been born into a home where nothing was what it seemed and the man who was supposed to love her unconditionally had used her as a weapon against Landry.

They were free of that. And Eliza would never again be a pawn.

But that didn't mean Landry couldn't appreciate Cal's smile, even if appreciation from a distance was as far as it would ever go.

Maisy abandoned her for Cal as soon as Cal reached them. "Maisy doesn't mind getting wet. But there's a spot a little farther down where we've strategically placed some rocks and logs. I'll show you."

His smile for her was genuine, but unless Landry was way off, Cal wasn't in a smiling mood. She ignored the inner voice that insisted on noticing that if she'd gotten to the point where she could dissect Cal's smiles, that might mean she paid way too much attention to them. "Everything okay?"

Cal waved a hand toward his side of the river. "Aunt Jacqueline's having a hard week. Mo and Meredith are . . . well, normally they would talk to each other. And they are, some. But neither of them wants to burden the other—"

"So they're burdening you?" Landry guessed.

"I don't mind. They're my cousins and my best friends. They were there for me when my life fell apart. Being there for them is the least I can do."

She believed him. She also knew there was more to it than that. "I'm sure you're doing a great job, being their support. But who's supporting you? I got the impression you're close to your aunt. This must be hard on you."

84

Cal grimaced. "Am I that easy to read?"

"I don't think you're easy to read. But this situation is a common one. Sometimes it's easy for family and friends to forget that the people in the support role are hurting too."

Maisy leaned hard against Cal until he bent down and gave her some attention. "Maisy's taking good care of me."

"I can see that. But Maisy, for all her admirable qualities, can't talk." Before she could stop herself, her mouth kept on going. "I realize you don't know me that well, but maybe in this situation, that's a positive. If you ever need to vent, I'd be happy to listen."

"I appreciate that." He sounded sincere. "But I think you have enough on your plate."

"Maybe. But"—she tried to slow down her thoughts, and her words—"I want to say this the right way, without it sounding like I'm a bitter old harpy. But your drama doesn't weigh me down. I don't know your aunt, or your cousins, really. So for me, while this is a sad thing my new friends are experiencing, it doesn't have the power to pull me under. That doesn't mean I don't care about what you're experiencing. I do. But there aren't any other ways I can help other than to listen. I'd be honored if you'd let me do that. If you ever need it." She yanked on her mental emergency brake. What was wrong with her? Every time she got around Cal, her mouth took off and left her hanging on for dear life.

"Thanks." Cal changed the subject to her house and the upcoming appointment with the architect.

She fought the heat that threatened to consume her. She'd done it this time. He probably thought she was a total loony bird and that the sooner he finished her house, the better.

Except that she was going to be his neighbor.

Forever.

She had to fix this. But how? If she started talking again, she might make it worse.

"Landry?"

Oh no. He'd been talking to her, and she'd been thinking about how she'd been talking too much, and now she didn't know what he'd said.

"Did I do something that's upset you?" His face clouded with concern. "Or embarrass you?"

Great. He'd noticed her Technicolor skin. And she still hadn't answered him. She had to speak. "I'm sorry. I talk too much when I'm nervous. And then I say something I think is dumb. Of course, I don't realize it's dumb until I say it, but then it's too late. And what I said before? About your drama not being personal to me? I didn't mean it like I don't care or anything. Because I do. No one should ever lose a parent or a family member they love. I hate it for you and for your entire family. You seem like such nice people. And I'm sure your aunt is lovely. I mean, she's Meredith and Mo's mom, after all, and they're both delightful. But—"

"Landry." Cal held out his hands in the universal sign for "stop already."

She nearly imploded from humiliation. She dropped her head.

"I'm going to shut up now." In her limited field of vision, she saw his feet stop a few inches from hers. He was so close she could hear him breathing.

Maisy leaned into Landry's legs, and it took all her self-control not to drop to her knees and bury her face in the dog's warm fur.

"Landry?"

She couldn't look at him. What was wrong with her?

"First of all, I don't want you to be nervous around me. If there's anything I can do to make you more comfortable, please tell me."

She didn't answer.

"Second"—his tone had hardened, and she caught a hint of command in his voice—"I don't know who made you doubt yourself, but what you said before? It wasn't dumb. It wasn't unkind. It was generous and affirming and gracious. I was the one who didn't know what to do with my emotions, so I changed the subject."

She blinked furiously but still didn't look at him.

"Please don't be upset. And please don't feel like you need to censor yourself around me. I'd much rather know what you think or how you're feeling than have to guess. And now, *I'm* going to stop talking. I'm fine if we pick up again like none of this ever happened. Even though we'll both know it did. But that doesn't mean we have to talk about it."

She dared to raise her head. He smiled, pointed to a tree with a ribbon around it, and said, "I can understand why you want to keep that tree. It's large and will give you a lot of shade. But if you keep it, we're going to need to adjust the footprint of the house. If we don't, we risk either damaging the roots during construction or having the roots damage the foundation later."

"It's a beautiful tree. How hard would it be to shift the house?"

"Not hard now. But the new footprint may take out a couple of trees on the other side." With Maisy underfoot, they proceeded to measure, discuss, and imagine the layout of her home for the next thirty minutes.

Landry wasn't sure when it had happened, but her skin had finally cooled to a normal temperature and her nerves dissipated. Cal never brought his cousins or his aunt into the conversation, but as they walked around the property and discussed her dream for a kiln and pottery studio of her own, Maisy slowly wandered away to explore. Landry took that as a good sign that Cal's emotions were in a better place than they'd been earlier.

When Cal said goodbye thirty minutes later, he smiled easily and jogged toward the river with Maisy running in big circles around him.

She watched until he slipped out of sight. As she drove back to The Haven, she did her usual postmortem of their conversation.

There'd been not one but two unfortunate verbal incidents. Her face heated at the memory. But Cal seemed to genuinely enjoy talking to her, and he'd been so gracious with the change of subject. Who knew? Maybe he'd eventually open up about his own fears for his aunt and cousins.

Regardless, one thing had been settled today.

She was going to enjoy having Cal Shaw as a neighbor.

NINE

Late Thursday morning, Cal's phone rang. He glanced at the screen and answered. "Hi, Mom."

"Hi, sweetheart. Are you planning to be in the office all day?"

There were a couple of reasons his mom would ask that question. Some were bad. Some neutral. But none were good—at least not for his ability to finish his to-do list today. "Yes, ma'am."

"I hate to ask, but could Minnie and Abby hang out at your office for an hour after school?"

All things considered, this was a minor ask. "Sure. What's going on?"

"I was supposed to be off this afternoon, but I have a patient in labor."

"Your favorite."

He could almost see his mom's smile through the phone. She was a family medicine doctor by training. But small-town mountain life meant that she took care of everyone from the cradle to the grave. And helping a mother bring a life into the world was a highlight for her. "She's alone. The dad ran off. I don't want her by herself at the hospital."

"Mom, you don't have to convince me. Do I need to come get Minnie?"

"No. If you can pick up Abby from school, someone will meet you there with Minnie."

"Got it. Go work your magic."

"Love you, sweetheart."

"Love you too."

Cal set an alarm—if he was late, Abby would never let him hear the end of it—and tried to cram four hours of work into two.

Cal pulled into the school parking lot at 2:30 p.m. on the dot and parked beside a familiar van. His uncle Mike opened the sliding door, and Aunt Minnie's smiling face peered out.

"Cal!" Hers was one of the most beautiful smiles in the world. Her voice had a hint of a lisp and was pitched just below ear-piercing levels. He stood by the door and waited for her to climb out of the van. Aunt Minnie was sixty-one. She'd been born during a time when common wisdom said her family should leave her in a nursing facility and go about their lives.

The only time he ever saw Granny Quinn lose her cool was when she told the story of the doctors explaining to her and Papa that bringing Minnie home would be a mistake. That they should think of their other children and forget Minnie had ever been born.

No one knew for sure what had happened to Aunt Minnie. His mother's current theory was that Minnie had had a stroke during delivery, but she wasn't certain. Even with the latest technology and testing available, Minnie was a mystery—and as far as their family was concerned, their own personal miracle.

She had been a fragile baby. They thought they would lose her more than once. But she always bounced back. It was years before she could walk, and she still had an unusual gait. She was short. Not quite five feet. And Granny had waged a war with Minnie's weight for decades. The war was complicated by the fact that Minnie didn't care that she wasn't supposed to have Oreos and ice cream and potato chips three times a day. Minnie's cognitive impairment was significant, and as Granny aged, caring for her had become more challenging.

A few years earlier, Cal's aunts and uncles called a family meeting and informed Papa and Granny that now that their own children were grown, there was no reason they couldn't help with Minnie. A schedule was drawn up, but it was loosely followed.

Taking care of Minnie was simply something their family did. And, if they could keep her out of the fridge, Minnie was easy. She was friendly and treated all her nieces, nephews, and great-nieces and nephews like they were her own personal minions.

No one minded.

"Minnie, want to walk with me to find Abby?"

Minnie's head bobbed enthusiastically. Abby was one of her favorites.

"Thanks, Cal. When your mom called, I told her it was fine for Minnie to stay with me, but I promised the boys I'd watch their practice this afternoon. She thought Minnie would prefer to hang out with you."

Minnie grinned. "Cal's office is fun."

Cal wrapped an arm around Minnie and pulled her close. "I'll have you know that I finished all my work. We aren't going to the office. We're going back to my house."

"With Abby?"

"With Abby."

Minnie's eyes rolled up and to the side. A sure sign that she was thinking about something. "Marshmallows?"

"I might have some marshmallows we can roast. And some graham crackers. And chocolate. But if Granny finds out, she'll skin us both."

Minnie's laughter was the best.

"I'll swing by your place later and pick her up." Uncle Mike laughed. "I promised her burgers for supper, so don't let her eat too much junk." Uncle Mike closed the van door.

Cal and Minnie waited until he was gone before crossing the parking lot.

Mrs. Bunney buzzed them inside and stood behind her desk as they entered. "Hey, Minnie! Hey, Cal! What are y'all up to today?" Mrs. Bunney had been the elementary school receptionist when Cal went to school there. She'd seen a lot of Quinns and Shaws walk through her doors. Not to mention that she'd gone to school with some of Cal's aunts and uncles, including Aunt Minnie.

"We're here to pick up Abby. But it wasn't planned, so I don't have the car tag or anything. I'm on the list though."

"Of course you are." Mrs. Bunney walked around her desk and made eye contact with Aunt Minnie. "And Minnie? What about you? I haven't seen you in ages. You doing all right?"

Minnie nodded. "We're getting marshmallows."

"Do I hear my sister out there?" Cal's Aunt Laura came out of her office, arms wide. Minnie ran to her, and they did that rocking-back-and-forth hug thing. "I thought you were with Carol today?"

Minnie shrugged. "A baby's coming."

Aunt Laura looked at Cal, and he explained the change in plans. She squeezed Minnie tight. "I wish I could stay and talk. Maybe I'll call Mike this afternoon and crash their supper."

"I'm sure he wouldn't mind."

Mrs. Bunney handed a pass to Cal. "You should keep this in your car. With Abby in kindergarten now, you're likely to be picking kids up more often than before."

"True." He studied the paper. "What does this pass mean?"

"It means they'll ask you who you're here for. They'll double check with me, and I'll tell them you can have her."

"Thank you so much. Do we need to get in the car line now?"

"Yes. School dismisses in twenty minutes. We try not to release students at this point because it's so disruptive."

Aunt Laura had been the principal of Gossamer Falls Elementary for twenty years. She ran a tight ship. And while she loved having various family members in her halls, she wasn't big on offering any special favors.

"Not a problem. Aunt Min and I will get in line. Abby's expecting Mom," Abby's expecting Mom, but I don't think she'll be too sad when she sees who I have with me."

"I'm sure she won't." Aunt Laura gave Aunt Minnie another hug.

They told Mrs. Bunney goodbye and a few minutes later, they were near the back of a stream of cars.

He glanced in his rearview mirror. "Well, hello, neighbor."

Landry recognized the big black truck as soon as she slid into the back of the car line.

What was Cal doing here?

In front of her, the truck shuddered slightly, then the door opened and Cal emerged from the driver's side. He spoke to someone in the car, then jogged back to her.

"Hello, neighbor." His smile was warm and welcoming. She could almost believe he didn't care that she'd rambled like a loony bird the last time they'd been in each other's presence.

"Hi. What brings you here?"

"I get to hang out with my best girls today."

Girls? Plural?

"I've got my Aunt Minnie with me. We're picking up Abby and going back to the house for a few hours."

"Oh." She'd heard about his aunt, a woman who was beloved in Gossamer Falls. "I'd love to meet her!"

Cal's face lit. "Sure. Come on." He led the way to the passenger side of his truck and opened the door.

A woman in her fifties or sixties peered out at Landry. "Hi. I'm Minnie." She extended a hand and Landry shook it. "We're getting Abby. Then marshmallows."

Landry couldn't help but smile. There was an innocence about her that made Landry's heart clench. "Hi, Minnie. I'm Landry. My daughter, Eliza, is good friends with Abby."

Minnie leaned toward her, still held in the truck by her seat belt. "Abby's my favorite. Mommy says I'm not supposed to have favorites. But"—her eyes widened—"I do."

Cal turned all the way around, and Landry suspected he was laughing. She did her best to hold herself together. "I've met Abby, and I can see why you feel that way."

A wet nose pushed toward her from behind Minnie. "Maisy!" Landry tried to pet her but could only get one finger on the edge of her nose. The nose disappeared, then Maisy's entire body came over the seat and into Minnie's lap.

Minnie didn't seem to be bothered in the least. She grinned and rested her face on Maisy's side. "Hey, Maisy."

Cal stretched out a hand. "Don't squish Minnie."

Minnie wrapped her arms around Maisy's neck. "Mine."

Cal leaned against the truck. "Just wait till Abby joins us. They'll fight over who Maisy sits with, and in the end I'll have to pull over, let Minnie get in the back, and then Maisy will sit between them."

His grumbling might have been more effective if so much genuine affection wasn't in his voice.

"Maybe, and this is just a suggestion, but maybe you could start out that way and save yourself some trouble." Landry shrugged in a "What do I know?" kind of way.

Cal snorted. "Why didn't I think of that?"

"I don't know. Probably because you secretly like the way they fuss over your dog."

Cal clutched at his chest. "Cruel woman." He shook his head mournfully. "It's the sweet ones who surprise you with their sharp tongues. You think, *Oh, she's pretty and friendly and nice*, and then, *wham*, she gets all up in your business." He looked at Maisy. "When will I ever learn, huh, girl?"

Landry's mind had stopped functioning somewhere around the "pretty and friendly" part. No. It was flattering, of course. But he couldn't mean anything by it.

Could he?

He was just making conversation. Being funny. Or he had been. Now he was looking at her like she'd sprouted a carrot from her elbow. She had to say something.

She was spared by the bell ringing, followed by a rapid succession of cars cranking and doors slamming as other parents who'd been visiting outside their vehicles jumped back in and prepared for their children to come out.

"I guess that's our cue." Cal made sure Minnie and Maisy were inside and closed their door. "See you around, Landry."

"See you." She doubted he'd heard her mumbled words as he jogged around the hood of his truck.

"Bye, Landry." Minnie's voice was a high-pitched sound that came through her closed windows.

"Bye, Minnie. It was lovely to meet you."

There. That wasn't so hard. Talking to people. Being polite. She knew how to do this. What was it about Cal that messed her up so much?

She walked back to her own car, slid behind the wheel, and

tried to think about anything and everything but Cal Shaw as she crept through the line.

It would have been a lot easier if he wasn't right in front of her.

———

Three hours later, she sat at Bronwyn's dining room table and studied the pages in front of her. "Bronwyn, we can't wait six months for Favors to be rebuilt."

"I know."

"What are we going to do?"

"That I don't know." Bronwyn slumped in her chair. "We need someone who can start immediately. But the good ones are booked solid."

Landry stared at the dates again. Not a single builder was available? She scanned the names. She recognized none of them. "Is there a reason you don't have a quote from SPQ?"

Bronwyn didn't sit up, but she lifted her head and glared at Landry. "How many reasons do you need?"

"How about one valid one?"

"If it were up to me, I'd hire them in a heartbeat."

Landry picked up the pages and stacked them into a neat pile. "I hate to have to point this out, but if I recall correctly, as of a few months ago, it *is* up to you."

"Just because I'm the CEO doesn't mean I have carte blanche to hire the Quinns."

"But what if the Quinns were available?" The idea had been simmering for a while, and now it refused to be silenced.

"The Quinns are the best. They'll be booked more solid than anyone else."

"Not necessarily."

"What do you mean?"

"I mean, that I happen to know for a fact that my house is the next thing on Cal's schedule."

"So?"

"So?" Was Bronwyn trying to be dense? "So, we switch it up. Have them build Favors first."

Bronwyn stared at her. Her mouth moved, but no sound came out.

Landry waited.

It felt like twenty minutes, but according to her watch, it had only been one minute—a very long minute—before Bronwyn spoke. "You can't."

"Wow. It took you a whole minute to come up with that crushing argument? Seems a bit weak. Like maybe you know I'm right and you don't want to admit it."

Bronwyn shook her head. "I was there the night Dylan died. I know what you left, I know why you left, and I know"—she pressed her hand over her heart—"how much having your own home means to you. I can't delay that. Why would you even ask me to?"

"Why? Because that home will cost money. A lot of money. I don't believe Cal is jacking up the prices or doing anything sketchy. But everything costs more these days. Every nail. Every piece of Sheetrock. Cal told me even the cost of outlet covers had gone up."

She took a breath. Bronwyn had dug in. It would take more than an impassioned argument about construction supplies to sway her.

"I have the money. I've saved for three years for two things. Attorney's fees and construction loans. The attorney's fees, at least so far, have proven to be far less than I anticipated. Which is good because the building will be a lot more."

Bronwyn pounced. "All the more reason to build it now."

"All the more reason to rebuild Favors now." Landry picked up a vase from the table. She'd given it to Bronwyn for her birthday.

"This is how I make money." She waved the vase around. "I make things. People buy them. If there's nothing to buy, guess what? I don't make any money."

"You have inventory—"

"That will be wiped out by Christmas. You know it as well as I do. The guests who come between now and Christmas will shop. They usually clean out my inventory, and that's when I'm not in the hole. I rely on that Christmas rush. I plan for it. I prepare for it. And I know what it does to my bank account."

She set the vase down, to Bronwyn's obvious relief. "The bottom line is simple. I'm in trouble either way. I've been at my wheel every spare second of the day, and I've done the math. If I work nonstop for the next six weeks, I still won't be able to replace the inventory. So even if we manage to sell it, even though we have no store and no means of doing so, I will take a hit this year. A big one."

Bronwyn dropped her head onto the table.

"And that's okay. If we focus on rebuilding Favors, it does two things. It gets me back in business sooner, and the small delay in starting my house gives me time to recover from this unexpected loss."

"I don't like this."

"I know you don't. But sleep on it. Please. I think you'll see that I'm right."

TEN

"Why are you nervous?" Landry asked Bronwyn. "Afraid they'll say no?"

"It's not that."

"Then what is it?"

"A lot of Quinns will be here."

"So?"

"There's some history I haven't fully explained to you."

"Involving the Quinns?"

"Involving one Quinn in particular." Bronwyn cut her eyes toward the back seat, where Eliza sat with her face pressed to the window. "I'll explain later. For now, let's focus on finding the Shaw brothers, saying what we have to say, and getting out of here."

Landry let it go. There would be plenty of time to pry the details out of Bronwyn when Eliza couldn't overhear.

Bronwyn eased the car around a curve, and Landry took in the scene. "Are all these people Quinns?" At least fifteen cars were parked alongside a fence that bordered the driveway and stopped a hundred yards from a large house. A wide porch wrapped around the three sides Landry could see. Rocking chairs, porch swings, and gliders filled the space, and most of the seating was taken. A flag football game was in progress on one side of the house, while the other side had what appeared to be a hotly contested cornhole game, based on the cheers and groans she could hear through the closed windows.

"Most of them are Quinns," Bronwyn said as she slid her car in between a bright red Jeep and a silver Camry. "Or Quinn-adjacent. Dating a Quinn, friends with a Quinn, or maybe they met a Quinn this morning. You can never tell."

Abby ran toward them and met Eliza beside the car. "Liza! Come play!"

Eliza paused long enough for Landry to give her a nod and a "Behave yourself" before she took off and was lost among the kids running all over the place.

"A month ago, I wouldn't have considered letting her out of my sight," Landry said to Bronwyn as they walked toward the house.

Bronwyn grinned. "I grew up running around this place. I'm glad she and Abby have hit it off. She's going to love it here."

"Bronwyn Pierce." A low, gravelly voice carried on the wind. "Bout time you came to see me. Who'd you bring with you?" The elderly man who approached them had a shock of white hair brushed back in a way that highlighted his widow's peak. He had on khaki pants and a long-sleeved plaid shirt.

"Papa Quinn. How are you?" Bronwyn gave the man a hug, then turned to Landry. "This is Landry Hutton. Abby and her daughter, Eliza, are best buds."

Recognition lit his wrinkled face as he extended a hand to Landry. "Abby's told me all about your Eliza. And Cal and Meredith have told me all about you." He gave her a wink, and Landry couldn't look away. His eyes were the same blue as Cal's. "It's a pleasure to meet you. I'm John Quinn, but everyone calls me Papa or Papa Quinn." He pointed to a white-haired woman in a rocking chair at the other end of the porch. "That there's my bride, Catherine." Catherine Quinn looked up from the crocheting she had in her lap, and her smile was so warm, Landry couldn't stop herself from relaxing as she followed Bronwyn to stand in front of her. Bronwyn leaned down and gave her a hug. "Granny Quinn, this is my friend Landry Hutton."

"I know who she is." Catherine Quinn stretched her hand toward Landry, and Landry took it. Her hand was small and thin with dark spots dotting her skin, but her grip was strong. "Good to know you, Landry. You're welcome anytime. Make yourself at home, dear."

There was something about Granny Quinn. A sense of peace? Contentment? Wholeness? Landry didn't know if those were the right words. But there was something deeply comforting about Granny Quinn. She'd never felt as sure of a welcome as she did in this moment. But she didn't trust herself not to start rambling, so she kept her response simple. "Thank you."

Ten minutes and too many aunts and uncles to remember later, Bronwyn and Landry made it to the back of the house.

The Shaw brothers were working on what Landry had learned since she moved to North Carolina was a well house. Or what remained of a well house. The three men hadn't noticed them yet, and they were laughing as they worked.

There were two stacks of lumber—one that looked old, the other new. She was no expert, but her recent home improvement show watching told her that they'd salvaged what they could, but this well house was getting an extreme makeover.

The one she assumed was Connor, the oldest, spotted them and said something to Chad and Cal. Landry hadn't met Connor yet, but there was no mistaking the relationship. He looked like a blond version of Cal. Chad, the middle son and father to Abby, was the shortest. Cal, the baby of the family, was the tallest.

All three men had stopped working and watched as she and Bronwyn approached. All three of them had the Quinn blue eyes. And all three were in blue jeans, T-shirts, and . . . tool belts.

Bronwyn nudged her arm. "That right there is a sight that has left many a Gossamer Falls woman appreciating the creativity of the Almighty."

Landry was spared from having to respond when Eliza ran into her legs. "Mama. Abby said if it's okay with you, I can stay and play all afternoon. Can I? Please?"

"Oh, um, I . . ."

Bronwyn started a conversation with Chad and Connor as Cal squatted down beside Eliza and pointed toward the porch. "Maisy is resting over there. You'd better go say hi to her before she thinks you've forgotten her."

"Be right back!" Eliza took off running.

Cal stood and brushed his hands together. When Eliza was out of earshot, he murmured low enough that Landry was the only one who could hear him, "No one will be offended if you don't want her to stay, but she's more than welcome to and will be watched carefully. With that said, our parents had a rule that if we ever put them on the spot, the answer was no."

Landry watched as Eliza knelt beside Maisy. "We'll be having that conversation tonight. But to be honest, it isn't a rule we've needed before, so I'm not inclined to enforce it today. But thank you for giving me the chance to escape the situation."

"Anytime." He turned to his brothers. "Chad, you've met Landry. Connor, this is Landry Hutton."

"Pleasure to finally meet you." There was a look of welcome in Connor's smile, but also something Landry couldn't quite put her finger on. It wasn't wariness. More . . . contemplativeness. Like he knew something about her that she didn't know herself. She'd almost decided she'd imagined it when she caught Cal giving his brother a look she recognized. It was the one that said "I know what you're doing, and you'd better stop it."

Connor clearly wasn't intimidated by his taller and younger

brother. "You should know that you've been the topic of quite a bit of discussion, Ms. Hutton."

"Oh?" Landry tried to keep her focus on Connor, but she could feel Cal's tension from two feet away.

"Abby talks about your Eliza all the time."

"But . . . wait." She pointed to Chad. "Abby's yours. Right?"

"She is. But we live next door to each other," Chad said. "Our kids treat both houses as their own. And Abby's a chatterbox."

"She gets it honest," Connor said with a pointed look at Chad.

"I'm not denying it." Chad grinned, and Landry thought the conversation had settled into safer territory—until he kept going. "Of course, Cal here isn't exactly quiet as a church mouse. He's been telling us about your house, and it sounds like the plans for your build are coming along nicely." Chad's expression was less speculative than Connor's had been, but it held a question, as if he were waiting for her to confirm or deny something. What that something was, she didn't know. Although she assumed it had something to do with Cal.

A quick look told her that Cal was all but grinding his teeth together. His jaw was so tight, it was probably a good thing his cousin was a dentist. Cal definitely didn't want her to know whatever it was his brothers were hinting at.

Despite her determination not to think about it, she hadn't forgotten his comment from the other day. The one about her being pretty. Was it possible that Cal had a, well, they were too old for crushes, but maybe Cal liked her? Surely not. He was young. Attractive. Well-educated. Successful. He probably had a girlfriend in Asheville or Greenville. At least, that's what she'd assumed.

All this flew through her mind in a flash, but before she could respond to Chad, Bronwyn spoke up. "That's what we're here to discuss with you."

The teasing light left Chad's and Connor's eyes, and Cal turned to face Landry, concern darkening his features. "Is something wrong?"

"No! We just, well, we have a proposal for you."

"A proposal?" Chad's eyebrows threatened to reach his hairline as he repeated the words.

"Not that kind of proposal, you moron." Bronwyn swatted Chad's arm. "I'm here as CEO of The Haven to officially ask you if SPQ Construction would build us a brand-new Favors."

Landry had never seen three men react in exactly the same way as the Shaw brothers did. It would've been funny if it hadn't been so serious. They straightened, cocked their heads to the side, and studied Bronwyn like she'd just told them she was a werewolf, but they didn't need to worry because she would never harm them or their families.

They made eye contact with each other and by some unspoken signal, elected Cal to be the spokesperson. "Beep, your family hasn't hired SPQ since your uncle left the business when we were kids."

"I'm aware." Bronwyn's tone held a touch of frost.

"What's changed?"

"What's changed is that I'm the decision-maker for this business now. I'm tired of substandard work or paying out the rear for quality work that has to drive in from out of town. We're friends. Our parents can carry on being childish if they want. But we have the opportunity to be better."

"Okay." Connor stretched out the word but added nothing further.

Bronwyn plunged ahead. "Landry and I had already been working on a design for Favors. We have the plans. We know where it needs to go. An architect has already signed off on everything. We were going to put it out for bid after the first of the year. But now we need it built yesterday. I don't want to put it out for bid. I want you to build it."

Connor, Chad, and Cal looked at each other, then back at Bronwyn. "We'd be happy to build it," Connor said, his voice a low rumble that held an emotion Landry suspected was pride and relief. "But"—he looked at Chad, who gave him a grim shake, and then at Cal, who frowned—"our schedules are packed."

Cal focused on Landry. "Your house is my next project. It will take us at least four months, maybe longer with weather." He shrugged. "Can you wait until after the first of the year?"

"We don't want to," Bronwyn said.

"I get that, but I don't see how to fix this."

"We have that figured out." Six vivid blue eyes landed on Landry. And then three heads shook, almost in unison. "Hear me out."

"You're going to say to build the store before your house." Chad's mouth thinned into a grim line.

"Bronwyn"—Connor's pride had turned to consternation—"you can't be okay with this."

"I wasn't." Bronwyn raised her hands in a placating gesture. "We've argued about it since Thursday. But she's very determined. And as much as I hate to admit it, she has a valid point."

"Which is?" Cal directed the question to Landry.

"Favors is my livelihood. If I don't have a place to sell my pottery, my income drops dramatically, which means I no longer have the money to build my house. It isn't that I don't want my house. But the architect told us that Favors wouldn't be a lengthy build. We're probably only talking a delay of two to three months. I can use that time to firm up the parts of the plans I haven't made final decisions on."

Cal didn't like this. Not one bit.

"As much as I hate to say it, I can see your point." Connor

gave Bronwyn an apologetic grin. "Sorry for jumping down your throat, baby sister."

Cal didn't miss the way Landry's eyes widened at the endearment. "I'll forgive you, you old goat. If"—Bronwyn paused—"you build our store as fast as possible so you can build Landry's forever home."

Connor pulled Bronwyn in for a hug. "You know you should put it out for bid."

Chad squeezed Bronwyn from the other side. "He's right."

Cal pointed to the three of them and directed his words to Landry. "You see this? This is why I could never get by with anything growing up. As soon as I decided to do something sketchy, Bronwyn would run to Connor and Chad. They were just enough older than we were that they thought they could boss us around."

"Nothing much has changed there," Connor said. "Which is why I still think you need to put it out for bid."

"Can you start work in a month?" Bronwyn asked.

Cal looked at Landry.

She leaned toward him. "Please, Cal. I want Favors finished first."

How was he supposed to say no when she was being all earnest and sweet? "If the weather holds, and if the plans are in order, and if we can get the permits, and the materials, then yes, technically we could start in a month. But there're a lot of ifs there."

"I checked with two other firms we've done business with." Bronwyn's grin was smug. "The earliest either of them could start is January. So without putting it out for bid, I can eliminate them from the equation based on that fact alone. One of my uncles contacted a firm that said they could start in two weeks, but I refuse to consider them. I'm still not convinced they weren't trying to sell photos to the paparazzi the last time we used them." Bronwyn squeezed Connor's arm. "I'd already decided to ask you to put a bid in. Bumping Landry's house wasn't on my radar. But she can be very persuasive when she wants something."

"Clearly." Chad rolled his eyes.

Bronwyn released Connor and laced her fingers together. "Can we agree to meet officially on Monday to review the plans and sign some contracts?"

Connor extended his hand. "We'll build you something beautiful, Bronwyn."

"I know."

"Thank you." Landry mouthed the words to Cal.

He couldn't bring himself to say "You're welcome." She'd been so excited when they met last week. Now she was putting everything on hold.

"Soup's on!" Uncle Michael called out.

"Are y'all gonna stay to eat?" Chad nodded toward the tables set up in the garage. "There's plenty."

Cal watched Landry for her reaction, but she was looking around the space, eyes darting everywhere with a hint of worry creeping in. Cal touched her elbow. "She's over there." He pointed to a group of kids standing around his Uncle Phillip. "Uncle Phillip's giving them the standard speech. Papa and Granny Quinn go first. Then the rest of the adults and any kids who still need their parents to help them. Kids old enough to get their own plate go last."

Landry took a step closer and whispered, "Are five-year-old girls trusted to get their own plates? Because if I leave Eliza to her own devices, she won't eat a single vegetable."

Cal pointed to where his grandmother had taken her place at the head of the line. "Granny's house. Granny's rules. It's been this way for as long as I can remember. Granny can be as tart as a crab apple. But when it comes to her grandchildren and great-grandchildren, she's as sweet as a cream puff."

Landry rubbed her forehead. "I guess it's okay." Chad rubbed his hands together. "Y'all can stand around and chat if you want. I'm starving. Come on, Landry, Naomi wants to talk to you about Abby's birthday party."

Connor wrapped an arm around Bronwyn's shoulders. "You too. Let's go. Carla will strangle me if I don't bring you to her right now. She's missed you something awful."

Cal watched as Landry was swept into the tide of Quinns. Her expression was a mixture of delight and befuddlement.

His dad, Craig Shaw, came to stand beside him. "That her?" He nodded in Landry's direction. "She the one who has you all in knots?"

Cal didn't bother to respond.

His dad kept going. "Good to see Bronwyn back."

"Yeah."

"Mo's in the house."

And now Cal knew why his dad had come over. "Thanks, Dad."

"No problem." He clapped Cal on the shoulder. "You know, your mother and I, we wouldn't say no to another granddaughter."

"Dad. Don't."

With a grin and a wink, Craig Shaw jogged to the line and inserted himself right between Landry and Bronwyn. He hugged Bronwyn. Shook Landry's hand. Both women smiled at him. Landry would be fine. He needed to find Mo.

As he walked, he scanned the group of kids until he spotted Eliza. She and Abby were giggling about something.

She's not your responsibility. Landry doesn't need your help.

He turned on that thought and marched into the house.

Mo sat in the den with his laptop. A glass of tea to his right. Maisy on his left. So that's where she'd gotten to.

The newly clean-shaven Mo didn't look up as Cal sat in the chair across from him. "Your dog is a pain in the rear."

"Yeah. She's a real pest."

Mo's response was a tiny quirk of his lips.

Cal dove in. "They stayed for lunch."

"I know."

"You can't avoid her forever."

That got Mo's attention. "I'm not avoiding *her*. I'm sparing my family any needless awkwardness. She's welcome here anytime. Always has been. Everyone loves her, and they've missed her."

"You miss her too."

Mo didn't deny it. "I'm used to it. Nothing's going to change there. Why don't you go eat? Flirt with Landry."

"That was a low blow."

"Not sorry." Mo's words were firm, but his hand left the keyboard and drifted over Maisy's head. He blew out a long breath. "Why are they here?"

Cal told him.

Mo closed the laptop. "You're going to do it?"

"Yeah."

Mo dropped his head back against the sofa.

"Is that going to be a problem? To be honest, I thought you'd approve."

"I do." Mo spoke to the ceiling.

"Funny way of showing it."

Mo's hand clenched in Maisy's fur. "I don't want to talk about it anymore."

"Okay. Let's talk about something else. Why'd you shave?"

Mo rubbed his jaw. "Seriously?"

"You've been living like a hermit for six months. Even your mom couldn't make you shave. Then you show up here looking fifteen years younger. Hair cut, face smooth, clothes that aren't loungewear. I hardly recognized you."

Mo lobbed a throw pillow at him.

"No kidding, Mo. I've been worried about you." Worried was an understatement. But telling his cousin and best friend that he was terrified for him wouldn't get Mo to open up.

"Yeah, and now that I've done what everyone wanted me to do, you're still worried."

"Because it came out of nowhere."

Mo looked out the window. Cal waited.

"I scared your little girl."

"What?" Cal scrambled to follow Mo's train of thought. Had his cousin finally snapped? He spoke with caution. "Mo, man, I . . . don't have a little girl."

That earned him a spectacular eye roll. "I know that, you big idiot."

The pieces clicked. "You're talking about Eliza."

"Of course I am." The "duh" was implied. "You show up at Meredith's with this gorgeous blond and her little girl. They're in trouble. And instead of everything being safe and cozy, I scared her. That's not who I am. I don't care what I look like for myself. Didn't think anyone else should care either. But I'm not the boogeyman. And I'm not okay with looking like one and freaking out five-year-olds."

Cal tried to hide his shock. He had no idea Mo had felt that way about Eliza's response. "She didn't mean anything by it, Mo. And she warmed right up to you."

"I know. She's a sweetheart. She brought me cookies the other day. Did they tell you?"

"No." Why had they brought Mo cookies? A hot pain speared through him. Mo had commented on Landry being beautiful. And Eliza being adorable. Was he . . .

"Don't get your shorts in a wad. I'm not interested in your girls. Not that way."

"Would you quit calling them my girls?"

NEVER FALL AGAIN

110

"Nope." Mo kept talking. "Anyway, I don't trust the barbers here. Remember that time Old Man Lester nearly sliced my ear off? Wasn't doing that again. So I had Meredith book me what I thought was a haircut and shave. What I got was a spa day. That brat scheduled the whole thing. They handed me a robe and slippers and told me to get comfortable."

Cal couldn't keep from laughing at the image of Mo—gnarly beard, shaggy hair, and bad attitude—finding himself in a spa.

"You laugh. Meredith texted me and told me that if I bailed, she couldn't get her money back and to do everything they said. Next thing I knew, I was getting a shave, then a haircut. A massage. A facial. And then a shower with about fifty shower heads. Which I needed to wash off all the lotions and oils."

Cal laughed so hard he couldn't breathe. "Please tell me you have pictures."

"You tell anyone, and I'll deny it."

When Cal caught his breath, he asked, "How was it?"

Mo smirked. "It was awesome. There's a hot tub. A sauna. I came out of there feeling more relaxed than I have in years. Doing it again in a few months."

Cal grinned. "My lips are sealed."

"That's good because you're coming with me next time."

"Not happening."

"What's not happening?" Meredith stood in the doorway with a smile Cal hadn't seen on her lips in a while. She came in and scootched Maisy to the side so she could sit beside Mo. He threw an arm around her shoulders, and she ran a hand over his face. "You look fabulous."

He pinched her arm, and she yelped. "You tricked me."

"I did what I had to do. I have no regrets," Meredith intoned solemnly. "Has Mom seen you?"

"Mom cried. Kept patting my cheeks and saying, 'There he is, my baby boy.' I felt like such a jerk. I didn't realize she cared that much."

Meredith's eyes welled with unshed tears. "She doesn't care about the beard or the hair. She cares about what the hair and beard mean."

Cal held perfectly still. This was dangerous territory.

"I'm not suicidal, Mer. I know everyone thinks I am. But I'm not. I just needed some time. And it was time."

Cal didn't buy it. He knew Meredith didn't either. But it was the first time Mo had acknowledged their fears without losing his temper.

Meredith's tears broke free. "I need you to be okay."

"I know. I will be." Mo squeezed her close and pressed a kiss to her hair. He winked at Cal. What was Mo up to? "So, baby sister, why don't you tell me and Cal about the time you've been spending with Gray?"

ELEVEN

It was a Quinn family characteristic. When the conversation got too heavy, they changed the subject. If you could change it to a topic that made everyone laugh, that was great. If you could shock everyone to the point that they completely forgot what they'd been talking about? Even better.

With his remark about Gray, Mo had succeeded.

Meredith jerked away from him. "What are you talking about?"

"Yes, Meredith. What *is* he talking about?" Cal pressed.

"I have no idea." Meredith set her jaw.

"For someone who has no idea what he's talking about, you sure reacted like someone lit your tail on fire."

It was Meredith's turn to throw a pillow at him. Cal now had all the pillows, and they were without ammunition.

"I was on the committee to spruce up the police station. We spent some time choosing paint colors. That's it." She lifted her chin. "And he's going to help me find a location for my next free clinic."

"Meredi—"

"This isn't up for discussion." Meredith held out her hands— one toward Cal, one to Mo's chest. "I know you're worried about me. I know there's some sketchy stuff going on higher up the mountain."

"Sketchy? How about dangerous, illegal, and downright deadly? That's the kind of stuff going on in the very place you want to go take care of people's teeth for free."

"I'm not clueless, Cal. I know that. But if Gray comes along, there's no need to worry. Gray's the police chief, for crying out loud. He was a Marine. A bomb tech. He can handle whatever they throw at us."

"Is that what he said? That he can handle it?" Cal watched Meredith closely.

"Not in so many words."

"What words did he use?" Mo asked. "His exact words."

Meredith huffed. "His exact words were that if I was foolish enough to go up there, he would have to go with me. Or I'd mess around and get myself killed, and he hadn't been chief long enough for his career to survive if he let the town's princess get blown up in a meth lab."

That sounded about right. Before Cal or Mo could express their opinions, Meredith put on a dazzling smile and said, "Enough about me. Let's talk about you, Cal. When I left the tent, Landry was deep in conversation with Aunt Carol."

Cal dropped his head. First his dad. Now his mom. He was doomed.

"Was she now?" Mo, the traitor, feigned intense fascination. "What were they discussing?"

"A little bit of everything. Landry's new house, the new Favors layout, Landry's pottery. They looked quite chummy."

"I bet they did." Mo grinned. "I bet Aunt Carol loves Landry. And Eliza."

"Enough. Both of you." Cal hadn't meant to speak in the tone he'd used, but it wiped all the humor from his cousins' expressions. He tried to speak calmly. "You know I can't. You know why I can't. Please don't make this any harder on me."

Mo dropped his head forward. Meredith bit down on her lip. "Sorry, Cal."

They sat in silence for a solid minute before Meredith spoke up. "Do you remember that time we were grounded? I don't even remember why. But we hadn't seen each other in two weeks, so we snuck out and met in the barn?"

Cal remembered. They were eleven or twelve. "I think we were grounded because we got in trouble for laughing during church."

"We totally disrupted Uncle John's sermon." Mo chuckled. "I don't remember what we thought was so funny."

"Did you notice that after they found us, they never tried to keep us from seeing each other. No matter how much trouble we were in, the punishment didn't include Cal," Meredith mused.

"I think they realized it was a lost cause. I heard Mom tell Dad one time that she'd given birth to three kids, but she might as well have had five. Chad and Connor are so much older than me, she was glad I had the two of you." Cal looked away. "I guess I am too."

"My point," Meredith said in a tone that refused to give in to Cal's teasing, "is that I've missed having you both around. I'm not happy about all the junk we've been through that's brought us here, but I'm so glad to have you both around all the time."

She stood. "And now that I've said that, I'm going to join the party. Catch up with some old friends. Make some new ones. If you two want to hide in here, that's fine. I'll find you later."

When the sound of her footsteps faded, Mo pointed at Cal. "You should go too."

"You coming?"

"Maybe later."

Before Cal could move, feminine laughter filtered down the hall. "The bathroom's right here, Eliza." Mo closed his eyes as

Bronwyn's voice reached them. "We'll be down the hall in that room on the right. Come find us when you're done."

And then Landry and Bronwyn were standing in the doorframe. Both of them stared at Mo. Landry looked confused. Bronwyn looked like she'd seen a ghost.

Cal waded in. "Having a good time?"

"Yes!" Landry's grin was infectious, and despite the tension in the room, Cal couldn't stop himself from smiling back. "Your family is hilarious."

"Are you sure you've been talking to my family?"

"I'm sure. They've been telling stories about you and Mo and Meredith when you were kids."

Mo groaned. "Lies. All lies."

Landry leaned against the doorframe. "You don't even know what they said."

"Doesn't matter." Mo doubled down. "All lies."

"Some of it was good." Landry spoke in a cajoling voice.

"That confirms it. You can't believe anything they say about us. The bad stuff wasn't nearly as bad. The good stuff wasn't nearly as good."

"So the story of how the three of you decided to hike to the top of the mountain but didn't tell anyone?" Landry gave Mo and Cal a questioning look.

"That's not entirely true." Bronwyn spoke.

"It isn't?" Landry frowned. "You didn't say anything while they were telling the tale."

Bronwyn held up a hand. "I just got back in. I'm not going to incriminate myself and get kicked out."

"So what part wasn't true?"

Bronwyn didn't answer, and her gaze locked on Mo, who, to Cal's intense shock, was smiling.

And then Mo spoke. "The part where no one knew."

"That part was true," Cal said. "We didn't tell anyone."

Mo and Bronwyn grimaced in unison.

"You told Beep?" Cal was walking a tightrope. This was the closest Mo and Bronwyn had come to having a conversation since Mo had moved back. Which meant it was the closest they'd come in years.

"Of course I told her. I wasn't foolish enough to go off without anyone knowing what we were doing. I figured if we didn't get back, she could let it slip. I didn't expect them to realize we were missing right away."

"Did you tell?" Landry asked Bronwyn.

"I never told. And now you're in the circle of trust, and you can't tell either."

Mo's lips twitched. "Welcome, Landry. You'll never escape, but it's not so bad."

Eliza chose that moment to burst into the room. She froze when she saw Mo. "What happened to your face?"

"Eliza!" Landry's horrified response was almost drowned out by Cal's, Mo's, and Bronwyn's laughter.

Mo patted his face. "What do you think?"

Eliza considered him. "I think you look like you now."

"Out of the mouths of babes." Bronwyn mouthed the words to Cal.

Eliza wasn't done. "Did it hurt?"

"No. But I may let a little of the beard grow back. Maybe a little bit like Cal does in the winter."

Eliza turned to Cal. "You don't have hair on your face."

"Not now." He rubbed his jaw. "But it gets cold up here. Having a beard keeps my face warm when I'm working outside."

Eliza studied him. "I'm not sure I would want you to have a beard."

Cal knelt beside her. "Tell you what. When winter rolls around, you can tell me if you like the beard or not."

"Will you shave it off if I don't like it?"

"Yes."

Landry gasped behind him. "Cal. You don't—"

"Okay." Satisfied, Eliza leaned against his arm. "Mom and Ms. Bronwyn have to leave for a while. But Abby said I can stay with her."

"What'd your mom say?"

"She said I could stay if I wanted to."

There was some hesitation in Eliza's words that Cal didn't understand. "Do you want to stay?"

Eliza scrunched up her face. "Are *you* staying?"

Her words, and her intent, nearly knocked the wind out of him. But he managed to keep his voice light. "I'm not going anywhere. I'll be here until bedtime."

"Good." Eliza gave a quick little nod. "Then I'm staying too."

"Okay. I'll be outside in a few minutes. You can holler if you need anything."

Eliza hugged her mom and Bronwyn, and after a moment of indecision, gave Mo a side hug before she ran outside to find Abby.

"Cal, I—"

"She'll be fine. Like I said before, there are plenty of adults to keep an eye on things. Mo and I were headed back out." Cal turned to Mo and he, thankfully, stood.

"Someone has to make sure this crowd stays in line."

Bronwyn huffed out a hint of a laugh. "Come on, Landry. We need to go so you can get back. This place will be a three-ring circus within minutes if these two are left in charge."

Cal and Mo walked Landry and Bronwyn to their car. When they pulled away, Cal put an arm on Mo's shoulder. "You okay?"

Mo nodded. "Yeah. Thanks."

Landry gave Bronwyn two minutes before she turned in her seat and demanded, "Spill. What's the deal with you and Mo Quinn?"

Bronwyn's hands tightened on the steering wheel. "It's a long story."

"And we've been friends a long time." Bronwyn didn't respond, and Landry knew. "He's the one, isn't he?"

"Yes."

Landry didn't ask any more questions. She didn't know the whole story, and she sensed that Bronwyn had shared all she was going to. All Landry knew was that there was a boy Bronwyn grew up with who had loved her. And she'd loved him. Just not the same way. She hadn't meant to do it, but she'd broken that boy's heart when she left home.

That boy was now a handsome man. A man who looked at Bronwyn like she was the source of every beautiful thing . . . and that beauty was forever out of his reach.

The ride back to The Haven was a quiet one. They went to work immediately and within an hour had all the plans and building information prepared for their meeting with the Shaw brothers on Monday.

"I'm going to head back to the Quinns to get Eliza." Landry pulled her keys from her purse. "Want to come with me?"

Bronwyn shook her head. "Thanks, but I think I've had all I can handle for today."

Landry gave her a quick hug and made the trek to the Quinns with ease. When she first moved from Arizona, driving the mountain roads was a teeth-gritting experience. Now she smiled as she pulled into the long drive and found a spot to park. The sun was on its way down, but it didn't look like anyone had left yet.

The house was lit and inviting, and before she went to find Eliza, she let herself inside and located the bathroom Bronwyn had shown them earlier. When she finished, she made a few wrong turns before she found the hallway she thought would take her back to the porch. Before she reached it, she heard voices coming through an open window.

"—what was her name again. A female voice. Older. Probably one of Cal's aunts.

"Landry. Unusual name, but I like it." Another female voice. This one with a little rasp, like she'd had a cold recently.

"Pretty girl."

"Very."

Both women heaved huge sighs.

"It's too bad." The raspy voice held disappointment and resignation.

"If it wasn't for the little girl, she'd be quite the catch for Cal." The first voice again. "But he'll never go for her. He's made that clear."

"Maybe we can set her up with Grayson. He needs a good woman. And I don't think he'd mind a little girl."

The women continued talking but they must have moved out of earshot.

Landry leaned against the wall and took three deep breaths. What was so wrong with Eliza that this family had the audacity to think she wasn't good enough for Cal? Not that she wanted Cal. But if she *did* want him . . .

Stop it.

Landry forced herself to focus on the facts. This family didn't seem to have any issues with race. Papa and Granny Quinn were as white as could be, but their offspring had married and adopted across a wide range of ethnicities and races. Over the course of the afternoon, she'd lost track of all the names and relationships, but there was a lot of brown skin in this family. Eliza blended in fine. So it couldn't be that.

Could it? Even in racially diverse families, there could be members who didn't approve. Surely Cal wasn't like that?

Why did it even matter? It didn't. She wasn't interested in dating—

"Hey!" Cal came down the hall toward her, a big smile on his face. "I saw the car and wondered where you were. I thought Aunt Minnie might have kidnapped you and taken you to her lair. I had to rescue Eliza and Abby a little while ago. They're both sporting purple nail polish now. Aunt Minnie is on a manicure kick."

Landry couldn't make herself speak. All she could hear was Cal's aunt saying "if it wasn't for the little girl."

"Landry?" Cal stepped closer. "Are you okay?"

"I need to talk to you." The words came out hoarse.

"Okay."

"Not here."

"Okay." This time Cal drew out the word. "They're getting ready to light the bonfire. Most everyone will be on that side of the house. And I've let Mom know about Eliza's asthma. She'll keep an eye on her and make sure she stays away from the smoke."

That was all nice and wonderful, but it didn't help her talk to Cal. "Good."

"Do you want to go for a walk? There's a path along the river a little way through the woods."

"That's fine." What was she doing? She didn't want to talk to him about this. But she had to. The questions would eat her up inside if she didn't.

"Give me a second to let Eliza know where I'll be." Cal waited for her to nod, then took off. He was back a minute later. "She said to tell you she's not ready to leave and to take a very long walk."

She should respond to that, but all she managed was a nod.

"You're kinda scaring me." Cal ushered her out a different door that led to the side of the house.

"I . . ." She couldn't think of a single thing to say.

"That wasn't an encouraging response. We'll be alone in a min-ute, and then I'm going to need you to share."

"Okay." She couldn't very well explain that she was afraid that once she started talking, she'd never stop. Why did it matter if the Quinns thought Eliza was a problem? That wasn't it. It mattered that Cal thought Eliza was a problem. If Eliza was objectionable to him, she needed to know now. Before she paid this man thousands of dollars to build her a house across the river from him.

She froze. She couldn't do this. She'd ask Bronwyn. Bronwyn would know, or she could find out. "I'm sorry. I shouldn't have . . . um . . . I need to go."

"Oh no you don't." Cal didn't touch her. Didn't do anything to physically restrain her. But something in his voice kept her from running away. "You've taken ten years off my life. You can't bail now."

Why was she still walking? Why was she following him into the trees?

They reached a small path that followed the edge of a river. Probably the same river that separated her property from Cal's. Cal didn't stop walking, but he didn't let it go either. "Let's hear it. What's got you worked up?"

Landry dug in her pocket for her ChapStick. Applied it. Kept walking. "I, um, I overheard something, and I must have misunderstood, or maybe I'm missing some information."

"What did you overhear?" Cal's voice was a low rumble of barely controlled fury. "Was someone unkind to you? To Eliza? I'll take care of it. Please tell me what's upset you."

She stopped walking and turned to face him. "Do you have a problem with Eliza?" There. It was out. She'd asked.

And in one horrible moment, everything changed. Because Cal's face said it all.

He *did* have a problem with her daughter.

122 NEVER FALL AGAIN

TWELVE

What could have given Landry the idea that he had a problem with Eliza? Cal's mind raced with possible scenarios and came up with nothing. "Eliza is precious. Funny. Smart. Cute as a button. Respectful. Polite. I could go on."

"You're lying to me." Her voice broke.

"I most certainly am not. You don't know me well enough to say that about me, or to know this about me, but if there's one thing I'll never do, it's lie to you."

Tears welled in her eyes.

"Landry, please tell me what brought this on."

"I"—she dropped her head and spoke to the ground—"I overheard two of your aunts talking. Or I think they were your aunts. I'm not sure. I didn't see them. And they were talking about me. And . . ."

"And?"

Even in the dimming light, he could see the flush that spread over her cheeks. "One of them said I was pretty, but that it was too bad about the little girl. That if it wasn't for Eliza, I would be quite the catch for you, but that you'd made it clear you weren't interested. Because of Eliza."

For a few seconds, Cal couldn't form a rational thought. This could not be happening. "My aunts are . . ." How could he describe them? "They want me to be happy. And they think the only way for that to happen is for me to find a good woman, settle down, and start a family."

Landry looked at him, eyes flashing. "I'm not looking for a man to settle down with, Cal. I just want to know what's wrong with my daughter."

"Nothing!" Cal ran a hand through his hair. "Nothing is wrong with you or Eliza. My aunts . . ." He couldn't believe he was about to do this, but he couldn't see a way around it. "Landry, please believe me. You and Eliza are wonderful. I think so. Everyone in my family thinks so. But I know why my aunts said what they did, and I'm happy to explain it. But it's not a short story, and it doesn't have a happy ending."

"You said Eliza wanted us to take a long walk." The words were a dare.

"You want me to explain now?"

"I do."

"Fine." He turned and walked along the river. Landry stayed with him. "But I need to give you some background so you'll understand."

Landry threw out a hand in a gesture telling him to get on with it.

"I'd always planned to move back to Gossamer Falls. My brothers are ten and eight years older than I am. Connor fell in love with Carla when they were fourteen. They eloped three days after graduation."

Landry's eyes were huge. "No way."

"Those two were crazy over each other, but everyone—my parents, her parents, the entire town—thought they were too young. So they ran off to Tennessee, got married, stayed gone a couple of days, then came home and told their families that it was done and they were going to have to deal with it."

Landry shook her head. "I'm having a hard time picturing this. Carla is just so—"

"Sensible? Responsible?"

"Exactly."

"She would say she knew she wasn't ever going to love anyone else. Anyway, that's a different story for a different time. The point is, he went to college and joined the Marines. Then came back home and joined the family business. Chad did the same."

"Chad eloped too?"

"No." Cal couldn't help but smile at that. "Chad met Naomi when he was a sophomore at NC State. He brought her home for Christmas. I was about twelve at the time, and I had the biggest crush on her. Told my brother if he let her go, he was insane."

"Obviously he didn't let her go."

"Asked her to marry him that summer. They were sensible and waited until after graduation. But again, they moved back here after Chad's service was up with the Marines, and he also joined the family business."

"So you followed in their footsteps?" Landry guessed.

"That was the plan. I figured I'd find the right girl. Get married. Serve my country. Come home. Raise a family here. It had worked out great for my brothers. And it's crucial that you don't tell them this, but I pretty much idolized both of them."

"My lips are sealed." Landry mimed zipping her lips.

If he wasn't mistaken, the hostility was leaving her as she listened to his story. He hoped it would stay away when he was done.

"I went to college, got my degree, and finished a deployment. But I still hadn't met the girl for me. I was stationed in the eastern part of North Carolina and that's when I met Gina."

"I have a bad feeling about this."

"Yeah, well, I didn't. We met at church."

"Uh-oh." Landry didn't sound like she was being sarcastic.

"What?"

"Mean church people are the worst kind of mean people." Her mouth had a hard edge to it.

If she was still speaking to him when this story was over, he'd have to find out what that was about. "I'd seen her with her kids. Two boys. No wedding ring. Didn't take long before I found out her husband had cheated on her and left her with a six-month-old and a two-year-old. She was from a town about two hours away, but she'd stayed because her job was there. She loved the church. Had lots of friends. I got to know her a little and asked her out. She told me that the only way she'd go out with me was if I agreed to stay away from her kids. That they were too young to understand if things didn't work out."

"Seems fair." Landry's mama-bear side was coming out, and Cal didn't mind that one bit.

"I had no problem with it. We dated for six months before she invited me to her house for dinner. The boys . . ." Cal swallowed. "The boys were three and five. Sebastian was potty training. Spencer was in kindergarten. They didn't have a shy bone in their little bodies. Gina went to the kitchen to get me a Coke, and I was on the floor playing with them."

"That doesn't surprise me. You're a kid magnet." Landry spoke softly. "But Cal, I think I can see where this is going. You don't need to say anymore. I . . . I shouldn't have insisted on an explanation. This is obviously something very personal, and—"

"No. It's okay. It's not something I go around talking about, but it isn't a secret either. And I think it's fair that you should hear it from me and not from my aunts' blabbing when they don't know the full story."

He led her to a small bench that Papa had put by the river so Granny could "watch the Lord put the day to bed," as she liked to put it. They sat, and he leaned forward and rested his elbows on his knees. "Over the next few months, our lives became more entwined. We started going out with the boys. I was on duty every other weekend, but when I was around, we were together."

"I feel like there's a huge disaster coming." Landry leaned forward and mimicked his posture.

"We'd been together over a year when I was deployed. The deployment wasn't a complete shock. I knew it was coming, but I thought I had a few more months. I only had three days to get everything sorted. When I left, I fully expected to come home to her, the boys, and restart our life."

Maisy came trotting down the path and joined them. How she knew to find him the way she did was a mystery, but he wasn't complaining. She sat between his leg and Landry's and rested her head on his knee.

"Every deployment is different. Sometimes you can call home, email, FaceTime. Sometimes you can't. In my case, I only had a small window about once every three weeks when I could touch base. The first time I called, it had been a month since I'd seen her and the boys. I was so excited to talk to them."

"She didn't answer?" Landry's voice held a potent combination of trepidation and indignation.

"Nope. I tried every number I had for her. No luck. I told myself that it happens. Time zones, schedules, the erratic nature of the communication. I was devastated, but I was more worried about how she would feel when she realized she'd missed my call." He tried, but he knew he hadn't kept the bitterness out of his voice.

"The next time I called, the same thing happened. I couldn't figure out what was going on, and I was starting to panic. What if something had happened to them? What if someone was sick? I ran into a buddy whose wife knew Gina and asked him to mention it when he talked to her. Three days later, he hunted me down. Told me he'd talked to his wife and that she'd talked with news about Gina."

Remembering that day, he could taste the dust on the wind and feel the sand on his skin. "Gina had left town. Taken the boys. Moved back to her hometown."

"She left while you were deployed?" Landry shifted so her body now faced his. "That's so wrong."

"I can't disagree with you there. The next week, I got a package. She'd written a note telling me she was sorry. That on those weekends when I was on duty, she'd taken the kids back to her parents to visit and reconnected with a high school boyfriend. He'd convinced her that the easiest way to handle it would be to wait until I left for the deployment and then move while I was gone. It would be, and I quote, 'less messy.'"

Landry snorted. "As in he was less likely to get his face rearranged by his girlfriend's Marine boyfriend."

Cal hadn't expected to laugh during this tale, but he did. "Something like that."

He wasn't sure how to end this part of the story. Up to this point, it had been mostly telling her the facts. Now he'd have to tell her how he responded.

And how he fell apart.

Landry wanted to find this Gina woman and punch her in the nose. What an idiot. She had a man like Cal, and she walked away?

"I'm almost afraid to ask, but the high school boyfriend? Was he rich?"

"How'd you guess?" Cal rubbed his hand over Maisy's head. "He wasn't millionaire wealthy, but he could give her a very comfortable life. He was a pretty-boy type. I showed Meredith a picture, and she said he was good-looking. It's not like she left me for a fat slob who spends his days watching TV and his nights in a bar."

"That's not much consolation."

"No. It wasn't. I did my job and kept my head down, but I was a wreck. I was grieving my relationship. And I lost a few friends while we were deployed. But I got out alive. Came home."

He rubbed his eyes. "I hadn't told anybody. But Mo and Meredith were waiting for me when I got off the plane. If they hadn't been, I don't know what I would have done."

"Were you going to go after her?"

"Maybe? I'm not sure. I wasn't in a good place mentally or emotionally."

"How did Mo and Meredith find out?"

"Meredith had gone to check on my place. I knew she was going to do that, and I appreciated it. I didn't realize that Gina had come over before she left town. She'd taken all her stuff and returned all mine. Meredith walked in and found a pile of sweatshirts, some books, a pair of sunglasses, and the jewelry I'd given Gina while we were dating. To say she was furious was an understatement. Meredith is very protective of those she loves."

"Oh boy." Meredith Quinn was a very nice lady. But Landry made a mental note to never get on her bad side.

"Yeah. Meredith called Mo. And he did what he does—he was Army intelligence and can find out anything."

Landry tried to keep her face impassive at that news. If Mo started digging into her past . . . she pulled her focus back to Cal.

"Mo got the whole story. Then he put a watch on my unit so he'd know when we came home. He and Meredith were ready for me. He'd taken leave, and she'd taken a week off too. They'd gone through my place and put everything away, cleaned it, stocked the fridge, and found a therapist for me."

"Which is what you meant about them being there for you in the past."

"Yeah."

"Did you ever talk to Gina again?" Landry wasn't sure how she was hoping he would answer that question.

"I was going to. But when Mo did his digging, he came across her marriage certificate. And her new husband was in the process of adopting the boys."

Cal's tone had been brisk and businesslike, but now it dripped with pain and loss. Landry couldn't stop herself from reaching for where his hand rested on Maisy's back. She squeezed. "Losing her was hard. Losing the boys must have been like a death."

He turned to her, a look of surprise on his face. "Yes, I'd dated before. Been dumped. Been the one doing the dumping. You move on. But with the boys? The last thing I'd said to them was that we'd talk soon."

She squeezed his hand again.

"It gutted me that they'd never hear me tell them how awesome they were again. That I hadn't told them I was proud of them. Or that no matter what, I'd always be there for them."

Cal stopped talking and looked out over the river. "Therapy helped. I got out of the Marines. Moved home. Meredith was still in the Raleigh area, and Mo was still in the Army, so they weren't here to help diffuse any of the stress. I was living in my parents' basement apartment and trying to get used to civilian life. My aunts, bless their hearts, thought I needed a girlfriend—and I needed one yesterday. They threw every eligible female they could find at me. I was twenty-eight when I moved back. They suggested a woman who was forty-two. I'm not saying a fourteen-year age gap is insurmountable, but that woman had been my high school biology teacher."

Landry couldn't help laughing at the horror in his voice.

"There was a woman from a town about fifteen miles from here, another from Asheville, one from Greenville. As far as I could tell, their only prerequisites were that the women had reasonable personal hygiene and knew how to read."

He leaned back and stared at the sky. "When they started with the single moms in town, I had to put a stop to it. My parents knew the gist of what had happened with Gina, but no one else did until the day Aunt Rhonda spent five minutes trying to convince me to call a girl I'd dated in high school. A girl who was divorced and had three kids under six. I'd seen her in town. Spoken to her. She's a nice woman. Her kids are cute. I think one of them is in Abby and Eliza's class. I tried to tell Aunt Rhonda I wasn't interested, but she wouldn't let it go. I held on to my frustration until she made a snide remark that at my age, I wasn't in a position to rule out single moms."

Landry had another bad feeling, but she didn't say that. "What happened?"

"We were eating under the tent, like we did today. I stood up from my chair, leaned down until I was about a foot from Aunt Rhonda's face, and told her, loud enough for the rest of the family to hear, that I'd dated a single mom before and had my heart shredded for my trouble. Then I said it would be a very cold day in a very hot place before I took that chance again."

"Did you actually say 'cold day in a hot place' or . . ."

"Oh, there's no cursing at Granny's house. I said it just like that. Granny was okay with it until Aunt Minnie got it all mixed up and told her it would be a hot day in a cold place before she would eat her broccoli."

"Aunt Minnie is a hoot."

"Yeah. But seriously, Granny didn't care. She'd gotten most of the story from Dad, and she understood."

Landry waited for him to go on, and when he didn't, she nudged his shoulder. "So you don't have a problem with Eliza, but you kind of do have a problem with Eliza."

He straightened. "No. Eliza is not a problem. I have problems. I have demons. I have issues. I have two boys out there in the world who have a piece of my heart, and they could walk past me on the street today and I wouldn't recognize them. And they wouldn't know me either. It guts me every time I think about it. I remember their birthdays, but I can't send them a card. It would be inappropriate, and I would never want to come between them and their new dad."

"I know you wouldn't."

"But the thing is, she took them and left. And she had every right to do that. I had no rights when it came to the boys. But in my heart, they were mine. And then they were someone else's. I realize this is going to sound weird, but if the boys hadn't been in the picture and she'd cheated on me and left me, I would've been hurt, but I would've moved on a lot easier."

"Have you moved on?" It didn't sound to her like he had.

"I think I have. Although I wouldn't blame you if you didn't believe me. When I first got back from my deployment, before I was out of the Marines, I tried to date a little. I asked a few women out."

"Too soon?"

"Too soon and all kinds of wrong. It took me a few dates to realize that I was using those women, and they didn't deserve that."

"How is asking a woman out using her?"

"Because I was asking them out to try to fix myself. To prove to myself that I was over Gina."

"I'm not sure I'm following you."

"When a man asks a woman out, it should be because he finds her intriguing. Because he wants to spend time with her. He should want to understand what makes her laugh or what makes her sigh. Why she likes certain books or why a particular song makes her cry. He should spend time with her because he's desperate to figure out what makes her tick. Not because he's afraid he'll never fall in love again or to prove to himself that he isn't hung up on a woman who clearly never loved him."

He took a deep breath. "I haven't dated since then because I refuse to use a woman that way. And because women with children scare me to death. I'm not sure I could handle another breakup that involved children."

THIRTEEN

Cal watched several emotions play across Landry's face and a tear slip down her cheek.

She swiped at the tear. "I'm sorry I put you in a situation where you felt you had to share that. There's some history that we don't need to get into right now, but it's made me quick to assume the worst. That has led me to hurting people who never intended to harm me. Which has taught me to speak up when something seems hinky. In the long run, it saves a lot of hurt feelings. Either I find out the person isn't who I thought they were, or I find out the truth, which is usually more complicated but also freeing."

"I don't feel like I was coerced. But I do need to ask you if they said anything else that I need to know about or that has you worried."

Landry twisted her lips to the side.

Oh no.

"They did say something about trying to set me up with the police chief."

"Gray?" Cal fought the surge of frustration welling inside him. He'd had the same thoughts himself. They would make a good couple. But there was that whole thing with Meredith . . .

"Yes. And if you could help me with that, I would appreciate it."

133

"You're interested in Gray?"

"Goodness no. I barely know him."

That was not relief flooding through his system. Or maybe it was, but that was because now things wouldn't be awkward with Meredith. "He's a great guy."

"I don't doubt that he is. But it would help if you could convey to them that I don't need to be set up. With anyone. Ever."

"You aren't interested in dating?"

"No." Flat. Unequivocal. "And since you shared your fears with me, I'll give you this for free, although I would appreciate it if you don't tell your aunts."

"It's in the vault."

"Thank you." She took a deep breath before she continued. "Your fear of women with children, especially in light of what you went through, is understandable. My fear is of so-called 'good Christian' men. The more often they go to church, the scarier they are. And this is coming from a woman who loves Jesus."

Cal didn't like where this was heading.

"My marriage was not happy, but no one in our church believed me. Dylan was such a *good man*. So faithful. I was blessed to have snagged him." Her voice had pitched into gossipy old lady territory. Then she shuddered. "I was young, naive, and in love. But the man I married was not the man I'd dated and been engaged to. He got me pregnant on our honeymoon. I realized later it was so he could control me. Eliza has no idea that the daddy she adored only saw her as a way to keep me in line."

Maisy lifted her head and placed it on Landry's leg. Landry ran her hand over Maisy's back. "She's a seriously amazing dog."

Cal didn't trust himself to speak. He went with a grunt.

"Anyway, when you say that you don't think you could ever open yourself up to that kind of vulnerability again, I get it. I'm sure there were red flags, but I swear I didn't see them. And now?

Even if I was willing to take the risk for myself, how could I ever put Eliza in that situation? How could I bring a man into her life who might someday hurt her? So no, I don't date. I'm not going to date. And it would be great if the matchmakers of Gossamer Falls understood that before I have to have a public showdown with one of them."

A horrible thought came to Cal, and even though he'd seen the death certificate, he had to ask. "Landry? Your husband. Is he really dead?"

"What?"

Unless she was hiding some serious acting chops, his question had surprised her.

"He's dead. I identified his body."

This time, there was no question it was relief that filled him. "I'm sorry to be so blunt. I wondered if you had left him and were hiding."

Maisy barked at something or someone in the tree line. Mo emerged a moment later. "Sorry to break this up, but the bonfire's starting to die down, and Eliza and Abby are plotting a sleepover. If you want to head them off at the pass, you're going to have to rejoin the party." He threw them a quick salute and melted back into the trees.

Cal and Landry made their way toward the house.

Landry stopped walking and said, "Cal?"

He stopped and looked at her. "Yes?"

She shifted from one foot to the other. Then shifted back. "Nothing. Never mind."

"Landry, given that we're going to be spending a lot of time together for, well, the rest of our lives, it might be a good idea for you to go ahead and learn that the whole 'never mind' thing doesn't work with me. It just makes me want to insist on getting it out of you."

She started to speak. Stopped. Then went for it. "Fine. I want to be your friend."

Of all the things she could have said, that was not what he'd expected. "I'd like that too."

"No. I mean. Great. But . . . I'm doing this wrong. What I mean is that I get it—that you don't want to date me. And you get that I don't want to date you. And we both get that it's nothing personal. We're in different places in life. And since we're on the same page, I think we could be great friends, without the drama of a romantic entanglement getting in the way."

Cal took a moment to process what she'd said, then extended his hand. "Deal."

Landry shook it. "Deal."

It took an hour for Landry to run the Quinn gauntlet of good-byes and make the drive back to The Haven. Eliza talked the entire way, filling her in on her afternoon. How Granny Quinn had let Eliza and Abby crochet a few stitches on the blanket she was making because it was important for everyone in the family to have helped, and how Cal had let them hold some of the boards he was nailing on the well house. How when they were done, she and Abby had taken turns being run around the yard in a wheelbarrow.

As far as Landry could tell, Eliza had made friends with nearly every Quinn present today, but most of her time had been spent with Cal, Chad, Naomi, Minnie, and "Abby's nana," who was Cal, Chad, and Connor's mom and also the town doctor.

By the time Landry turned off the engine, Eliza had shifted into a thrilling retelling of how a cat had brought a dead mouse to Papa Quinn.

"Come with me to the studio, baby. I want to check a few pieces before bed."

Eliza, still chattering, hopped from the car and held Landry's hand as they walked the hundred yards from their home to the studio.

A man approached on the walkway and tipped an imaginary hat. "Evening, ladies." The deep voice was familiar.

Landry didn't stop walking but spoke as they passed. "You're back again, Jensen? We're going to have to get you a permanent cabin if this keeps up."

"Fine by me." He'd turned and was walking backward now.

"Hey, will you be in the studio tomorrow?"

"I'll be around. Not sure when," Landry called over her shoulder.

"Okay, I'll catch you later. Want to see about some Christmas gifts."

"Sounds good. See you tomorrow."

"Tomorrow."

Eliza didn't say anything until they were inside the studio and the doors were closed behind them. "Jensen comes around a lot."

"He does." Landry checked her notes and looked at a vase she'd made the day before. "He has a stressful job. He likes coming here because he can hike all day and come back to a warm fire and a delicious meal."

"Is he rich?" Eliza asked.

"He is."

"Do you think he'll buy a lot of pottery tomorrow?"

Landry sat at her desk. "Come here, baby."

Eliza did as she was told. Landry patted her lap and Eliza climbed into it. Landry wrapped her arms around her and pressed her cheek to her daughter's head. "What's all this about?"

"Are we poor?"

"No. We have everything we need and a lot of what we want."

137

"But we aren't rich."

"Compared to the guests at The Haven, we aren't rich. But compared to the rest of the world? We are. Where's this coming from?"

Eliza squirmed. "You said you needed to sell more pottery to be able to have Mr. Cal build our house. And that you need Favors built first so we can have our house."

Landry bit back a groan. Little ears. Always listening. Before she could respond, Eliza went on. "I said something about Mr. Cal building our house, and Jerry at school said Mr. Cal only builds houses for rich people and that I was lying."

Jerry had been a problem from day one. The teachers knew. The kids knew. His parents? Yeah, they thought Jerry was an angel. "You can't let Jerry bother you with stuff like that. You know you weren't lying. Cal *is* going to build our house. But I asked him to build Favors first because I need a place to show the pottery. And Jerry probably overheard something he doesn't fully understand. Cal builds big houses for rich people. He also builds small houses. Even tiny houses."

Eliza's eyes lit up. "He built his house. And he built the houses for Miss Meredith and Mr. Mo."

"That's right." Landry snuggled Eliza close to her side. "We're going to have a beautiful house. A new studio that has a spot just for you. We'll plant a garden. And flowers. And we can have your room painted any color you want."

Eliza grinned at her. "Purple."

Last week she'd said pink. The week before that, she'd said green. "We'll see what color you want when it's time to paint."

"What color do you want your room to be, Mommy?"

"Gray." Landry could almost picture it. Pale gray walls. Bedding in blues—navy, light blue, teal—a fluffy rug on the floor that would feel good on her bare feet when she climbed out of bed. She curled her toes in her shoes just thinking about it.

Eliza scrunched up her nose. "What about red?"

Landry kissed her nose. "Definitely not red."

Eliza giggled and then yawned.

"You've had a big day. You need some sleep."

"Mmm." Eliza put her head on Landry's chest and snuggled closer.

"I love you, baby. If anything ever worries you, you can always come and talk to me. You know that, right?"

"I know."

"Did you tell the teacher what Jerry said?"

"She heard him. She said that she'd known Cal forever and he built beautiful houses. Then she said she couldn't wait to see our new house."

Landry let it go. Not that she would forget. This was the part of parenting no one warned you about. It was imperative that Eliza learn how to stand up for herself. But should she already have to learn at five?

Landry didn't miss Dylan. Not for a second. But she missed the dream of what parenting could be like with a true partner. Someone she could vent to after Eliza was asleep. Someone who would validate her concerns.

But Eliza was hers and only hers. And like she'd told Cal tonight, she had no intention of changing that. So if this Jerry became a bigger problem, she would deal with it.

She pushed the thoughts of Jerry and Dylan and pipe dreams from her mind. Eliza didn't often stop moving long enough to cuddle, and Landry took full advantage of this moment. She rested her cheek on Eliza's hair. Normally she smelled of her favorite apple shampoo. But tonight she smelled of woodsmoke, marshmallows, and the mountains on a fall day.

Landry held Eliza close until she squirmed. Five minutes later she locked the doors to her studio, and she and Eliza walked back to their home. Her phone buzzed as she opened their door, and she glanced at the text. It was from Cal.

From one friend to another: Eliza was a hit. So were you. Granny said to make sure you know you're welcome anytime. And that neither I nor Abby need to be present. She also said if you haven't started teaching Eliza how to crochet that you should get on that because "she's not too young to learn." At this point I suggested that Granny text you herself.

She asked Eliza about the crocheting. "Abby doesn't like it, but I do. Granny said I was a natural."

"Did she?"

"She said she could teach me how to make a doll blanket."

"Would you like that?"

"I guess so."

Landry closed the door and locked it.

After Eliza was in bed, she grabbed her phone and replied.

Hey, friend. How'd Granny respond to that?

The three little dots appeared almost immediately.

So Granny's not big on texting?

There may have been some snide remarks about me not being too old to get myself taken to the woodshed for sassing my granny.

Granny's not big on technology in general. She prefers a hands-on approach to everything. But she did have me put your number in her phone. I should warn you that she also had me put you in the "Quinn Extended Family" group text. Feel free to mute it.

Landry stared at her phone. She'd lived in Gossamer Falls for three years and made exactly zero friends with the locals. She had pleasant conversations with some of the regulars at The Haven, but she couldn't call any of them friends. Her circle was small. She was friends with Bronwyn. Cordial with her coworkers. A few of them could be called friends. Maybe.

So how was it that in the space of a month, she'd managed to make several friends and get herself semi-adopted?

She had no idea.

But she didn't hate it.

FOURTEEN

Monday morning Cal drove to The Haven with Chad and Connor behind him in their own vehicles. When he arrived at the gate, he rolled down his window. The security guard was an old friend. "Barry, good to see you."

"You take a wrong turn somewhere, brother?" Barry looked behind Cal's truck and his eyes widened. "Um, Cal, man, I . . ."

Cal tapped the door of his truck. "Relax. Call Bronwyn. We have a meeting with her this morning."

"You do?" Barry blew out a huge breath. "Thank heaven. I thought y'all had decided to storm the castle or something."

"Nah. This is a friendly invasion."

"Never thought I'd see the day. Hang on a minute." Barry stepped back into his guardhouse and lifted a phone to his ear. The call was brief, but Barry spent another minute opening a locked drawer. He returned to Cal's truck with three cards. "Bronwyn said to give you each one of these." He handed one to Cal.

"What is it?"

"It's a pass to enter the grounds from the employee entrance. You know where that is?"

"Yeah."

"That'll keep you from getting stuck here if there's a new guest coming in."

"Appreciate it."

"You gonna tell me what's going on?"

Cal slipped the card into a cubby in his truck dash. "Did Bronwyn not tell you?"

"I didn't ask her. Figured I'd ask you."

"No can do."

Barry was disappointed but recovered quickly. "I'll find out soon enough. She said to tell you to drive to the main admin building. That y'all would walk from there."

"Thanks. Have a good one."

"You too."

The drive through The Haven's grounds was beautiful. Gentle curves wound through the forested property on a paved road that did its best to blend into the landscape. Quinn land was prettier, but Pierce land was nothing to sneeze at.

He reached the admin building and found Bronwyn and Landry waiting on the sidewalk.

Once everyone had gathered, Bronwyn smirked at him. "You three fighting or something?"

"No."

"You couldn't ride together? Where's your concern for the environment? Or your gas bill?"

Connor crossed his arms. "Oh, I see how it is. We're on your turf now, so you're going to hassle us?"

"Of course." Bronwyn's grin was full of mischief. "Seriously, though, why three trucks?"

"We're going in three different directions after we leave. In fact" — Chad pointed at Cal— "we're going to leave him to do all the paperwork while we" —Chad nodded at Connor— "go get our hands dirty."

Landry had been watching the exchange, and she turned to Cal. "What did you ever do to make them hate you so much?"

Connor slapped Cal on the back. "He's the baby. We make him do everything we don't want to do."

Cal leaned toward Landry and spoke in a conspiratorial whisper. "It's best for the business if I handle these things. These two?" He grimaced dramatically. "We try not to talk about it, but they're getting up in years an—"

"He's eight years younger than me," Chad said, "but to hear him tell it, I'm just a few years from retirement."

Bronwyn interrupted. "Okay, okay."

"You started it," Connor said.

"And now I'm ending it. You three are impossible. Let's look at the building site and talk about money."

They walked around the charred remains of Favors and down a small, paved path marked with an understated STAFF ONLY sign. Bronwyn was sandwiched between Connor and Chad, which left Cal and Landry to follow behind. Cal let them pull ahead a little before he asked Landry, "Any word on when Gray's going to release the old site?"

"He says maybe this week."

Cal heard hesitation in her response, and there was no way he could ignore it. "You sound worried."

"I can't shake the feeling that he's found something and that's why he's held off on releasing the scene. And given that he's shared no details, it makes me wonder who he suspects."

Cal dropped his voice. "Like who?"

Landry wouldn't meet his eyes. "Not everyone loves Bronwyn the way your family seems to. Maybe you should mention that to your brothers."

"We know." Cal was close to most of his cousins, and cordial with all of them, but the Pierce family had a split. One side could be reasonable. The other? Papa Quinn had been known to compare them to mules. Once they made up their minds about something being a good idea or a bad idea, it was almost impossible to get them to change. And some of them had a very different view from Bronwyn about how The Haven should be run.

"I think Gray suspects it could have been an inside job. But even with the family squabbles, I can't see any of the Pierces doing this. They're practical people. Burning down their own building makes no sense."

"Who else would have done it?"

Landry pursed her lips. "I can't see the guests doing this. For one thing, our guests are happy here."

"What's the other reason?"

"Why go to the trouble when you have the power to create a social media firestorm?"

Cal paused on the path, and Landry stopped with him. "You've given this a lot of thought, haven't you?"

"It feels like it's all I've thought about since it happened."

"Is that part of why you want the new shop built first? To thwart whatever purpose was behind the arson?"

"Maybe. But given that we're completely in the dark, I don't know if we're slowing them down or playing right into their hands. What I do know is that rebuilding in a better location and with a better layout is the right decision. It needed to happen regardless, so we'll do the best we can with what we do know and trust that what we don't know will sort itself out in good time."

"Sounds like a well-thought-out decision."

Landry cut her eyes to him. "Does this mean you'll stop grumping about putting Favors ahead of my house?"

Cal widened his eyes in mock shock. "Me? Grump?" When she laughed, he played up the drama. "I'll have you know that in high school, I was voted Most Likely to Get Kicked Out of a Funeral for Laughing."

Landry didn't miss a beat. "That just tells me you have poor self-control in somber situations."

"Mean!" Cal bumped her shoulder as they walked. "But seriously, I apologize for the grump routine. I'm excited for the house and for you and Eliza to have your own place."

"I can't help but notice that you didn't say you were excited to have me for a neighbor." Landry feigned outrage.

"My apologies. That's the best part. Eliza will be awesome to have as a neighbor. I've already talked to Mo and Meredith about fixing the little bridge over the river. Meredith had opinions." He put opinions in air quotes.

"I don't think I've ever had an opinion about a bridge."

"Meredith has opinions about everything. The annoying thing is that she's usually right. She has an eye for color and spatial elements."

"I noticed that in her house. She used every bit of space and still made it seem open. What does she have in mind for the bridge?"

Cal didn't try to hide his frustration when he answered. "She wants it to be an arch. Said it would blend into the environment and be more aesthetically pleasing. The fact that it will take longer and cost more? That's not her problem. According to her, she's the brains behind the operation. Mo and I are the brawn."

Landry tried not to laugh at Cal's consternation. She could tell that it was only partly real. From what she'd seen, he would do just about anything Meredith asked him to do. Before she thought it through, she said, "When you get ready to build, if you'll let us know, Eliza and I would like to help. I mean, if that's okay, I'm not any good at building, but I'm a decent gopher. And based on the way Eliza rambled on and on about how you let her shoot a nail gun on Saturday . . ."

Cal had the decency to appear to be abashed. She didn't believe it. She tapped her finger on her bottom lip. "I'm going to go out on a limb and say that you have an experiential childrearing philosophy."

As soon as the words left her mouth, she regretted them. After what he'd shared? How could she bring up something like childrearing philosophy to a man who'd lost the boys he thought were going to be his?

She scrambled to come up with an apology that wouldn't make things even more awkward, but Cal didn't seem upset. "By and large, that's the Shaw and Quinn philosophy. Once they're old enough to run around mostly unsupervised, they're old enough to hold a board, fetch a tool, or"—he winked—"shoot a nail gun. But we don't give kids sharp objects or power tools without safety briefings and close observation. As for the nail gun, I don't think you need to worry. She and Abby squealed like, well, like five-year-old girls when they shot in the nails. And neither of them has the arm strength to hold the thing or the right hand size to pull the trigger unassisted."

"So you're saying my fears are unwarranted?" She wasn't mad. In fact, she was pleasantly surprised and relieved.

"Not unwarranted. Nail guns can hurt the people using them or the people around them. But for the girls it was a chance to say they helped with the roof of the well house, the same way they helped crochet stitches on Granny's blanket."

Landry didn't trust herself to speak right away. When she did, her voice wavered more than she would have liked. "Your family is quite welcoming."

"We try. We aren't perfect. Not by a long shot, as you've already learned."

"It's okay. I-I still feel bad that I basically forced you into sharing your pain with a near stranger."

To her surprise, Cal grinned. "But I didn't. I shared it with my friend. She's a new friend. Still figuring her out. But so far, so good. She hasn't beaten me up for letting her daughter use a nail gun. She didn't lose her mind when I mentioned the word *roof* a moment ago, and she seems to be the kind of person who wants to hear the truth for herself rather than jumping to conclusions. I can work with that."

"Did you say *roof?*"

Cal's laughter echoed around them and got the attention of the three in front of them.

"What's so funny?" Connor asked.

"Did you let my daughter get on a roof?" Landry asked. Connor and Chad exchanged a look.

"That means yes." Bronwyn was grinning.

Cal, still chuckling, said, "The roof was five feet off the ground, Landry."

She punched his shoulder.

"Ow! What was that for?"

"For giving me a heart attack!"

Bronwyn, Connor, and Chad stopped, and they all turned to face the area Bronwyn pointed to. "Right there."

Landry pointed out the blazes on trees where Bronwyn had gotten a little happy with a can of spray paint. The new space would be significantly larger and a bit removed from the rest of the resort. Landry couldn't wait.

"Why here?"

"That's the best part!" Landry didn't try to hide her excitement. "This is the first phase of several new buildings that will need to be constructed over the next few years. We need to grow in this direction, and the guests have no trouble finding the out-of-the-way areas. They like the way the restaurant and fitness studios are tucked to the side. This will continue that tradition."

Bronwyn picked up the thread. "We'll have room for the shop area and Landry's classroom space. She wants to move her main studio and kilns to her property once her house is built, but I've convinced her that she needs an on-site studio for the guests who want pottery lessons."

Cal, Connor, and Chad asked questions about square footage and drainage and water supply and electrical supply, most of which Bronwyn and Landry were able to answer because they'd already covered these details with the architect they'd met with in the spring. Cal jotted notes on some kind of stainless-steel storage clipboard that looked to Landry like it might have been used as a hammer more than once. It wasn't dirty, but it was scratched and dented.

"You know," she said in a low voice, "in this century, we have these things called tablets."

He tapped the clipboard. "Never runs out of battery. Doesn't break when I sit on it. Gets the job done."

Landry pinched her lips together to keep from laughing. Cal had a shiny truck with all the bells and whistles. His phone was the latest model. And his office had a multiscreen Mac setup. He wasn't afraid of technology. But for some reason, he was attached to that clipboard.

They spent an hour discussing the project before Connor and Chad left to check on other jobs. Cal took some measurements, asked more questions, and thirty minutes later declared he was ready for lunch. "Can I invite you ladies to Triple Ts?"

Landry loved Triple Ts. The official name was Through Thick and Thin, but she'd never heard anyone call it that. It was only a few miles from The Haven, and she took Eliza there every couple of months for burgers and milkshakes.

"I'm so in," Bronwyn said. "Landry?"

"Sure. I cleared my schedule for today so we could talk about the shop." If they finished lunch early enough, she planned to work in her studio before Eliza came home.

"Great." Cal pointed toward the path. "I'm starving. And when we finish lunch, I have to go stare at my computer until my eyes cross so I can get you an estimate as soon as possible."

"It doesn't have to be done today." Bronwyn pushed a branch out of the way as she maneuvered through the woods. "I know these things take time."

"They do, but the sooner we get this place done, the sooner Landry gets her house."

"Fair enough."

Before Landry could add her thoughts to the discussion, Bronwyn's phone rang. "Bronwyn Pierce." Bronwyn listened intently, then closed her eyes and shook her head.

Landry met Cal's gaze and widened her eyes.

Cal mimicked her and whispered, "Beep is *not* happy."

Bronwyn frowned at them and walked several steps away.

"Any guesses what that's about?" Cal nodded toward Bronwyn.

"It could be anything." Landry had no idea how Bronwyn managed everything she did. "Anything from a guest complaint to an employee who wants a day off when it would leave us short-staffed." Cal's expression darkened. "Neither of those things should be in her job description. Doesn't she have a general manager?"

"She does." Landry let her disdain color her words.

"Let me guess. One of her cousins?"

"Bingo."

"My father's never been a fan of The Haven, but he was good friends with one of the Pierces. Hence the SPQ business name. People thought it was a big deal when he left, but Dad and Uncle Douglas never had any drama with him. Dad wanted The Haven to be a success and to do what the Pierces said it would do. And for the most part, The Haven has met or exceeded every expectation the Pierces had for it. It hasn't destroyed the town. It's a source of income and training for people all over the area. They pay a huge amount in taxes, which benefits everyone."

"I sense a *but* coming."

Cal pointed toward Bronwyn. "Dad contended from the beginning that Bronwyn's side of the Pierces needed to completely buy out the other side as soon as they could. They have two different philosophies on almost everything. Dad says family businesses only work when everyone's pulling in the same direction. I have a feeling that The Haven is going to experience some growing pains before it's all resolved."

Landry didn't want to betray Bronwyn's confidence, but Cal had the picture right. Bronwyn's cousin was a lazy moron. And Bronwyn planned to fire him. This latest drama would probably be another nail in the coffin that idiot was building around himself.

In the long run, it would help to get rid of him. In the short run?

Bronwyn slid her phone into her pocket with a force that threatened to rip the pocket right off her pants. "You two go on to lunch without me. I have to take care of this."

What? Wait. What?

"Anything we can help with? I'm pretty handy," Cal offered before he had any idea what the problem might be, and Landry sensed that the offer was genuine, with no strings attached.

"I'd take you up on that if I could. But sadly, this isn't structural. This is a guest disputing their bill."

"Don't these people have money to burn?" Cal didn't ask the question as rhetorical, and Bronwyn didn't take it as one.

"In my experience, the people with the most money are some of the pickiest. They ask for discounts for every perceived slight or inconvenience, and they expect their wishes to be honored because they starred in a movie or their daddy made billions in oil." Bronwyn puffed her cheeks and blew out a breath. "I'm going to run to my office to freshen up before I face the demon . . . I mean, the delicate flower who has decided she should get a free night because one night the chef ran out of asparagus."

"I could come with." Cal cracked his neck and frowned. "I can be menacing."

His dramatics made Bronwyn smile. For about half a second.

"No. But thanks for the offer." They'd reached the fork in the path that led to the parking lot on the left and Bronwyn's office on the right.

"Text us when you get done, okay?" Landry gave Bronwyn a quick hug.

"Want us to bring you a burger?" Cal asked.

Bronwyn's eyes lit up. "Yes. Please!"

"Consider it done. Let's see. As I recall, you'll want lots of mayo and mustard—"

Bronwyn smacked his arm. "Keep your disgusting condiments off my burger."

Cal winked at her. "Lettuce, tomato, cheese, and pickle. We'll check it before we leave the premises."

"You'd better." Bronwyn squared her shoulders and walked to her office.

"Want to ride with me?" Cal pointed to his truck. "I'll swing you back when we're done."

Landry's car was a half mile away. "Sure. That sounds great." Cal held out his hand. "After you." He opened the door for her, and when she had climbed into his behemoth of a vehicle, he closed it and jogged around to the driver's side.

He wasn't smooth and polished the way the rich, famous, and occasionally talented but usually mediocre actors who deigned to visit The Haven were. He was . . . real.

And it was a good thing they'd decided to be friends, because she could enjoy lunch out without having to worry about him catching feelings for her.

The thought should have soothed the butterflies in her stomach that refused to settle, but it didn't.

FIFTEEN

Several weeks later, Landry smiled at the men standing in her studio. They were regulars who regularly flirted with her. Today, they decided to take their art efforts to a new level, but the results were less than they'd hoped for.

"They're awful," Silas, a thirtysomething pro athlete, groaned. "It looks like something I would have made in kindergarten."

Landry looked at the canvas. "You're very good with your hands, but it's possible painting isn't going to be where you find your greatest creative joy."

Derrick chortled. "At least you can tell what his is supposed to be. Mine looks like blood spatter." He would know. He was a forensic scientist who now consulted on several popular television crime procedurals. The money in consulting wasn't typically enough to make someone a regular at The Haven, but Derrick had married an up-and-coming star. When she cheated on him, he destroyed her in court. He lived more than comfortably now. He'd also made friends in the entertainment industry who were quick to invite him to The Haven whenever they visited.

One of those friends, Ignacio, made the trip to The Haven at least three times a year. Ignacio, who was known by that one name and no other, was a well-known stunt actor. He was in high demand

and made money from the stunts he did himself, the consulting he did for stunts others did, and in the last few years, endorsements. Landry would bet he was the one who'd convinced his buddies to come to the group art class today.

The women who'd attended had kept to themselves, painted their pictures, and left. The men had laughed, sipped their drinks, and dared each other to try random techniques and color combinations. They'd had fun, which was the point. But their canvases left a lot to be desired.

Ignacio shoved Silas. "I would say you should take private lessons, but I'm not sure even Landry could sort you out."

Silas waggled his eyebrows. "What do you say, Landry?" His words dripped with innuendo. "Could I interest you in some *private* lessons?"

Ignacio smacked him on the head. "I didn't say for you to *give* the lessons. I said for you to *take* them."

"I heard you." Silas winked at Landry. "Whatdya say?" Landry deflected, as she did every time. "I'll have to decline your kind offer." She waved toward the canvases. "Should I have them shipped to you?"

Silas and Derrick shook their heads.

"Could you burn them?" Derrick wasn't joking. "I don't want any proof of this experience. This is one of those times when I'm so glad no one has a phone on them." Phones weren't allowed in any of the public areas of The Haven. Guests kept them in their rooms, and posting to social media was strictly prohibited for privacy purposes. "No offense, Landry. You were amazing as ever."

She didn't say what she wanted to say—that if they drank less and paid more attention, they could have come up with something lovely. As it was, only Ignacio had produced a painting that resembled the one she'd modeled for them.

NEVER FALL AGAIN

Ignacio pointed to his painting. "Keep it. I'm headed for Eastern Europe and won't be home for at least a month."

"Eastern Europe?" Ignacio was a nice guy, but Landry fully expected to see news one day that he'd died a violent death. He took risks no one should take. "Can you tell us what you'll be doing?"

"Sorry, Landry. I didn't read the entire contract. But my lawyer assured me there was no wiggle room for speaking of it in any way. I probably shouldn't have even told you where I was headed."

"I have no idea how you make your life work, man." Silas took another sip of his drink. "Do you even know what you're doing after this job?"

Ignacio shrugged. "I think it's in Africa. Or maybe Alaska? My agent will tell me. That's what I pay him for."

"I don't trust my agent as far as I can throw him." That meant more coming from Silas than almost anyone Landry knew. Silas was a pitcher. She'd watched him play on TV. "I monitor everything he does."

"Life's too short for that mess." Ignacio slapped him on the back.

"Your life, maybe." Derrick handed Landry a twenty-dollar bill. "Thanks again, Landry. Maybe next time we can paint something intentionally abstract."

"Yeah." Silas handed Landry another twenty. "Knowing you, if you go for abstract, you'll wind up with a landscape."

"It'd be better than that." Derrick pointed to his own painting, then winked at Landry. "Later, doll."

Ignacio handed her a folded bill. "Thank you for putting up with them today."

"They're perfect gentlemen compared to some of the guests. Be safe in Europe. And Africa. Or Alaska."

"What would be the fun in that?" He grinned, and she wondered, again, if this was the last time she'd see him.

When the art studio was empty at last, Landry looked at the bill. A crisp hundred. She'd known it would be. Ignacio was a great tipper. She appreciated it, but she suspected it spoke more to his reckless nature than to a generous spirit.

It took her almost an hour to restore the space to her preferred pristine state. Landry always made sure the room was serene and inviting before she left. For the men today, the art had been a way to hang out with friends and have fun. And that was fine. Art should be accessible to everyone for whatever they needed it to be.

But for some people, art was therapy. On Monday she had a guest coming who'd requested a one-on-one lesson and another who'd requested supplies and a private space. The one who wanted the lesson had endured a brutal social media attack earlier in the year. His therapist had suggested art, and he was going to use his time at The Haven wisely. He had some real talent, but that wasn't why he painted.

The one who wanted the private space was a woman whose voice could—and frequently did—make people weep from the sheer beauty of it. She painted because she knew she was bad at it. She claimed it was freeing to play without any expectation of a beautiful result.

Landry locked the doors behind her and made her way toward the site of the new shop. She was done for the day, and she wanted to see the progress they'd made. SPQ had obtained the permits so quickly that Cal accused Bronwyn of greasing the wheels with food bribery. Bronwyn told him there were no laws forbidding her from making her great-aunt some of her famous peanut butter cookies, and it wasn't her fault her great-aunt was the one in charge of processing the permits.

Cal told her he'd look the other way if she gave him some peanut butter cookies. Which she did.

The reality was that Bronwyn had bent herself into a pretzel in her attempts to keep everything aboveboard. But small-town life meant there was no way to avoid having your relatives in places of authority. And sometimes those relatives put your project on the top of the list.

The weather had been cool but dry, which had allowed them to do all the grading and foundation work in record time. And even though Bronwyn had a strict policy that forbade Cal's crew from beginning work before 9:00 a.m., she did allow them to work until dark and they frequently did. They also worked on Saturdays.

The crews were thrilled with the overtime. Bronwyn was thrilled with the progress.

It was a win-win for everyone.

Landry stopped twenty yards from the low fence around the work zone. The women who'd been in her class were now huddled together watching the men work.

Landry said, "Excuse me," and tried to skirt the group, but Chantal, a Chicago socialite, stopped her. "Do you know those men?"

"Some of them. Why? Is there a problem?"

The women burst into laughter. Jess, Chantal's sister, spoke up. "The problem is that Chanti's determined to have herself a mountain man, but she can't seem to catch one."

Chantal's aggrieved expression bordered on tragic. "I told Bronwyn it's a crime the way she's hidden these hotties from us. Who knew there were so many gorgeous men in these mountains? I've been coming here for five years, and I had no idea this kind of . . . scenery . . . existed."

She pointed through the fence. "Landry, I want to meet that one. The one with the ball cap on backward."

At least six men had their ball caps on backward, but Landry knew who Chantal was looking at. Maybe that's why it was easy for her to shoot the woman down. "Chantal, I'm sorry, but the men have been given strict orders to stay away from the guests."

Chantal pouted. "But what if the guests want them to come say hello?" She flipped her hair. "I'm going to talk to Bronwyn. This is a ridiculous rule. Come on."

Without another word to Landry, Chantal walked away, her entourage behind her like baby ducks following their mother. Landry waited until they were out of sight before she approached the fence. She watched and waited. About a minute into her surveillance, a man tapped Cal on the shoulder, then pointed in her direction.

Cal's smile was brilliant against the dust and dirt on his face. He held up two fingers. She nodded and waited.

He climbed down from the ladder he'd been on, wiped his face with a cloth he pulled from his tool belt, and grabbed a bottle of water from a cooler before he made his way to her. "Hey there."

"Hey yourself."

Cal chugged the water, his throat moving rhythmically—whoa. Nope. She was not going to think about Cal like that. He was her friend. She focused on the construction crew while he finished drinking.

"Sorry. I haven't taken a break."

"No problem."

"Can we thank you for getting rid of the groupies?" Cal pointed to the trail where she'd come from.

"You knew they were there?"

"That crowd's been showing up off and on all week." Cal took another swig.

"One of them has her sights set on you."

Cal choked. "I'm sorry. What?"

Landry laughed at his horrified expression. "The privacy and happiness of the guests is our utmost priority." She did her best to keep her expression neutral. "Normally, we do whatever we can to ensure their stay is pleasant and all their expectations are fulfilled. However, in this case, I did tell her that your crew had been told to stay away from the guests."

"Thank you."

"She didn't like that, and they headed to Bronwyn to complain."

"Please tell me you're joking."

"Nope. Bronwyn won't give in, but I thought you should have a heads-up. Chantal is persistent. I wouldn't put it past her to leave the property and look for you."

"I'll talk to Bronwyn. We've discussed putting up another row of netting along the fence to block the view."

"Might be a good idea. Apparently, she's determined to, and I quote, 'have herself a mountain man,' and she specifically asked about you."

"Please tell me you didn't give her my name."

Landry shoved at him through the fence. "What kind of friend do you take me for?"

Something flickered in Cal's gaze before it morphed to a look of relief. "Thank you, again."

"You're welcome."

"Want to come in and see what we've done? There's been a lot of progress since you were last here."

"I'd love to. But I don't want to interrupt your workday."

Cal grimaced. "We *are* in the middle of something. Why don't you and Eliza come back around three thirty. We're wrapping early today so everyone can go to the harvest festival tonight."

"Don't you have to be at the festival early?" He'd said something about cooking. Or serving. Landry wasn't sure. This would be her first Gossamer Falls Harvest Festival. She'd begged off the last few years, but Eliza was giddy about tonight's festivities.

"My shift starts at five thirty. I'll have time to show you around. I probably need to head out by four."

"Okay."

Cal checked his watch. Again.

The morning had flown by. The afternoon? Not so much. He was ready to call it a day. He didn't always work on the jobs he managed, but one of his crew leaders had taken the day off because his daughter was having her wisdom teeth out.

Darryl had sent them a video of Betsy post-surgery. During lunch, the entire crew got a good laugh out of it. Betsy was normally an easy-going girl, but in her anesthesia-induced state, she'd been sassy and snarky. The video shook so much that Cal could picture Darryl laughing as Betsy ranted about the color of her seat belt.

He'd have to show Landry. She'd get a kick out of it.

Landry.

Cal checked his watch again. Thirty more minutes.

Focus. He'd write up anyone on his crew who was daydreaming while standing thirty feet up on scaffolding. If this kept on, he'd have to write *himself* up. He and Emmett were almost done. One more board and they'd climb down and pack up for the weekend. The crew was enjoying the extra hours, but everyone agreed to take off early today and not work on Saturday. The annual harvest festival was that big of a deal.

"That pretty blond gonna come back later?" Emmett, the manager for this team, hammered a nail in with one skilled hit. Then another.

"Landry?"

"That's the one."

"She wants to see what we've done this week."

"Be sure to ask her about those windows. We need to know by next week."

"I will."

Emmett sent another nail home. "She comes by a lot."

"She helped design the building, and she's invested in the outcome."

Emmett smirked. "I've been here every day since we started this job. Noticed a few things."

Cal didn't bite.

"Noticed she doesn't come by when you aren't here."

Cal focused on his work.

"Noticed you drop everything to talk to her when she comes by."

"We're friends, Em." Cal congratulated himself for the way he put a touch of humor in his voice.

"Noticed that." He shifted his position on the scaffolding before adding, "Looks like you're real good friends."

Cal had no good options. If he acknowledged Emmett's remark, he'd be giving the man more fuel for the fire. But if he ignored Em and said nothing, he might as well be flying a flag that said "Cal likes Landry more than he's supposed to."

Before he could decide how to handle Emmett's nosy nature, Eliza's voice cut through the sounds of the rest of the crew packing up. "Mr. Cal! Mr. Cal! Mommy said you're going to show me what you're working on!"

Emmett had the decency to keep his laughter quiet as he clapped Cal on the back. "I got this. You'd better go get your girls."

Cal gave Emmett the dirtiest look he could, then turned to wave at Eliza, who jumped up and down by the fence like she had springs in her shoes. "Hey, Liza Lou. Hang on a minute. I'll be right down."

He refused to make eye contact with Emmett, who was now

laughing so hard he was hanging on to the scaffolding bar for support.

"Can I climb up there with you?" Eliza yelled to him.

"No!" Cal and Landry replied in unison. Eliza stopped jumping.

Landry mouthed "Thank you" to him.

"You'll have to be older before you can start scrambling around on the scaffolding."

"How much older?"

"Much, much older." Landry widened her eyes at him as she answered Eliza.

"You heard your mom." Cal opened the gate, and Eliza and Landry walked inside. "Let's go wait in the trailer while the guys clear out."

"I know we're early, Somebody"—Landry nodded to Eliza—"couldn't wait and then ran almost the whole way."

"It's no problem." He led them into the small trailer where he had a desk. The walls were covered with blueprints, and a small refrigerator was stocked with water, soft drinks, and recently, juice boxes.

Maisy greeted them with exuberant woofs. She nudged Cal's leg, then Landry's, before succumbing to Eliza's embrace. Eliza put her arms around Maisy's neck and was rewarded with a lick to her cheek. Eliza pointed to the fridge. "May I have a drink?" It was unclear to Cal who she was asking, but Landry spoke up. "Go ahead."

Eliza went to the fridge, and Cal asked Landry, "Would you like anything?"

"No. I'm good."

Eliza made herself comfortable in an ancient chair that had made the move with the trailer since Cal was a kid. Maisy jumped into the chair and took over most of it while Landry studied the blueprints on the wall. "It's amazing to me how you take this

162

two-dimensional drawing and turn it into a three-dimensional building."

"Well, it's amazing to me how you take a lump of clay and make beautiful pottery with it."

She looked over her shoulder and smiled, and he could not make himself look away.

Not good. Except she wasn't looking away either.

Emmett stomped into the trailer. "Ma'am." He touched his hat. "I'll be out of here in a second."

Manners were important, and Cal had no choice but to introduce Emmett, the fiend. "Landry Hutton, please meet Emmett Carver. He's the manager of the crew on this job. Emmett." Cal tried to send a mental message to Emmett to behave himself. "This is Landry Hutton, and this firecracker—"—he winked at Eliza—"is Lucy."

"It's not Lucy!" He and Eliza had played this game before, and she giggled.

"So nice to meet you, Lucy." Emmett had kids and played along.

"It's not Lucy, it's—"

Cal slapped a hand to his forehead. "Em, man. I'm sorry. I get it wrong sometimes. Her name isn't Lucy. It's Veronica."

Eliza smacked her hand on the arm of the chair. "My name is—"

"You know, she doesn't look like a Veronica," Emmett said. "She looks more like a—"

"Eliza!" Eliza stood in the chair. "My name is Eliza!" She was laughing so hard, Cal worried she would fall.

"Eliza. Wow. I was way off." Cal widened his eyes and went for over-the-top confusion and remorse. "Sorry about that."

Eliza hopped from the chair and ran to him. He scooped her up and tossed her into the air. She wrapped her arms around his neck. "You're funny, LumLum."

Landry burst out laughing, and Cal fixed her with a death glare. "Did you put her up to that?"

She gave him the fakest innocent expression he'd ever seen. "As I recall, you're the one who mentioned it. It's not my fault she remembered."

"LumLum." Emmett laughed so hard he was wheezing. "LumLum."

Cal glared at Emmett. "Weren't you leaving?"

"Sadly, I hate to leave. This show is pretty entertaining." He winked at Eliza. "I owe you one, Miss Eliza." He nodded toward Landry. "Ma'am." Then, "LumLum. See you tonight."

If Cal had anything to throw at Emmett, he would have done it. As it was, he waited until the door closed behind him to set Eliza on the floor, cross his arms, and focus his ire on Landry. Or he tried to. He held his laughter in for all of three seconds before it came out in a disgruntled chuckle. He didn't want to laugh. The crews would be calling him LumLum now. Emmett would text them before he got to his truck.

But he hadn't expected it. Not from Landry. Their friendship was still . . . fragile? No. That implied it could break easily, and he didn't think that was the case. Nebulous? Maybe. They hadn't figured out who they were to each other. There was an undercurrent that he tried not to focus on but couldn't deny. A sense that if their pasts had been different, their futures might have—

No. Not going there. He focused on Eliza. "All right, you little stinker. Let's go see the fireplace."

"Yes!" Eliza led the way out of the trailer. It took them almost ten minutes to get to the fireplace because Landry kept stopping to exclaim over something that hadn't been there last week. But the moment she saw the fireplace, she froze. "Oh."

Her eyes filled with tears that she blinked back. "It's perfect." Her words were a quiet whisper. "It's exactly right." Then she turned to him and pressed a kiss to his cheek. "Thank you."

Cal watched as Landry and Eliza examined every inch of the

fireplace. A fireplace he'd spent hours working on this week. A fireplace he thought might be one of the best things he'd ever designed or created.

He tried to focus on what they said and not the way their delight burned through him. He hadn't expected their response to impact him. And on the heels of that kiss . . . .

He'd put Landry in the close platonic friend/family category with the other important women in his life. His cousin. His sisters-in-law. They were all affectionate. All kissed his cheek regularly. He thought nothing of it.

But he could still feel the softness of her lips. Could still catch the way her unique scent—something floral mixed with the earthiness of clay—intensified as she drew near, then faded as she walked away. He could still hear that soft "thank you" and . . . .

He was in so much trouble.

SIXTEEN

At 6:00 that evening, Landry pulled into the parking lot of the Gossamer Falls Church. The parking lot wasn't full yet, but it was close. She fought every compulsion to turn around and go home. Her mind told her that these people were wolves in sheep's clothing. That they would stab her in the back the moment the opportunity struck, and then they would blame her for being a "poor testimony" to the unbelievers in the world.

Landry believed Jesus died for her and that trusting him and his sacrifice was the only way to restore the relationship between her and a holy God. She could expound on doctrine for hours. She knew all the terminology, all the Christianese.

And she hadn't stepped foot through the doors of a church since she'd walked out after her husband's funeral three years ago.

Her faith in God wasn't an issue.

Her faith in the people who claimed to know God? *That* was the issue.

On an intellectual level, she knew she couldn't lump all church-going followers of Christ into one cesspool of hypocrisy and deceit. But her heart didn't care. With every frantic beat, it warned her of the risk she took if she got out of the car.

"I see Abby!" Eliza's excited cry broke through Landry's near meltdown and pulled her firmly back on solid ground. She wasn't joining the church. She wasn't even attending a worship service. She was here because, a decade ago, the people of Gossamer Falls decided that trick-or-treating on dark mountain roads was a bad idea. So every year the three main churches worked together—something Landry still found difficult to believe—to put on a harvest festival on the Friday night closest to Halloween.

It was such a success that, to her knowledge, the children of Gossamer Falls assumed everyone dressed up in costumes and walked along their Main Street. Stores and restaurants had booths set up on the sidewalks where they handed out what, if the rumors were true, was an alarming amount of candy. At the beginning, middle, and end of the street, the crowds detoured into the parking lots and well-tended lawns of the three churches where they were treated to hot dogs, pulled-pork sandwiches, fried chicken, tea, and lemonade on one end, and homemade ice-cream sundaes with all the fixings on the other end. In the middle was a small grandstand with live music—bluegrass, heavy on the banjos and fiddles—and booths serving popcorn, cotton candy, and hot chocolate.

Every bit of it was free. A gift from the churches of Gossamer Falls to the town.

Landry didn't buy it. There was a catch. She was sure of it. But now that Eliza was in kindergarten, all she had talked about for the past month was the harvest festival. Landry hadn't been able to bring herself to squash Eliza's anticipatory delight, so she'd gone along with the idea.

And when Eliza came to her, begging to get a costume that matched Abby's? Well . . . that hadn't been a hard sell.

Landry opened her door, climbed out, and helped Eliza from the back seat.

Eliza adjusted the small tool belt at her waist and grinned up at Landry from under a pink hardhat. "How do I look?"

"Like you're ready to be put to work on a construction crew. If you aren't careful, Cal will hire you tonight and put you to work on Monday."

Eliza threw her arms around Landry's waist. "Thank you, Mommy."

And that was why she was in a church parking lot on a cool Friday evening with her daughter dressed not as a princess or a ballerina but as a construction worker.

They joined Chad, Naomi, and Abby at the back of their car, and Chad gave the girls his seal of approval on their costumes. "You two look fabulous." He smiled at Landry, "Thanks for coming tonight. You'll love it." Apparently, Abby's older brothers had been given freedom to begin their jaunt down the street, but there was no way Landry would allow Eliza to go running off into the throng of pirates, ghosts, and what looked like an entire bag of M&M's.

Chad bent down and looked both girls in the eyes. "Someday you'll be allowed to go on your own. But that's still several years off. For now, you need to be able to see one of us." He pointed to himself, then Naomi, then Landry. "And more importantly, we must be able to see you. If you want to stop at a booth, make eye contact so we know where you are. Is that clear?"

Both girls nodded in unison.

"We walk down this side of the street until we get to the Main Street Church. Then we'll eat dinner. On our way back down the other side, you can stop for hot chocolate or candy, and we'll wind up back here for ice cream."

The girls were nearly levitating with excitement. Landry could picture them spinning their legs like cartoon characters before they took off.

Chad clapped his hands. "Okay. Let's go get so much candy that we single-handedly keep Aunt Meredith in business."

Landry hadn't thought of that. Dentists weren't typically big on candy-infused holidays. "Where is Meredith?"

"She has her own booth." Naomi fell into step beside Landry while Chad herded the girls toward the chaos. "She gives out toothbrushes, floss, toothpaste, and lots of business cards."

"Do the kids stop at her booth?"

"Everyone does. I don't want to spoil the surprise. When you see it, you'll understand." Landry had a feeling Meredith Quinn could make anything fun. But that didn't mean she had a clue what Meredith did to ensure everyone stopped at her booth.

Despite her misgivings, Landry had to admit that the atmosphere was festive and friendly. Everywhere she looked people were smiling and laughing. The street had been closed to everything except pedestrian traffic, and older kids ran from booth to booth with minimal supervision. But they weren't running wild. Landry saw several teenage boys stop short when an older gentleman called them down for running through the crowd. They apologized and slowed to a trot. The man shook his head with an indulgent smile. Maybe the entire town was watching out for all the kids, regardless of who they belonged to.

Gossamer Falls wasn't perfect, but tonight was shaping up to be a magical night. The kind of night kids remembered when they grew up.

As they walked down the street, Chad and Naomi spoke to almost everyone they saw and introduced Landry and Eliza. "I'll never remember all these people," Landry told Naomi.

"They won't expect you to. You're meeting hundreds of new people. They're only meeting you. If someone starts chatting you up in a store or at the library or whatever, just go with it. You can always try to take a photo on the sly and send it to me. I'll tell you who they are."

Naomi wasn't a Gossamer Falls native, but she'd lived here long enough that Landry didn't doubt her ability to identify everyone in town.

They convinced the kids to bypass the hot chocolate and candy corn and keep going until they were almost to the Main Street Church parking lot.

That's when she saw Meredith's booth and understood. Meredith had a giant chomping mouth that groups of kids ran through. You never knew when the teeth, conveniently encased in foam and completely flexible, would close. When they did, squeals of laughter and shouts of dismay would rumble down the street. It was easily the most popular booth of the entire event. And each child left with a small bag filled with dental supplies.

"Meredith's a genius."

Chad chuckled. "That she is."

They spent several minutes talking to Meredith, then chatted with other parents whose kids were being devoured by the chomping gums. All of them walked away with huge smiles.

Eliza tugged on Landry's arm. "I'm starving." She stretched out the word and added a moan to bring the point home. Abby mimicked her.

Naomi ran a hand down Abby's sleek ponytail. "I'm hungry too. Let's go load up on enough grease to clog our arteries for a decade."

The girls ran ahead, although they followed the rules and stayed in sight. They entered the Main Street Church parking lot and joined the queue for the fried chicken dinner.

Landry spotted Cal standing beside a rather cute woman, probably in her midtwenties. The woman scooted around Cal, and . . . oh no she didn't. Oh yes she did. That little flirt brushed against Cal. And was that a hip bump as she walked by? Who did she think she was?

They were laughing. Not the way acquaintances shared a moment of humor. They were doubled over, laughing so hard that the woman was dabbing tears from the corners of her eyes.

That was when the girls broke ranks and darted away from the line, straight toward Cal and the woman who was now leaning against his arm.

"Uncle Cal!" Abby's sweet voice broke through the sounds of the gathering, and Cal turned to her. His eyes lit with joy that was so pure, it nearly took Landry's breath away. He jogged toward where Abby and Eliza had stopped and put his hands on each of their little pink hard hats.

Then his eyes met hers for a long moment before he returned to his animated conversation with the girls.

Landry stared at her shoes and tried to stop the color she could feel on her face from creeping all over her body. What was wrong with her? What was her problem? Who did *she* think *she* was? She had no claim on Cal Shaw. He was her friend. Her good friend. And if he wanted that cute little thing helping him fry chicken? Well, that was his business.

Maybe they would all be good friends?

No.

The realization hit Landry and spiraled through her, pressing in on all her scarred places that would never heal. Cal Shaw would never be more than her friend, and Landry would never be friends with the woman who someday claimed his heart.

Cal couldn't get over the vision before his eyes.

Abby and Eliza dressed as construction workers. They were so cute it made his heart hurt.

Pink hard hats, leather tool belts, jeans, even tiny scuffed-up work boots.

He searched the crowd again for Landry. He spotted the top of her blond head, but her face was turned down. He'd catch up to her in a few minutes.

"These are the best costumes I've seen all night." Abby and Eliza grinned at him like he just handed them an award. "Are you here to say hi or to eat?"

Abby rubbed her stomach. "We're starving."

He tweaked her nose. "Me too. I've been cooking for hours, and I think I'm going to pass out if I don't eat something soon." The girls giggled. "Tell your mom and dad to save me a seat. My shift is over, so I'll join you."

"Yay!" Both girls shouted and took off back to the line.

"Cassie?" Cal found his cousin standing around the corner of the fry station, talking to their replacements. He waited until she'd passed the chicken-frying baton. "You ready to go? Chad and Naomi are in line to eat."

"I'll come say hi, but I'm running over to Leah's to shower, and then I'm meeting Donovan at eight. I don't want to smell like fried chicken tonight." Cassie waggled her eyes at him.

"You have a date with Donovan Bledsoe?" Cal pushed all the Marine officer voice he had into those words.

It appeared to have no impact on Cassie. She lifted her chin. "He's nice."

He crossed his arms and went with the stern older brother approach. "He's older than I am."

"By two years."

"Which makes him eight years older than you."

"Which is hardly worth mentioning."

Cal played his last card. "You know you're always going to be a baby to me. I don't want to see you hurt."

"I know, and I love that about you." Cassie stretched onto her toes and kissed his cheek. "He's nice, Cal. I . . . I like him a lot."

Cal pulled her into a hug. "Okay. But if he hurts you—"

"He'll have the entire Quinn clan out for blood. Don't you think he already knows that?"

"I'm going to ask Gray about him." Gray had hired Donovan a year earlier—which, though he would never admit it to Cassie, was a point in Donovan's favor.

"Fine." Cassie flashed a brilliant smile. "And I'm going to go introduce myself to that gorgeous blond over there who's trying very hard to kill me with her eyes."

Before Cal could stop her, Cassie jogged over to where Landry stood with Eliza. It took one glance to see that Cassie was right. But why would Landry have an issue with Cassie? Cassie was one of the sweetest people on earth.

Cassie spoke to Landry and extended her hand. Cal reached them in time to hear her say, "Landry and Eliza. I finally get to meet you. I've heard all about you from Abby, of course." Cassie gave Abby a fist bump. "And Granny Quinn. And pretty much my entire family."

Before Landry could reply, Chad gave Cassie a peck on the cheek. "I've heard nothing but good things about the food, Cass."

Cassie bent down and spoke in a loud whisper to the girls. "Cal's coming to take credit for all my cooking. It's a good thing he's my favorite cousin, or I'd have to get mad."

The girls laughed. Chad feigned offense. And Landry? Landry looked like she'd been burning at the stake and someone just doused her with water.

What had Cassie said? *"That gorgeous blond over there who's trying very hard to kill me with her eyes."* Was Landry . . . jealous?

Cal tried to act like his mind wasn't swirling in a million directions as he joined the group. "Please. I taught her everything she knows."

Cassie shrieked in outrage before walking off in a pretend huff. "I'm out of here. I can't stay where someone is trying to steal all my glory." She blew kisses as she skirted around the crowds.

"Why didn't she stay?" Abby's shoulders slumped. "Cassie's my favorite."

Eliza nodded in agreement. "She was funny."

"She also"—Cal made it a point to look at Chad and not Landry—"has a date."

Naomi wrapped Chad's arms around her and squeezed. "You two stay out of it. Cassie can date whomever she wants."

"No, she can't," Chad and Cal said in unison, and Cal allowed himself to glance at Landry. A smile flirted with her lips.

"Protective much?" she asked.

"You have no idea." Naomi pointed to Cal. "They're all bad, but he's the worst."

"Hey!" Cal took a shift in the line as an opportunity to stand closer to Landry. "I was Team Naomi from day one. You're supposed to be nice to me." He turned to Landry. "I'm not saying Chad was going to mess it up, but if it wasn't for me—"

"Lies," Chad groused. "Don't listen to him, girls. I'll have you know I swept my Naomi off her feet, then I ran off with her heart before she had the chance to come to her senses."

"Funny what old age does to a man's mind." Cal touched his head. "You start forgetting how your little brother saved your bacon."

"And yet"—Chad tapped his own head—"you remember that your little brother nearly ruined your proposal."

"Enough." Naomi put one hand on each of their chests. "I prefer to remember that I got the man of my dreams for a husband and picked up an awesome little brother in the bargain."

Cal exchanged a look with Chad. "She always does this. Ruins our fun by being all nice."

Chad, not looking like anything was ruined at all, turned Naomi into his arms and planted one on her. Cal made a point not to glance at Landry.

"Enough." This time it was Abby, and she sounded exactly like her mother. She squeezed in between Naomi and Chad. "Stop smooching. It's time to eat." She turned to Eliza. "They do this all the time. You'll get used to it."

A little girl Cal thought he recognized from Abby and Eliza's class walked up to them, and their chatter, oddly enough, gave Cal his first opportunity to speak to Landry. "Hey."

"Hey."

Okay. That was . . . well, he'd led with a one-word greeting, so he couldn't complain about her following up with one. He'd been expecting . . . something? More warmth? Or some of the jealousy he'd picked up on earlier? Or . . . what?

They'd never had trouble talking before. What was the problem now? He scrambled for a safe topic. "Eliza's costume is amazing."

"Thanks."

They lapsed into silence again. This was all Cassie's fault. She'd put the idea in his head that Landry was jealous. But as far as he could tell, Landry wasn't jealous of anything. She didn't seem to even care if she talked to him. Which was fine.

Completely fine.

They were friends, after all. And friends didn't need to fill every second with conversation.

"So"—Landry fiddled with the zipper on her jacket—"how is Cassie related? Because I didn't see her at your grandparents' house, and I don't think I've seen her anywhere before. Not that I would have seen her around. I mean, I haven't exactly been around much myself. I was just wondering where she fits into the family tree."

SEVENTEEN

Landry fought the urge to clap her hand over her mouth. What was wrong with her? First, she was jealous of Cal laughing with a girl. Then she found it almost impossible to even speak to that girl. A girl who turned out to be lovely, sweet, funny, and so obviously a Quinn that Landry wasn't sure how she'd missed it. She even had the Quinn blue eyes.

But what if she hadn't been? Her response to Cal being with someone else was not okay.

No. There was no "else" in this. Her response to Cal being with someone, period, was ridiculous. And then she'd been so overcome with relief that she hadn't been able to speak to Cal. He'd tried to engage her in conversation, and she'd replied with short answers.

Until the words—so many words—flew out of her mouth, and now he was sure to think she'd finally cracked. She forced herself to look at him and wasn't prepared for the obvious relief on his face or the way his entire body had relaxed. She hadn't realized how tense he'd been until the tension was gone. What was *that* about?

She tried to steady her breathing and slow her heart rate as Cal explained. "Cassie is my cousin John's daughter. John is the son of my Uncle John and Aunt Rhonda. Uncle John is the oldest, while my mom is the sixth in line, and Meredith and Mo's dad is the baby of the family. So my first cousins—John and Jessica—were more like an uncle and aunt. The same way I am to Abby. Cassie and I grew up as cousins, but technically she's my first cousin once removed. I think? She's the child of my first cousin. So . . . yeah. That's right."

Abby and Eliza were herded into the line in front of Chad and Naomi. Naomi turned and mouthed "I've got her," so Landry stayed where she was with Cal.

"As for where she's been . . . Cassie's been in Georgia the past few years. After she graduated from culinary school, she worked at a couple of high-end restaurants around Atlanta. Right now, she's running a small restaurant here in town. High-end Southern comfort food. She wants to stay in Gossamer Falls, but I'm afraid her talents are going to take her to bigger cities. It's going to be hard for her to thrive here."

He stood in line behind Landry as they picked up plates, napkins, and plastic cutlery. "I wish I could figure out how she could fulfill her dream here. But there just aren't enough people in Gossamer Falls who want her kind of food."

Landry pointed to the crowds. "Seems like a lot of people want her kind of food."

Cal laughed, and Landry felt ten feet tall. "Okay. So everyone wants her food. But there isn't a large enough population for her to have a restaurant here. If we're lucky, she's probably going to wind up in Asheville. Maybe Charlotte. Or back to Georgia, poor thing."

"Not a Georgia fan?" Landry tried to keep her voice light and teasing.

"Not a fan of my baby cousin living so far away when she wants to live here."

"Wow. Naomi wasn't kidding."

Cal held out his plate for the server to pile a scoop of mashed potatoes on it. "Kidding about what?"

"You're protective of everyone, aren't you?" Her own plate was loaded down with macaroni and cheese, fried chicken, mashed potatoes, gravy, green beans, and a biscuit that was so beautiful, she almost hated the thought of eating it.

Almost.

He was beside her as they made their way to the table where Chad and Naomi had already settled Eliza and Abby. "Not everyone." Cal adjusted the plate in his hand and pulled out her chair for her.

"Just the people I care about."

Cal and Landry took their seats and dove into their food.

Landry had never enjoyed eating fried chicken in public. Should she cut it with a knife? Use her fingers? Some combination of the two?

She scanned the tables to either side. No one was using cutlery to eat their chicken. The kids were going in face-first. The adults were following suit with the smaller pieces. Thighs and breasts were being pulled apart with fingers.

Landry pulled a small piece from the chicken breast on her plate. Juices ran down her fingers before she could get it in her mouth. But once she tasted it, she simply didn't care what she looked like. "This is the best chicken I've ever eaten." She spoke to Cal around bites. "How is it possible that Cassie isn't already married? I would think chicken like this would garner marriage proposals by the dozens."

Cal didn't stop eating but gave her a look that said he agreed with her. He took a drink and muttered, "I hope Donovan was on duty and hasn't had any of this tonight. Otherwise, we'll be planning a wedding for spring."

"What's your problem with Donovan?" Naomi asked from her spot across from Landry. "He's a nice guy. Gray likes him. He hasn't been dating his way through the female population like that other officer did. Do you know something the rest of us don't?"

"I know lots of things the rest of you don't." Cal spoke with false solemnity. "The stories I could tell . . ."

"Oh, hush." Naomi waved a chicken leg in his direction. "Fine. You know stuff about Donovan. Is it related to his character? Or just that he has a past? Everyone has baggage. You can't protect Cassie from that. In fact, maybe we should be warning Donovan. Cassie's own baggage is heavy."

Landry listened to the exchange with unabashed curiosity. Cassie? That bubbly young woman? She seemed light and carefree. But Landry knew better than most that young women weren't immune to darkness.

"Donovan's a good guy. I'll stay out of it." Cal frowned at his plate.

Naomi laughed. "Heaven help us all if you ever have a little girl. Poor thing will have to move out of the country if she wants to date."

At Naomi's words, Cal stiffened. Just for a second. Landry didn't think she would have noticed had she not been sitting right beside him, their elbows occasionally brushing as they ate. He laughed at Naomi's remark, and the laughter was close to real but somehow . . . off.

A round, balding man who desperately needed someone to discuss nose hair trimmers with him approached from the left, and Cal and Chad both stood, extended their hands, and made introductions. The man, who turned out to be the middle school principal, took a seat to Cal's left. Chad and Cal returned to their seats and their meals while continuing the conversation about what sounded like a project the principal wanted them to help with.

Landry suspected that under normal circumstances, Cal would have been annoyed by the intrusion about work on his evening off, but she couldn't shake the feeling that tonight he was grateful for it.

179

He had so much. A warm family. A loving community. He was brave, had served his country, and on the surface, had it all. But Naomi's off-the-cuff remark had hurt him, and Landry found herself unwilling to let that go. Under the table, she reached out her hand, placed it on Cal's leg right above his knee, and squeezed. Before she could pull her hand back, his hand covered hers and returned the squeeze.

Then they both went back to eating and chatting, and apparently, pretending that nothing had happened.

———

It took Cal a full three minutes to pull himself together enough before he could look at Landry. When Mr. Brevis left to accost some other poor soul about opportunities to advertise their business in the middle school's new gym, Cal turned in his seat so his body language hopefully indicated that he didn't wish to be approached by anyone else.

He made eye contact with Chad. The kind that even their age difference hadn't prevented them from perfecting over the years. Chad didn't like Mr. Brevis. He particularly didn't like it when people tried to talk business while he was with his family.

Naomi patted Chad's arm. "Thank you for not making things difficult with Brevis. Danté has spent enough time in the man's office this year. No need to give him any more reason to think the worst of him."

"It's extortion is what it is." Chad stabbed a green bean. "You see who he's talking to now? The Lancasters."

Naomi leaned toward Landry and said, "Gretchen Lancaster spends more time in Brevis's office than Danté."

Landry pinched her lips together. "Are Gretchen and Danté friends?"

Chad rolled his eyes. "Those two will either change the world for the better—"

"Or become criminal masterminds," Naomi finished the thought. "Brevis better be careful. The Lancasters are fed up with his treatment of Gretchen. He's going to get himself called up before the school board."

Landry leaned toward Naomi and whispered, "I had no idea there was so much drama in Gossamer Falls."

"Oh, honey. You have no idea."

They finished their meal, and Cal joined them as they made the trek back down Main Street. The adults spoke to friends while the girls stopped at every booth and loaded up on candy. Cal could sense Naomi's remark hovering on the edge of his consciousness, but he refused to give in to the temptation to wallow.

Maybe, someday, he'd have a little girl. And he'd rock being a girl dad. The same way he would have rocked being a boy dad. But he couldn't think about that. Because then he'd start thinking about the boys and wondering what they'd dressed up as this weekend. Or if they'd decided they were too old for such nonsense.

That kind of thinking could put a man into a depression. Been there. Done that. Got the therapy. Knew how to keep from spiraling again. He stayed in the present, and when they made it back to the church parking lot and sat down for dessert, he was able to enjoy the look on Eliza's face when she tasted Cassie's banana pudding.

"This is amazing." Eliza held a spoon filled with yellow custard toward Landry. "You have to try it, Mommy."

Landry obliged. Her eyes closed, and she sighed. "Delicious."

"Granny Quinn used to have the best banana pudding in the county. And hers is good. But Cassie's is next level." Cal savored a bite of his own. "She makes me one every year on my birthday, and I eat the entire thing."

Landry almost choked on her next bite. "You're kidding."

"Nope. I eat it for breakfast, after lunch, in the afternoon, and after dinner."

"You eat an entire banana pudding in a day?" Landry took another bite, her expression contemplative. "Never mind. I can see it. This stuff *is* amazing."

Cal and Landry had taken seats across from Chad and Naomi again. The girls inhaled their dessert and asked if they could go play on the playground at the back of the church. Naomi and Landry exchanged looks, and Landry spoke. "It's okay with me, as long as you stay where you can see us and don't leave the playground."

The girls jumped from their seats and, after being reminded to take their trash to the garbage can, ran to the swings.

The Lancasters walked over to them and leaned toward Chad and Naomi. "Sorry to interrupt your dessert, but could we have a word?" Larry had a grip on his wife's hand that made Cal suspect the woman was ready to punch someone's lights out. And that someone was probably Mr. Brevis.

Landry's hand landed on his knee again, and she gave him a squeeze. Cal knew this was not the same as before. How he understood the message, he had no idea, but he scooted back in his chair. "Y'all take our seats. We're done."

Landry popped from her chair like a jack-in-the-box and grabbed her plate and his. "Yes. Here you go." She turned to Naomi and Chad. "We'll catch up to you in a little bit."

Chad lifted his chin at Cal. "I'll text you when we're ready to go."

Cal took both their cups and followed her to the garbage. They dumped the trash, and by unspoken agreement, walked to the edge of the parking lot.

Cal bumped her elbow. "Thanks for getting us out of there."

"I hoped you'd be okay with that."

"Okay? Are you kidding? I was afraid it was going to be one of those awkward situations where you get stuck sitting in the middle of two people, or in this case, four, having a conversation that you not only have nothing to contribute to but also feel very uncomfortable even hearing."

"Exactly!" Landry came up on her toes, her eyes animated, and leaned closer. "And that Gretchen's mom is about to go off on someone. I try to keep a low profile. The last thing I need is to be caught in the middle of a brawl at the harvest festival. Can't you see the headlines?"

Cal tried not to get hung up on Landry's low-profile comment and kept the conversation light. He made air quotes. "Irate parents attack middle school principal with banana pudding."

Landry laughed, and they settled into a silence that was neither awkward nor comfortable. Something had shifted between them, and Cal didn't know if they were going to be able to keep their footing or if they were about to crash.

A scream ripped through the night.

Then another.

And another.

Cal didn't wait for Landry but ran straight for the playground. He knew exactly where two little girls in pink hard hats were playing, and he had no thought but to reach them and get them out of there.

The problem was that both girls were running away from him and into the woods at the back of the playground. He called out, "Eliza! Abby!" But his words were lost in the chaos of frightened children and their arguably more terrified parents.

He glanced around to keep from running into small children and random playground equipment until he was close enough for the girls to hear him. He called out again, "Eliza! Abby!"

This time they stopped, turned around, and ran to him. He

dropped to his knees, and they ran straight into his arms. He scooped them both up. Only once he had them—their tiny faces streaked with tears, their arms wrapped around his neck to the point of choking him—did he attempt to figure out what had caused the commotion.

"Shhh. Shhh." He tried to soothe the girls. "What happened?" Abby hiccupped into his shoulder and said something, but Cal couldn't catch it. Chad ran up then and took Abby. "Come on." His expression was grim. "One of the older kids said there was a man with a gun."

"It was a big gun." Eliza spoke just as Landry reached them. "What?" Landry's face was ashen, and she reached for Eliza. Eliza removed one hand from Cal's neck but kept the other one tight around him. "Mommy!" With her grip on Cal, and Landry tugging on Eliza, Cal found himself in a tight huddle with both of them.

He scanned the crowd while he listened to Landry murmur to Eliza. He knew every face, and while some of them might have been carrying a weapon, he couldn't imagine anyone flashing a gun around kids.

Gray approached, all business, and with a gentleness not many people saw, spoke to the girls. "Miss Eliza, Miss Abby, are you ladies okay?"

Abby nodded. Eliza pointed toward the seesaws. "The man was over there. He had a weird mask on. He pointed the gun at us and said he was sorry."

Cal shifted Eliza to his left hip and pulled Landry in close to his right side. Her arm wrapped around his waist, and he took most of her weight.

"He asked us what our names are." Abby looked at Chad. "But I told him I didn't give my name to strangers."

"Good girl." Chad touched his forehead to Abby's.

"Do you know who screamed?"

"Mallory." Eliza pointed to a girl on the opposite side of the parking lot. "Her brother was with her, and he yelled for everyone to run, so we ran."

A small sound came from Landry, and Cal squeezed her closer. Gray ran a hand over his chin. "You two are very smart. Thank you for talking to me. I have one more question, then I'm going to go talk to Mallory and her brother."

"Her brother's name is Leo," Eliza said. "He's in sixth grade."

"Good to know. Now, you said the man had on a weird mask. What was weird about it?"

The girls exchanged looks, and their confusion was evident. When Abby spoke, her voice was filled with uncertainty. "It was kinda dark. But his mask looked like a person's face. Sort of. But not really."

"You've both been very helpful. If you think of anything else about the mask, tell your parents, okay?"

"We will," the girls responded in unison.

Gray made eye contact with the adults. "I'd say the best plan for tonight is to get these ladies home for the evening. I'll touch base tomorrow."

Chad handed Landry a large bag that Cal realized was Eliza's haul from the evening. They must have grabbed it when they left the table. With a nod, Chad and Naomi headed to their car with Abby.

Cal paused by Gray, Landry and Eliza still attached to him. "Do you need any help tonight?"

Gray looked from Landry to Eliza to Cal. "No. Get your girls home. I'll call you if anything changes."

EIGHTEEN

Landry didn't argue as Cal, still holding Eliza on one hip and her against his other side, maneuvered them through the dispersing crowds and toward her car. When they reached it, she had to disengage from his side to dig her keys from her pocket. She'd left her purse locked in the trunk and kept her keys and phone in her jeans and her license, some cash, and a credit card in a small pocket in the inner lining of her jacket.

Her hand shook as she tried to find the right button on the fob. It took a few tries, but she got the doors unlocked, and Cal gently extricated Eliza's arms from his neck. "Okay, Liza Lou."

"No." Eliza clamped herself around Cal again.

"Sweetheart." Cal knelt beside the car, setting Eliza on her feet even as her arms stayed locked around him. "The safest place for you to be is at The Haven. Safe and sound in your own bed. Abby's going to her house right now." He pointed to the spot a few cars down where Chad had pulled out of the parking space.

"Can you come home with us?"

At Eliza's query, Landry sagged against the car. She'd never wanted her child to experience any sort of trauma. And now, her five-year-old stood clinging to Cal, trembling with fear. She expected Cal to tell Eliza no.

"I can follow you to your house and make sure you get tucked in. Would that work?" Cal's voice held a barely controlled emotion that Landry couldn't quite define. Was it anger? Fear? Whatever it was, he had it in check. All he was showing Eliza was gentleness and compassion.

Eliza nodded.

Landry turned to Cal. "Where are you parked?"

He pointed to the far side of the church. "I'm over there. Why don't you drive me to my truck?"

She agreed. There were so many things she wanted to say. So many questions she wanted to ask. So much she didn't understand. But the only thing she knew for sure was that the right thing was to take care of Eliza—mind, body, and soul. And what Eliza needed was the assurance that the man who was now buckling her into the car would make sure she made it home.

Cal climbed into the passenger seat without a word, and the car was silent until she put it in park beside his truck. He opened the door, then turned to her. "Could I have a word?"

"Of course." She undid her seat belt and climbed out of the car. Cal met her at the rear bumper. "I'll stay right behind you. And I'm coming inside when we get to your place. I won't leave until Eliza's settled. Okay?"

For the first time in Eliza's entire life, and that included the two years her father was alive, Landry didn't feel the full weight of responsibility for managing the situation. Cal was here. Cal was going to stay until they were settled. Cal . . .

She shut down those thoughts. She *was* responsible. Cal wasn't. Cal never would be, and she would do well to remember that.

"You don't have to——"

"I would have followed you home whether Eliza asked or not." Cal moved until he was mere inches from her. He kept his voice low, but his eyes burned with intensity. "There's no way I'm letting

187

you out of my sight until I know you're safely behind the doors of your home."

"Okay." She could have argued with him, but why? She didn't mind. And his presence would make navigating the dark, winding road to The Haven far less stressful. A creeping anxiety flitted around the edge of her mind, and Cal's presence was the only thing keeping it from tackling her and putting her in a submission hold she wouldn't be able to break.

Cal walked to her door and opened it. "Lock your doors, and don't leave the parking lot until I'm behind you. When we get to your place, stay in your car until I'm parked and beside you."

"Got it." She climbed back in, buckled up, and twisted to give Eliza a reassuring smile.

"Is he still coming?" Eliza asked.

"Of course. Cal will be right behind us."

"Good." The quaver in her voice had Landry second-guessing every decision she'd made in the last few weeks.

When they were ensconced on the grounds of The Haven, rarely leaving or interacting with anyone in town, they'd avoided drama. Since she'd decided it was time to not only build a house but also have a life in Gossamer Falls, Favors had burned to the ground and the perpetrator had left a note that might or might not have been intended for Landry and Eliza.

And now? A gun-toting masked man on a playground after dark. A man who spoke to her daughter? She bit back the scream of frustration that tingled on her lips.

Why had he wanted to know Eliza's name?

Why was he even there?

What would have happened if the girls had told him their names?

The questions flooded through her for the entire twenty-minute drive to The Haven's gates.

As promised, Cal stayed directly behind her. Far enough not to blind her as she drove but close enough that no car could squeeze between them. When she drove through the gates, he stayed on her tail. And when she parked in her assigned space, he pulled into the space beside her, then backed out and pulled behind her, parking perpendicular to her car.

She stayed in her seat until he opened her door. He offered her his hand, and she took it. When she was out of the car, he opened the back door and repeated the action for Eliza.

"Do you have everything?" He tapped Eliza on her hard hat.

"Looks like you came away with some good loot there, Liza Lou."

Landry had her house keys in her hand and led the way to the door. Behind her, she heard Eliza chattering away. "I think I did. It's heavy."

"Heavy's a good sign. Let's get it inside so you can show me."

Landry opened the door and ushered everyone in. As soon as they were in, she turned to lock the door. Cal leaned close and whispered, "I'm going to clear the house. Keep Eliza beside you. It will take thirty seconds."

Before she could react, he slipped away.

She pulled Eliza close to her. "You were so brave, sweetheart. I'm so proud of you." Cal wasn't back yet, so she kept going. "I love you. So much."

"I love you too, Mommy."

Landry squeezed her again until Eliza squirmed for release. But she didn't let go until Cal came back and gave her a thumbs-up. "Before you do anything else, go to your bathroom and wash your hands."

"Yes, ma'am." Eliza paused at the edge of the room. "Don't leave, Cal. We have to look at my stuff."

"I'll be here."

As soon as she heard the door close, Landry turned to Cal. "Why did you want to check the house?"

189

"We can't be too careful."

Landry couldn't stop the shiver that ran through her. Even though there was no reason to suspect that the gun-wielding man on the playground tonight had been there for Eliza, the nagging voice in her mind that she'd been the target refused to be silent.

"Do you think—" The bathroom door opened, and Eliza ran out. "Fastest hand washing in history, sweet girl." Landry's admonishment carried no real heat, and Eliza's smile told Cal that she knew she wasn't really in trouble.

Eliza grabbed her bag. She poured the contents on the kitchen table and eagerly sorted through the candy, ignoring anything that looked remotely healthy or educational.

Landry gave her ten minutes, then called a halt to the post-game analysis. "Bath time. Bedtime."

Eliza obeyed, albeit in slow motion. Cal knew this tactic. Abby was a professional slug at bedtime. A trip to the kitchen for a glass of water could take fifteen minutes.

Thirty minutes later, bath time was over, teeth had been brushed, and Eliza came back into the living room to tell him good night. She gave him a hug and went to bed without any fuss.

Landry returned to the living room and flopped into a recliner. "She almost fell asleep in the bath. She should conk out soon."

Cal pointed to the pile of candy on the table. "Think she'd notice if I snagged a Snickers?"

"I was planning to take a Milky Way, but I forgot to get it before I sat down. Now I don't think it's worth it."

"Allow me." Cal went to the table, sorted through the candy, and returned to the living room with three fun-sized Milky Ways for Landry and one Snickers for himself.

"Want something to drink?" she asked.

"Nah. I'm good."

Landry unwrapped one candy bar and glanced toward Eliza's room before saying, "Do you think he was after my baby?"

"I don't know. Do you want to tell me why you think he might have been?"

She ate two of the three candy bars before she responded. "Do I want to? No. Nothing personal. I avoid talking about it in general." She tucked her feet under her legs and leaned toward him. "But you probably should know the whole story. I think I need some outside eyes to tell me if I messed up—well, worse than I already know I did."

Cal braced for her revelation, but she surprised him when she continued. "But not tonight. I need sunshine and fresh air for that conversation."

"That doesn't give me a warm, fuzzy feeling."

"It isn't a warm, fuzzy story." Landry folded one of the wrappers into a precise square. "For tonight, what you need to know is that my husband's family made it clear they didn't believe I was a fit mother and they would be better able to care for Eliza."

Cal lurched to his feet at her words. He went back to the table and returned with another Snickers. Rather than resuming his seat, he paced back and forth behind the sofa. "You have to be kidding me."

"I wish I was." Landry's sad smile nearly broke him. "When I left, I did my best to hide my whereabouts. I changed my name back to my maiden name and changed Eliza's as well. I kept my head down, broke all ties to that area, and worked to establish myself. I was newly widowed with no employment history and no proof that I could provide for my child when I left. But now I have a successful business and a steady income. My child is healthy and happy."

Cal rested his hands on the back of the sofa. "Your child is amazing. As are you."

"Thank you. She is, for sure." She set the folded candy wrapper on the small table beside her chair. "Before Eliza started school, I checked with three different attorneys. All agreed that at this point, no judge in the land would let anyone take her from me. They said I had more than proven my competence."

"You're so much more than competent."

"I'm inclined to agree with you, but his side of the family has money, influence, and a track record of totally disregarding the truth. With that said, I've never believed they would stoop to doing anything undeniably illegal. Unethical? Sure. But illegal? No."

"So does that mean you think they're behind this? Or not? I'm not sure what you're saying."

"I'm not saying anything." Landry threw up her hands. "I just know that since we came out of isolation, we've had two major incidents." She clambered to her feet and faced him across the sofa. "And don't you dare tell me I'm imagining it. If you didn't think there was any chance we could be at risk, you wouldn't have cleared the house."

Cal's own annoyance bled through as he replied. "I don't know anything either. I have nothing to base my concerns on beyond the very little you've shared about Eliza's father, his family, and what brought you to Gossamer Falls. But I'd rather be dead wrong than be wrong and you and Eliza wind up dead."

Landry balled her hands into fists and looked at the ceiling. "Why is this happening?"

Cal wasn't sure if she was praying or venting, although maybe it was both. One thing he knew for sure was that a bit of divine guidance would be welcome right about now.

When she looked at him, the anger was gone, but the stark fear that remained was threatening to destroy him. He walked around the couch and approached her slowly. In his experience, wounded people were significantly more dangerous than any wounded animal could ever be. They could lash out and land blows that forced the people trying to help to abandon their attempt so they could tend their own injuries.

Before he could get to her, she dropped her head. "I'm sorry, Cal. None of this is your fault. And it isn't your problem."

He was about to cross a line. A line they'd both drawn in extra bold permanent marker. And he didn't hesitate. When he reached her, he rested one hand on her hip, and placed his other hand on her cheek with his thumb under her chin. Her hands landed at his waist, but he did nothing to pull her body any closer to his. Instead, he tilted her face up and waited until her eyes met his. "Don't ever apologize for allowing me to see the truth of you, Landry."

"The truth of me is not always a pretty thing to see."

"I disagree. I'll take your tough truth over a deceitful mask any day." He tucked a few strands of hair behind her ear. "But I'm guessing you've had enough truth for tonight."

Her laugh was shaky. "Yeah."

Cal pulled her in and gave her a quick hug, then stepped back before he forgot that as far as she knew, they were just friends. "I'll call you tomorrow."

"Okay."

There was two feet between them. He could close that distance—

Landry's phone rang. She blinked several times before she dug the phone from her purse. Had she been as caught up in the moment as he'd been?

"Hello?" A pause. "Yes." She pulled the phone away from her ear, tapped the screen, and Gray's voice came through the speaker.

"Sorry to bother you so late, Landry. I wanted to be sure you made it home safe and that Eliza's okay."

Landry didn't seem to mind Gray's interruption in the slightest.

"Oh, that's so kind of you. We're home. Eliza's gone through her candy and is already asleep."

A simple "Yes, thank you" would have sufficed.

"Good. Did Cal follow you home?"

Landry didn't meet Cal's eyes. "He did."

"He still there?"

That was enough of that. "What do you want, Gray?"

Gray cleared his throat. "Just making sure Landry and Eliza are okay."

"As Landry said, they're fine."

"Thought you might stop by the station on your way home."

"You could've called me."

Gray cleared his throat again. "I did. Three times."

Cal pulled the phone from his pocket. Sure enough. Missed calls. More than three. "Sorry, man. I guess it's on Do Not Disturb." He went to the settings tab.

"Maybe you can take it off?"

"Doing that now."

"Good. Are you coming by?"

"Of course."

"Anytime soon?"

"I'm leaving now."

Landry leaned toward the phone. "Gray, excuse me, but do you have something I need to hear?"

"Sorry, Landry, but no. I wanted to bounce a few things off Cal. When you blow the sawdust out of his ears, he has an excellent mind for law enforcement."

Landry laughed. Cal was less than amused. "If you don't have anything important to say, then I'm disconnecting this call now."

"Have a good night, Landry."

Cal hit the end button before Gray could say anything else that might cement Cal's need to strangle his former best friend.

"Do you really think there's nothing I need to know?" Landry asked.

"If he has anything important to say, I'll let you know."

"Thank you."

"Okay. So, I'm headed out." Cal walked to the door. Landry followed him, and when he stepped outside, she waited at the door.

He turned to her. "Gotta be honest. I don't want to leave."

Landry's skin turned pink, and she looked down at her phone but didn't respond.

He didn't say anything else. Just turned and walked to his truck. *Idiot. Couldn't leave well enough alone. Messed it up big.*

"Cal?" He could hear the anxiety in her voice. He'd put that there. He stopped but didn't turn around.

He heard footsteps, then felt a small hand on his arm. "Cal?"

"Yeah."

"Thank you."

"Anytime." He meant it. He also needed to get away from her.

"Cal?"

"Yeah."

"Will you text me when you get home? Let me know you made it?"

"Sure."

"Okay. Thanks." Before she dropped her hand, she leaned closer and whispered, "You have no idea how much I wish you could stay." She ran inside, then closed and locked the door.

NINETEEN

Cal climbed into his truck, cranked the engine, and stared at Landry's door. He had no idea what he was doing. He didn't think Landry knew either. And for tonight, leaving well enough alone was the best outcome.

Before he drove away from The Haven, he read the text messages that waited for him.

From his mother in a group text with his father:

Ten minutes later:

I've messaged Mo.

From Mo:

Cal? If you don't answer your phone, I'm sending out a search party. Where are you?

From Meredith:

Aunt Carol is losing her mind. Call your mother, you idiot.

Cal? Are you okay? Is Landry? How's Eliza? Call me. I need details.

196

From Chad:

Call me.

From Connor:

Call me.

From Connor in a group text with Chad:

Are you seriously at Landry's and not answering the phone? You've got some explaining to do, bro.

From his father in the group text with his mother:

Mo tells us your phone is at The Haven. Chad tells us you were following Landry home. I'm assuming you're still there, but fair warning . . . your mother is calling Gray.

And that explained why Gray had called Landry. He typed a quick text.

Leaving Landry's. Wanted to make sure Eliza was settled. Headed to Gray's office. Will text more later. Love you.

He copied it and sent it to his mom, dad, brothers, Meredith, and Mo.

Then he waited. No real surprise that Mo called him first. He answered the call with no greeting. "Did you track my phone?"

"You had the entire family in an uproar." Mo wasn't the least bit apologetic. "I thought Aunt Carol was going to cry when she called me. Who finally got you to answer the phone?"

"No one. Gray called Landry."

Mo's laughter almost made this entire debacle worthwhile. He was still laughing when Cal heard Meredith's voice asking, "Is that Cal? What's so funny?" Then she was on the phone. "I put you on speaker. What's wrong with you? You can't disappear after a masked gunman was in the park. How could you not expect a general roll call? I hope Aunt Carol has called Granny Quinn. And what has Mo laughing?"

"Is that laughter? Sounds like he's trying to pass a kidney stone."

"Cal! This is serious." Meredith's words were intense, but her laughter ruined her efforts to bring any sort of decorum to the situation.

Cal's phone beeped. It was Chad. "Mer, Chad's calling. Get Mo to fill you in." He swapped over to Chad's call before Meredith could respond. "How's Abby?"

"Sacked out. Seems to be fine. How's Eliza?"

"Same."

Cal let the silence stretch.

"You talked to Mom yet?"

"No. Sent her a text. Before I could call anyone, Mo called. Then you."

"Call Mom."

Chad disconnected. Cal spoke into the silence. "Hey, Siri, call Mom's mobile."

His mom picked up on the first ring. "Cal?" The relief in her voice hit Cal hard. He hadn't meant to worry her or anyone else.

"Sorry, Mom."

"Were you really with Landry?" His mom's relief had morphed into unveiled curiosity in the space of half a second.

"Yes. Eliza was pretty shaken up, and she wanted me to follow them home, so I did. But once she got home and went through all her candy, she went to bed easy. Landry's pretty anxious, but she's home and behind locked doors for the night. I'm on my way to Gray's office."

"Chad said the man specifically asked the girls for their names."

His father's voice came through the speaker.

"That's what they told Gray. And I don't get that at all. They don't look alike."

"They don't look alike to *you*," his mom corrected. "They were dressed in identical costumes, they both have brown skin, they're similar in height, and with those hard hats on, the difference in their hair would have been hidden."

Both girls had brown skin, brown eyes, and eyelashes that their mothers envied. Cal had never thought about eyelashes until Abby came home and every female in the Quinn/Shaw family lost their collective minds over hers. Then they did the same thing when they met Eliza.

Despite those similarities, no one who saw them without hats would ever confuse them.

Abby's hair was black and straight and reached to her midback. She frequently wore it in a long braid and desperately wished for curls.

Eliza's hair was dark brown with glints of bronze threaded through bouncing curls. She sometimes wore it in a pouf on top of her head, and she desperately wished for straight hair.

Tonight, the girls had told him that Naomi and Landry had promised to curl/straighten their respective hair over the Thanksgiving break. They were ecstatic.

Cal knew better than to comment on the topic, but he didn't want Eliza's hair straightened any more than he wanted Abby's in curls. Cal wasn't ignorant of the girls' ethnicities and didn't want to be, but as far as he was concerned, they were each perfect exactly as they were.

Abby had been adopted from an orphanage in India. No one knew anything about her birth family, but there was no reason to think she was anything other than Indian.

Eliza didn't have a clearly defined ethnicity. Eliza's birth father had also been adopted, and according to one of the few things Landry had told him about the man, no one knew for sure what his genetic makeup was. His adoptive family was white and Latino. They'd assumed he was some combination of Latino, African American, and Native American.

Landry had told Cal she'd never given it much thought until she was signing Eliza up for school and realized she had no idea what to check on the "race" box.

Abby's skin was darker than Eliza's, but in the dim light of the playground . . .

Had the gun-wielding stranger been looking for Eliza? Or Abby? Or someone completely different?

But the man didn't ask anyone else for their name. Just the girls.

"I'll talk to Gray about it."

"Good. Let me know what he says. Good night." His dad signed off.

"Cal." His mom wasn't quite done with him. No surprise.

"What do you know about Landry? Before she came here."

"Not much." Not enough. He pulled into the police station.

"Mom, I'm here to talk to Gray. I need to go."

"Okay, honey. Just one more question." She didn't say anything for several seconds.

"Mom?"

"Mom?"

"Honey, I try to stay out of your business——"

"Mom——"

"Is she important? I mean, I know she's important. But is she important . . . to you?"

"I'm not sure what she is to me, but yes, she's important."

"Okay, sweetheart. Talk to Gray. And while you're there, tell him if he cancels another checkup with me, I'm going to make an office visit and check him out at his desk."

"I'll tell him."

Cal disconnected the call and climbed from his truck.

Gray met him at the front door and unlocked it. "Took you long enough."

"Sorry. Had to talk to everyone in the family."

Gray relocked the doors, and Cal followed him to his office. Gray indicated a chair for him to sit in, and he took the seat behind his desk. "I'll be quick. Bottom line—no one has any idea who the guy was."

"The one night of the year a stranger could walk around Gossamer Falls, and he picks tonight? That's not a coincidence."

"No." Gray leaned back in his chair and studied Cal. "I'm going to ask Landry for more details about what brought her to Gossamer Falls."

Cal refused to break the eye contact. "Okay."

"You don't care?" Gray was fishing.

On a normal night, Cal would have laughed at the bait. But this was not a normal night. "As long as you aren't planning to talk to her over dinner, I don't have a problem with it."

Gray popped upright in his chair. "I knew it. What's going on with you?"

"Nothing."

"Who do you think you're talking to? You just warned me off from dating her, and now you're sitting there doing that 'I'm a cool operator' thing when I know full well you're as prickly as a porcupine when it comes to Landry and Eliza Hutton."

The mention of Eliza sent a wave of anxiety through Cal. He'd sworn he would never, ever go there again. No more kids. He couldn't get attached to her.

Except . . . tonight when he'd seen her in that little construction worker costume?

Gray watched him with unconcealed satisfaction. "I'm happy for you, man."

"There's nothing to be happy about."

"But there will be. You aren't cut out for single life. You're a family, man through and through. Wife, kids, in a house by the river? I can see it."

"Yeah?" Cal leaned back in his seat. It was time to treat Gray to a taste of his own medicine. "When are you going to quit messing around and ask Meredith out?"

Gray's amusement vanished. "What?"

Cal took pity on his friend. The poor guy's dark skin had turned a little gray. "Don't worry. You've got my approval. Mo's too."

"Cal . . ." Gray looked genuinely pained. Had Cal missed something important? "Meredith is a lovely woman. Funny, intelligent, kind, fearless."

"And?"

"And way too good for the likes of me." Gray picked up a file and tapped it on the desk. Cal took the hint and let it drop. "As for the Hutton ladies, I sent Bronwyn a text earlier. The security team at The Haven has been alerted to pay close attention to their whereabouts. I'm sure you'll be doing the same. Let your brothers know. The guys on the crew working at The Haven too."

"You think she's in danger?"

"Do you?"

Cal grimaced. "Yes. Something about this . . . that note . . . it's personal. Too personal."

"We'll figure out what's going on. We'll keep them safe."

Gray meant every word. Cal knew it.

Didn't mean he didn't wish he was driving back to Landry's instead of to his tiny house on the river. Alone.

Landry woke the next morning to twenty-seven text messages. She stared at the notification number on her phone. Had she ever had twenty-seven messages at one time?

She walked into the kitchen and scanned the screen. Five from Bronwyn. Four from Naomi. Two from Gray. One from Meredith. One from Granny Quinn. Granny Quinn texted?

Landry. This is Granny Quinn. You let us know if you need anything. Hope you and Eliza slept well.

The remaining messages were from two different group texts that she had not been part of when she'd gone to bed last night.

The first one was Meredith, Mo, and Cal. Meredith had added her, and it was short and to the point.

Landry—this is Meredith, Mo, and Cal. Let us know how you and Eliza are.

The next one was a larger group. It took her three texts to real-ize that it included Chad, Naomi, Connor, Carla, Cal, and . . . oh, sweet mercy . . . Cal's mom and dad, Craig and Carol.

She'd been added to the Shaw family group text.

She set the phone down on the counter. She needed coffee. Lots of coffee.

All. The. Coffee.

She took her time getting the coffee exactly right. Then, cup held tight in both hands, she looked at her screen and read the first message.

Hi Landry. Sorry for bringing you into this chaos. Just wanted you to know that we're here for you. We wanted to check on you and Eliza this morning. We also wanted to check on Abby, and to see how Chad and Naomi are. So it seemed easier to just send one big text. You'll find that I (Carol) text.

Dad (Craig) rarely texts, but he reads them and gets his feelings hurt if we don't include him.

From a new number:

From Carol:

I don't get my feelings hurt. And I do text. Especially when I'm being maligned.

From Craig:

Well, at least I malign you to your face and not behind your back.

I'm a blessed man.

From Connor:

Landry took a sip.

From Carla:

Run, Landry! It's not too late. Get out while you can!

Carla had included a laughing emoji and a winking emoji.

From Connor:

Sorry you've been dragged into this, Landry.

Hey!

From Carla:

Love you, babe.

From Chad:

We're fine. Thanks for asking, Landry; ignore everyone else.

From Naomi:

Abby slept fine. I did not. Landry—I sincerely hope we haven't messed up your sleep with our special brand of crazy. I'm going back to bed. Abby's still asleep.

Landry reread the thread. Nope. Not her imagination. She was in a group text with Cal's entire family.

She pulled up the texts from Cal.

Oh my word. My mother. I love her. But she should have asked before subjecting you to this.

I hope you slept well. And that Eliza wakes up full of confidence and joy.

Don't feel like you have to respond to the group.

Landry could imagine what was happening in a text loop she wasn't a part of—one where Cal, Chad, and Connor were giving Carol grief for the group text.

She grabbed her phone and responded to Cal first.

It's fine. A bit of a surprise, but that's okay. I appreciate the concern. Eliza's still asleep. I just got up. I slept okay. When did you get home?

Then she replied to the group text.

Good morning, everyone. Thank you for checking on us. We're fine. Eliza is still asleep. I slept okay. Just not long enough.

Cal responded almost immediately.

Glad you're okay. What's on your agenda for the day?

She hadn't had much time to process everything that had happened last night. Especially the part where Cal had acted like far more than a good friend.

No, it wasn't his actions. A good friend—male or female—might have followed her home and made sure she and Eliza were okay. It was the way he looked at her, the way he held her gaze, the way he worried. It wasn't any one specific thing she could put her finger on, but something was different.

And then the way he'd held her face. And that weirdness before he left.

A smart woman would put some distance between them.

> I planned to spend most of the day in my studio. I'm still rebuilding my stock. But right now, I'm not sure I can stand to be inside. We may drive out to the property and dream about our house.
>
> Let me know if you want some company. I'll be around.

Three hours later, Landry packed some books, blankets, pillows, and a picnic basket filled with enough food to feed a few extra people, and she and Eliza drove to the three acres of North Carolina that belonged to them.

She parked in the spot she envisioned would one day hold her studio and opened Eliza's door. Eliza clambered out and headed for the river. "Stay where I can see you." Landry grabbed the books, blankets, and pillows and followed Eliza. She found the tree that had become her absolute favorite spot and spread out the blankets. She left the pillows and books and went back for the basket. By the time she returned to the tree, Eliza was headed back.

And she wasn't alone.

Maisy was on one side. And Cal was on the other. When he

reached her, he dropped his head. Almost like he was . . . shy? "I'm sorry about this, Landry." His voice was low, and his body was turned so Eliza couldn't see his face. "Maisy and I were playing fetch. When we saw Eliza, Maisy ran for her. Then Eliza insisted I come with her."

"You're more than welcome, Cal. I'm glad you're here." Cal's dubious expression bugged her. "Why do I get the feeling you don't believe me?"

"I feel like I'm intruding on your day with Eliza."

"Not at all."

Cal pulled his ball cap off his head and looked over her shoulder. "I, um . . . I thought that maybe you'd rather not see me."

"What would make you think that?"

"I . . ." Cal shifted from one foot to the other.

She had never seen him so off-kilter, and she didn't like it. "What's wrong? You're acting weird."

Cal made a frustrated sound and then made eye contact. "I told you to let me know if you wanted company. You didn't text. I don't want to assume you want me to be here."

Oh.

Cal's neck had a bright red flush creeping up it and darkening by the second.

"I thought about texting you. And then I didn't. I couldn't quite figure out what to say."

Cal frowned. "What's hard about saying 'I'm on my way'?"

She didn't have an answer. "I thought I'd text you after I was already here and invite you to join us for lunch."

Cal slammed his hat back on his head. "You don't have to say that just because I'm already here."

"I'm not!"

"It's fine."

"What's wrong with you?" She stepped toward him until there

was no more than a few inches between them. "What do I have to do to prove to you that I want you to be here?"

"You don't have to prove anything."

"It certainly seems like I do."

The entire conversation had taken place in hushed tones and hissed whispers. Now, they stared at each other. Landry didn't know what Cal saw on her face, but she could guess. She was confused, aggravated, embarrassed, and trying desperately to avoid saying things out loud that she was not ready to say. Or, for that matter, think.

"Are we fighting over whether or not we want to have lunch together?" Cal's question was laced with humor. The hostility was gone.

I have no idea what we're fighting about. In fact, I didn't think we were fighting. I thought we were doing a terrible job of communicating, but I didn't think we were mad about it." Landry didn't like the way the idea of him being mad at her made her ache. She'd tiptoed around a man for far too long. She would never do that again.

"I'm not mad. I'm making a mess of things. I'm sorry. I'm being ridiculous, insecure, and as you put it, weird. Please let me start again."

Landry took a step back. She had to. If she didn't, she was going to throw herself into his arms and kiss him. Instead, she gave him her brightest smile and offered the do-over he'd requested. "Cal! You're here. I'm so glad."

She must have done something right, because the tension bled out of him, and the smile he gave her was the real one she'd found herself chasing these past few months.

"I'm glad too." He dipped his head and whispered, "Thank you." Then he pointed to the basket. "What's for lunch?"

She sat on the blanket, grateful for the space between them so she could catch her breath, and opened the lid. "We have chicken and beef burritos. Chips, queso, salsa—"

"Is this your famous homemade salsa?" Cal reached for the jar.

"It is." When had he gotten so close? He was kneeling on the blanket beside her, staring into the basket as she shifted the items around. "We also have brownies——"

"The caramel brownies?"

"Yes. The ones you liked so much that you declared me to be your favorite baker, even though I've told you at least ten times that they come from a box and require zero baking skills."

"I don't care how you bake them. I just care that you do because they're awesome. Why mess with perfection?"

She pulled a bottle of water from the basket and handed it to him. "Are you ready to eat? Or we can wait. There's no rush."

"Are you crazy? What is this? Some sort of cruel Tex-Mex torture? Are you secretly working for the CIA on new interrogation techniques? Show a man his favorite foods but don't let him eat them?"

TWENTY

Landry's laughter echoed off the surrounding trees and settled into Cal. He'd been so nervous about seeing her. And then he'd botched the whole thing because he thought she hadn't wanted to see him.

He was lucky she *wasn't* the type to let anything slide—and also lucky she *was* the type to give a man another chance.

Now they were laughing and pulling burritos and chips from the basket. Landry had brought all his favorite foods to this picnic. There was no way she hadn't been planning to invite him.

Could he be more of an idiot?

The brownies—his favorite—were warm. She'd gotten up this morning to make them. And what had he done? All but accused her of not wanting him around because he couldn't say what he wanted to say.

They were friends.

F-R-I-E-N-D-S.

She'd had so much on her mind last night she probably hadn't noticed the way he'd behaved. All possessive and a little bit crazy and way more like a boyfriend than a buddy.

And friends were what they would stay. At least, as far as she was concerned. He'd had all night to consider the dilemma of Landry Hutton, and he'd concluded that as long as he kept himself in line, there was no reason they couldn't continue as they had been. It wasn't necessary for him to clue her in to the fact that his feelings for her were shifting into something he apparently had no control over.

But he would find some control. Because if he lost it completely, he'd lose her.

And that wasn't okay.

After a wonderful lunch, he took Landry and Eliza across the river and to his workshop. Eliza was fascinated by everything, and he let her help him sand a few of the small candy dishes he'd made last week. Despite Eliza's pleading, he followed the unmistakable wishes in Landry's eyes and didn't allow the little girl to help him run the electric current through the wood to create the gorgeous patterns that made his work unique.

Eliza recovered from her disappointment when he showed her how to rub the blue polymer into the areas etched by the electric current. Landry didn't seem terribly upset that Eliza's fingertips were blue—and would probably remain so for a few days.

When they were done, he promised that when the stain was dry on the bowls they'd worked on, he would bring her one to keep on her dresser.

And all the while, he tried very hard not to let Eliza squirm into his heart.

They started the walk back to Landry's property. Eliza got permission to run ahead, with Cal and Landry bringing up the rear.

Landry heaved a huge sigh, looked up at the puffy clouds, and then down at the ground. "It's sunny, bright, and happy here, and I don't want to ruin our day. But I did promise you some answers."

Cal tried to keep his cool. "I haven't made it a secret that I'm curious about your life before The Haven and what led you to Gossamer Falls. But you don't have to talk about it if you don't want to."

"You're just being nice because I accused you of being a horrible person, and you had to out yourself in order to prove you weren't." Landry's grin was sardonic. "But it won't work. It isn't fair for you not to have the whole story."

He didn't know if fairness had anything to do with it, but if that's how she felt, he wouldn't argue with her.

"I hate talking about it because there's no way to tell the story without highlighting my own stupidity and bad decision-making and pretty much pointing out to you how much of a moron I am."

"You aren't a moron."

"You haven't heard the story."

"I didn't say you had never been a moron. You've heard my story. You know how dumb I was."

"You weren't dumb! She was a deceptive shrew!"

Well, that was interesting. "Regardless, maybe I should have noticed all those trips to her folks' or the way she danced around it whenever I mentioned marriage or the way she refused to make vacation reservations."

"She gave you good reasons for all of it."

"She did. And I was a moron for believing her."

"Cal!"

He couldn't stop himself from laughing. "If I see myself as a moron for my behavior, and you don't, why would you be surprised that I would see your situation quite differently than you do?"

Landry's expression grew pensive. "Maybe. But you haven't heard it yet. So stop interrupting me."

"Yes, ma'am."

Landry leaned against a tree where she had a full view of Eliza by the edge of the river, building a tower of rocks. "I have to be careful. I never want Eliza to think she isn't wanted. Or that I have a second of regret when it comes to her. I don't. She's the best thing that ever happened to me. I never say that I wish I'd never met Dylan, or that I hadn't married him, because then I wouldn't have her."

"Understandable."

"But I do have regrets, Cal. So many."

Cal planted himself against a tree near Landry. Close enough that she wouldn't have to raise her voice to be heard but far enough to the side that she wouldn't have to make unwanted eye contact.

"My childhood was okay. There was food in the house. And I had clothes, although I do remember frequently going for a while without shoes that fit. But for the most part, my most basic needs were met. I went to school because I liked it. I went to church because my grandmother took me. I took a bath at least once a day. I liked at school said you should take a bath once a day. I didn't realize until recently how much my parents didn't do. I thought it was normal for little kids to be left alone for hours at a time. I didn't realize parents were supposed to make sure their kids ate. And slept. And went to school. My parents weren't abusive the way most would define it. They never hit me. They never yelled. But they were neglectful."

Landry spoke in an almost monotone. She truly didn't sound bitter about her childhood. More like ambivalent.

"I was mostly on my own. I don't have siblings. If I have cousins, I've never met them. I got a scholarship and went to college and realized how much other people's parents did for them." She chuckled. "Remind me some time to tell you about my first roommate's mom. Wow."

"A nightmare?" Cal asked.

"No. A clean freak." She waved a hand. "Anyway, I could go on and on. The point is, without realizing it, I was in a desperate emotional situation. I dated some in college, but not a lot. I was focused on school. I graduated, landed a job in sales, and started my life. Or thought I had."

"Two years after graduation, I landed a job several hours away from my home. I made the move, settled in, and started attending the church his father pastored. That's when I met Dylan." The old bitterness crept into her voice. She tried to force it away.

"I don't know if Dylan recognized my emotional vulnerability immediately, or if it was a case of someone who had no spine falling in love with someone who turned out to be a narcissist. Regardless, when he first asked me out, I said no. He was handsome, and he said he loved the Lord. He was at church every week. But I was traveling at the time for my job, and I didn't think it would be a good idea."

She paused as Eliza ran over to them. Sometimes she could see Dylan in Eliza's face. Certain expressions and mannerisms had to be genetic, because he hadn't lived long enough for Eliza to learn them by watching him.

"Look, Mommy! Cal!" Eliza held her palm flat, and a rock glimmered in the sunlight. She touched it with the index finger of her other hand. "It's shaped like a heart!"

"Wow!" Landry studied it. How unusual. "Want me to hold on to it for you?"

"Yes! I'm going to see if I can find more."

"Be careful."

Eliza responded with a wave of her hand as she ran back to the riverbank.

Landry fingered the rock. "Dylan was persistent. I didn't say yes until I was twenty-five. By then, I'd discovered pottery and bought my first kiln. I spent my weekends making all kinds of crazy messes. At the time, he claimed it was charming. Delightful. One of the many things he loved about me."

She traced the heart shape. "He didn't want to date long or have a long engagement. He sent flowers and candy to me at work. He held doors and said nice things. In hindsight, I can see it for what it was."

"What was it?" Cal's voice was a hoarse whisper.

"An act. A well-thought-out, carefully choreographed maneuver. I was a believer. I had no family. My grandmother died before I graduated from high school. My parents moved to Missouri while I was in college. I'd been on my own for years. That's how I started volunteering at the, um, the place where I met Bronwyn."

She'd almost slipped. Bronwyn was a big part of her story, but Bronwyn's story wasn't hers to tell.

Cal coughed. "I don't know everything, but I know she met you at a rehab clinic. She talked about you a lot before you moved here. She credits you with keeping her sane."

Relief flooded through her. "Like I said, I was alone. And the rehab clinic gave me a place to teach pottery and art, something I'd always enjoyed. They discourage the staff from becoming friends with the patients. So even though we hit it off, I tried to keep some distance between us."

Cal snorted. "Bronwyn's good at keeping her distance from other people, but if she wants to be around you, she's almost impossible to avoid."

"Precisely. When she got out of the inpatient part of her rehab, she chose to stay in the area for the next year. It was during that time that we became friends. I started dating Dylan a week after Bronwyn moved back here."

"Is there a correlation?"

Landry looked at him. "I don't want to believe there is, but it's possible. I was lonely, and he was persistent. And once I said yes the first time, things moved so fast. I should have realized it was too fast. But I didn't have anyone in my life who could see what was happening and warn me. And sadly, the people in my church were either too oblivious or too weak to stand up to his family. So they watched it all play out but did nothing to intervene."

TWENTY-ONE

Cal didn't like where this was going. Not even a little bit. "Did he . . . did he force you, Landry?"

"No. Not like that." Landry's face flushed, but Cal believed her. "He didn't get physical until the very end. But he was a master at emotional bullying."

Cal kicked his foot into the tree behind him. "So he hounded you until you said yes, then he won you over by being sweet and wooing you."

"Pretty much. The thing is, I ached with loneliness. I had this gaping hole in my soul, and somehow I thought having a family would fill it. It made me susceptible to his charms. But I was still an idiot. I should have seen it for what it was. He knew I was alone. He knew once he had me, he could isolate me and keep me bound to him because there was no one for me to run to and nowhere for me to go."

She sighed. "But I didn't see it. And to be honest, while at the time I thought I was in love with him, I'm not sure I was. I think I was in love with the idea of a family, of marriage, of children, of security and stability. And he was kind and gentle and attentive. I thought maybe the kind of love that takes your breath away was for other people. Or maybe it would grow in time."

Cal bit back a growl.

"Anyway, when he proposed, I said yes. And when he wanted a small ceremony, I was fine with that. It wasn't like I had anyone to invite."

Landry fell silent, and Cal knew that the bad stuff was about to come.

"I can't honestly say I enjoyed the honeymoon. And knowing what I know now, part of the reason I felt that way was that my husband was far more experienced than he'd claimed he was. Anyway, he made me cry for the first time on the third day of our honeymoon. By the time we flew home, I knew I'd made a horrible mistake. He was not the man I'd thought I'd married. And even though I truly believe marriage is forever and vows aren't meant to ever be broken, I considered leaving."

"But you were pregnant." Cal could see it. How this Dylan had trapped her.

"Yep. My pregnancy was a bizarre experience. Dylan was almost as sweet as he'd been before we got married. I even started to wonder if I'd imagined the whole thing."

"Gaslighting at its finest." Cal wished he could punch something.

"I know now that he was just trying to keep me happy and content because he didn't want anything to happen to Eliza. As soon as she was born, he shed his cloak of civility and paraded around in his true form."

Her words painted a dark and disturbing picture. "Did he ever hit you?"

"Not until the very end."

Cal couldn't keep his distance any longer. He walked over to stand in front of her. "What happened?"

"The one thing I'd kept from my former life was my volunteer work at the rehab center. It looked good to his family and the church, so he didn't argue about it. And I'd stayed friends with

Bronwyn. I only ever talked to her when I was at the center. I'd take Eliza with me, and I'd teach art and pottery, and I never let on how bad things were at home."

"And then?"

"Then Bronwyn flew out to surprise me."

Cal dropped his head. "Let me guess. She came to your house."

"She did. Knocked on the door. Dylan opened it. Bronwyn breezed in, gushing and happy, and I knew I was in big trouble. She told me later that she knew the minute she walked in that there was a problem, but she hoped by playing dumb she could minimize the damage until she talked to me about it later. She claimed she had a layover in Phoenix and was flying out the next morning, and she only stayed for about thirty minutes."

Cal stepped away from Landry. He had a feeling he was going to need some space for what came next.

"I put Eliza in bed and came back out to the living room. He'd been drinking. He'd already had a couple before Bronwyn stopped by. I'm not sure how many he had while I was with Eliza. Regardless, when I came out, he grabbed me. Pinned me to the wall by my throat. Screamed. Yelled."

She stopped talking.

Cal took a few steps away. "I don't need more details. Please don't feel like you have to share them."

She swallowed. "The next day when he left for work, I went to the rehab clinic. Bronwyn was there. She went with me to tell the director what had happened. We made a plan. I was so afraid. His family . . . they're well-off and well-respected. I'd gone to my mother-in-law and father-in-law to ask for advice early in our marriage. They told me to be a better wife. I'd mentioned a few problems to someone I thought was a friend at church. She told me to pray for forgiveness—that Dylan was a godly man and I needed to strive to be a godly wife."

She gave him a weak smile. "Then she told her husband, who told Dylan, who came home that night and told me if I ever ran my mouth about our marriage again, I would regret it." She swallowed hard. "I believed him. And I never said another word."

She pointed to Eliza. "He told me that if I left, he would sue for custody, and he would win. That no one would believe my story. That I had no money. No job. No way to provide for Eliza. He used her to keep me with him. But after that day, I knew I had to leave. I just didn't know how."

So many things made sense now. Horrible, awful sense. "Bronwyn suggested you move here."

"She said I would have a place to stay and a job. Once that was sorted, the staff at the rehab facility knew people who ran a nearby women's shelter, and they came, took statements and affidavits, and laid the groundwork for what would happen after I left. I went home to pack."

A shudder rippled through her. "I thought he'd be at work all day, but he came home early."

Cal didn't know how much more of this he could take. "He caught you packing?"

"He walked in, looked around, realized what was happening, and lost it. He slapped me. Shoved me into a chair. Pulled my hair. Screamed at me. Eliza was asleep, but she woke up and started crying. He told me to make her hush. Then he locked me in the bedroom with her. He took my phone. Took the computer. Took everything."

Cal had reached his limit. "Landry?"

"Yes?"

"Could I please hold your hand?"

He wanted to hold her hand? Landry didn't sense any flirtatiousness or teasing. He was quite serious. "Of course. Are you okay?"

"Am I okay? No, I'm not okay. I know you survived." He laced his fingers with hers. "I know you're alive and Eliza's alive, and I can see you and hear you. But touch grounds me. And I don't want to call Maisy, because if I do, Eliza will come. And if you don't tell me the end of this story and quickly, I will not be okay."

Landry decided it was time to jump straight to the end. "I don't know for sure what happened after that. Even in a rage, he was careful. He did hit me. He did hurt me. I'm sure his handprint on my cheek was there for a while, but by the time night fell, there was no evidence of an assault."

"How long did he keep you locked in the room?"

"Three hours? Maybe four? Then he came in and yelled at me for a while. Most of it was incomprehensible. His breath reeked so I assumed he'd been drinking for a while. Then he said he was leaving and that I'd better not do anything stupid while he was gone."

"Did he lock you in the room again?"

"No. I think he would have, but he was drunk. I should have told him not to drive, but I was so desperate for him to leave, all I could do was pray he wouldn't hurt anyone."

"Did you leave that night?"

"No."

"No?" Cal's shock and outrage filled the air around them. "Why didn't you run?"

"I'm getting there."

"Please get there a little faster. I'm dying over here."

"Okay. As soon as he left, I started running around, trying to gather everything. He'd unpacked all my bags, thrown stuff around, the house was trashed. Then there was a knock at the door. Before

I could scream, I heard Bronwyn calling my name. When I didn't show up at the rehab center, she came to the house. But she'd had the good sense not to come in."

Landry looked at Cal. "Her life, after she left here, wasn't easy. She has street smarts. The kind you don't get growing up in Gossamer Falls."

"I believe that." Cal acknowledged it with a grimace. "In some ways, she's still our Beep. But in other ways? She's a stranger."

"Well, her skills came in handy that night. She'd snuck around our house, heard some of what was said, and called the women's shelter for reinforcements."

"Why not call the police?"

"Because Dylan's best friend was on the force."

"Of course he was." Cal kicked at some leaves.

"Anyway, Bronwyn had been planning to try to get into the house, but when Dylan left, she didn't mess around. She came to the door. Three other people came in who I'd never seen before and I never saw again. The plan was we'd pack everything, we'd split, and once we were safely away, we'd sort it all out."

"What happened?"

"Before we got the first car packed, a police car pulled up in the driveway. I was convinced Dylan had somehow figured out a way to get me arrested or take Eliza away. Bronwyn went to the door while I hid in the back. She told the officers I couldn't come out. Asked them if they had a warrant. All kinds of stuff. They're supposed to notify the next of kin first, but Bronwyn was insistent. They finally told her they weren't there for any reason but to tell me that my husband was dead."

Landry closed her eyes, and she was back in that hallway, listening. The shock, the fear, the relief all battered against her.

"Dylan had wrapped his car around a telephone pole. No one else was hurt. But Dylan was dead."

"Wow." Cal stared at her. "But, if he was dead, then you were free. Why come here?"

"I wasn't free. I was free of Dylan. But his family was another matter entirely. His mother and father despised me. Oh, at church we were one big happy, God-fearing family. But at home? I was the one who made their sweet Dylan miserable. I hadn't given him another child. I hadn't submitted to him the way a wife should. I was terrified they would try to take Eliza."

"So what did you do?"

"Bronwyn stayed with me for the next week. She was at my side through the funeral. Either she or I always kept Eliza in our sights. I played the grieving widow. And I was grieving. Just not for the reasons everyone thought. My father-in-law approached me after the funeral and suggested I move in with them. I told him I'd think about it."

"As in, you'd think about how to make sure it never happened?"

"Exactly. That night, Bronwyn and I left. She'd been slowly packing up the house during the week. While we were at the funeral, she had those same friends put everything we'd staged for them into a small U-Haul. It was mostly Eliza's stuff, as well as my baby kiln and pottery and art supplies. Some books. A few things from my grandmother. I left everything else. They parked the U-Haul at a restaurant about an hour out of town, then came back and gave the keys to Bronwyn. When we left, she rode with me until we got to the U-Haul. Then she drove it, and we cara-vanned all the way here."

TWENTY-TWO

Cal had so many things he wanted to say. So many more questions he wanted answered. But Maisy was running at them full force.

Instead of digging deeper into Landry's past, he released her hand and said, "I'm so very sorry that happened. But I'm so glad God brought you here."

"Me too." That was all Landry had time to say before Eliza came careening toward them.

"Mommy, Cal showed us how he makes his bowls and vases. We should take him home and show him how you make yours."

Cal expected Landry to give Eliza one of those exasperated looks that parents gave their children when they backed them into a corner. But when she looked at him, her expression was bashful, not bothered. "We definitely will have to do that, baby. Although I don't know if today is a good time. I'm sure Cal has other things he needs to get done."

"No, he doesn't." Eliza spoke with childlike confidence. "He said he didn't have anywhere to be."

Landry pinched her lips together and held her hands out in surrender. "Fine. Cal, if you have time today, that would be great. If not, another time. But we would love to show you the studio and throw a few bowls."

He couldn't resist teasing her. "Is that pottery terminology?" He mimicked throwing a frisbee. "Seems like throwing pottery around is a good way to break it."

Eliza giggled. "You don't throw it, throw it."

Cal tweaked her nose. "You don't?"

"No. That's what it's called when you work the clay on the wheel."

"I guess I have a lot to learn."

Eliza patted his arm. "Mommy will teach you. She's a great teacher."

He winked at Eliza. "She'll have to be. I'm not a great student."

It took them almost forty-five minutes to get back to Landry's side of the river, pack up the picnic, load the car, and get on the road. Cal ran home and caught up to them before they got to town, then followed them the rest of the way to The Haven.

The sun was gone from the sky, the fall evening coming on fast, when he parked beside Landry.

Eliza led the way to the studio, skipping ahead of them.

"You have to be getting tired of making this trip." Landry scooted to the side to allow a guest to pass.

"What do you mean?" Cal asked.

"You're driving here almost every day."

"Most of my jobs are farther away than this one. And given that Bronwyn won't let us start work before nine in order to protect the slumber of her guests, I have time to get some work done in my office before I arrive. It's turned into a very pleasant project." And the work hours had nothing to do with it.

Eliza danced around the studio door. "Hurry up, Mommy! I want to show Cal what I made this week."

"I can't wait to see it." He pulled Eliza to the side so Landry could use the keypad to open the door. "Hold up, jitterbug. Let me tie your shoe." Eliza stood still while he leaned down to tie it, and Landry stepped inside the studio.

Her gasp was the first warning that something was wrong. He grabbed Eliza's hand and pulled her behind him as Landry backed out of the doorway. Slowly at first, but then she picked up speed until she ran into him, her back to his chest. He wrapped his free hand around her waist, held her tight against him, and then led both Landry and Eliza to the side of the building.

"What is it?" He whispered the words against Landry's ear.

"It's . . . there's . . ." She shook her head.

"Do I need to call Gray?"

She nodded.

He had no idea what was going on. All he wanted to do was get them as far away from the studio as he could. He twisted around until he had both Eliza and Landry standing in front of him. He gently pulled Eliza's hand from his and tucked it into Landry's. Then he knelt down to eye level and said in a voice that he hoped was calm and reassuring, "Eliza, I need you to walk back to your house with your mom, okay?"

When she started to speak, he put one finger up. "No questions right now, sweetheart. Can you do that for me?"

Eliza, eyes huge, nodded yes.

"Thank you."

Tears were leaking from Landry's eyes, but she held on to Eliza with one hand while her other hand gripped Cal's forearm. Cal used his free hand to pull his phone from his pocket. Landry didn't release him, even when it got awkward as he pulled up Gray's contact info. Gray answered on the first ring. "Yo, Cal. Everything okay?"

Cal glanced toward Landry and Eliza. "Not exactly. Gonna need you to come out to The Haven."

"What happened?" Gray had gone from mildly concerned to full-on cop mode in the space of a second.

"I'm walking the Hutton ladies back to their house right now. I'll call you back in a few minutes. Head this way, okay?"

"I'm guessing you can't discuss it at the moment."

"That's correct."

"I'm on my way. Call me back as soon as you can talk freely."

"Will do."

"Do I need to bring backup?"

Cal glanced at Landry. She was crying, but she wasn't panicking. He had no idea what that meant. "Unclear."

"Awesome." Gray could always be counted on for pointed sarcasm. "Call me soon." Heavy emphasis on *soon*.

"Yep." Cal disconnected and put the phone back in his pocket. They were almost to the house. Landry's tears were silent. Eliza had gone quiet the way young children do when they know something is very wrong but they don't know what's happened. They reached the front door. "I need you to wait right here. I'll be fast." There was no good option. He wanted them inside, but what if the person who'd done whatever they did to the studio was in her house?

Cal cleared the space in record time, then escorted them inside and closed and locked the door.

Cal knelt by Eliza again. Her fear was palpable, and he didn't think about what he was doing. He pulled her close and squeezed her tight. "It's going to be okay."

She trembled in his arms. "Mommy's scared."

"She is. But it's going to be okay. Right now, can you go play in your room for a few minutes while I talk to her?"

Eliza's response was to dash to her room. When she was out of sight, Cal stood and put his hands on either side of Landry's face and used his thumbs to brush away the tears. "Talk to me."

"It's ruined." Her pain screamed through the whispered words, and she dropped her forehead to his chest. "Someone destroyed my studio. There were words . . . on the wall."

Landry gulped several breaths of air.

"They were red."

More air. It took everything he had not to rush her. She was shaking, and he wrapped his arms tight around her, then dipped his head so his mouth was at her ear. "Landry. Honey. What did it say?"

A shudder ran through her. She pulled back so she was looking at him and said, "Time's up."

Even with her eyes closed, Landry could see her ruined studio. Shelves of pieces she'd abandoned, pieces she'd been experimenting with, pieces that held sentimental value, and some that were there for no reason other than because she found them inspiring—all destroyed.

All the work she'd done over the past few months—the hours and hours she'd spent churning out bowls and vases and mugs—all of it had been for nothing. The finished pieces she'd been storing, pieces to fill the shelves of the new Favors, were shattered.

The pumpkins. Those were what she'd seen first. She'd finished ten of them a week ago, and they had come out of the final firing yesterday.

They'd been gorgeous. Some of her best work. They would have sold to The Haven guests.

Destroyed. She had no way to bring in income.

Her boxes of clay had been cut open. Her glazes thrown around like a Jackson Pollock painting.

"Everything's ruined, Cal." Her voice sounded strange to her. Like she was speaking into a paper towel roll. Maybe that was because she was speaking into Cal's shirt.

"We'll fix it, baby. We'll fix it."

"Some things can't be fixed."

Instead of arguing with her, which she'd expected, he set his phone on the side table and dialed. Then his arm came back around her.

He must have put it on speaker because she could hear it ringing.

"What's going on?" Gray's voice.

"Landry and Eliza have been at their property and my place since noon." He looked at Landry. "Did you go to the studio this morning?"

She shook her head no.

"So yesterday was the last time you were in there?"

She nodded. "Before I came to see you. Eliza and I popped in so I could show her the pumpkins." Her voice broke, and more tears flooded down her cheeks. She couldn't stop them.

"Gray, the last time she was in the studio was around three thirty on Friday afternoon. We got here a few minutes ago." He filled him in on everything that had happened since.

Landry could hear a siren chirping, then Gray's muttered, "Get out of the way, people." Another chirp. "I'm on my way. I'll call my team. No one goes inside that studio. Clear?"

"Got it."

"Ten minutes." Gray disconnected.

Cal released her and dialed another number. The phone rang.

"Cal?" This time it was Bronwyn's voice.

"I need you at Landry's. Now."

"Is she okay? What's going on?"

"She's uninjured. But she's not okay."

"Five minutes."

Cal pushed a few more buttons on the phone. The phone rang. This time it was a male voice. "Yo."

"Is it movie night?"

"Yeah. Why?" Now she recognized the voice. Chad.

"Can Eliza join you?"

"Of course. What's wrong? You sound angry."

"Someone trashed Landry's studio. That's all we know. Gray's on his way. We need a safe place for Eliza."

"Of course. Abby and I will come get her. Is it safe to assume Landry's okay with this plan?"

She appreciated that Chad had asked, but right now, she had no ability to think of any plans. She was drifting. And she would follow Cal's lead. "It's fine. She may be a bit emotional."

"We're experts on big emotions over here." Chad's unruffled response made her heart settle a tiny fraction.

"Thank you."

"No problem."

"Chad." Cal leaned slightly toward the phone. "Locked and loaded."

"Already on it. I'll call Connor on my way. Bring him up to speed."

"Thank you."

The phone disconnected and Cal wrapped both arms around her in a tight hold.

"What's locked and loaded?" Landry didn't move, but Cal's face was close enough to hers that she was sure he could hear her.

"He'll be carrying in the truck. And he has a rifle. When he gets home, he'll set the security system, he'll make sure he has weapons at the doors, and he'll keep his personal weapon with him. He'll tell Connor. Connor will do the same at his house. If anyone tries to get on the property, they'll be in for a rude welcome. I trust them to keep her safe."

Fear clawed at Landry's chest. "I hadn't thought about that. Maybe she should stay here."

Cal dropped his head onto her hair. "Landry, I hate to have to say this so bluntly, but The Haven isn't safe for you. Not anymore. Someone got into your studio. It's only a hundred yards from your house. My brothers are Marines. My nephews have all been through multiple gun safety courses. All know how to shoot. One of Connor's boys is on the marksmanship team at school. He never misses. So for tonight, I think it's the safest place for Eliza while we deal with this."

The shock was wearing off, and fury was taking its place. Why? Why now? Who was behind this?

Cal gave her a gentle squeeze. "Besides the words, what else did you see?"

She told him. He listened. And as he listened, his hold on her tightened until she whispered, "Cal?"

"Huh?"

"I'm having trouble breathing."

"Sorry!" He released her. Completely. Took a step back and everything. That was not what she'd been going for at all. She'd just needed a little bit of room for her lungs to expand. But now that there was some distance between them, she didn't know how to shorten it.

She didn't need to shorten the distance! She needed to put up a ten-foot-high wall.

Who was she even kidding? She'd just climb it.

She dropped her head into her hands. "I can't believe this."

And just like that, he was back. His arms were gentle as he guided her to the sofa. He sat first, then pulled her down beside him. He kept one arm around her shoulders, and it just made sense for her to rest her cheek against him. "What are we doing, Cal?"

He took her left hand in his and laced their fingers together. "I have no idea."

Landry stared at their hands for a moment. "I'm scared."

A low chuckle rumbled through Cal's chest. "I'm terrified. But we don't have to figure anything out right now. Let's get through tonight. Then we'll get through tomorrow. And the day after that."

"Okay."

A long moment passed, and Cal said, "I want to ask you something. You might think it's weird."

"What?"

"Would you mind if I prayed?"

Landry looked up at him. "Pray? Now?"

"Now seems like a good time."

"You aren't wrong about that. Go for it."

He squeezed her hand, dropped his head to hers, and spoke. "Father, we don't know what's going on. We don't know where the danger's coming from. And we don't like it. We don't like being afraid, and speaking for myself here, I'm sick to death of people breaking Landry's pottery. Please give Gray and his officers wisdom. Give Bronwyn wisdom. Give Landry peace, Father. The kind of peace that comes only from you. Please help us know how best to protect Eliza and Landry. Shield them from evil and give them rest from their enemies."

A sharp knock at the door interrupted his prayer, but Cal didn't move.

"Open us up to what you want to do, Father. Help us not to hold on so hard to the past that we miss the future you have for us. In Jesus's name, Amen."

Another knock.

"Stay here." Cal disentangled himself and stood. Landry swiped at a rogue tear, and the hard shell around her heart that she'd built, layer upon layer, against envy, deceit, lies, and meanness cracked. It didn't fall away, but it broke enough for her to see light on the other side.

Voices came from behind her, and she caught enough to know that Cal was filling Bronwyn in. She could have kissed him for that. How did he know that she didn't have the mental or emotional energy to tell anyone else?

Then Bronwyn slid into Cal's spot.

"I'm so sorry. We'll fix everything. We have insurance. You won't have to replace the supplies on your own. I'll call that clay supplier from Asheville and see if they can get us what you need."

Bronwyn wrapped her arms around Landry, and it was her friend's tears that finally broke the dam of Landry's horror. She sobbed, Bronwyn sobbed, and she expected their combined sorrow to scare Cal off.

But she was wrong.

He came around behind the sofa and put his arms around both of them. "We'll figure this out."

Another knock on the door. Firm. Insistent.

"Be right back."

Landry pulled away from Bronwyn, and they wiped their faces.

"I promised you'd be safe here." Bronwyn sniffled. "I promised."

"This isn't your fault." Landry got up and retrieved a box of tissues from the coffee table. She took one and handed the box to Bronwyn. "You should probably visit the bathroom and fix your face. You don't need to give anyone ammunition by being a 'weepy female.'" She put air quotes around *weepy female*, words Bronwyn's uncle had used in his argument against making her the CEO.

Bronwyn blew her nose and headed toward the bathroom. "If my family is behind this, Landry, so help me . . ." Landry patted her arm as she walked by.

Cal and Gray were still talking by the door. She could hear their voices enough to recognize them but not enough to hear what they were saying.

She looked around her home. It was a nice place. Plenty of space for her and Eliza. Had she been wrong to want more? To plan for a place of her own?

No. One of her favorite therapists at the rehab center had a

233

favorite saying. "Never doubt in the dark what God revealed to you in the light." She'd been so sure, so settled, so at peace about the property and the house.

Despite the fear she lived with every day, she'd been confident that God loved her and that even if no one else understood her, he did. She'd seen the property and the timing and everything as being a gift from him.

She wouldn't see it as anything else.

Cal would be surprised to know how often she prayed. She wasn't big on praying out loud, but sometimes as she sat at her wheel, she prayed for the people around her. She prayed for whoever would someday own the piece she was creating. It delighted her to imagine the vases and bowls she'd prayed over being carried as light into the homes of people who lived and worked in a dark world.

That darkness had crept into her world in Gossamer Falls. But it wouldn't succeed. She closed her eyes and asked for peace and protection. Then she joined Cal and Gray at the door.

TWENTY-THREE

Cal, wearing booties, gloves, and an oh-so-fashionable hair net, stood just inside Landry's studio door.

It had been a long night. Gray had refused to let anyone into the studio until they determined no explosives were present. That had meant waiting for an explosives team from Asheville to arrive.

Fortunately, the guy who ran the team was a former Marine buddy, and he'd hurried his people up. They arrived around 4:00 a.m. They found a small explosive at 5:00 a.m. It was almost 7:00 a.m. before they declared the studio safe to enter.

The devastation was overwhelming. He understood why Landry had backed away. And why she currently sat in her house with Bronwyn, answering questions and giving a statement to Donovan, the officer who'd had a date with Cassie after the harvest festival.

"Thanks for the extra set of eyes." Gray, similarly attired, stood to his right. "I just want you to give me your impressions about the crime."

Cal studied the space. Landry's studio was a roughly forty-foot square building. One corner held her office area. The other corner held three kilns.

When he'd first seen them weeks earlier, he'd expected the kilns to be bigger. One was about three feet high and four feet around.

The other was smaller and slightly more oval than round. Then there was the one Landry called her baby. It was the first kiln she'd ever owned, and she brought it with her from Arizona.

It didn't take a genius to see that the kilns were destroyed. It looked like someone had detonated small charges. The lids were blown off. The electronic control panels fried. One of the kilns lay on its side, and from where Cal was standing, it looked like someone had poured acid inside it.

"What is that?" Cal pointed to the kiln and threw the question out.

"A very strong acid is all I can tell you right now," a young tech said. In all the gear, Cal couldn't tell who it was. "It's eaten through the sides of these things. I don't know anything about pottery, but I'd say these are a total loss."

"Bronwyn said they're insured." Gray said it almost like he was trying to convince himself everything would be okay.

"Some things can't be fixed." Cal could hear Landry saying those words and knew this would only help cement the concept in her mind. Cal pointed to the shelves of pottery now lying cracked and broken on the floor. "She's worked so hard to replace her inventory, Bronwyn can buy new kilns. No one can replace the time, the energy, the creative output."

Gray put a hand on Cal's shoulder. "I need you to level with me. If you can't handle this, that's okay. No shame in it. You can go sit with Landry and be her emotional support person."

Cal wanted to brush off Gray's words, but he understood the truth, and the friendship, behind them.

"No. Give me a minute. Let me take it all in."

What he took in made his stomach churn. Her pumpkins. The angels she'd started working on. The platters. The vases. The destruction of Favors had been devastating. The destruction of her studio could be debilitating to her creative spirit, her future at The Haven, and her income.

It was dangerous to assume, but if the person behind this was the same person behind the fire at Favors, Cal had to think they were escalating at an alarming rate. And that for whatever reason, they were trying to drive Landry away from The Haven.

The words—*Time's Up*—made him wonder if the escalation had an external trigger. Had something happened in the perpetrator's life to make him ramp things up this way? Or had Landry done something that he was using to justify this behavior? Or was he a twisted psychopath and none of it made sense?

He shared his thoughts with Gray.

Gray studied the wall. "Has she told you yet? About her husband?"

"She has. Today, or, well, I guess yesterday."

Gray nodded. "I don't have details. She told me, back when Favors burned, that her husband's family might want Eliza. But she also said she didn't think they would go to these kinds of levels."

He pointed to the studio. "After seeing this, and knowing what you know, do you agree with her?"

"I don't know. There's a lot of rage here. But I can't see how this makes it more likely for them to get their hands on Eliza. From what Landry told me, they despise her. They wouldn't want to do anything that would drum up sympathy for Landry. No one could see this and not feel bad for her."

"True. But she told one of my officers last night, that while the equipment is insured and Bronwyn has promised to replace everything, the kilns are currently backordered by as much as four months because of some critical part shortage. If she can't get new kilns, she can't replenish her stock, which means her income takes a serious hit. She still has her salary from Bronwyn and tips from the guests, which she said would put food on the table. But it won't pay for a new house."

"So what's the motive here?"

"I have no idea. Landry claims to have no known enemies other than her husband's family."

"Deceased husband."

Gray quirked an eyebrow. "My apologies. Her deceased husband's family."

Cal wasn't in the mood to joke about the wretch who had made Landry's life a misery. "He wasn't a good man, Gray."

"So I gathered. She give you details?"

"A few. The world's a better place without him."

"Good to know. Aside from her deceased husband's family, everyone else in the known universe loves Landry, Bronwyn says she consistently gets the highest possible scores on her guest surveys. People have even left remarks like 'If you ever get rid of her, we won't be back.'"

Cal frowned. "Seriously?"

"Yeah. Why?"

"I think saying you won't come back like that sounds a bit possessive. I know we considered it when Favors caught on fire. Maybe we need to revisit it, treating this as a new data point."

"Most of the guests here wouldn't know how to do this stuff."

"No, but some of their bodyguards would."

"Bodyguards?"

"Yeah. Some of these people bring staff. Sometimes they call them their personal assistant. But there was one lady who had a guy with her who was at least thirty years younger than she was, and he was built like a football player."

"Doesn't mean he was her bodyguard, Cal."

"Bronwyn confirmed it. Some of these bodyguard types are former military, former Special Forces even."

"Or former criminals." Gray studied the scene. "We're missing something."

"Except the part where we're sure this is about Landry now."

"Probably."

"Gray, what do you mean, probably? This person trashed her studio. He didn't trash the restaurant or the fitness area. He trashed her private space."

"Maybe someone in the family wants her gone to discredit Bronwyn."

Cal studied his friend as best as he could through their protective garb. "You don't believe that."

"No. But my job is to look at every possible angle. And right now, we have too many angles." He signed a document that a tech brought over. "With that said, I made a phone call last night." "To whom?"

Cal had no idea where Gray was going with this. "To whom?"

"To Meredith."

"About?"

"Letting Landry and Eliza crash at her place for a few weeks. Maybe longer. Until we get this sorted."

"You're kidding."

"I'm not. I don't have the manpower to put them under guard. And without a more specific threat, I don't see Landry agreeing to disappear for a while. If they stay at Meredith's, they have you and Mo on either side. Anyone trying to get to them will have several miles of Quinn land to traverse before they get to the house. And according to Meredith, Mo's been playing around with added surveillance that will give him a heads-up if anyone comes within three hundred yards of the place. Even if they come up the river or through the woods."

Cal knew Mo had been up to something but hadn't wanted to discuss it yet. "Mo gets a little paranoid sometimes."

"It's not paranoia when the threat is real." Gray stepped away and spoke to someone, then returned and picked up like there'd been no pause. "Meredith says this is the excuse she's been looking for."

Cal understood. "She wants to stay with her mom and dad. The last month has been hard, and Aunt J has a full month of chemo to go, but she's been insisting that she doesn't, and I quote, 'need a live-in nanny.'"

"Well, she's about to get one whether she wants one or not. Meredith said she has no qualms whatsoever about using this situation to guilt her mother into letting her stay—and to get Landry to agree to stay in her house."

Cal moved over to let another gowned and masked person walk by. "Let that be a lesson to you. Everyone thinks Meredith's an angel, but she has a manipulative streak."

Gray held out his gloved hands. "As long as she uses her powers for good, I don't care."

"Famous last words."

Landry stood in her bedroom and stared out the window. She hadn't cried since her breakdown with Bronwyn last night. She didn't cry when she talked about her kilns. Or the time it would take to put everything together. She didn't cry when she did the math and realized she wouldn't be able to build a house after all. She didn't even cry when the police told her they'd found a bomb in her studio. She'd almost taken her daughter into that building. A building that could have exploded and killed her.

She wasn't sad anymore. She was furious.

A light tap on the door didn't encourage her to move. She didn't care who it was. She managed a weak "Come in" but didn't turn around to see.

The door opened, the door closed, and the person standing behind her didn't approach for ten seconds. Then, he spoke, "Landry."

That's all he said, but at her name, the dam broke.

She whirled to face him. "What did I ever do to deserve this? I don't bother anyone. I don't ask for much. I want my daughter to grow up in a safe place. I want her to grow up knowing she's loved. I want her to grow up knowing how precious she is."

She threw a hand at the window. "But you know what I didn't want? I didn't want my daughter's first sleepover with a friend to be because some lunatic destroyed her mother's studio and now it isn't safe for her to sleep in her own bed!"

Cal nodded.

"I didn't even pack her pajamas! She went to her first sleepover with no toothbrush or pillow or clean underwear! What kind of a mother am I? Is this what she'll remember when she's grown up? That her mom's life was such a train wreck that she frequently messed up the important things?"

Cal took two steps toward her. Then stopped and held out his arms. "Landry?"

"What?" The question was a whip of anger and frustration and terror.

"Come here."

His words were a plea. His arms were an invitation. And she didn't have the strength to tell him no. She might never have the strength again, and right now, she didn't care. She walked into his embrace and rested her head against his chest. Her arms went around his waist, and his wrapped around her back.

"You're an amazing mother. Eliza is living proof. I already received a text this morning. Everyone's staying home from church. Naomi made a big deal out of the fact that there was no point in putting on clean clothes when the girls were going to get covered in dirt anyway, and she sent them outside to rake leaves. We'll pack Eliza a bag, and Carla has volunteered to come get it. By the time the girls are done playing outside and ready for hot chocolate and a movie, there will be clean clothes, a toothbrush, and whatever else she needs."

"It shouldn't have been this way," Landry's words were muffled by Cal's shirt.

"I agree."

"I want it to stop."

"Me too." Cal's head rested on hers. "But I'm not going anywhere, Landry. Unless you send me away, I'll be here. We'll get through this. Gray's got his best people on it. Mo's been doing some digging, and trust me, when Mo starts digging, he doesn't stop until he finds something."

"I'm not sure if that's a positive trait or a negative one."

"We aren't either. His code name was Badger. Badgers are the world's fastest diggers. They can even dig through asphalt."

"Well, thank you, Nat Geo." She wanted to bite her tongue. This wasn't the time for sarcasm.

But Cal clearly thought it was funny. His laughter was contagious, and she leaned back enough so she could see his face. She didn't move her arms, and he didn't release her.

"Ready to pack Eliza's bag?"

"In a minute. What did you come in here for? Because it wasn't to tell me about Mo being a badger."

"No. I came in to talk to you about something else. But it can wait. Why don't you pack for Eliza first? That way it's done. Naomi and Chad didn't want to leave the house. Carla had to take something to the church for her Sunday school class. Once she drops it off, she's going to swing by." Cal glanced at his watch. "I'd say we have maybe twenty minutes."

"What will your family think about everyone missing church? Did you know I was going to go today? I'd already decided. My issues with church notwithstanding, I want Eliza to go. And maybe your church will change my mind. But no one's ever going to believe it. Now they'll think I'm a bad influence."

"No, they won't. It's a small town. None of the officers will be at church either. Our entire family knows what's going on. No one's going to get their shorts in a twist. Just relax."

Didn't he know that telling a woman to relax never worked?

"Your family is being so kind. I don't know how I can ever repay——"

Cal's finger over her lips froze the words in her throat. "No."

He was so solemn, she swallowed but didn't speak, even after he moved his finger. "You're ours, Landry Hutton. There's no repayment. That's not how family works. I realize your experience with family didn't teach you that. But in our family, you help when it's needed, and then you accept help when you need it. There's no ledger. No tally sheet. No scorekeeper."

"That's not how the real world works. Someone is always keeping score."

"Welcome to Gossamer Falls. Where we do things the way we want to. You can learn to do it our way, or you can leave."

"That's not the town motto."

"Sure it is. Unofficially."

At some point, he was going to realize he was holding her. And he was going to let go. And she was going to let him.

She could let go first.

The idea hurt her. She didn't want to let go.

Not now.

Not ever.

"While you're packing Eliza's bag, I have something else for you to think about."

Her entire body tensed. "What?"

"Meredith is moving in with her parents for the next month. Aunt Jacqueline is struggling with her treatments, and someone needs to be there."

"I thought there was a rotation?"

"There is. And it will continue. But Meredith can't walk away. It's not in her nature. She's wired to help, and she's determined to be there for her mom and dad. Mo's there too. A lot. But Aunt Jacqueline doesn't want her thirty-two-year-old son helping her to the bathroom. Not that she wants Meredith to do it either, but it's different."

"I get that."

"And Uncle Douglas has to get some sleep. He's been a zombie. I told him if he slept three nights straight, I'd put him to work on Favors. He's still got two nights to go. Meredith thinks her dad will settle if she's there."

"I know where this is going. You want me and Eliza to move into Meredith's."

"Well, Gray does."

Wait a minute. "You don't? Why not?"

A grin tugged at Cal's lips. "Of course I want you to come. Maisy's going to deliver her puppies soon. I'm sure Eliza would love to be around for that. And Mo's added surveillance to our security system. You'll be safer at our place than you are here."

"But you're blaming Gray?"

"I'm not blaming anyone. I'm"—Cal blew out a breath—"strategically arranging the playing field so that when you decide to tackle someone, I'm not in the way."

She poked him in the ribs. He jumped, but instead of moving away from her, he jumped toward her. They wound up touching from chin to toe. Cal's gaze held hers. "I know we have a lot to discuss, and now isn't the time. But please come to Meredith's. I had to force myself to leave Friday night. After all this, I can't stand the thought of being far away from you."

It was an easy capitulation. "Okay. We'll come." There was no way she could stay here. The Haven, despite its robust security measures, wasn't safe for her right now.

She wasn't an idiot. She knew Cal, Meredith, and Gray had discussed it and come up with a situation that would be hard to refuse. But she didn't care. She needed to feel safe, and right now, the only time she felt safe was when she was with Cal.

"I'll pack a bag for Eliza to have at Abby's. And I'll pack for each of us to stay at Meredith's for a while."

Cal's relief was evident. "Thank you."

"Is there something else?"

"Gray wants you to focus on guests of The Haven. Anyone who flirted with you, made comments about you, or asked you out—or even someone you consider to be a friend and nothing more."

Landry groaned.

"I know you don't want to." Cal ran a thumb over her cheek, and her train of thought derailed.

When had they gotten this close? When did it become okay for him to do this? When did she realize that not only did she not mind, but she craved this? Just the two of them. Talking. Touching. Together.

She couldn't think about it right now. Shouldn't think about it ever. She'd said she'd never fall again.

But she hadn't expected falling to feel so right.

TWENTY-FOUR

A quick tap on the door preceded Bronwyn's appearance. "Hey. Oh. Sorry, I'll come back."

"Get in here." Cal let go of Landry, but he didn't get in a hurry about it. And she didn't seem to be in a hurry to move either.

Bronwyn cleared her throat. "Landry, did Cal talk to you about staying at Meredith's?"

"He did." Landry held up her hands in a placating gesture. "I'll go. I don't like it, but I'm not going to throw a fit about it."

"Oh. Well . . ." Bronwyn blinked twice. "Good. I'm . . . thrilled. Okay. So, that was my first order of business. Second order of business is that I've pulled together a portfolio of guests. It wasn't hard since I did this after the fire. Last time we were more focused on people who might've had a grudge against The Haven or people with some random connection to Landry's former family."

Landry sank into the sofa, and at her wave, Cal joined her. "Sit down, Bronwyn. I don't have the energy to do this right now. If I keep standing, I'll tip over."

"Sorry." Bronwyn sat in the chair across from the sofa. "Anyway, we didn't find anything concerning last time. This time, I've changed it up. Mo"—she stumbled a bit over his name—"emailed me with suggestions."

"What kind of suggestions?" If Landry noticed Bronwyn's slip, she didn't let on.

"He suggested I focus on regulars who take your classes and have an excellent rapport with you. The types no one would ever expect."

"Awesome."

"I made the list."

"And?"

"You aren't going to like it." Bronwyn pulled a piece of paper from her pocket. "I have the full portfolio with photos and details in my office. This is just the list of names."

Cal peered over Landry's shoulder as she read. He recognized several names from pro sports and the music industry.

Landry slumped in her seat. "Bronwyn. Seriously?"

"They always take an art class. They tip well. They leave great reviews."

Cal peered at the paper. "Who are we talking about?"

Landry pointed to a group of names in the middle. "These men are the least likely to ever destroy my studio. They come in every time they're here."

"And they're here a lot." Bronwyn put her feet up on the coffee table. "Our average guest is a first-timer. At any given moment, at least half the guests have never been here. Our stats tell us that anywhere from fifty to seventy-five percent of first-time guests will return within five years. Twenty-five percent of our guests fall into the frequent category, which for us means they've been here at least three times in a five-year period."

Cal slid an arm around Landry's shoulder—to focus better on the paper, of course. "How often do these guys visit?"

"Between the six of them? They've each been here at least twice a year for three years. The three-year number is significant because——"

"I've been here three years." Landry tapped the paper. "Three of the six are married men."

"Married men who, conveniently enough, don't bring their wives when they visit." Bronwyn didn't look happy about it, but she did look a bit smug. "I double-checked. Four of the six have been visiting for more than five years. But their frequency tripled or quadrupled in the last three years."

"Anyone stand out?" Cal directed the question to both ladies. Bronwyn leaned toward them, pen in hand. "I'll preface this by saying that I don't think any of these men are guilty of anything more than maybe having a wee bit of a crush on our Landry."

Landry grabbed for the pen, but Bronwyn jerked it back.

"But these two are the most frequent." She circled two names.

Ignacio and Derrick.

"No last names?" Cal would find out, but it would be easier if Bronwyn shared on her own.

"Not yet. I'm already skating on thin ice here, Cal. If our guests get a hint that we aren't protecting their privacy, they'll bolt."

"Guests who break the law can't expect to be afforded protection here." Cal pointed in the direction of Landry's studio. "You're making a strong statement that you protect your staff and your guests by chasing down criminals using whatever means necessary."

"I agree." Bronwyn jumped to her feet and paced the space behind her chair. "My family is losing their collective minds. I'm in the hot seat. If it were up to me, I'd give you every guest portfolio I have and tell you to question them all. But if I'm not here, The Haven becomes a very different place, Cal. You wouldn't believe some of the cockamamie ideas some of my cousins have floated around. I'm holding back the tide. If The Haven goes the way some of them want, none of us will be safe here. We'll lose our livelihoods and our town. I'm trying to be sure that doesn't happen."

"Hey. I get it. I do. I'm sorry. I'm just—"

Cal dropped his head to Landry's shoulder for a moment, and the contact sent a jolt of affection and desire and a little bit of desperation through him. He raised his head to look at Bronwyn.

"I'm not okay right now, Beep." He'd left Maisy with Mo yesterday. She ran all over the place with Eliza and was tired. If she were here, she'd have her head in his lap and be doing her thing to help him settle down.

"I know you aren't. I'm sorry."

"I can't lose anyone else. Not this way. Not *any* way." He turned to Landry. "I know you don't want to think about these men this way. I respect that. But try to see it not as accusing them of anything but as absolving them of involvement."

"That does sound better." Landry smiled. "I can do that."

"Great." Bronwyn clapped her hands together. "Let's go through this list so I can send it to Mo."

"What?" Cal couldn't believe his ears. Willing interaction between Bronwyn and Mo?

"Don't make a big deal out of it, and it won't be a big deal." Bronwyn returned to her seat. "He said he'll run the names through his databases, and he has a contact somewhere in the middle of the state who's a genius at tracking down stuff like this."

"If Mo thinks he's a genius——"

"She. She's a genius." Bronwyn corrected him with a smile. "Don't make that mistake to Mo. He'll bite your head off and accuse you of misogyny. Ask me how I know."

"Noted. So, if he thinks she's a genius, then she must be off the charts. Mo's no slouch."

Bronwyn shook out her arms and tapped the paper. "Okay, let's focus, people. We need names."

Landry made comments about every person.

"He's nice."

"His wife is an actress, and he comes when she's overseas."

"He's a flirt, but he's never been inappropriate."

"He never talks. Ever. I don't know anything about him."

"He's hilarious. And madly in love with his girlfriend. He's planning an epic proposal."

Finally, they got to Bronwyn's two top contenders.

"Derrick—he was a forensic scientist." Landry filled them in on what she knew about his career and first wife. "After the divorce, he went on a long bimbo binge—that's his description, by the way—before settling down to work on his career. If he's dating anyone, he's kept it under wraps."

Cal whistled. "You know a lot about him."

"Like Bronwyn said, he's a regular. But he's not interested in me. He loves his great big life in the great big city. He likes the attention, the media, all of it. If you check, he almost always comes with someone else. He likes it here. Likes the food. Likes the hiking. And he likes that he can disappear and make the paps wonder where he went. But as soon as he gets home, he dives back in. He's not interested in me. He's trying to find the next ex."

Cal looked back at the list. "What about this next person, Ignacio? Wait a minute. Is that Ignacio the stunt guy?"

Bronwyn and Landry shared a look. A look Cal didn't like.

"Landry?"

"Yes. But you can't say anything. He's very private. And half the time when he's here, he's not supposed to be here."

"What does that mean?"

Bronwyn answered. "It means he's booked solid. And sometimes his contracts include language prohibiting him from travel or engaging in certain activities because they're trying to ensure that he lives long enough to do the job."

"He's a daredevil. You have to be to do the kind of work he does. But over the past few years he's been doing fewer and fewer stunts, and instead, he's been designing and directing them. He's making a fortune doing it, and he likes it. But sometimes he gets an itch to do something stupid, like bungee jump in a developing country with poor quality control." Landry shuddered.

Bronwyn picked up the tale. "Or flying a plane through a canyon. Or seeing how deep he can dive before he passes out."

"You both like him, don't you?" Cal asked.

"He's hard not to like," Landry said. "He's sweet. Tips great. Always respectful. But I worry for him. I'm afraid whatever high he's seeking will get him killed one of these days. Every time I tell him goodbye, I wonder if it's the last time we'll see him alive."

Bronwyn nodded in agreement. "We respect his privacy. He comes here when the pressure gets to be too much. And he visits a lot."

"Regardless, you can take him off the list." Landry pointed to his name. "He told me he was headed to Eastern Europe. Then Africa or Alaska—he wasn't sure which. He said he leaves all that up to his agent. But then he told me he shouldn't have even said he was headed to Eastern Europe—it was all very hush-hush."

When they were done, Cal declared there were six names in need of immediate follow-up. He promised to get the list to Mo immediately.

Bronwyn, miracle of miracles, took the hint and left. As soon as she was gone, Cal grabbed Landry's hand and pulled her close. Not as close as they'd been earlier, but not friend close either. "Do you want me to help you pack?"

"No. I can handle it."

"Can you go ahead and pack a bag for Eliza?"

"I'll do that first thing."

"Landry?"

"Cal?"

The knock on the door had Cal groaning. "Every single time."

He went to the door. Opened it. Donovan walked in carrying a carryout container. "Sorry to disturb you again, Landry, but Cassie stopped by, I wasn't sure when you'd eaten last."

Landry's heart squeezed. "Thank you. And please tell Cassie thank you as well."

"Will do." Donovan tipped his cap and left.

Landry opened the box. A cinnamon roll the size of a frisbee stared back at her. There were two forks. She held out the box to Cal. "Care to join me?"

He snagged a fork, then they set the box on the kitchen counter and dove in. "This is delicious."

"Cassie's a genius."

Bronwyn reentered with a barely there knock. "Sorry to barge in. Donovan said you had a—" Her eyes lit up. "I need a fork." She rummaged in the silverware drawer and came back to join them.

"Hope I'm interrupting something."

She took a huge bite. Cal stabbed at Bronwyn's fork when she tried to get another piece. "He brought this for Landry."

"Yeah? You don't look like Landry to me. And I'm starving."

"So is she."

"Please. This thing will feed a family of five."

Two minutes later, the cinnamon roll was gone.

"I guess that means we're now a family of five." Landry threw the box in the trash to the sounds of Cal's and Bronwyn's laughter. "Did you come back for another reason? Or just to poach my cinnamon roll?"

Bronwyn wiped her mouth. "Another reason. Gray said to ask you to please come to the studio as soon as you're ready."

"He'll be waiting a while."

"I told him you had to pack a bag for Eliza."

"I don't think that's what she was talking about, Beep." Cal gave her arm a squeeze. "Tell Gray that as soon as we get Eliza sorted, we'll be up there. Do you mind?"

"Nah. No problem. Thanks for the food."

Landry went to Eliza's room and packed her bag on autopilot. It only took a few minutes, and she returned to the living room.

Cal was on the phone. He saw the bag and grinned. "Perfect timing, Carla. She just finished. Why don't you let me get one of the valets to take it down to the main entrance. That way you don't have to drive all the way in."

A pause. A grunt. "Thanks. Love you, sis."

He picked up The Haven phone that sat on Landry's kitchen counter and dialed a number. Moments later, he said, "Yes. I need to have a package for Eliza Hutton delivered to the guardhouse. Feel free to confirm with Bronwyn." Whatever the other person said made Cal grin. "As soon as possible. The police chief wants us at the studio."

Cal put the phone back on the receiver. "Can you make it a few more hours?"

"Do I have a choice?"

"Sadly, no. But tonight we'll get you and Eliza settled in at Meredith's. We'll have a fire in the firepit. Maisy will lay on your feet. Then you'll go to bed and sleep. And tomorrow, there'll be breakfast waiting for you."

Cal opened the door to a quiet knock, handed Eliza's bag to the valet along with a five-dollar bill, then held the door for Landry to join him.

"Will there be blueberry pancakes?"

"No. Blueberries don't belong in pancakes. Sacrilege. Wash your mouth out with soap, young lady."

Despite herself, Landry laughed. "Then what will we have? But fair warning. If you say cereal, I'll have to seek alternative lodging."

"Oh, ye of little faith." Cal pretended to sulk. "There will be Belgian waffles. Powdered sugar. Sliced strawberries. Real maple syrup. Thick-cut bacon. And, if you're very, very good, coffee."

"I can't wait."

He held the door for her and stayed by her side as they walked to the studio. "Cal?"

"Yeah?"

"Nothing."

"We've covered this already, haven't we? Saying 'nothing' just makes me determined to get the truth out of you."

"It's just . . . Eliza . . . she doesn't know about her dad. I mean, she knows she had a dad, obviously. And that he died. And that we moved here to start our new lives. She hasn't asked much about him, but I think that's because we've been so isolated at The Haven. Now that she's in school, she's asked a few questions about him—and his family. Her grandparents. That kind of thing."

"And you don't want her overhearing something she isn't supposed to know."

How did he do that? How did he know what she meant when she was stumbling through her explanations?

"Something like that. I'm sure that someday I'll have to tell her. Not the details, but the general idea. But I'd prefer to spare her that. I don't talk about Dylan. Ever. That's probably unfair. But he wasn't a good father. She loved him the way kids do, but he didn't love her the way a father should and—"

"Landry." Cal pulled her to a stop before they went inside. "I would cut out my own eyes before I let anyone hurt her. I'll make a couple of phone calls, a few discreet remarks, and we'll make sure the topic of her father is a nonstarter. We'll do everything we can to protect her. Not just physically, but emotionally."

"Thank you." She had an almost unquenchable desire to fall

254

against him. To let him hold her. To snuggle close and know that his arm would fall over her shoulders.

Gray poked his head out of the door. "There you are. Everything okay?"

Cal reached him first. "Just a heads-up. As we're talking about this case, Eliza's father needs to stay out of any conversation Eliza might overhear. Or *any* little ears might overhear. He's a topic that needs to be off-limits."

"Got it. Come on in."

Landry stared at the space that had been her sanctuary. She couldn't make her mind make sense of it. She tried to see it the way it had been. Was it just yesterday?

Gray led them to a back corner. "We figured out how he got in." He pointed to the corner behind the kilns.

"Am I supposed to be amazed right now?" Landry pinched her lips together. Her mouth was going to get the best of her. She rambled when she was anxious. She got super sarcastic when she was scared or tired. And she was all three. Which meant if she wasn't careful, she was going to ramble sarcastically.

Wouldn't that be a treat for everyone? And now she was being sarcastic to herself. "Sorry, Gray. That was rude. What am I missing?"

TWENTY-FIVE

Cal pointed around the building. "Your studio has one way in and out. The windows on the front of the building aren't functional. And they're visible to the guests and security staff. The keypad is monitored. The code is changed frequently, and the keypad worked last night. There's no evidence of tampering. The glass on the windows is intact. That means there are only two possible scenarios. Either our bad guy knew the code and waltzed in through the front door, or he got in a different way."

"But there is no other way," Landry's eyes narrowed. "So you guys decided to see how he got in through a solid wall?"

"Exactly. I am curious. Why is the studio built this way? It isn't like anything else at The Haven. You have trees almost touching the back and sides. And no windows back here."

"We wanted it to blend in as much as possible but not be accessible to guests. I didn't want guests showing up while I'm working. That's also why the windows on the front are set high on the walls and don't function. I wanted natural light, but I didn't want people to gawk at me while I worked. I get enough of that during classes. And I didn't want an exit into the woods. Mainly because I didn't want there to be an entrance from the woods. I spend hours in the studio. I needed a place where I felt safe. This building is exactly what I wanted." Landry's words were calm and reasonable, but her skin was turning an adorable shade of "you're ticking me off" red.

He wanted to kiss her. He needed to kiss her. Soon.

But not now.

"That makes sense. Thank you for explaining it to me. Now, back to our bad guy. Once he realized that the windows in front weren't functional, he had to go around back at some point. We have to assume that once he got back there, he saw that while there was no way in, there was a lot of privacy."

"I'm still not following you." Landry looked from Gray to Cal and back to Gray.

Gray whistled and got the attention of one of his officers. "Open her up."

The young man spoke into a walkie-talkie type thing on his shoulder and walked over to the corner Gray had indicated earlier. A moment later, a two-foot square of wall moved.

Landry jolted, then stared. It moved again. And again. And then the officer inside the building grabbed it, pulled, and the whole thing came out. A young man peered at them from outside. "Want us to put it back?"

"In a minute." Gray turned to Landry. "I hate to say it, but it was elegantly done. He managed to choose a location that didn't have any electrical wires running through it. You had shelves back here before, so it would have been highly unlikely that you would have noticed the damage. And even if you had, he'd camouflaged it."

"He what?" Landry leaned closer.

"We don't know for sure"—Gray pointed to the cube now sitting on the floor—"but we suspect that he created this ingress before now. It's been here for a while. He cut out the square, crawled inside, then wrapped it." Gray put a gloved hand on the cube, then tilted it onto one side. "He put straps on it that he could use to pull it back into place from the outside." He nodded to his officer. "Show her."

As she watched, the officer outside reached through, grabbed straps on the top and bottom, hefted it up, and slid it back into place. Within a few seconds, if she hadn't known what she was looking for, she never would have seen it.

"Like I said. Elegantly done. This wasn't a heat-of-the-moment opportunity. This was meticulously planned."

"The biggest problem is the size of the opening." Gray rubbed his jaw. "I tried. Even going at an angle, putting my hands through first, shifting around—nothing I did allowed me to fit through there. But a few of the guys were able to shimmy through. So we're looking for a man with a narrower build than mine and the tenacity to plan something like this."

Landry dropped her head and groaned. "You need to look at Ignacio."

"Who?" Gray pulled a pen and notebook from his pocket. Landry explained who Ignacio was, what he did for a living, and why he'd made it onto her short list of possible suspects.

Gray wrote furiously. "Any idea where he is now?"

"He told me he was headed to Eastern Europe, but"—Landry held out her hands—"I don't want to accuse an innocent man of anything. He's never been anything but kind. He asks about Eliza. He tips well. He always makes it a point to take a class of some type from me while he's here. And he's almost never here alone. He always brings a friend or two, and they make a big party out of it."

Gray wrote for another thirty seconds, then turned his attention to Cal. "Do you think Mo could find a guy who doesn't want to be found in Eastern Europe?"

Cal considered it. "If he can't, he knows someone who can."

"Let's get him on it." Gray slid his notebook into his pocket and focused on Landry. "Are you going to Meredith's?"

"Yes."

"Good. I think you should plan to stay there for a while."

"So I've been told." Landry cut her eyes to Cal.

"He's not wrong." Gray patted her arm. "We'll get your life back for you, Landry. Hang in there."

Cal followed Landry back to her place and hung out on her porch while she packed. When she was ready to go, he followed her to his carport and unloaded her bags.

Landry barely spoke.

"I'm getting the feeling you need some space."

She sat on Meredith's sofa and rubbed her hand on her throat.

"I don't want to be ungrateful, Cal. But I need a few minutes before Eliza gets here to pull myself together. I don't know what's wrong. I'm just very tired."

"If you want to take a nap, I'm sure Naomi and Chad—"

"No. I appreciate everything they've done. So much. But I need her here with me."

"Okay." Cal took a step toward the door. "I'll get out of your hair."

"Cal?"

He paused. "Yeah?"

"Sometimes I need space."

"Okay."

"That's how I'm wired. It doesn't mean I . . . I don't . . . or I . . ."

Cal took the three steps necessary to reach Landry. He squatted down beside her. "You don't have to explain. I like my space too." She waved her hand around them. "Your living arrangement would argue against that."

"My living arrangement is *proof* of that. We could have built one house and moved in together. We talked about it for about thirty seconds, then we laughed for thirty minutes. You've been surrounded by people for hours. Needing a little distance is normal."

"I don't need a lot of distance. Just a little. For a little while."

Cal was going to lose his mind if he didn't kiss her. *Not now. Not now.* "Good. Because I'm only going to be about thirty feet away, and I won't be gone long."

"Okay."

He stood and beat a hasty retreat to Mo's place. If he'd stayed another second . . .

No. Nope. Nada. Not now.

Later?

Definitely.

He entered Mo's place without knocking. "I need you to focus on Ignacio."

Mo looked up from the bank of computers that he all but lived behind. "The stunt guy?"

"That's the one."

"He spend much time at The Haven?"

"Yep."

"Weird." Mo's fingers flew across the keyboard.

"What's weird about it?"

"I'm assuming you mean beyond the obvious. Because burning down stores and vandalizing pottery studios isn't normal behavior."

Cal didn't bother to respond.

"Fine. He's all wrong for Landry."

"What?"

"Ignacio. Landry needs a grown-up who's still young enough to grow with. She doesn't need a guy who hasn't learned how to be a man. And she also doesn't need a man with a death wish. I've seen a few of his stunts, and I have serious doubts about his mental health."

Mo paused typing, made eye contact with Cal and grinned, then started typing again. "I'm thinking she needs a guy who's a partner in his family business, has a college degree, has served his country with distinction, loves his family, and thinks his mama walks on water but isn't attached to her apron strings."

"Oh, really?"

"Yeah. You know anyone like that?" Mo's ability to type and talk was impressive, but Cal wished he would shut up and concentrate.

"Yeah. I do. Now, can you find this guy or not?"

"It's been thirty seconds. I'm good, but I'm not that good."

"How long?"

"A few days, unless he pops up somewhere obvious. Eastern Europe's not the most specific location."

"Thanks. Holler when you know something."

The typing stopped. "Cal?"

"Yeah?"

"I know you're scared out of your mind, but don't be stupid. Don't let her get away. Be happy. Okay. I need . . ." The typing resumed and almost, but not quite, succeeded in drowning out Mo's final words. "I need to see that it works out for somebody."

Cal wished he could fix everything that had gone wrong for Mo. But maybe he could give him this. "I'm working on it."

"Work harder." Mo looked at a screen to his right. "Chad's on his way in with Eliza."

Cal walked over so he could see Mo's screen. "Is it motion-triggered?"

"Yeah. Resolution stinks. But it's good enough to recognize the main outline, and I think I can clean it up to get license plates if we need them."

"Cool. Thanks." Cal walked to the door. "And Mo?"

"Not talking anymore, Cal."

Cal knew better than to push it. "Okay. Later."

"Later."

Cal stepped outside and waited until Chad's truck came into

view and parked. Chad, Naomi, Abby, and Eliza all spilled from the vehicle. The girls were their usual giggly selves. Chad and Naomi were keeping up appearances for the girls, but Cal could read their tension.

Landry came out of Meredith's house, and Eliza ran into her arms. "Mommy!"

Cal had to dig his heels into the gravel to keep from joining their little huddle. The ache for them to be his was ridiculous. He'd been a fool to ever think he could just decide not to fall again. His heart didn't give a flip about the danger. About the possible heartache. He just wanted them to be his.

Landry didn't think she could live in a tiny house on a regular basis, but for tonight, it was perfect. It felt safe and cozy, and the chicken concoction she had in the oven made the entire space smell like the best parts of a Southern kitchen.

Meredith's refrigerator was filled to the brim. She'd come by that afternoon to grab her Kindle and talked Landry through the dishes.

"This chicken—you should have it tonight. It's amazing. The crust bubbles up from the bottom somehow. I don't know how it works, but it's delicious." She pointed to a salad. "This salad and vinaigrette"—she touched a small mason jar—"are from Cassie. She makes the vinaigrette from scratch. You'll never want any other salad dressing again."

There were two different soups, a pot roast, and a lasagna for main courses. A fruit salad, two different green salads, garlic bread, and a jar of homemade honey butter to go with the yeast rolls that were in the freezer.

"We'll never be able to eat all of this."

"Don't be so sure. Cal and Mo will smell it and come knocking." Meredith's phone buzzed, and her happy expression fell. "Mom wants me to pick up some ginger ale before I come home."

"I'm sorry about your mom." Landry didn't know what else to say.

"Thanks. She's a fighter. And as bad as things are right now, the doctors say her prognosis is good. We just have to get her through the treatment."

"I can't wait to meet her."

Meredith's eyes lit. "She's excited to meet you. And Eliza. She's heard all about you from Aunt Carol. And Granny Quinn. And Papa Quinn. Pretty much everyone."

Landry closed her eyes and willed her face not to turn pink. Not that it worked. "I'm not sure if that's a good thing or not."

"Oh, it is." Meredith looked around and spotted Eliza outside playing with Maisy. "We've all been wondering who would finally break through Cal's shields."

"I—"

"I know." There was no teasing light in Meredith's eyes. "I was there, Landry. I know what that woman did to him. And I know he swore he'd never take that risk again. But I don't think he took into account the fact that sometimes even though the brain acknowledges the risk, the heart realizes that playing it safe is riskier." Meredith grinned. "I think you're a chance worth taking. So does everyone else in the family. Cal knows it too."

Landry had no idea what to say to that. Fortunately, Meredith didn't seem to need an answer. She changed the subject, talked the entire way to her car, then waved and honked on her way down the driveway.

Five minutes later, Bronwyn texted and informed her that Meredith had told her about the food in the fridge, and that she would be there for supper at six.

263

As much as Landry wanted to sleep, she knew that sleeping now was a mistake. If she could hold on until she put Eliza in bed, then she could crash. Her head hurt, her eyes ached, and her back complained with every move she made. She hadn't pulled an all-nighter in years, but she hadn't expected her body to rebel this way. Surely thirty-two wasn't too old to occasionally lose a night of sleep?

She opened the oven door to check on the casserole. It did look amazing. She closed the door and groaned. It made absolutely no sense that her hands would hurt from lack of sleep.

Eliza clattered down the stairs from her little loft. "What's wrong, Mommy?"

"Oh, nothing, sweetheart. I'm just tired. Miss Bronwyn's going to come over for dinner, but she won't stay long. Then you and I are going to call it a night."

"Okay. Should I go tell Mr. Cal and Mr. Mo what we're having?"

Landry opened the refrigerator to give herself a few moments to think. They were both welcome, but with Bronwyn here, would Mo come? If he didn't, how would she explain that to Eliza? And if he did, would it be awkward?

Short answer? Very.

But they couldn't invite Cal and not Mo. And it was possible Meredith had already spoken to them and they were expecting an invitation. She pulled one of the salads out of the fridge. "Sure. Go tell them Miss Bronwyn will be here at six."

Eliza dashed outside, and Landry watched through the window as she covered the short distance to Cal's house. His door opened, and he knelt down so he was at eye level with Eliza. They chatted for several minutes, and it wasn't until the oven timer beeped that Landry realized she'd been standing there watching them. She covered the casserole with foil, as she'd been directed to do, and reset the timer as fast as she could. She returned to the same spot in time to see Cal and Eliza walk to Mo's and knock.

When Cal opened the door but neither he nor Eliza walked inside, Landry guessed that Mo had hollered for them to come in. They stood in his doorway for less than thirty seconds, then stepped away. Cal closed the door behind them and gave Eliza a fist bump before they both walked to Meredith's.

Eliza ran inside, but Cal waited at the door. Landry walked over to him. "Thank you for going with her to Mo's."

He cut his eyes toward Mo's house. "I wouldn't count on him coming over. Thank you for giving him the warning about . . ."

"No problem. Full disclosure. I don't know the whole story there."

"I don't think anyone but the two of them do." Cal sighed. "But I haven't given up hope."

Landry held on to those words when Mo tapped on the door at 6:02 p.m. Bronwyn was pouring tea for everyone, and to her credit, only sloshed a tiny bit onto the counter when she saw Mo at the door. Landry waved him in, and so began the strangest dinner party of her entire life. And that included the fiascos she'd endured at Dylan's parents' home.

Eliza scarfed down her food and then went up to her loft to enjoy a few minutes of screen time. Everyone else was extremely polite. There was a lot of laughter and even some teasing. Initially, Landry thought it was going quite well. And then it dawned on her that while everyone participated in the conversation, Mo and Bronwyn avoided making eye contact or speaking to each other. Landry wasn't quite sure how they managed it.

The crazy thing was that the distance between them, while painfully obvious to everyone except Eliza, wasn't like the simmering hostility of a demilitarized zone. It was more like the tentative way someone sipped their coffee after burning their tongue on the first try. There was a hint of desperation and longing but also the fear of experiencing that pain again.

In a house the size of Meredith's, there was nowhere she could go to talk to Cal privately, but when Mo stepped outside to take a call and Bronwyn excused herself to use the restroom, Landry nearly collapsed in relief when Cal stood beside her in the kitchen, hip to hip, and said, "Are you as stressed as I am with those two?"

"I'm dying."

"Want me to wrap things up?" Cal's deep voice settled around her like a cozy blanket on a cool night, and for a few seconds, she considered telling him no.

"I don't want *you* to leave, but I'm so tired I can barely think." Had she just said that out loud? She turned her head oh-so-slowly and . . . yep . . . Cal's smug expression confirmed it. "Oh, don't look so full of yourself. You know it's true."

His arm slid around her waist, and his lips brushed her ear. "What I know is that we're way overdue for a long conversation."

She had no resistance left in her. Couldn't even remember why she'd ever tried to resist him. He was big and strong and warm, and without thinking about it, she leaned into him and rested her cheek on his chest. He rolled her so she was facing him. His expression started out filled with flirtatiousness, but his brows furrowed, and his free hand came to rest on her forehead. "Landry, honey, you're burning up."

"Am I?"

"Yes. You are."

"I think it's the fatigue from being up all night. I'll be fine after I sleep."

He gave her a dubious look, and when the door opened a few seconds later, he spoke to Mo. "Landry's not feeling well. We're going to need to cut this short."

266

Bronwyn came down the short hall. "You're sick?"

Landry tried to stop a yawn. Especially when yawning made her throat hurt. "I'm just tired."

Bronwyn picked up the plates from the table and called up to Eliza. "Sweetie, can you start getting ready for bed? Your mom's not feeling great. We need to get things cleaned up and get you settled."

Mo, Bronwyn, and Cal made short work of the kitchen, and almost before she knew what was happening, Bronwyn and Mo had said good night and were on the porch not talking to each other. Cal hesitated. "I'm right there"—he pointed to his house—"if you need anything."

"Thanks."

She and Eliza, already in her pajamas, told him good night. She tucked Eliza in and dragged herself to the bathroom for a quick shower. She took some ibuprofen and climbed the stairs to her bed. Every step sent a spear of pain through her body. She remembered Meredith's bed being comfortable and cozy. But tonight, she huddled under the blankets, cold and shivering and more tired than she could ever remember being. Fatigue dragged her under.

TWENTY-SIX

Cal woke to the sound of Maisy yipping at the door. He threw back the covers, grabbed his phone, and jogged down the stairs. "What is it, girl?" She wasn't barking like there was an intruder, but she was definitely trying to get his attention. Pregnancy had made her a bit more protective than normal, but this wasn't typical behavior. He rubbed her head and flipped on his porch light.

Nothing he could have imagined would have prepared him for the sight that greeted him. Eliza stood there in pajamas and bare feet, her small hand knocking tentatively on the door. He unlocked the door, opened it, and pulled the sobbing girl inside. "Eliza? What's wrong? Where's your mom?"

She looked at him with so much sorrow that he could feel his heart splintering. *Please, please, God. Let Landry be okay.*

Eliza grabbed his hand and tugged. "Mommy's sick."

He thought she'd had a fever earlier, but she'd said she was just tired. No surprise after being up all night. But clearly it had been more than that.

He scooped Eliza into his arms and ran to Meredith's house, Maisy hot on his heels. The door was open, and he didn't hesitate to enter. "Where is she?"

Eliza pointed to the small bathroom door. "She can't get up."

Panic crept through every inch of his skin.

"She told me to go back to bed, but . . ."

Some of the panic faded. If Landry was talking, that was a good sign. He set Eliza on the sofa and wiped the tears from her face. "It's going to be okay. You did good. Sit here while I check on your mom." He turned to Maisy and patted the sofa. "Maisy. Stay."

Eliza sniffled and nodded. Maisy hopped up beside her and rested her head on Eliza's legs. He grabbed a throw blanket from a basket and tucked it around them both. Then he called out, "Landry? I'm coming in."

He pushed the bathroom door open. Landry was slumped against the wall. Her skin was pale, her eyes were bright, and her hand trembled when she held it out toward him. "Go away. I don't need—"

She didn't get the rest of her sentence out before she scrambled to her knees and bent over the toilet. Cal walked behind her, sat on the edge of the tub, and pulled her hair away from her face. Then he held it with one hand and rubbed her back with the other until she was able to reach out and flush the toilet.

Her skin blazed beneath her pajamas.

He hopped up and took a washcloth from the small shelf on the wall and wet it in the sink. When he handed it to Landry, she took it with a sigh.

"Thank you." She wiped her face and resumed her earlier position against the wall. "How'd you get in?" A tremor shook her body, and she put a hand to her throat.

"Eliza came to my place. She's worried about you."

Landry looked at the door. "Where is she?"

"In the living room. Let me get her so she can see you're alive. Then I'll get her back into bed."

He leaned into the small hallway and motioned for Eliza to join him. When she moved toward Landry, he stopped her with a hand on her shoulder. "Sweetheart, your mom's pretty sick. Probably best if you don't get too close to her germs. Tell her good night, and then let's get you back into bed. You have school in a few hours."

Cal could see Eliza's face reflected in the mirror, and it was taut with tension. "I'm sorry I disobeyed, Mommy."

Landry's eyes shone as she studied her daughter. "We'll talk about it later. I know you thought I needed help. Going to Cal was a good decision."

Relief flooded Eliza's expression. "He'll take care of you."

"Yes." Cal squeezed her shoulder. "I will. But first, let's get you back upstairs."

"Good night, Mommy." Eliza blew Landry a kiss.

"Good night, pumpkin." Landry pretended to catch the kiss, then blew one back.

Cal led Eliza back to the stairs and up to the loft where her bed was located. She climbed in without complaint, and when he pulled the covers over her, she snuggled in, her face at peace. Maisy jumped on the bed and curled up at her feet. Clearly, Eliza was hers to protect.

"Night, Cal."

"Good night." Her eyes closed, and her breathing was soft and even. She was probably asleep by the time he made it down the stairs.

He paused in the kitchen to fix a glass of water for Landry, then returned to the bathroom. She sat, eyes closed, face in a grimace.

"I brought you some water."

Her eyes fluttered open, and she reached for the glass. "Thank you." She took a small sip, and her entire body went rigid.

"What's wrong?"

"Throat. So sore. Hurts to swallow." She set the glass on the floor. "I'm achy all over, but my throat's the worst. It might be the flu. But I'll be fine, Cal."

"Yeah." He pulled his phone from his pocket and turned on the flashlight. "Open up. Let me see that throat."

270

She frowned at him. "Since when are you a doctor?"

"I'm the son of a doctor. I'm also someone who's had strep throat enough in his lifetime to know the symptoms. Nausea, fever, sore throat, body aches—all hitting fast? You might have the flu. But in my professional strep-throat-survivor opinion, you have strep. Let me see."

Landry opened her mouth, and Cal shined his light toward the back. Her throat was so red and swollen, it was no wonder it hurt to swallow. And it was covered in white spots.

"My mother will tell you that white spots and sore throats don't necessarily mean strep. But you're going to get tested for it."

"I can't leave the house." Landry waved a slender hand around the bathroom. "I'm afraid to move."

"Well, that's where you're in luck." He turned off the flashlight function on his phone and called his mom.

She answered on the third ring. "Cal? What's wrong?"

"Sorry to wake you, Mom."

"You didn't. I was already up." Dr. Carol Shaw had been an early riser Cal's entire life, but he seriously doubted that she was up at 4:30 a.m.

"Sure you were."

"I couldn't sleep. Got up around four, made coffee, and settled in to read my Bible and start my day. Looks like God knew I needed to get up, given that my baby boy is calling me now, expecting to wake me up."

"It's Landry. She's sick."

There was a brief pause. "You're with Landry?"

"Yes. Eliza came and got me. Landry's burning up with a fever and has a raging sore throat. I took a look, and her throat is red, super swollen, and covered in white spots. She's throwing up so much she can't get out of the bathroom, and her body aches."

"Let me get dressed and get my bag. I'll be there in a few minutes."

271

"Can I give her anything for the pain?" Cal brushed Landry's hair from her forehead. Her eyelids twitched at his touch but didn't open. "She's so miserable."

"Ah, sweetheart. If you give her anything, she probably won't keep it down. For now, try to keep her as comfortable as possible. I'll be there soon."

"Thanks, Mom. Love you."

"Love you too, baby boy."

Cal disconnected the phone.

"Did she call you 'baby boy'?" Landry's voice was a hoarse whisper, but there was amusement and disbelief in her words.

"Yes." His mom had called him "baby boy" his entire life. Since he'd hit his teens, she kept it to private conversations. He hated it when he was younger. But sometime in his late twenties, he decided she could call him that if she wanted to. It didn't hurt him. Didn't make him less of a man to let his mother use a term of affection. And while she called him her baby, she didn't treat him like one.

So it was fine.

As long as she didn't say it in public.

"That's sweet." Landry didn't open her eyes when she spoke.

"She loves you."

"She does. I love her too. She's awesome. And she's on her way here."

"Cal." There was a whine in Landry's voice now. "I don't go to the doctor every time I get sick."

"Maybe you didn't before, but you do now."

"Bossy." If she was trying to make him mad, it wouldn't work. If she was trying to tease him, that wouldn't work either. He didn't care one way or the other right now. She was so sick, she couldn't get off the bathroom floor. He couldn't fix her, but he wouldn't sit by and watch her suffer without making sure she was getting the best possible care.

And in Gossamer Falls—or, in his opinion, anywhere—that meant she needed his mom.

He slid to the floor beside her, and she didn't complain when he pulled her toward him so her head rested against his arm. They sat that way until his mom arrived. She texted that she was out front, and he told her to come on in. When she entered the bathroom, she shook her head in sympathy. "Poor girl. Let's get you checked out."

She banished Cal from the bathroom, so he tiptoed up the stairs to check on Eliza. She was passed out. He checked his watch. 5:30 a.m. School started at 8:00, but Eliza liked to be early because Carla dropped Abby off no later than 7:40 so she could get the older boys to the middle school in time for class.

Even a town as small as Gossamer Falls had car lines that made parents a little crazy.

It would take him fifteen minutes to get to the school. He set an alarm on his phone for 6:30. Surely he could get one little girl ready for school in forty-five minutes.

He went back downstairs and made a pot of coffee. He could hear his mom's alto murmurs but couldn't quite make out what she was saying. Based on the pauses, he assumed Landry answered.

When he did hear something five minutes later, it wasn't what he wanted to hear. He poured another glass of water and took it to the bathroom. He tapped on the door and pushed it open a few inches but didn't look inside. "I have some water."

"Thank you." His mom opened the door farther, and he could see Landry slumped against the wall, pale, wiping her mouth with a washcloth. When she took the glass from his mom, the water sloshed so violently he wasn't sure she'd be able to get it to her mouth.

"Mom?" He loaded all his concern and fear and frustration into that word. "What's the verdict?"

"She's sick, but it's nothing we can't fix. I brought a rapid strep test with me, and it's positive."

Cal felt simultaneous relief and frustration. Strep was no joke. It was fixable, but it was misery waiting for the meds to kick in.

His mom tossed something into the trash can, then washed her hands. "She'll need antibiotics, but there's no point in starting them until we get her nausea under control. I'm going to run to my office and get something for her. I'll be back as soon as I can."

"That sounds great, Mom. But will she be able to keep it down?"

"She will because I'm going to give her a shot. It should settle her stomach and knock her out. Once we get her stomach settled, we'll be able to get her into bed. She'll rest so much better there. I'll call in the antibiotics as soon as Heather opens, and you can pick them up for her."

That wouldn't be happening. He'd send Mo.

"Eliza," Landry whispered.

"I've got her." He tried to give her his most encouraging smile.

"I'll take her to school. She'll be fine."

"I can—"

"No." The word came from Cal and his mom at the same time. "Landry, you can't get off the floor. And after Mom's through with you, you won't be able to keep your eyes open. You're going to bed and nowhere else."

She looked so very small and lost, and when she swallowed, her entire body contorted.

"Mom, what about the pain?"

"I'll take care of that too." She patted his hand. "I should be back in the next forty-five minutes." She ran a finger across Landry's cheek. "Hang in there, sweet girl."

At the affectionate remark, something that looked suspiciously like tears sprang into Landry's eyes, but Cal pretended not to notice.

"Cal, walk me to the door. Landry, don't even think about getting up."

Cal obeyed. When they were outside, his mom turned to him. "Her throat is a mess. I'm not sure how she isn't sobbing in agony. Probably trying to be brave for Eliza. I'm going to give her a shot of nausea medicine, pain medicine, and antibiotics to jumpstart the healing process. Then you'll need to be sure she gets the rest of the meds throughout the day."

"Thanks, Mom."

"I would do it for anyone, but I especially don't mind doing it for your girl."

"She's not mine, Mom."

His mother rose on her tiptoes, he bent down, and she kissed him on the cheek. "You don't have to trust me with the details yet, but don't lie to me or to yourself."

"It's beyond complicated—"

"You thrive on complicated."

TWENTY-SEVEN

Cal sat with Landry until his mom returned. She was only with Landry for a few minutes and when she came out, she handed him a piece of paper with written instructions for Landry's care.

"Once the meds kick in and she can keep something down, she has to drink. She won't want to, but she has to. I'll call around lunch. If she hasn't been able to keep any fluids down, we'll need to start an IV."

"She won't want to go to the clinic."

"She made that abundantly clear. Which is why I'm making it clear that she has to drink. Make her some sweet tea. You always liked sweet tea when you had a sore throat."

"I'm on it."

"I'm headed back to my office. I saw four patients on Saturday with strep, and my schedule is already full for the day. It's going around." She pointed over her shoulder toward the bathroom.

"Give her about fifteen minutes. Then help her to bed."

"Okay."

He returned to the bathroom. He'd have to congratulate Meredith on her foresight. The bathroom at his house was barely big enough for him to turn around in. Meredith had insisted it was

276

worth the square footage to have a decent-sized room, and as he slid to the floor—again—he was thankful for it.

Landry's eyes were heavy, and she sagged against him. "This is so embarrassing."

"It is not. It's strep throat. Which, in my expert opinion, comes straight from the devil. It's evil."

"I agree with you on that." A shiver ran through her. "I need to make Eliza's lunch."

Cal didn't try to stop the frustrated growl that built in his throat. "What's it going to take for you to believe me when I tell you? I. Have. This."

She lifted her head from his arm and looked at him, a furrow between her brows.

"She's mine, Cal. She doesn't have anyone else."

"She *didn't* have anyone else. Now, she does. I'm perfectly capable of packing her lunch and getting her to school. You're going to drink some water for me, and then you're going to let me help you up the stairs and into bed."

"I think I'll stay here. It's safer."

"I'm not leaving you on the bathroom floor. You're going to sleep in a bed with warm blankets and a soft pillow. I'll bring you a trash can."

"When I'm not loopy on drugs, we're going to have to discuss this bossy side of you."

"Tell you what. Next time I have strep and I'm trying to sleep on a bathroom floor, you can boss me around all you want."

"I won't forget this."

Neither would he. Heaven help him. Neither would he.

Ten minutes later, he helped her to her feet. She swayed like a sapling in a thunderstorm. He caught her and put one arm around her waist. The other he locked onto the bicep that rested against his chest. "Just take it slow. Lean on me as much as you need to."

They shuffled out of the bathroom and up the stairs. She was wobbly and leaned into him with each step. But at least it was a short trip. When they reached the bed, she all but fell into it. He helped her settle and pulled the covers over her.

Landry's eyes closed and didn't reopen.

Her mouth, however, did.

"Cal—"

"Yes?"

"What're we doing?" Her words were slurred.

"We'll figure it out. For now, rest and know that I'm not going anywhere."

"I'm not what you're looking for."

No. She wasn't. She was so much more. But he had no plans to confess his feelings—feelings he wasn't even sure he could articulate yet—while she was like this. "Maybe not. But I like surprises."

"Surprise." The world trailed off as she sank into peaceful oblivion. Her body relaxed under the covers, and Cal closed his eyes in relief. She'd be okay. Not today. But tomorrow would be better. By the weekend she'd be back at work.

Where would that leave him? He had no idea.

The alarm on his phone chimed. Time to get Eliza ready for school.

He eased down the stairs and then back up to the loft where Eliza slept. "Liza Lou?" He kept his voice just above a whisper. The last thing he wanted to do was startle her. It wasn't like she was used to having a man wake her in the morning.

She lifted her arms above her head and stretched. "Sleep." She rolled over and settled onto her side.

"School first. Sleep later."

She didn't move. Maisy stood and licked her face. That got her moving. And giggling.

"If you get up and get dressed fast enough, we'll have time to eat some of Meredith's muffins before school."

Eliza sat up. "What kind?"

"I checked the freezer. She has chocolate chip and blueberry."

"Blueberry." Eliza rubbed her eyes.

"Blueberry it is. And some oatmeal. But you have to help me out and get a move on."

She yawned and blinked at him a few times. Then she frowned. "Where's Mommy?"

"In bed asleep. My mom came over and took care of her. She's had medicine and she's resting."

"What's wrong?"

"She has something called strep throat. When kids get it, it's not fun. But sometimes when adults get it, it makes them very sick. Looks like your mom is one of those people. But she'll be okay. She needs to rest and take some medicine, and then she'll be as good as new."

Eliza threw herself into his arms. "I knew you'd know what to do."

He held her close, savoring the trust and affection and ignoring the little voice screaming warnings from the still-shattered parts of his heart.

Thirty minutes later, and thanks in large part to the fact that Eliza needed very little assistance, he put a bowl of oatmeal and a blueberry muffin in front of her while he sipped his coffee.

"Aren't you going to eat?"

"I'll eat later. Right now I'm going to pack your lunch."

Eliza told him her favorite lunch items and, given that her list included orange slices and turkey roll-ups, he didn't worry that Landry would have a conniption when she found out that he put a few Oreos in the box before he zipped it.

He jogged up the stairs. Landry was out cold. Sometime during breakfast, Maisy had abandoned him and Eliza and made her way to Landry. She lay sprawled across the empty side of the bed and gave Cal a look that said, "Leave us alone and let us rest."

He jogged back down, grabbed his keys, Eliza's backpack, and his coffee, and they went to his truck. Mo stepped outside, a matching coffee thermos in his hand. "What's going on?"

Cal gave him a quick rundown. "Will you sit inside until I get back? Just in case she needs anything? Maisy's on the bed with her."

"Got it." Mo winked at Eliza. "You'll tell me if he drives too crazy, right?"

"Right." She grinned at him and clambered into the back of the truck and into the booster seat he kept there for Abby. Cal made sure she was securely buckled, gave Mo a small salute, and headed to the elementary school.

He'd had plenty of opportunities to take his nephews and niece to school over the years, so he knew how the drop-off system worked. He got in the line and inched his way toward where the teachers and aides stood, opening car doors and greeting students and parents.

When he reached the drop-off point, the woman who opened the door was someone he'd known since elementary school. He'd also dated her sister a long time ago. Lisa gave him a look that he understood all too well. Thankfully, she kept the innuendo out of her voice as she helped Eliza from the truck. "Good morning, Eliza. Look at you, riding in the back of this big old truck. What did you do to get Cal to bring you to school this morning?"

"My mommy's sick." Eliza turned to Cal. "Thanks, Cal."

"Have a good day, Liza Lou. I'll be here to pick you up after school."

"Okay." As soon as her feet hit the sidewalk, she took off like a rocket.

Lisa quirked an eyebrow. "Getting domestic, are we, Cal?"

He gave her his politest smile. "Just helping a friend. Landry has strep throat, and she's pretty sick today."

Genuine concern replaced her sarcasm. "We have three teachers out, and my guess is we'll have a lot of students out today too. It's going around something awful."

"Mom said it was bad."

"She'll be hopping today, I'm sure." Lisa nodded toward where Eliza now stood with some other kindergarteners. "We'll keep an eye on her. I'll make sure Mrs. Wilson knows about Landry."

"Thanks."

Cal drove straight to Meredith's house.

When he walked inside, Mo walked out. "She's asleep. Maisy's still with her. You going to work?"

"No. I'm going to take a nap on the sofa. Then I'll work from home. Can you go to the pharmacy in a little while and get her medicine? Mom was going to call it in when Heather opened."

"I'll take care of it. Get some rest."

"Thanks."

Cal couldn't resist peeking in on Landry. Just like Mo had said, she was asleep. He reached a tentative hand to her forehead. It was warm but not blazing like a few hours ago. Good.

He'd made sweet tea while Eliza ate breakfast. Now he put it in the fridge to chill, took five minutes to clean up, then set an alarm for two hours and lay on the sofa.

When his alarm woke him, he noticed a distinctive white bag sitting inside the door. He picked it up and found a note in Mo's scrawl that said, "You were asleep. Figured you needed the rest more than anything else."

Cal hated to wake Landry, but he did it anyway. He cajoled her into drinking some tea and swallowing the meds Mo had dropped off. He helped her walk down the stairs to the bathroom, then back up before tucking her in. She was a little loopy and said her body still hurt all over, but it wasn't as bad as it had been. She was asleep again ten minutes later. Maisy resumed her guard post.

He set a new alarm on his phone for 2:00 p.m. and lay back down on the sofa. His phone ringing woke him, and he stared at the screen in confusion. For one thing, the phone claimed that it was 1:15 p.m., so this wasn't the alarm he'd set. The number also confused him. Something was familiar about it. "Cal Shaw."

"Hey, Cal. It's Aunt Laura. Carol called and told me what was going on with Landry. How's she doing?"

"Good. Listen. I hate to do this to her, but I need her to come pick up Eliza from school."

"What?"

"Eliza's sick. Sore throat. Fever."

"Oh no."

"Yeah."

"I'll come get her and take her to Mom."

"Landry and I had a meeting at the beginning of the school year. She was very clear that the only other person who could pick up Eliza was Bronwyn Pierce. I can't violate that trust, Cal. Not even for you."

"I know, Aunt Laura. And I appreciate that. But if you check Eliza's records, you'll see that the list of people approved to pick her up has grown since school started."

"Are you on the list?"

"I am." He'd been on it since he volunteered to pick up Eliza and Abby one day a few weeks earlier. "So are Naomi and Chad."

"Oh, thank heaven." Aunt Laura blew out a long breath. "So can you come get her? Or should I call Naomi?"

"I'll get her."

"Okay, I'll let the nurse know you're on the way."

"Thanks."

He left still-sleeping Landry a note and drove to the school. On the way, he called his mom, who informed him that he wasn't allowed to make medical decisions for Eliza and that her office was booked solid until 6:00 p.m. "Take her home, give her some Tylenol, and let her rest. I'll swing by with a strep test when I get done."

"Thanks, Mom."

The Eliza who met him at the door to the nurse's office wasn't the same girl he'd dropped off this morning. "I don't feel good, Cal."

"I know. Let's get you home."

She fell asleep on the way home, and he carried her into the house. Landry poked her head over the rail. "Is she okay?"

"Probably has strep too. Sore throat. Nurse said there are white spots, and her fever's around 102. Mom said to give her some Tylenol, and then she'll come by tonight with a strep test."

"Your mom's an angel."

"She's pretty awesome."

Landry started for the stairs.

"Don't you dare. Wait for me."

"What?"

"You've almost fallen up and down those stairs the last few times you've made the trip. We've got the strep on the ropes. Let's not add broken bones to the mix."

He settled Eliza, who was still asleep, onto the sofa and then jogged up the stairs. He didn't know everything there was to know about parenting, but he knew better than to keep a mama away from her sick child. He helped Landry down the stairs and hovered as she cuddled with Eliza.

Landry's color was better, but he'd bet she was running a fever again. Her skin felt too warm to him, and it had been over four hours since her last dose of pain medicine.

She told him where to find the children's Tylenol and managed to get the dose into Eliza. Cal was then sent to find Eliza's pajamas. He went upstairs to give them some privacy while Landry helped Eliza change. Once she was dressed, he carried her to her bed.

After Eliza was settled, he focused on Landry. "Okay. Your turn." The meds and tea went okay, but when she grimaced and pushed the blueberry muffin away, he knew she was done. "Back to bed for you."

He got her settled and resumed his spot on the sofa. He pulled out his phone and checked his email, made a few phone calls, and tried to make sure he hadn't dropped any balls. An hour later, he heard footsteps on the stairs. Eliza came down dragging a purple blanket and a ginormous stuffed tiger. She didn't say anything. She just crawled into his lap, rested her feverish cheek on his chest, and promptly went back to sleep.

Cal stroked her hair and conceded defeat.

The fight was over.

Landry and Eliza Hutton were his.

TWENTY-EIGHT

The trip to full consciousness started with a stretch and ended when Landry tried to swallow.

It still hurt. Bad. But not as bad as it had yesterday. Or was it today? Or last night?

She peered through half-closed eyes. Was the day almost over or just beginning? She yawned and rubbed her hand on the pillow and bedding until she located her phone.

5:24 p.m.

Wait. What? Landry went from prone to standing in the space of two heartbeats. Eliza. Sick. Landry swayed a little and grasped the rail that kept the master bedroom loft from being a death trap.

The view that met her gaze froze her in place.

Below her, Cal sat on the sofa with Eliza draped over him like a starfish. He had one hand on her back, rubbing up and down in a soothing rhythm. The other arm wrapped around Eliza's waist. He was holding her. Comforting her. Protecting her.

Eliza was sound asleep in a man's arms for the first time in her young life. Her own father had never held her with the same tenderness.

This wasn't the way a man determined to protect his heart acted.

This was the way a daddy cuddled with his baby girl when she was sick.

Landry watched them for another minute before a fuzzy memory hit her brain. She'd helped Eliza get tucked into bed. But obviously she hadn't stayed there. At some point, either she'd walked down to Cal or he'd gone to get her.

She wasn't taking any more of those pain pills. They worked, but they worked too well. Landry couldn't be so out of it that she lost track of her daughter.

She waited for the fear to crash through her at the realization that she'd slept so hard. But it didn't come.

Because of Cal.

She trusted him with Eliza. When had *that* happened?

She wrapped her robe around herself, held on to the rail, and eased down the stairs.

Cal turned his head and watched her, concern and something else in his eyes. "Feeling better?"

She read his lips more than heard his words. And she didn't try to respond until she was standing beside him. "Not one hundred percent. Maybe fifty?"

"It's progress."

"Definitely." She pointed to the bathroom. "I'll be right back." She closed herself in the bathroom and decided once and for all that tiny house living wasn't for her. The door was closed, but Cal was just a few feet away. It didn't feel like she had any privacy.

She took care of business, brushed her teeth, ran a brush through her hair, and returned to the sofa. She waved a hand to encompass Cal and Eliza. "How did this happen?"

Cal's expression was bemused. "I have no idea. She slept upstairs for an hour or so, then decided I would make a better bed. So here we are."

His expression turned serious, and he patted the sofa cushion beside him. "Join us?"

"I'd love to." As soon as she sat, his arm wrapped around her shoulder, and she didn't fight it when he pulled her closer. She dropped her head to the free spot right above his heart.

This was definitely not what a man who wanted to stay friends would do.

At least, she didn't think he would. The Quinns and Shaws were an affectionate family. Hugs, pats, and squeezes were regular occurrences between the aunts, uncles, and cousins.

But this didn't feel friendly. This felt like . . . she wasn't sure if she could even think the thought.

Her breathing sped up.

Cal pressed his cheek to the top of her head. "You okay? Comfortable?"

"Mm-hmm."

Cal didn't move his head.

Yeah. This wasn't friend-zone behavior. This was edging into happily-ever-after territory. At least, it was for her. And if she'd read the situation wrong, she needed to know yesterday. But today would have to do. If she was wrong, this had to stop—and stop now—because she *and* Eliza were already in way too deep with Cal.

The timing was terrible. She was sick. Eliza was sick. His mom was on her way here. What if she said something now, but he wasn't ready yet? This conversation could ruin everything.

Or it might be amazing.

They sat that way for a full minute before she couldn't take it anymore. "Cal?"

"Hmm?"

"Um . . . do you remember when we were talking and I, uh, I told you that even if I ever got to the point where I was willing to take a chance on a relationship again, that I couldn't imagine a scenario where I would be comfortable putting Eliza's safety in jeopardy?"

Beside her and around her, Cal's body had gone from languid and relaxed to tense. Battle ready. But when he spoke, his voice was calm. "I remember."

"When I woke up and saw y'all down here? I realized that I was right. I couldn't imagine it then. And now, I don't have to imagine it. Because I *know* Eliza is safe with you."

Cal squeezed her shoulder. "What about you."

"What about me?"

"You said you knew Eliza was safe with me. But what about you? Do you know *you're* safe with me?"

Landry took a deep breath and went for it. "I know that if you ever got to the point where you were willing to risk it, I would be safe with you."

"Landry, this"—a quick squeeze—"isn't risky. This is right." She lifted her head and smiled at him. When she did, his lips swept over hers in a fleeting caress that promised more . . . later. He rested his forehead against hers. "You're killing me, Landry. When you're feeling better, and"—he nodded toward Eliza—"when we're alone, I'm going to kiss you properly. And often."

Before she could respond, headlights flickered in the driveway.

"That's Mom." Cal groaned. "This isn't the best timing, but I need to say this before she comes in, just so we're on the same page."

"Okay."

"I can't be just friends. Not anymore. You know where I'm coming from, so I'm not going to hold back. I want everything. I want you for you. I want you and Eliza in my life. I want dates with you and movies and pizza nights with both of you. I want phone calls and texts. I want to hold your hand in public and kiss you senseless in private."

She could feel her skin heating, and when Cal's lips curled into a smug smile, she knew he'd noticed.

But still, he asked. "I need to know. Are we on the same page?"

As if he didn't already know. She leaned into him. "Same page. Same line, same word, same letter."

Eliza stirred, and her eyes fluttered. "Mommy?"

Cal groaned. "Get better soon, Landry. We have so much to discuss."

———

To no one's surprise, Eliza had strep. But after a few doses of antibiotics and a day piled on the sofa with Landry and Cal watching all her favorite movies, she was raring to go.

Cal had taken her to school on Wednesday morning, then reluctantly went to the office. He came to check on Landry at lunch, picked up Eliza from school, and somehow failed to return to work after he dropped her off at home.

Landry was still weak, but her throat didn't hurt anymore. She hadn't run a fever in twenty-four hours, and her skin no longer felt like it was going to split apart if someone breathed on her.

She hadn't had pain medicine in thirty-six hours, and she finally believed she was going to return to her former health.

It was cool out, but she didn't need more than a jacket when she stepped outside. Eliza was asleep, and she'd expected to find Cal at the firepit with Mo. But he wasn't there.

"He's walking by the river." Mo pointed to a trail that led from the firepit to the river. Small solar lights dotted the path. "Maisy's with him."

"Oh." Landry looked back at the house, then toward the river. Three days ago, she wouldn't have considered hunting him down.

But things had changed. And he'd been quiet tonight. He'd stayed long enough to tuck Eliza in, but then slipped out. What if he wanted to be alone?

What if he was having second thoughts?

"Landry?" Mo pinched his lips together and pointed toward the river. "If you're worried about Eliza, I'll sit out here until you come back." He winked. "No rush."

"I, uh . . ."

"I don't mind."

"Oh. No. I . . . it's not that."

"Nervous?"

She caught a hint of wicked glee on Mo's face before it returned to its usual flat state.

"No." The word came out a bit more defiantly than she'd intended.

Mo shook his head. "Head to the river. He'll find you."

Landry figured he would. Probably because Mo would text him as soon as she got out of sight.

She wavered. But she missed Cal. And they'd had almost no time alone since they'd officially taken their relationship in a new direction. They needed to talk.

And she needed reassurance.

She started walking down the path toward the river. Ugh. She didn't like this part of herself. But there was no denying it. Dylan had done a number on her confidence. Right now, things with Cal felt like the moment when she finished a piece on her wheel and it was time to take it off the bat and move it to her drying rack. The shape was there, but the clay was still wet and easily pulled out of shape. One wrong move, and the piece could be ruined.

It could be fixed. But it would never be exactly the same again. Sometimes it was better than the original. Sometimes there was nothing to do but start all over.

She didn't want to start over.

Maisy reached her first, but not by much. She bent over to give Maisy a rub. Then two strong hands landed on her waist, and a very content male voice spoke in her ear. "There you are."

"Hi." She stood. What should she do? Face him? Stay where she was, his chest to her back? Where should she put her hands? Why was everything so weird in her head?

"What's wrong?"

"I'm nervous." The words flew right out of her mouth before she could stop them. They were true. But really? *Way to play it cool, Landry.*

Cal gently turned her to face him. He stepped back but didn't release her. He took both her hands in his, and his thumbs swept across her skin. "Want to walk with me? Just a short walk."

"I'd love to." He kept one of her hands and laced their fingers together as he led them toward the river. "It's a beautiful night." She'd led with a conversation about the weather? "Sorry. I'm——"

Cal pulled her against him, then his lips found hers.

And her nerves were gone.

She slid her hands up his chest and locked her arms around his neck. The last coherent thought she managed was that she hoped they were far enough down the path that Mo couldn't see them.

When they broke apart, she dropped her head against his chest. "Hi again."

He chuckled. A very satisfied male chuckle. "Hi."

They walked along the river with their arms around each other's waists. "I assume Mo knows?"

"I don't kiss and tell."

"Then——"

"My mother, however, apparently has a big mouth. My phone rang all morning. That's part of the reason I stayed here this afternoon. Dad called first thing. Then Granny called. Mo, Meredith,

Bronwyn—and speaking of Bronwyn, I didn't tell her, but apparently you did."

"She asked. I wasn't going to lie."

"I should hope not. I'm not planning to keep us a secret."

"Me neither."

He stole a quick kiss. "Good. Because I'm pretty sure we'd do about as well at keeping us a secret as we did at being friends."

"Hey! We were great friends."

"We *are* great friends. But we're going to be even better together." Cal tilted his head in her direction. "Are you . . . I mean, you *were* on drugs at the time. Any regrets now that you're back in the land of clear thinking?"

He was nervous too? She shouldn't be surprised. In fact, given his history, she should have expected it. Maybe they'd both need reassurance. At least for a little while. She pulled him to a stop, rose on her tiptoes, and whispered against his lips. "My only regret is that I didn't get strep throat a month ago."

After that, they discussed many things.

They didn't use words.

TWENTY-NINE

On Friday morning, Landry dropped Eliza off at school for the first time that week. Cal had volunteered, again, but she needed to get back in the groove.

Eliza was back in fighting form and had been since Tuesday afternoon. The way kids bounced back was impressive.

Landry didn't know if she would ever be back to her normal self. Her throat wasn't sore. Her body didn't ache. But she couldn't seem to return to her typical energy levels.

Thanks to one of the many documentaries she'd watched this week, she now knew a lot about the world's slowest animals. Including that sloths, while the slowest land mammals, were slightly faster than snails. This week she'd been a snail.

Today's goal? Sloth.

Maybe by tomorrow she'd hit koala speed. Then she'd be well on her way to her normal worker-bee pace by next week.

On the one hand, the timing had been . . . perfect. If there ever was such a thing. Her studio remained a crime scene because they were waiting on some expert to come in to do something. They told her, but she couldn't remember what they said. The bottom line? She couldn't access her studio.

It hurt her heart to think of it. Pottery destroyed. Kilns ruined.

But she had work to do. She needed to order supplies, update her website, and pick up a few things from her house.

Cal had kissed her goodbye this morning and told her he would see her at work. Then he'd headed to The Haven.

She touched her fingers to her lips. Mercy, Cal kissed like it was his mission and failure wasn't an option. Not that she was complaining. Far from it. Some kisses were sweet and tender. Some made her wonder if it was possible to melt from the heat generated by another person.

If his kisses were smoking, the look he gave her when he spotted her standing outside the fence of the construction site was scorching. She'd gone straight to the office when she arrived and taken care of the work that had to be done. She was exhausted, but there was no way she was leaving without seeing him.

They'd discussed their relationship, and while they had no plans to keep it a secret, they were trying to be discreet for Eliza's benefit. Her world had been turned upside down enough.

But keeping it from Eliza meant avoiding any and all forms of PDA. Because while Mo, Meredith, Bronwyn, and, heaven help her, Cal's entire immediate family were in the know, no one else knew. As soon as they did, it would spread like wildfire, and then it was just a matter of time before someone—probably that punk kid in Eliza's class—said something to her about it.

They planned to talk to Eliza this weekend, and then they'd go public. Although anyone who'd seen that look from Cal wouldn't need any other proof.

Cal came out of the building and stood at the fence. "Hi."

"You have to stop looking at me like that."

Cal feigned innocence. "Like what, exactly?"

"You know what." Her skin heated. That look, up close and personal, was even more potent than it had been at a distance.

"I can't help it. I've missed you. It's been"—he looked at his watch—"four hours since I talked to you last. I can't touch you right now. Can't kiss you through the fence. Can't give you a hug. All I can do is look. It's not my fault if my emotions and desires show."

How could she be upset about that? She couldn't. She wasn't. The truth was that while it had only been a few days, she'd already come to realize that she'd never been loved the way Cal Shaw loved her. Oh, he hadn't said the words. Neither had she. But she knew what this was, and she knew that any woman who could resist Cal's level of devotion would have to have a heart of stone.

As much as it had hurt him, in the deepest, darkest part of Landry's heart, she was glad Gina had been that kind of woman. Her loss was Landry's gain.

"Can I take you to lunch?" Cal slid two fingers through the fence, low enough that it wouldn't be visible to anyone who might be watching.

She locked two of her fingers with his. "I want to, but I don't think I can manage it. I'm exhausted."

Cal squeezed her fingers. "Want me to drive you home?"

"Thank you, but no. I can drive. I'm going to go back to the house and take a nap before car line."

"Why don't you let me pick up Eliza? Then you can take as long of a nap as you need."

"You've picked her up all week. I know you're behind at work."

Cal waved it off. As if missing hours of work was no big deal. "I can work tonight after the two of you fall asleep. And I can work tomorrow. It's fine."

"Cal." Her voice was firm.

"Landry." His mimicked hers.

"Is this the part where you're going to get all bossy again? Don't think I've forgotten about that."

His grin was full of mischief. "I'm not being bossy, beautiful.

I'm being selfish. If you let me pick up Eliza, then I get home three hours earlier than I would otherwise. That's three extra hours I can spend with you."

"Oh." Landry leaned against the fence. "Well . . . when you put it that way."

Cal winked at her. "Go home and get some sleep. Eliza and I will be back around three. Unless . . ."

"Unless?"

"Unless we decide to make a pit stop."

"A pit stop?"

She suspected Cal was going for innocent, but what he was pulling off was decidedly sneaky. "Fine. Keep your secrets."

Cal squeezed her fingers. "Let's not do that. No secrets."

Landry had never wanted to climb through a fence so much in all her life. "Secrets aren't good. I agree. And I don't want that either. I've had enough for a lifetime. But . . ."

"But?"

"I trust you. And trust means leaving room for surprises."

A slow smile spread across his face. "I like the way you think. So, do you like surprises?"

"I like fun surprises."

"What's a fun surprise?"

"Unexpected gifts, visits, food, experiences. Secrets bring despair. Surprises bring delight."

"I like that distinction. And I agree. I think I should warn you that as far as I'm concerned, surprises should always be part of who we are."

"Who we are?"

"Yes. You and me. Us. Our . . . our family."

A shiver ran across Landry's skin, and it wasn't an unwelcome experience.

"I want to keep you on your toes. Not with anxiety, but with

296

anticipation. I want you to know that I'm always up to something, always plotting a fun surprise."

Mercy, but she loved this man. "Do *you* like surprises?"

Cal blinked like a confused owl. "Me?"

"Yes, you. Why would you think you're the only one who can do the surprising?"

Cal rubbed a hand across his face. "Honestly? I'm not sure I've been on the receiving end of many good surprises."

It took a great deal of effort, but Landry squelched her fury at Gina, and any of the other women he'd dated, for the way they'd taken advantage of Cal's heart. This man gave and gave and gave. It was high time he received. "Then I guess your life's about to get very interesting."

This time, the smile on his face gave her a glimpse into what he must have looked like as a little boy. There was innocence and wonder. When he spoke, his voice held no teasing, just tenderness. "I can't wait."

"Yo! Cal!" a male voice called out from somewhere high. Probably someone on the roof.

Cal responded with a wave. "Be right there." He turned to Landry. "Gotta go." He ran his fingertip across the fingers she still had through the fence. "I hope Eliza takes the news okay. I don't want to freak her out, but I'm not sure how much longer I can go without being able to touch you whenever I want."

"She's five, and she adores you. She may have questions, but she'll roll with it. In a few years, maybe less, she won't even remember there was ever a time when you weren't in her life."

"A few years, huh?"

Landry realized what she'd said. They hadn't talked about the future. She'd assumed. And after a second of terror, her anxiety dissipated. Cal wasn't interested in a fling. He didn't have to tell her he was in this for the long haul. She already knew. And he knew she'd never go public without knowing where things stood. This thing between them was too new to talk about forever, but forever was where they were headed. "Do you have a problem with that?"

Cal groaned. "None whatsoever. Now go home. Take a nap. I'm going to need you awake when I get home so we can tell Eliza and quit sneaking around like teenagers."

Landry thought of their walk by the river last night after Eliza had gone to sleep and whispered, "I don't know. It's kind of fun."

Cal took a step back. "Kind of?"

Landry laughed. "Very fun."

Cal took another step. "Don't worry, baby. It'll be even more fun once everyone knows you're mine."

THIRTY

An hour later, Cal could still hear Landry's delighted laughter in his head as he climbed out of his truck. He needed some desk time before he picked up Eliza, and today was the perfect day for it. Carla had taken off at noon for an afternoon date with Connor. Chad was on a job site and wouldn't be back until six.

He'd just opened the door when his cell phone rang. He paused, settled his clipboard in his other arm, and with the keys still in the doorknob, dug his phone from his pocket.

Something heavy slammed into him, knocking him completely inside the office. He turned and tried to shove away from whatever had hit him. A tingling sensation spread through his arm, and before he could fight back, his right arm went numb, his legs followed suit, and he crumpled to the floor. His vision blurred, and the only sense left was his hearing.

His thoughts were thickening, as if even the nerves of his brain had filled with sludge. He fought to focus. Whatever this was would wear off eventually. The more he could remember, the better.

A jingle of metal told him that someone had retrieved his keys from the doorknob. He had no idea how much time had passed before loud footsteps approached. A grunt was the only warning that his body was being moved. Even his hearing was fading.

His last conscious thought was a prayer. *God, please protect my girls.*

A knock on the door jolted Landry from her nap. She glanced at the clock.

2:10.

She stretched, groaned, and called out, "Coming."

The light-filtering curtains were drawn, making everything nice and cozy for a nap but minimizing her ability to see to the deck outside.

The sound of a key sliding into the doorknob froze her at the bottom of the stairs. Someone was coming in. Before she could make herself move, the door opened.

"Cal?"

He came toward her and put his arms around her. No. He kind of looked like Cal, but he wasn't Cal. Her body already knew how she felt in Cal's arms. This wasn't Cal.

"Hello, sweetheart. It's time to go home."

A sharp pinch at her neck was all the warning she had before the room spun.

"I've got you. You'll be safe now." The face was Cal's. The voice was wrong.

She tried to speak, but her mouth wouldn't move. She couldn't even tell if her eyes were open or closed, but either way, she couldn't see anything. Her mind tried to hang on, but everything had slowed.

No one could get on the property without alerting Mo. He was home, and he'd see . . .

The man who wasn't Cal touched her arm. She screamed, but no sound came out. "Don't worry, my sweet angel. I won't hurt you. No one will ever hurt you again. I've grabbed a few of Eliza's toys. I already have everything you'll need in our new home. If you want something from your place, we'll get it later."

Landry's brain continued to fight against the temptation to rest. He planned to get Eliza too? He wouldn't be able to. No one who wasn't on the list could pick her up.

"Just so you know, I've taken care of Callum Shaw. He'll never bother you again. We'll be able to be the family we always wanted to be. It's going to be glorious, darling."

The last flicker of hope died. What had he done to Cal?

———

"Mommy. Wake up. Please, Mommy. Please wake up." Eliza's pleading voice penetrated the swirling fog in Landry's brain. She tried to open her eyes, but all she managed was to crack them enough for a tiny bit of light to filter through. She tried again, and this time she could make out the blurry shape of Eliza's face. A few more blinks, each one easier than the one before, and the room came into focus.

She cleared her throat. "Eliza?" Her voice worked again.

"Mommy, where are we?"

"I don't know, sweetheart. We'll figure it out, okay?"

Her mind screamed warnings. She had to wake up. Had to think. Had to move. She forced herself to sit up. A wave of dizziness rushed over her as she ran her hands over Eliza's face. "Are you hurt? How'd you get here?"

"I thought he was Cal. He was in Cal's truck. And you were asleep in the truck. I got in, and we drove away. And then I don't remember anything else after that until I woke up a little while ago." Eliza's voice trembled. "He looks like Cal, but he's not Cal."

The room refused to be still, so Landry lay back down. It wasn't like she could rescue them in her current condition. "How do you know he isn't Cal?"

"His voice is wrong. And he said my name wrong."

How could anyone mess up *Eliza*? It was a straightforward name. "How did he say it?"

"He said it like everyone else says it. But not like Cal says it."

Landry couldn't process that. She swallowed, thankful that her mouth and arms were working again. She tested her legs. She could move them, but she wasn't sure they could be trusted to hold her up. "Where is he now?"

"I'm right here, sweetheart."

Landry opened her eyes.

The mask was gone.

"You!"

THIRTY-ONE

Cal lay still. Something was wrong, but he couldn't remember . . . anything.

His thoughts were sluggish, but eventually he realized that he couldn't move. His brain was sending the signals, but his body wasn't responding.

Cal wasn't sure how long it took him to get his eyes open, but wherever he was, it was pitch black.

What happened?

He tested his body again. He could blink. He could move his head a small amount. But his arms and legs weren't responding right.

He fought the panic creeping around the edges of his mind by trying to remember how he'd wound up here. Wherever here was.

All he could remember was getting up and going to Meredith's place to have breakfast with Landry and Eliza. Everything after that was blank.

Landry.

Eliza.

The panic wasn't creeping anymore. It was squeezing him like a vise.

He forced himself to think, and the day began to reform in his

303

thoughts. He had gone to work early. He was behind on every-thing, but he didn't care. This had been the best week of his life.

Landry, *God, please let her be okay. Please.*

She came to see him at the job site. They talked through the fence.

Eliza. Did he pick her up from school? No. Wait, did he? He couldn't remember.

Landry left. He went back to work. He went to the office before going to get Eliza.

The office. Something had happened at the office, but he couldn't get a handle on it. The only thing he knew for sure was that he wasn't at the office now. Wherever he was, it was cold, dark, and he couldn't move.

This had to be about Landry. Where was she now? Was she safe? Was she alone? Was she hurt?

Cal had no idea how long he lay there, praying for his girls, when he became aware of Maisy barking.

No, not barking.

Maisy was losing her ever-loving mind. He'd never heard her bark like that. She didn't sound hurt, but she did sound frantic.

He tried to move his body again. He thought he might be on his side. His fingers twitched, and when they did, he felt something. On the left, he thought he could feel his hand touching his leg. Maybe. The material felt like his pants. He couldn't move his left arm. But he managed to move his right arm a small amount. Some kind of scratchy fabric was touching it. His legs still wouldn't move.

No. Not wouldn't. Couldn't.

The muscles were trying, but something was holding them down. His mind cleared away another layer of cobwebs, and with it came the realization that he was enclosed in something. A blanket? No. A blanket wouldn't be this heavy. And it would be softer. He could feel the scratchy material against his left cheek now.

Why couldn't he move?

Maisy's barking was nearby now. He tried to call out to her.

"Maisy!"

His voice sounded muffled, but Maisy's bark grew more insistent.

Then he heard the voices. Deep, high, terrified.

"No!"

"You don't think . . ."

"We need a shovel."

"Not a shovel, you idiot."

"How would you suggest——"

There was a vibration, something shifted, and whatever he was wrapped in collapsed onto his face and with it went the final cobwebs.

That's when he knew.

He'd been buried alive.

The vibrations around him grew closer. The voices grew clearer. And then the pressure on his legs lessened. He kicked out with as much force as he could manage in the cramped space, and a yell went out from somewhere close. "Cal? Cal? Is that you?"

The voice was close enough that he could distinguish it. That was Mo. He tried to call out. "Mo!"

"Cal!" That was Meredith.

"Faster!" Connor.

"I think these are his legs." Chad. "Focus over there. Get his face uncovered." Cal felt the shift in their efforts. The pressure around his face was less than it had been before. "We have to get him some air. No one can survive long——" The word choked off.

"Cal, man, if you can hear us, try not to move. We need to get this off you. It isn't deep. Hang in there, bro." Connor, taking charge as usual.

"Not going anywhere." Cal did his best to project his voice.

It must have worked, because the next thing he heard was Chad. "Well, this confirms our suspicions. He's going to have a smart mouth until he's dead—and probably even after."

They were close enough now that Cal could hear the emotion in Chad's voice. He had so many questions, but one couldn't wait. "Landry?"

Silence. And that told him everything he didn't want to know.

"Get me out of here!"

A frantic thirty seconds later, the final weight lifted from his face. "Cal, don't move, man." Connor again. "You're in some kind of burlap. I'm going to cut it open. Don't want to slice your face."

Cal fought his growing desperation to get out of the ground and lay still. When the burlap split, he saw Chad and Connor peering down at him. Tears streaked their faces.

Chad gripped one side of the material, Connor the other, and they yanked it apart.

Chad reached toward him, his hand landing on Cal's chest. "Talk to me."

Cal gulped in a lungful of air.

"He's going to need oxygen." Connor took Cal's face in his hands. "I don't think he's firing on all cylinders yet."

"Well, of course he isn't," Mo said as he continued to dig near Cal's legs. "It's a full-blown, no-doubt-about-it miracle that he's alive. If he'd taken the time to pack down the soil . . . if we'd been ten minutes later . . ." Mo cleared his throat. "I didn't expect him to be alive."

"Mo, thank you for keeping that tidbit to yourself." Meredith's voice was thick with emotion. "I don't care how it happened. I'm just thankful he survived."

Cal continued to focus on his breathing. The more oxygen he took in, the clearer his thinking became. "I'm with Mer on this one. I don't need to know. I just need to get out."

"Working on it, bro." Connor leaned toward him again. "Thank heaven he buried your legs deeper than your head."

"Where's Landry?"

No answer.

"Eliza?"

Still no answer.

"Chad?" Chad never could keep anything from him.

From his position on the ground, he saw Chad's Adam's apple bob. "They're both missing. Half the town's looking for them. The other half's been looking for you."

Somewhere nearby, he heard Meredith. "Gray. We've got Cal. He was buried in a shallow hole on Landry's property. Yeah. Maisy led us to him." A pause. "No idea." Another pause. "Yeah. Will do."

They had his arms free now, but he still couldn't sit up because his legs were pinned. Chad, Connor, and Mo scooped out the dirt around him with their hands.

Meredith knelt beside him and traced his face with her fingertips. "Cal."

"Tell me what happened." Maisy danced around the hole, and he reached for her and held her close to get her to calm down.

"We don't know exactly. But we're almost positive Ignacio is the one behind it. Mo found something."

"I tried to call you. You didn't pick up. I figured you were busy. Should have kept calling. But because I didn't, no one knew anything was wrong until Carla and Connor stopped by the SPQ office after school." Mo's face was a mask of anger and frustration.

When it was clear he wasn't going to say more, Meredith continued with the story. "Carla and the kids stayed in the car. Connor ran in to get something from his desk. He walked in and saw your clipboard on the floor under the coffee table. Then he noticed that some of the chairs weren't in the right spot. He went to straighten them and saw some kind of needle on the floor."

"I think I was drugged or . . . something."

"Connor called you. You didn't answer. He tried Landry. She didn't answer. He called Mo, who said he saw your truck pull up to the house around two. You went inside my house. Mo didn't think anything of it and went back to work."

"Because there was no way I wanted to interrupt you and Landry if you were having another one of your discussions like the one I interrupted yesterday," Mo grumbled as he scooped more dirt from Cal's leg. "I was going to give you thirty minutes, then I was going to come tell you what I'd found. Stupid. Should have made sure."

Meredith shushed him. "Anyway, after Connor called, Mo pulled up the security cameras, and that's when he saw you carrying Landry out of the house and putting her in your truck."

"I don't remember that."

"That's because it wasn't you."

"What?" Cal managed to get one leg to move. "What do you mean it wasn't me?"

"Dude. You've been in the ground." Mo threw a handful of dirt over his shoulder. "That psychopath was wearing a mask of your face."

Cal dropped back to his side. Maisy lay beside the hole, watching him. None of this made sense. "I'm confused."

"That's because Mo interrupted me." Meredith's frustration was evident in her tone. "Once Mo saw that footage, he called Connor and told him what he'd seen. Connor called the school. Aunt Laura remembers seeing you"—Cal could hear the air quotes she put around *you*—"driving through the car line. Your truck. Landry was asleep in the passenger seat. No one questioned it. Everyone knows she's been sick."

"He must have drugged her too."

"Probably." Connor grunted and tugged on the burlap around Cal's legs.

"Don't be too mad about that." Mo studied him. "I think that drug is what saved your life."

"What?" Four voices responded to Mo's claim.

"His respirations would have been shallow and slow because of the drug. He didn't know he'd been buried, so he couldn't panic about it. If he'd been conscious, he would have used up all his air in a few minutes. The loose soil and the drug are why he's still alive."

Cal knew that at some point in the future, he would have to think about how close he'd come to dying. But that point wasn't here yet.

"Anyway"—Meredith huffed out a breath—"Mo ran a GPS tracker on your truck. It was on an old logging road about fifteen minutes out of town. There were tire tracks for a different truck. Best guess is that Ignacio, or whoever, abducted Landry and Eliza, parked the truck there, drove yours out of town, then switched vehicles."

One huge tug later, Cal was free. Hands grabbed his arms, legs, and chest, and he was out of the hole. After a round of hugs, back slaps, and more than a few tears, he knelt to give Maisy as much love and praise as he could manage in his current state. He scanned the area. "He buried me on Landry's land."

"Pretty sure this guy hates you, bro." Chad pulled his phone from his pocket. "I need to let everyone know you're okay."

Connor approached and held out his phone. "Talk to Mom before she skins our hides."

Cal took the phone. "Mom. I'm okay."

A stifled sob was the only response. Then his dad's voice came through the speaker. "We're on the other side of town. Coming back toward you. Connor said you were drugged and buried alive. Your mother wants you on oxygen, and she's going to need to do some bloodwork before she's convinced you're okay."

"I know. But we have to find Landry and Eliza first." Cal could still hear his mom crying.

"Agreed. If you get any leads, call us. If we don't hear anything, we're heading to your mom's office to get the oxygen and prep a bag."

Cal didn't need his dad to explain further. She wanted to be ready to take care of everything from gunshots to scratches.

"Thanks, Dad. And tell Mom I really am okay." Physically. His mind was clearing with each breath of fresh air. But he wouldn't be truly okay until they got Landry and Eliza back. He refused to consider a scenario in which he didn't get them back. He disconnected the call and handed the phone back to Connor.

Then he turned to Mo. "How do we find them?"

THIRTY-TWO

Landry held Eliza's hand and angled her body so she stood mostly in front of her.

Ignacio laughed and rolled his eyes. "Surprise! A good surprise, no?"

"No, Ignacio. This isn't okay."

Ignacio took her free hand in his and pulled her toward him. "Let me show you what I've done. You'll love it here."

She wasn't sure what told her to keep her mouth shut, but something was giving her a strong "just go with it" vibe. She turned to Eliza and widened her eyes. That look usually meant "You're in big trouble when we get home," but she hoped Eliza would understand it to mean "This guy's a lunatic, and we're going to try to keep him from snapping until we can get out of here."

It was probably more than she could reasonably hope to convey in one look, but whatever Eliza thought she meant didn't matter. What mattered was that Eliza stayed quiet.

"Ignacio, help me understand. I thought you were in Eastern Europe. Now you're here?"

He winked. "That was all part of the plan to free you, my darling." His eyes softened, and for one horrifying moment Landry thought he was going to kiss her. "I think I played my role too well. I never let on, and you didn't know what I had planned. I understand that you're confused. Don't worry. You'll see. We're going to have a beautiful life together. Come. Let me show you the house."

She followed him as he showed them Eliza's room. It smelled of fresh paint. "I had gone with pink, but then I heard you wanted purple." He grinned at Eliza. "You made me work hard, but it was worth it. You're going to love your room."

Eliza's eyes were wet, but she mumbled, "Thank you." Then she hid behind Landry's body.

Ignacio squeezed Landry's hand and leaned closer to her. "She's confused. I understand. We'll give her time. Once she figures out how happy we are, she'll settle."

Landry had to try to get through to him. "Ignacio—"

He put a finger to her lips. "Come, my love. Let me show you our room."

Landry's blood iced over, and she managed to gasp out, "*Our* room?"

"You'll love it." He opened a door at the end of the hall. The room was gorgeous. Pale gray walls, soft peach and turquoise bedding and accents, a sitting area with a loveseat, a cozy chair, and a TV, and a bed larger than any she'd ever seen.

He patted the bed. "Only the finest, my darling. I special ordered this behemoth. This is an Alaskan king." He winked at her again, and this time there was an unmistakable predatory glint in his eyes.

The tour continued for several minutes. There was a guest room "for when we have company." A theater room, complete with popcorn maker, "to watch all the movies we want." And a nursery. "For our baby."

Landry had never been much of an actor, and her ability to hide her terror under a veneer of fake interest was waning. She'd known

Ignacio was unstable. She'd expected him to die doing something stupid. She'd never anticipated that when his mind broke, it would devolve into this particular form of madness.

When he'd shown her every room in the house, they wound up back in the kitchen, and Ignacio opened the fridge. It was stocked with fresh fruit, veggies, milk, eggs, yogurt, and assorted condiments. He scratched his face. "I need to grab a shower. That mask is rough on my skin." He waved to the kitchen. "Why don't you whip us up some dinner? We'll have our first meal as a real family tonight before we tuck Eliza into bed."

Seriously? He was going to leave them alone in the kitchen? This was her chance. She'd made a note of the bowl in the entryway that held his keys. She had no idea where this house was located, but if she could get to the truck, they could get to the road. Then they'd find someone with a phone.

He walked toward the master bedroom. "And oh, don't worry about anything, Landry, darling. You're completely safe here. I have sensors on all the doors and windows. My phone will alert if anything is opened. And I have cameras and surveillance set up all along the driveway. No one can get in or out without me knowing."

Her hopes crashed around her. If it were just her, even in her physically weakened state, she'd have made a run for it. But she couldn't run with Eliza. So far, Ignacio had given no indication that he planned to harm Eliza. But as erratic as his mental state was, that could change in a heartbeat.

As soon as the door closed behind Ignacio, she turned to Eliza. "Did you see Cal at all?"

Eliza's lips trembled. "No, Mommy. Is Cal okay?"

"I don't know, sweetheart. We're going to pray that he is."

Ignacio said he'd taken care of Cal. But what did that mean? She couldn't let herself imagine a scenario where he wasn't fine.

"We should pray for God to show us how to get away from Ignacio. God will help us." Eliza spoke with all the faith and confidence of a five-year-old. Landry didn't think she would ever have truly childlike faith again. She knew God didn't always choose to help. He didn't always fix things, at least not the way Landry wanted them fixed. But he could help. She knew that. He might not, but it wouldn't hurt to ask.

"Okay, baby. Let's pray."

Eliza grinned. "I'll go first." She folded her hands and bowed her head. "Jesus, there's something wrong with Mr. Ignacio, and we need to go home and find someone to get him some help. Please help Mommy know how to get us out of here. And help Mr. Cal to be okay. In Jesus's name, Amen."

Landry ran a hand over Eliza's hair. "I don't think there's anything I can add to that, sweetheart." In her mind, she pleaded, *God, please. I don't deserve it. I know I don't. But for Eliza. Please help us.*

Landry stared into the still-open refrigerator. "Regardless of anything else, we need to take our antibiotics." She found her purse lying on the floor near the door. She dug through it, and her fingers wrapped around a pill bottle. She pulled it out, stared at the label, and an idea hit her.

It might not work.

Or it might work too well.

But she had to try. She poured the pills out of the bottle and put them in her pocket. Then she dug around some more until she found her antibiotic.

Ignacio bolted through the bathroom door and barreled toward them, a huge grin on his face. "Fastest shower ever, huh? I couldn't wait to be back with you. I'm so glad you're here. What's for dinner?"

She hadn't had time to warn Eliza about her plan. Hopefully she'd go with it. "Eliza and I are both on antibiotics. The doctor told me we need to consume yogurt. You know, to help keep the good bacteria in our gut."

Ignacio nodded. "Makes sense."

"So I need to make us some smoothies first thing. Then I'll figure out what to do next."

"Awesome." Ignacio pulled a massive blender from a cabinet. "Will this help?"

He'd stocked the kitchen. "That will be great. Thank you."

"Okay. I'm going to watch a little TV." He grabbed her and pulled her into a bear hug. "Isn't this amazing? Our new life together. So good."

He released her and walked into the den. "Eliza! What do you want to watch?"

Eliza looked at Landry, terror in her eyes. Landry called out. "I need her to stay with me so I can give her the antibiotic. We'll join you in a few minutes."

"Sounds good, darling."

Landry couldn't figure Ignacio out. On the one hand, he acted like he had no idea that she was not okay with this. On the other hand, he was giving her some space—but not much. That really had been the fastest shower in the history of showers. And now the open layout of the home meant that even though he was in the other room, he could still see them. Was he waiting for her to react? To throw a fit? To run?

It didn't matter. She had to do whatever she could to get them out of here. She had no idea where they were. No way to call for help. And no way to know if anyone was coming.

Eliza wrapped her arms around Landry's waist. "Mommy?" The question was quiet, the fear unmistakable.

Landry found the Greek yogurt, fruit, and a few other items in the fridge and poured them into the blender with some ice.

Before she turned it on, she took a dishcloth, laid it on the counter, and set the six pain pills she'd found earlier on it. Then she covered them with another layer of the dishcloth and turned on the blender. As soon as the blender hit peak volume, she smacked them three times with a meat mallet she'd located in a silverware drawer.

She lifted the cloth. The pills were now in small pieces. Hopefully small enough that even if they weren't completely crushed by the blender, it wouldn't be obvious what they were. She poured out small cups—one for her, one for Eliza—and then dumped the pills in.

She pulsed the blender a few more times.

She poured the doctored smoothie into a glass. "We're coming!" she called out in her cheeriest voice.

Lord, please, please, please let this work.

Eliza followed her into the living room. Landry settled her into the corner of a sofa, as far away from Ignacio as she could get, and then took the glass to Ignacio. "Join us, won't you? We'll have a smoothie toast to our new life."

"Sounds great!" Ignacio took the glass and raised it, then Landry clinked hers with his. They all drank their smoothies. Landry watched, and when Ignacio got to the end of his glass, she hopped up from where she'd gone to sit by Eliza. "Let me take that for you."

She took it, walked to the kitchen, and rinsed it out. She didn't see any obvious signs of the pills she'd put in there. Hopefully that meant they were now swimming through his digestive tract on their way to dampen his nervous system and ultimately put him into a sleep deep enough for them to escape.

They watched TV—some show about special effects in movies—for fifteen minutes. Landry watched Ignacio, looking for any sign of fatigue. She'd almost given up when he lowered the leg rest of the recliner, stood, and then stumbled toward the spot where she and Eliza sat on the couch. He knelt beside her, one hand on her knee.

"I realize this has all been a bit of a shock to you."

A bit? Because being kidnapped in broad daylight by a man

316

wearing a mask of your boyfriend's face and driving your boyfriend's truck was so close to a normal day that it was hardly worth mentioning? Landry did her best to remain calm. "I have to admit, I was unaware of your feelings for me."

"Oh, my love. You've had my heart from the first day. I knew. I flew home and immediately started making plans for our home and our life together."

"Why didn't you tell me?"

"I must confess that I did some digging into your past. I knew about your husband, and I knew it was too soon. So I made my plans and waited until your heart had healed enough to move on. When you bought the property from Bronwyn, I knew it was time to put everything in motion."

"So was all of that you? Burning down the store?"

Ignacio preened. "The store took months to plan, an hour and a bit of good fortune to set up, and a second to start. The fire was glorious. I'll be using that method in my next movie. Minimal risk to the parties involved, maximum damage." He tapped her nose. "I thought when you saw the destruction, you'd be ready to move on." He tsked at her. "But no. Not my brave warrior. Not my Landry. You went straight to rebuilding. And that's when I realized I would have to do a little more to convince you that it was time to join me."

"I'm not sure how destroying my studio was supposed to accomplish that, Ignacio." She was on thin ice, and she knew it. But what kind of sick mind came up with a plan like this?

"Oh no. Look." He grabbed her hand and pulled her to a curio cabinet she'd paid no attention to before.

Now she stared at the pieces inside. "Are these . . ."

"Yes. All yours. The pieces that won awards and the pieces that had sentimental value. I took them from the store and from your studio. I would never hurt you that way. No, my darling. I wasn't trying to hurt you or frighten you. I was laying the groundwork for your departure. After what happened at your studio, even Bronwyn will understand when you tell her you aren't going back."

"I'm not?"

"Of course not! You can create here. I have a studio for you behind the house. Several kilns, a wheel, all the tools, the clay, the glazes. It's all there. You'll be back at work whenever you feel up to it. You can continue to sell your work online. But there will be no pressure. None at all. I have more than enough money to provide for us. You can create what you want when you want." He beamed at her, obviously proud of his efforts on her behalf.

He yawned and shook his head. Was it her imagination, or were his blinks slowing down? "Darling, this isn't exactly the way I'd hoped the evening would go, but I think it's time we go to bed." The hand at her knee crept up her thigh. "I've been awake for well over twenty-four hours in my last-minute push to get everything ready for you. I need to get some rest."

Landry forced a smile and stood up. His hand fell away and this time, it wasn't her imagination. He was wobbly. *Please let it be enough.* She'd managed to avoid making him mad so far, but she didn't know how much longer that would last. She needed to keep him content until the meds knocked him out.

"I'll need to help Eliza before I come to bed." She leaned toward him and tried to make her voice sound conspiratorial. "She has a routine. If we stick to it, she sleeps like a champ. If we don't?"—Landry made big eyes at Ignacio—"she'll be up every thirty minutes."

Ignacio was suitably horrified by the thought of Eliza's nighttime antics. "Definitely do whatever you need to do. I'll be waiting for you, my darling." He ran his fingers along her cheek. She couldn't stop the shiver that trembled through her body. He mistook it for desire, and his expression grew smug. "Just don't be too long."

Oh, she was going to be long. Far longer than he knew.

THIRTY-THREE

Cal paced around Mo's house. "Why didn't we build this place bigger?"

Mo kept typing. "This place has all the room I need. You're welcome to go wear out the floors in your own house."

"Anything?"

"What? Anything on this highly illegal search of personal records that I have no authorization, warrant, or approval for?"

"Yeah. That."

"Almost."

"Why are you so sure it's Ignacio that's behind this? Because if we're wrong and we're looking in the wrong place . . . " Cal couldn't make himself finish the thought. "If it is Ignacio, he could have taken them anywhere. They could be on their way to Eastern Europe by now."

"No." Mo sounded confident. "They're close. Ignacio hasn't been in Eastern Europe . . . or anywhere . . . lately."

"He told La—"

"I know what he told her. But I've been looking for him since the incident at the studio, and that's why I was calling you this afternoon. Unless he's been traveling under forged paperwork, Ignacio hasn't left the country in the past six months. He's dropped off the grid entirely. Everyone assumed that was because he was working. But he wasn't."

Mo handed an iPad to Meredith. "Can you pull up that article about him bailing on a job?"

Meredith tapped the screen a few times, then turned it toward them. A headline read, "Where is Ignacio?"

"He disappeared?" Cal leaned toward her screen.

"According to this, he flaked on his last role. Never showed up. No one seems to know what happened to him. And it's not the first time. About five years ago, he pulled a similar stunt. Disappeared for a year. Reappeared with no explanation and went back to work."

Meredith scrolled down. "This article says that his contracts for the next several years included massive penalties if he didn't show. But that once he appeared to be settled in, they dropped that clause."

"How is that even possible?"

"It's Hollywood. People get addicted, go to rehab, don't want to talk about it. Come back. People don't ask." Meredith rattled this off as if she were a society reporter and knew what she was talking about.

The crazy thing was, it kind of made sense.

Mo continued typing. "This afternoon I realized that I wasn't going to find him in Europe because he isn't there. I found one thread that might be him, and when I pulled it, it led me back to North Carolina. Specifically, a real estate deal somewhere around here. I was digging into his possible whereabouts when Connor called."

"Do you have any proof?"

"No. It's all circumstantial evidence at the moment. But it won't be for long. I'm about ten minutes away from his banking records, so if you two want to keep it down, that would be great." Mo accentuated the point by pulling on a pair of noise-cancelling headphones.

"Okay." Cal turned to Meredith. "If I were Ignacio and I wanted to buy real estate around here but didn't want anyone to know where I was, how would I do it?"

Meredith tapped a finger to her lips. "I'd buy the old Drake place."

"Mer, that place is condemned."

"The land's worth a fortune. Tear down the house. Build fresh." Meredith shrugged. "It's beautiful property."

"Yeah. It is. But I was out there with Chad and Connor a couple of months ago, looking at a nearby property. There's one gravel road, barely more than a path, in and out of that place. We parked near the path and hiked in just to check on it. There's nothing out there."

Cal closed his eyes. *Please help me. Where would they be?* He mentally made a circuit around the county. The old homes where no one lived anymore. Property that would someday sell for an outrageous sum but so far remained untouched. When he circled back to Quinn land, he expanded his search.

His eyes popped open. "Mo. Mo!"

Mo lowered his headphones.

"Who bought the old Bradsher place?"

Mo's eyes widened, then his fingers flew.

"Someone bought it?" Meredith put down her laptop and stood behind Mo.

"Yeah. It was anonymous. I thought at the time that it would make sense for it to be some celebrity from The Haven." Cal smacked his hat on his knee. "I should have thought of it sooner. But it was at least two years ago."

Mo sat back. "Ignacio."

Cal looked at the screen. "That says John Smith."

"And John Smith"—Mo opened another screen—"has the same social security number and date of birth as Ignacio."

Cal took Meredith's phone from where it lay on the counter and dialed Gray. "We need to go to the old Bradsher place. It's technically in Chief Kirby's jurisdiction. Can you call him and let him know what's going on?"

"Cal, you can't storm private property, and I have no authority there. You—"

Cal handed the phone to Meredith. "You talk to him." He turned to Mo. "You in?"

Mo stood and grabbed a jacket. "Let's go."

Before the door closed behind them, Cal heard Meredith. "Gray, they're gone. You need to tell Kirby that if his guys do anything to block any of the Quinns from going after Landry, he won't spend another day in office."

He didn't speak until he and Mo were off their property and blazing down the road toward the old Bradsher place. "Mo?"

"Yeah."

"What's Meredith got on Chief Kirby?"

"No idea." Mo looked ready to spit nails. "She's done a couple of those charity dental clinics up there in his neck of the woods. There's no telling what she's gotten herself mixed up in."

Cal took a curve thirty miles per hour faster than he should have. "We'll get Landry sorted. Then we'll get Meredith straightened out."

"Have you met Meredith?" Mo's dry tone did nothing to hide his frustration—or his fear. "What's the plan?"

"The plan?"

Mo turned in his seat. "Cal. A seriously deranged man has run a multiyear op that culminated in him nearly killing you, impersonating you to get to Landry and Eliza, and then disappearing with the two of them. What exactly do you plan to do? Drive up to the place, knock on the door, and say, 'Yo, man, give me my woman back?'"

Cal scratched his neck. "I need to get close. Then we'll reevaluate. But I'm not sitting on my thumbs waiting for a warrant. Gray can haul my rear to jail if he wants to. I'm getting into that house. Tonight."

Mo's phone chirped. He looked at it. Answered it with the speaker phone. "Mer."

"Gray's already got the warrant, and they're on their way. Chief Kirby was on the other side of his county, but he's on his way now too. I don't trust Kirby, but I don't think he'd allow this to stand. Not for an outsider like Ignacio."

He had a lot to unpack there, but now wasn't the time.

"Kirby told Gray that someone's been doing a lot of work on the place off and on for over a year."

"Thanks, Mer."

"Mo? Cal? Be careful. Bring them home. Love you both bunches."

"Love you." Both men spoke in unison. The phone went dead. They didn't speak for the next twenty minutes. There was nothing to say.

All that was left was to get Landry and Eliza back.

They came around a bend and found the road blocked. Cal put the truck in park, then climbed from the vehicle. Mo joined him.

As they approached the nearest police car, Mo put his hand on Cal's arm. "I think you should let me do the talking. I'm less likely to get thrown in jail."

Landry had no idea how long she could expect the pain pills to keep Ignacio knocked out. Or if, heaven forbid, she'd given him so many that she'd killed him.

She didn't want to kill him.

She tiptoed to the master bedroom. It had been twenty-two minutes since Ignacio had stumbled through the door and disappeared from view. She'd used the time to explain her plan, such as it was, to Eliza. They'd both used the bathroom, then they pilfered through the closet and dresser where they found a large selection of clothing in Eliza's size.

Landry tried—and failed—not to be creeped out by that. But given that she had no idea what they were about to walk into, she helped Eliza put on several more layers under her jacket. She stuffed a few pairs of socks into her coat pockets, and then sent Eliza to wait by the door to the garage.

Now, she stood in the doorway. Ignacio lay sprawled across the bed. Face down. Snoring.

He was alive.

She didn't know what to do. If an alarm went off when they exited the house, and she fully expected that to happen, then he would come after them. Or try to.

But staying wasn't an option. They had to get out. And this was the best chance they would have.

She closed the door and scanned the hallway, looking for anything she could use to barricade him inside. But there was nothing she could move on her own without making a racket. She gave up on the idea and hurried down the stairs.

His phone lay on the end table. She took it. If nothing else, she could make an emergency call. She put the phone in Eliza's jeans pocket, then held Eliza's hand with her left and the keys in her right. She made eye contact with Eliza. "We're going straight to the truck. We're getting in and leaving. When I say go, we run. Are you ready?"

Eliza nodded.

"Go!" They ran for it.

An alarm sounded the second the door opened. She hit the button to activate the garage door, and ran to the driver's side of the truck.

She scooped Eliza into her arms and helped her inside. "Climb in the back." Eliza obeyed and Landry scrambled into the seat, started the engine, and threw it in reverse. "Buckle up, sweetheart." Landry hit the lights, backed out of the garage, and floored it down the driveway.

"You aren't buckled, Mommy."

"I'll buckle in a minute. Right now, we have to get away. Do you still have Ignacio's phone?"

"Yes, Mommy."

The terror in Eliza's voice nearly crushed Landry. She'd get her all the therapy she needed as soon as they were safe. "Does it have a password?"

Eliza answered a moment later. "It's locked."

"Try 526379."

"Five, two, six, three, seven, nine." A pause. "That worked!"

Of course it did. He had used her name to create his password. This wasn't the time to be creeped out by how much Ignacio had deluded himself about her. "Okay, now I need you to call Cal." She gave Eliza the number. She didn't expect Cal to answer. Not after what Ignacio had claimed he'd done. But maybe someone would answer. "Can you put it on speaker?"

A moment later she could hear the phone ringing. "Callum Shaw."

Landry almost hit the brakes. The relief that flooded through her at his voice was overwhelming. "Cal?"

A pause. "Landry! Landry! Where are you? Where's Eliza?"

"I'm right here." Eliza's little chirpy voice broke through Landry's momentary freeze.

"Cal. Is it really you?" Landry asked.

"Yes, it's me. Where are you?"

"We escaped. We're . . . I don't know where we are. We're in his truck. We have his phone. And we're going as far away from the house as we can get. I'm afraid to stop. Can you track the phone?"

"Landry, Honey, Keep driving but get ready to stop."

"What?" Through the trees, Landry noticed a flickering light that grew in intensity until she came around a curve. Police cars, private vehicles, an ambulance, and standing in the flashing lights . . . Cal.

She hit the brakes and put the truck in park right in the middle of the road. She'd barely stopped when Cal yanked her door open. "Cal!" She threw her arms around his neck and held on for dear life.

"Landry!" His lips brushed hers. He probably meant for it to be a sweet little kiss. But Landry had spent the past several hours convinced he was dead. She pulled his head back toward her and claimed his mouth with her own. She didn't care who saw. She didn't care who knew. Cal Shaw was hers. She loved him. And she was never letting him out of her sight.

Cal held her close and took over the kiss, saying all the same things with his kiss that she'd said with hers.

THIRTY-FOUR

ONE MONTH LATER

"We're here tonight to celebrate new beginnings and new relationships." Bronwyn made eye contact with Cal. "The partnership we've developed with SPQ Construction over the past few months has reaped more rewards than we could have possibly imagined."

Cal squeezed Landry's hand and murmured, "Definitely more than I had ever dared to dream."

She blushed beautifully and leaned into him as Bronwyn continued. "I want to personally thank the SPQ crew members who are here tonight. Thank you especially to Cal Shaw for not only ensuring a smooth project that was completed in record time, but also for the original design of the fireplace and the artistry of our new pottery section."

Bronwyn paused and smiled directly at Landry. "And of course, to my partner in crime, our phenomenal artist-in-residence, Landry Hutton. She has worked tirelessly over the past month to ensure that we could reopen before Christmas, and I can't wait for you to experience her vision for Favors and what this space could be for our Haven guests."

Bronwyn stood, surrounded by Pierces of all ages, and with

a giant pair of scissors cut through the ribbon Landry had tied across the porch rails a few hours earlier. "Welcome, everyone! Please, come in!"

As the crowd surged forward, Landry let out a huge sigh, her shoulders slumped and her expression grim. "I have to go inside now. Find me later?"

"Always." He pressed a kiss to her forehead. "This is supposed to be fun. Enjoy it." When the unease didn't leave her face, he pulled her into his arms and whispered in her ear, "You're safe. Eliza's safe. If you need me, send me a text."

Landry cuddled closer for a few seconds, then stepped back. "Okay. See you in a bit." She turned to Eliza. "Be good for Cal." He scooped Eliza into his arms. "We're going to find Abby, and then we're going to hit the ice-cream station, aren't we?"

Eliza's laughter seemed to eliminate the rest of Landry's tension, and she walked into the building ahead of them.

Cal hadn't been inside since they'd finished a few final touchups five days earlier. Bronwyn had pulled out all the stops for tonight's event. In a move few in her family agreed with, she'd opted to christen Favors with a by-invitation-only party before opening the store for business.

She'd invited the men and women who'd worked tirelessly to create the space they now wandered through, and she'd encouraged them to bring their families to see what they'd done. Despite the busyness of the season, almost everyone invited was in attendance.

Electricians showed off lighting features to girlfriends and curious teenagers. Construction workers pointed out the vaulted ceilings and intricate moldings to wives and parents.

Tables were laden with hors d'oeuvres, bite-size desserts, and homemade ice cream with a buffet of toppings, and even though almost everyone had a plate, it didn't look like the crowd had put a dent in the food.

Cal helped Eliza and Abby with their ice-cream sundaes but kept Landry in his sights. Every now and then she'd scan the crowd, and when their eyes met, the smile she gave him sent a shiver down his spine. Every time. He wanted to stand beside her all night, but he made himself mingle as much as he could with his two pint-sized charges.

His parents had come, and both of his brothers and their families were also here. Mo was supposed to put in an appearance, but Cal hadn't seen him yet.

Gray, in full uniform, was cornered by an octogenarian and her granddaughter. Cal didn't miss the way Gray's gaze strayed to Meredith as she floated through the throng like the town princess Gray said she was.

It was the highest concentration of Quinns on Pierce property in years. Maybe ever. And while Bronwyn was the only Pierce who spoke to any of the Quinns, no one had stomped off and everyone was being civil.

It was progress.

The girls finished their ice cream, and Abby tugged on his arm. "Can we go see Nana?"

"Of course. If we can find her."

"She's talking to Mommy." Eliza pointed toward the small crowd around Landry. A crowd made up entirely of Cal's family.

When they reached them, the girls squirmed their way through the aunts, uncles, and siblings until they reached Cal's mom, Carol, who was deep in conversation with Landry, Naomi, and Carla.

"Hey, Nana!" Both Eliza and Abby spoke. In unison.

Carol Shaw turned at the greeting, and her eyes welled with tears. "Well, hello there, my precious ones. Are you having fun?"

Landry's eyes widened, and her gaze landed on Cal.

Before Cal could do more than try to give her a reassuring smile, his dad spoke up, voice full of feigned outrage, hands on his hips. "Whoa. You say hi to Nana and not to me?"

Both girls ran to him. "Hey, Papa!" Then they each grabbed onto his arms. He pretended to try to lift them and made a big deal out of how he couldn't do it because they were too grown-up. He knelt beside the girls and kept their attention focused on him. Cal knew it was to give the rest of them time to pull themselves together, because everyone who'd seen the interaction was blinking back tears. Naomi was openly crying.

Meredith breezed into their circle and handed out tissues. "Why are we crying? What did I miss?"

"Eliza called them Nana and Papa." Naomi dabbed her eyes. Meredith pressed a hand to her heart. "Well, that explains that." She grinned at Landry. "You do realize you're never getting out. Our family is like the mountain mafia. There's no escape."

Carol pulled Cal down for a quick hug. "You do beautiful work, my sweet boy. And you have excellent taste, as evidenced by your designs and the lovely ladies you've brought into our family."

"Mom." Cal tried to infuse his voice with caution. He loved Landry and Eliza. He wanted to keep them forever. But he was trying to give Landry time to adjust to the idea of it all. To him. To his crazy family. To the idea of forever. It had all happened so fast, and he didn't want to scare her off.

"Don't worry." His mom patted his arm. "I can bring us back from the brink." She shifted her focus to his brothers and their wives, while still including Cal and Landry. "Since I have everyone in one spot, I need to warn you that Granny Quinn has once again ignored our suggestion that she not buy Christmas presents for everyone this year."

Landry leaned against Cal and listened as her new family discussed their plans for Christmas.

"Are they scaring you?" Cal kissed the top of her ear.

"Never." She pulled Cal back down so she could speak softly. "I don't know where that came from though. Your mom and dad didn't seem to mind but . . . "

Before Cal could respond, Mo joined their huddle. "Landry, this place is amazing."

Landry didn't try to hide her shock. "Amazing" was high praise from Mo. "Thank you. Of course, I can't take credit for all of it. Bronwyn did a ton of work."

"She's just saying that because she saw me coming." Bronwyn laughed as she accepted hugs from all the Shaws and Meredith. Mo, however, made no effort to speak to her. Or as far as Landry could tell, even to make eye contact. But he did stay in their circle for several more minutes before Meredith said, "Mo, would you do me a favor? Mrs. Cunningham has had Gray locked down for twenty minutes. Could you rescue him?"

"How do you expect me to do that?"

"Just walk up to them. She'll go away." Meredith was joking, but based on the way Mo's face hardened, Landry didn't think Mo took it that way.

When he spoke, he confirmed her suspicions. "Why? Because I'm so scary?"

Then Eliza's little voice broke through the moment. "You aren't scary, Uncle Mo." Eliza stood beside him, her face fierce. "You're grumpy. That's not the same thing as scary."

Landry did her best not to laugh. Cal, however, made no such attempt. "She's got you pegged, *Uncle Mo*."

Mo turned a fake glare on Eliza. "If you aren't careful, little miss smarty pants, I'll change my mind about giving you and Abby a ride in the Jeep."

Both girls squealed in delight. "Can we go now? Please!" They danced around him.

"We'll go in a few minutes." Mo turned his smirk on Meredith.

"First, I have to rescue *Uncle* Gray from a little old lady." Meredith's eyes flashed, and she hissed, "Watch it, Mo." With a satisfied grin, he pointed at the girls. "Give me five minutes. Ask your moms."

"Mommy, please?" Eliza dragged out the word *please*. "Please?" Landry had no idea what Mo did on these little Jeep rides that had made it a favorite activity for the girls. She suspected it involved junk food. She gave her assent, and Eliza joined Abby in her attempt to convince Chad and Naomi to allow her to go.

"Eliza's calling him Uncle Mo now?" Bronwyn asked from just behind Cal.

"She is." Meredith answered the question. "And Uncle Craig and Aunt Carol are now Nana and Papa."

"Oooh!" Bronwyn squeezed Landry's arm.

Landry tried to communicate with her eyes and every form of friend bonding they shared to drop it. It didn't work.

Bronwyn turned her grin on Cal. "Well, Cal, I guess you're next." Landry wanted to melt into the floor. "You're dead to me, Beep." Bronwyn blew her a kiss. "You don't mean it." A server waved in Bronwyn's direction, and the traitor left her there to deal with the fallout.

Landry knew Cal loved her, and she loved him, but since they'd officially gotten together, they hadn't discussed their future. Everyone was assuming it was a done deal.

Everyone but her.

THIRTY-FIVE

The next afternoon, Cal and Landry left Eliza with her nana and papa and snuck away for a few hours to themselves.

They'd hiked for twenty minutes on property that was privately owned, ironically enough, by the Pierce family. But their destination was a specific spot on Quinn land.

"Where are you taking me?" Landry asked for the tenth time.

"You'll see."

"Are we almost there?"

He stopped on the barely-there path and turned around to face her. "What's the rush?" He stepped closer, slid his arms around her, and kissed her. She melted into him, and he savored the feel of her body against his. He pulled back but didn't release her. Instead, he rested his cheek against the top of her head. "Better?"

She snuggled closer. "Yes."

Landry had come close to having a panic attack when she learned that Cal had been buried alive. They'd decided it was best if Eliza didn't know that part of the story, but the weight of it had threatened to crush Landry. They didn't talk about it much, but they'd both experienced moments when they simply needed to be held. They needed the reassurance that they had survived.

Maisy had outdone herself with her attempts to keep them

both comforted. She was happiest when they were together and she could snuggle between them or lie at their feet. They'd left her at home for this adventure. Cal didn't know if hiking was bad for pregnant golden retrievers, but he didn't want to risk it. After the trauma she'd experienced when he was buried alive, it only seemed reasonable to make sure they kept things as easy for her as possible.

"It isn't much farther." Cal squeezed Landry tight, then released her. He would have kept her hand in his, but the trail only allowed single-file passage. "I promise it's worth it."

Landry's smile held no fear, only trust. "I believe you."

Five minutes later, the path emptied them onto the rock-strewn edge of a waterfall basin. "Oh, Cal! This is . . ." Landry shook her head in wonder as she stared up at the cascade. The spray bit against their cheeks, and the roar was enough that they had to yell to be heard. "Does it have a name?"

"Papa calls this Nina's Falls."

"Why Nina?"

"You won't hear it often, but Nina is his nickname for Granny Quinn. Every now and then he'll say, 'Now, Nina, leave them be,' and it's like some kind of magic. Granny Quinn isn't known for backing down, but when Papa calls her Nina?" Cal shook his head a little. "Honestly, I try not to read too much into it. It's special to them. That's what matters."

"It's lovely." Landry's eyes shone "Thank you for bringing me here."

Cal opened his backpack and spread a waterproof blanket on the ground. From the thermos he'd packed, he poured a cup of hot chocolate for each of them, then they settled on the blanket. Her back to his chest. They sipped their drinks and enjoyed the peace of the space. There were no cars, no voices. Cell phones didn't work here. It was a place that, for Cal, had always been somewhat sacred. He knew others in the family came here, but it was as if this spot was private for each of them.

After he'd returned to Gossamer Falls, he sat by the edge of the pool and screamed at the top of his lungs. He hadn't been back since.

But today, he planned to reclaim these falls. Not as a place that held his pain, but as a place that birthed his future.

He brushed a few strands of hair off Landry's cheek and tucked them behind her ear. "I need to talk to you about something."

She shifted so her face was inches from his. "Okay."

"Now that we're done with Favors, your house is the next thing on the construction schedule."

"Right." Did she sound less enthusiastic than she'd sounded previously? That was a good sign.

"I was wondering if you'd consider postponing?"

"Postponing?" Landry frowned. "Why?"

Cal tucked a finger under her chin and pulled her close for a quick kiss. "I own thirty acres across from your three."

"I'm aware."

"And I was wondering if you'd consider building your house on my side of the river. And making it *our* house. I wouldn't want to change much. I love your design. But I think it would need to be larger. Have a few more bedrooms, a bigger kitchen, that kind of thing. We could build your studio on your land, and I'll even agree to that ridiculous bridge across the river that Meredith designed."

Landry's skin had gone bright red. Her eyes were huge. Her body trembled in his arms. "Cal?"

"If you think it's too soon, I understand. But I want to marry you, Landry. I want you to be mine. I want to adopt Eliza. And I want to live with you forever. I understand if you can't say yes now. But please wait to build your house. Give me a chance to convince you that we can build something better if we build it together."

Landry smiled. "Callum Shaw. Are you asking me to marry

you? Because I think maybe you think you are. But I haven't heard those actual words come out of your mouth yet."

He scrambled around so he was kneeling in front of her. Forget one knee. He was on both knees. He held her hands in his. "Landry Hutton, would you do me the honor of becoming my wife? I promise to love you every moment of every day, I promise to take care of you and to let you take care of me. I promise to play with you and to annoy you. I promise to tackle every decision—easy or difficult—with your heart and happiness at the forefront of my thoughts. I love you."

At some point during his speech, Landry had removed her hands from his and slid them to either side of his face. His hands now rested on her hips, and he felt the slight motion that settled her lips against his.

"I love you."

He knew she did. That wasn't up for debate. But he hadn't planned to go through with the full proposal today. He didn't want to force her to make a decision before she was ready.

"I would marry you today. As soon as we got back to town. Gray could make it official before nightfall."

Something Cal didn't know he'd been carrying lifted from his body. Everything felt warm. Light. Free. "What?"

"But"—she pressed a kiss to the side of his mouth—"if we deny Eliza and Abby the joy of being flower girls"—another kiss landed on the other side of his mouth—"we'll scar them for life." This time the kiss landed on his chin. "I think we should plan it for spring. It will still be quick, but that should give us enough time to pull something beautiful together. I would imagine Meredith and Bronwyn can—"

Landry's words were cut off by Cal's kiss. He wasn't playing. He held her face in his hands. "Landry Hutton. Are you saying you'll marry me? Because I think you are. But I haven't heard an actual yes come out of your mouth."

She grinned. "Yes! Yes! I'll marry you. And we'll redesign the house and build it on your side of the river."

"With more bedrooms?" Cal asked.

"How many do you think we'll need?" Landry tilted her head.

"I'm not getting any younger here."

"I don't know. Three or four."

"It was already going to be a three-bedroom house. Are you saying we'll need seven bedrooms? Because that might be a bit more than what I had in mind."

Cal laughed at her and nuzzled a kiss to her neck. "Maybe five bedrooms? Three for the kids. One for us. One as a guest room. Or, you know, in case we needed it for another child along the way?"

"Five bedrooms sounds perfect." Landry wrapped her arms around his neck. "Do you think you'll have it built before the wedding? Because honestly, your place is a bit small for me and Eliza."

Cal grinned. "I don't think we'll have it finished before a spring wedding, but I've already been tweaking the plans. I think we could have it finished by summer."

"Do I get to see the plans?"

"Of course. I happen to have them right here." He patted the backpack. But rather than opening it, he reached into his pocket. "But I thought maybe you'd like to see this first."

He opened the lid of the small box and removed the diamond ring. He hadn't planned to propose, but he'd packed it just in case. "This ring holds both the past and the present. The diamond belonged to my Granny Shaw. She left it to Dad and told him to give it to me if I ever sorted myself out and found a woman worthy of it. I knew about the diamond, but I had never asked Dad to give it to me until a few weeks ago. I took it to a jeweler in Asheville. They made the band."

He held up the band, which was made entirely of small diamonds, for Landry's examination. The stone was a round solitaire. It was large, but the setting made it look even bigger.

Landry's hand trembled as Cal slid the ring onto her finger.

Six months later, he carried her over the threshold of their new house.

"Welcome home, Mrs. Shaw."

DON'T MISS

LYNN H. BLACKBURN'S
THRILLING NOVELLA

COMING SOON

Cassie Quinn dropped her speed as she approached the employee entrance to The Haven. Everyone in the small town of Gossamer Falls knew Cassie had a lead foot. But violating the fifteen-mph speed limit within the gates of The Haven was a one-way ticket to unemployment.

And Cassie wasn't about to risk that. Especially today, when she was on her way in for a meeting with her boss and The Haven's CEO, Bronwyn Pierce.

She waved her badge in front of the sensor and gave a tiny salute to the security guard she knew watched her from the cameras placed along the top of the walls. The massive iron gates opened, and she drove her Jeep inside. A quick check in her rearview mirror confirmed the closure of the gate mere seconds after she was through.

No one could get inside the grounds of The Haven without permission. Bronwyn had a zero-tolerance policy for trespassing. That didn't mean people didn't try, but the few who managed to get a toe across the property line found themselves spending the night in a Gossamer Falls jail cell.

The last time it had happened, she'd still been dating Officer Donovan Bledsoe.

Cassie reached up and popped herself on the back of the head. *Don't go there.* The three months they'd dated had been shoved into the same vault where she'd stuffed the four months of trauma she'd experienced in Atlanta.

Heartbreak came in many forms. Some, like the Atlanta fiasco, she knew she'd never put herself through again. That was in the

341

vault because she didn't need to relive that. Ever. But Donovan? He'd never been anything but a dream come true.

Right up until the night he ended everything.

So he'd gone into the vault that held the dust of her dreams.

Would her time as chef at Hideaway join him there? Maybe. But when Bronwyn had called her a month earlier, desperate after the head chef had a heart attack, Cassie hadn't had to think twice before she took the risk.

Just like she knew if Donovan ever came to her and said he'd made a mistake, she'd give him another chance.

Because some dreams were worth it. Weren't they?

A glance at her speedometer pulled her back to the present. She eased off the gas and settled in for the worst part of her day—the creeping drive through the grounds. It was beautiful, but it would be so much more fun if she could take it just a little faster.

Five minutes later, she pulled into her reserved parking spot and checked her watch. She was early, but not by much. The walk to Bronwyn's office was a short one, but she couldn't dawdle. She checked her makeup in the mirror and climbed out. She was reaching into the back seat to grab her bag when a horn beeped.

A few seconds later, Bronwyn parked beside her.

Cassie waited for Bronwyn to exit her car and smiled at the woman who'd given her an opportunity she'd never dared dream of. Was she going to end the dream today?

"Cassie! Great timing!" Bronwyn's grin held no tension. So, maybe this wasn't going to be a bad day? *Lord, please let it be good news.* "Want to walk with me over to the breakfast kitchen? I need coffee."

"Sure." Cassie fell into step with Bronwyn. The Haven catered to an exclusive clientele. Celebrities, politicians, and business moguls came to the mountains of North Carolina to get away from it all. But just because they wanted a mountain escape didn't mean they wanted to rough it. They wanted luxury linens, high-end everything, and room service. Lots of room service. Three years earlier, Bronwyn had a separate kitchen built to accommodate the myriad requests for everything from chocolate milk to The Haven's most popular dish—a fried green tomato BLT.

The breakfast kitchen handled room service requests, twenty-four hours a day. Breakfast, lunch, and snacks were provided through the breakfast kitchen and delivered to the individual cabins by resort staff.

Dinner was another matter entirely. The Haven's fine dining restaurant, Hideaway, had made a quiet name for itself for its intimate atmosphere, professional service, and unique seasonal menu, which featured sophisticated Southern cuisine. Reservations were required and were only available to The Haven's guests. Dinner was served from six to nine. No exceptions.

Cassie loved everything about it. Well, almost everything.

"Thanks for meeting me so early," Bronwyn said. "When did you get out of here last night?"

"I left around one."

Bronwyn tugged on her arm and stopped them in the middle of the path. "One—a.m.? Why? You should be out of here before then."

Cassie couldn't meet Bronwyn's eyes. She'd been hoping to avoid this conversation.

"Cass? What's going on?"

Cassie stared at the ground and tried to come up with a way to answer that wouldn't get anyone in trouble. "I didn't want to say anything. It's a temporary situation, and I can handle it."

"Explain." Bronwyn's voice had shifted from concerned friend to concerned CEO.

But Cassie wasn't prepared to give in. "I'm not a rat. And it isn't my kitchen. If it were, I'd handle this differently. But Chef

Louis has been nothing but gracious, and I won't ruin what he has worked so hard to put together."

Bronwyn shook her head, her frustration obvious. "Fine. We can table this discussion temporarily. After we talk, you may have a different answer."

That didn't sound ominous at all.

Before Cassie could ask what she meant, Bronwyn pasted on a smile. "Let's grab coffee and a pastry and go back to Hideaway to talk. I don't want to be overheard, and my office will have too many people there now."

They chatted about safer topics as they picked up coffees, a muffin for Cassie, and a chocolate croissant for Bronwyn.

"I heard you had a date last week." Bronwyn's oh-so-casual tone didn't fool Cassie.

"Who told you that? Was it Cal or Meredith?" Cassie didn't ask if it had been Mo. Her cousins, Cal, Meredith, and Mo, had grown up with Bronwyn, then drifted apart. Cal and Meredith got along with Bronwyn just fine. She had no idea what had happened between Bronwyn and Mo, but she knew enough not to bring him up.

Bronwyn's laughter held so much mischievous glee that Cassie groaned. "Spill it." She took a bite of her muffin and stared Bronwyn down until she answered.

"I heard it from our very own sheriff."

The muffin went down all kinds of wrong. Cassie coughed and spluttered, and tiny crumbs flew out of her mouth. She wanted to die of embarrassment. She couldn't stop coughing, but Bronwyn was laughing so hard, she was doubled over. Hopefully she'd missed the crumb debacle.

Chief Grayson Ward was Donovan's boss. If Gray knew then . . ."

Cassie finally got the coughing under control and ran a finger under each eye in hopes of preventing her makeup from running down her cheeks. When she refocused on Bronwyn, it was to see that the laughter had been replaced by concern. "Cassie, I'm sorry." There was no way to miss her sincerity. "I didn't expect you to nearly choke to death. And I've just realized why this isn't funny to you. If it helps, Gray heard it from Cal at breakfast. Donovan was on a night shift, so I doubt he heard anything about it. If you care about that?"

Cassie took a sip of her coffee. Then another. She didn't respond until they were almost to the back door of Hideaway's kitchen. "I don't know why I reacted that way. I'm free to date whomever I want. And it shouldn't matter if anyone"—she refused to say his name—"overheard or knows. I didn't realize I cared. But I guess I do."

Bronwyn put an arm around her and squeezed. "Oh, Cassie. I understand so much more than you know." With a final squeeze, Bronwyn slid her ID card in front of the security sensor to unlock the door. "Aside from anything else, how was the date? Good?"

Cassie followed her inside. "It was—"

Bronwyn had flipped on the lights and they both stared at the kitchen. A kitchen that had been pristine when she'd left it just a few hours ago but now looked like someone had taken a chainsaw to the appliances.

The kitchen had been destroyed. The cooking surfaces were warped and jagged. Glass was shattered everywhere. Ceramic cracked. Counters dented. The refrigerator door had a hole large enough for a gallon of milk to fit through it.

Cassie didn't even know how that was possible.

On the floor, written in a red sauce was one word.

Oops.

ACKNOWLEDGMENTS

No one ever writes a book on their own. My eternal gratitude to:

Darlene Brady, potter/owner of The Dirt Dauber Pottery, for answering all my questions and helping me create my own little pieces of art. Your kindness and expertise were crucial to the development of this story. Thank you for sharing your skills and your art with me.

Jason and Russ Hart, brothers/artists/owners of Turned and Burned, for letting me hang out in your shop, for answering my questions, and for allowing me to watch you electrocute some wood and spend some time breathing in sawdust! The design and creation of your vases and bowls were the inspirations for some of the scenes in this story and in the stories to come in this series. Thank you for being so generous with your time.

My family—Brian, Emma, James, Drew, Jennifer, Mom, and Dad—for your constant encouragement and love.

Lynette Eason, for your brainstorming brilliance and friendship that goes beyond the words.

My sisters of The Light Brigade, for praying me through, even when I'm MIA.

Deborah Clack and Debb Hackett, for holding my hand across continents and oceans. I don't think I could do this without you, and I never want to try.

Kelsey Bowen, for your encouragement to try something new and for your excitement for Gossamer Falls!

Amy Ballor, for always finding the plot holes.

Robin Turici, for jumping in and seeing this book through to the end.

The remarkable team at Revell, for being the absolute best in the business and the best to work with!

Tamela Hancock Murray, my ever-supportive agent.

Most of all, to my Savior, the Ultimate Storyteller, for allowing me to write stories for you.

Let the words of my mouth and the meditation of my heart
      be acceptable in your sight,
O LORD, my rock and my redeemer. (Psalm 19:14)

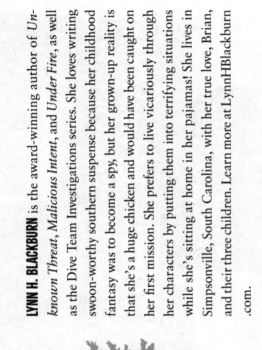

LYNN H. BLACKBURN is the award-winning author of *Unknown Threat*, *Malicious Intent*, and *Under Fire*, as well as the Dive Team Investigations series. She loves writing swoon-worthy southern suspense because her childhood fantasy was to become a spy, but her grown-up reality is that she's a huge chicken and would have been caught on her first mission. She prefers to live vicariously through her characters by putting them into terrifying situations while she's sitting at home in her pajamas! She lives in Simpsonville, South Carolina, with her true love, Brian, and their three children. Learn more at LynnHBlackburn .com.

Plunge into the enthralling cases of

DIVE TEAM INVESTIGATIONS

MEET LYNN